THE GOO
DOCTOR

D0530347

THE GOOD
DOCTOR

CAROLA GROOM

Phoenix House
LONDON

1

Doctor Ryder was seen running down Water Lane, Burlas, in a state of some agitation, shortly after ten o'clock on the fifteenth of August, 1870. He was breathless. It was a warm day and his hair was darkened with sweat – those blond curls, the merits of which had been debated among his lady patients . . .

Water Lane was a little-used thoroughfare. It ran directly out of town, towards nowhere in particular. The doctor wore good quality drill and tweed, and as he ran he looked about himself in panic. In a quiet suburb in quiet times his demeanour was notable.

He was exhausted, but at last he saw someone he recognised. A joiner, who had panelled the doctor's study in oak the previous year, was walking up the lane towards him. Ryder stopped him with a raised hand then hesitated, catching his wind.

'I need help! There's a man up on the hillside with a bullet wound, possibly mortal. I must fetch my bag. Can you find transport to take us there, and a plank or something to bear him down to the road?'

The joiner was shocked, but saw his chance to play a part in a rare drama. He agreed to do what he could and began to ask for more details. Ryder interrupted with a note of authority.

'He is desperate. He tried to kill me,' he said, breaking into a run once more.

2

Inspector Oswald Tutt laboured uphill through the tangle of bracken and heather. Ahead stood a small group of men. As he drew closer they parted to let him through. In the centre, with his back to Tutt, the doctor crouched in white shirtsleeves, intent. Another man lay lifeless, both arms outstretched, one hand still clutching the tooled white stock of a low-calibre revolver. Tutt looked quickly at the supine figure, the unconscious face exposed to the full glare of the sun.

'Evenden!' he cried with ill-suppressed excitement. Then, 'I am sorry, Doctor Ryder. I did not mean to startle you.'

The doctor, who had tensed involuntarily at Tutt's first word spoken so suddenly behind him, bent his head again over his work. Tutt reached down and carefully prised the gun away. When he dropped the hand it fell back limply. The onlookers shifted, relieved.

'Fired recently,' he said, still panting a little, 'but the other chambers are empty.'

'I know little of guns,' said the doctor, as if called to respond. 'I did not consider that he might have to re-load. I just ran. I should have stayed.' The little crowd made murmurings of dissent. 'I think I know you,' Ryder went on, glancing up.

'My name is Tutt, Inspector Oswald Tutt.' As he answered, he did not take his eyes off Evenden's face. 'Perhaps you have seen me. I have sometimes seen you and Mrs Ryder about town, you know.'

'Oh yes.'

The response was toneless. Ryder looked scarce more than a pink-cheeked youth, with his dank hair now softening and lightening in the sun.

The smell of blood hung around them. Tutt swallowed as he saw the scarlet against Evenden's smooth white skin.

'Can you help me here?' the surgeon asked. He showed Tutt how to hold a portion of sheeting, already soaked with carbolic acid, taut and horizontal in the air a foot or two above the wound. 'It will shield you from the sight, if that concerns you. But there is a medical purpose. Though the atmosphere out here in the country is not so pathogenic as elsewhere, the lowering quality of this weather is not helpful.'

Another man was given a rag with chloroform and a brief, clear injunction to use them if Evenden stirred. Tutt, his view obscured by the sheeting, could sense the progress of the operation from the expression on the doctor's face and his general aspect.

'You will want a statement from me?' Ryder asked.

'Later will do.'

'I can tell it briefly now.' He looked up into the Inspector's eyes for a second. 'Perhaps later in more detail.'

'I understand.'

Ryder produced scalpel and long, slender forceps from his bag, checked Evenden's breathing, then began his incision and his account.

'I called on Mr Evenden earlier this morning. You know he lives out this way – the big house on the way to Frith?'

'I know. I took some note when he returned to this country. And one always knew his inheritance.'

'Yes. One moment – '

Tutt deduced that a delicate cut was being made. The doctor's account was punctuated with pauses made necessary by his concentration on his patient.

'Well, I called and spoke with him and I am afraid we disputed violently. I left and walked across country. Around here, I realised that I would soon come back down into Water Lane. I stopped – I stopped to compose myself. Suddenly he was upon me; he must have been following me. He was in a worse passion than before, shouting – I saw him start to pull the gun from his belt, and I seized hold to turn it from me.'

At this point the doctor put down one tool of his trade and took up another.

'We struggled. I believe I was gripping his fist and the barrel of his gun. Then I felt it twisting between us and his finger must have been wrenched against the trigger. There was an explosion. I saw he was badly hurt. But he started to raise the gun again and – I ran. I knew that before long his injury would greatly weaken him, at the least. So in Water Lane I fetched my bag and gathered these men to help me; we commandeered a carriage. A carrier was passing and we told him to go to the police office. *There!*'

Ryder held up the bloody forceps for a second, showing a small object pinched between the tips. Then he cleaned them and used them to pick up a rag, deftly dipping it in carbolic. His hands disappeared beneath the sheeting once more as he cleaned into the deep recesses of the wound. A moment later he indicated that Tutt could discard the cloth he had been holding. As he lowered it Tutt saw that a first dressing of carbolised lint was already pressed over the injury.

'You will have many questions, Mr Tutt, but for now can I ask you to help me dress the wound?'

Awkwardly, Tutt moved to stand astride Evenden and raise him by the waist. The task was not difficult; like the doctor, Evenden was young and free of fat. With an effort Tutt maintained the balance of firmness and gentleness required. Ryder swiftly passed and re-passed a wide roller bandage underneath and across the exposed part of the body.

Once the process was complete, Tutt straightened. The knot of onlookers stirred and put ready a scullery table top that had been brought to act as makeshift stretcher. Many hands assisted with the lifting of Evenden onto this litter. The awkwardness of it, rather than the weight alone, required four to carry it back to the stile, leaving only Tutt and Ryder keeping slow step behind.

Tutt moved heavily over the rough ground. 'Doctor Ryder, you said that he was in a passion. Would you say that he was deranged when he attacked you?'

'The thought occurred to me, when I had a chance to think, before he produced the gun. It is difficult to make a clinical judgment in the circumstances. But, yes, in layman's terms that would describe his behaviour.'

'That will complicate any trial of course. Will he live?'

'Probably.'

Tutt paused before saying, 'I shall have to take a full statement.'

'Of course. I can be at your service any time today.'

'Thank you. And shall Mrs Ryder be at home?'

This produced an effect, Tutt thought. Ryder stopped, but he might only have been allowing the stretcher party space to negotiate a short steep descent. Tutt saw that his eyes had closed and a sick pallor had overspread his face. It was curious that a practised surgeon should be so affected by the bloody scene just enacted. Ryder put a hand to his temple and shook his head.

'I beg your pardon. Why do you ask after my wife? You mentioned her before.'

'Violence generally has a cause. I know of only one factor connecting you with Evenden, and that is Miss James, as was.'

'You are further ahead than I was myself, until this morning.' He paused, with an intake of breath. 'I found her gone, and when I went to him he as good as – ' Again he closed his eyes and shook his head as if to stave off another attack of weakness. 'When I said I would not divorce her, he said I would not stand in their way. They must be free. Free!' Ryder made ready to stride after his patient, adding only: 'And you, a stranger – so quickly you know and understand it all!'

Tutt, uncovered in the heat, followed in silence, one hand holding his hat as he steadied himself with the other.

The board with its load was manoeuvred over the stile. The carrier's cart which had fetched Tutt was still waiting in the lane beyond.

At the Infirmary, Tutt took the names of the other helpers in the

7

rescue and then dismissed them, entrusting one with a note to his office. He was alone for a time, sitting in a coolly shadowed passageway. Each nurse who passed would look at him, as at a large insanitary object. Their efficiency discomposed him.

Tutt waited while unfathomable medical rites were performed out of sight. He always disliked the early stages of a case, when outcomes were uncertain. He found some satisfaction in the thought of the cleaning, ordering, disciplining operations being carried out on Evenden's person.

'He seems comfortable now. He may come round soon, but there has been a great loss of blood and he will be weak,' said Ryder as he emerged.

'I must be there, when he wakes.'

'Very well.'

The doctor took him into the room. They stood for some while in silence. Evenden now lay washed and undressed, covered in fresh starched linen. Tutt tried idly to find the supposed mark of high birth in his face; but as ever he could not see in what this 'good breeding' consisted.

Evenden's eyes opened, glittering and unfocused. Tutt leaned forward and asked first the question he most wanted answered.

'Where is Mrs Ryder?'

'Safe,' said Evenden in a low voice.

'Not from justice, if she conspired with you.'

'Is it Tutt, and still a fool?' The patient's articulation was slow but clear. 'She is innocent.'

'Were I ten times the fool I am I could send you down this time.'

'Two people have wanted me dead. Here they both are.' Evenden's eyes were fixed on Ryder but his words were for Tutt. 'Did he tell you that he shot me?'

'He told me what happened, and others besides myself can testify that he then saved your life.'

'I thank him for it!' This with some sarcasm, but with eyes glazing as they closed again.

Tutt spoke close against his ear. 'You took a gun and followed Doctor Ryder, and you tried to shoot him.'

After a pause, the whispered 'Yes' hung softly in the air.

Out in the corridor Tutt spoke with the doctor.

'My thanks for your forbearance. I think your staying quiet goaded him.'

'I could not trust myself to speak. But he is right on one point. My wife is surely innocent of any knowledge of his intentions against my person – wherever she is. My faith in that is absolute.'

'After this morning?'

Ryder looked at him angrily, then lowered his eyes. 'I should like to go home and change. Gather my thoughts. When must I call on you – and where should I go? I don't know.'

'I shall call on you, sir, in a couple of hours. I know where to find you.'

Tutt watched the doctor leave before moving himself. It was past one, and he had breakfasted before six. He went to find his luncheon.

3

Two hours later, having meanwhile instigated enquiries with the object of locating Mrs Ryder, Tutt made his way on foot to the Ryders' house in Water Lane.

The maid was ready to show him straight into the doctor's study, as if she had been told to expect him. He made her wait a moment while he used his large handkerchief to mop his head. Then at his indication she preceded him into the room.

They both halted just within the doorway, the scene being laid out at the same moment to each. Across the room and at right angles to them was the doctor's desk. Ryder himself was seated in the chair but his head and upper body rested motionless over the blotter. The face was turned towards the doorway; the doctor's eyes, which had been handsome, bulged like a pair of baked fish-heads. His fair skin was darkly suffused. A gobbet of thick blackened spittle hung on the chin. There was no sound but for the ticking of a clock, and no movement but for small tremors in the lace at the open window.

No-one could suspect that Tutt's was one of those personalities governed by secret fear. He lived alone and worked mostly alone, with no-one to swat the daily demons for him, to dilute and challenge each passing doubt. He had devised a method of facing the day wherein he made a faith for himself, that if he feared *enough* the worst premonitions would not come to pass. Today his faith had failed him.

'Lord have mercy upon us.'

Tutt concluded that the maid had spoken and he himself said quite loudly, 'Amen!'

He stepped round her and approached the desk. Ryder's farther elbow rested against the edge of a tray on which were tea things and the remains of a plate of toast and relish; the soiled knife had been placed across the top of the open jar, clear of the white tray-cloth. The domestic detailing contrasted with the awful contorted rigidity of the doctor.

Tutt did not touch the body; there was no need. On the unobscured portion of paper on the blotter were the words WILLIAM FREDERICK EVENDEN underscored, followed by the beginnings of a clear medical description of the injuries sustained by that gentleman. The doctor had been making up his notes. After a paragraph there was a space, then unevenly scrawled the letter K and then, more faintly, ALICE.

Tutt moved the knife, picked up the jar, and peered and sniffed at the contents. He became aware of small noises behind him. The maid was struggling to suppress her panic. For a minute she only gasped, then she brought her voice under control and spoke. She sounded clipped and precise, something Tutt knew to be not inconsistent with shock and high emotion but a more rare response in woman.

'Ah, no. I did not think he was *so* desperate.'

Tutt turned to her.

'Is this kept in a special place?' he asked, carefully replacing the lid on the jar of relish before wrapping it in his handkerchief.

He questioned her on several matters. For most of the time they were standing in the hallway having closed the door behind them on the scene in the study.

Her name was Mercy Meadows.

'The wages of fear,' he said.

'Sir?'

' "His mercy is on them that fear Him." '

She responded promptly, 'Amen.'

He asked if she knew where her mistress was and she replied that she did not, though she did know of the disappearance, having

11

found a note to herself in the fold of the counterpane on Mrs Ryder's bed that morning. She had not shown it to the doctor, but she drew it from the pocket of her apron and gave it to Tutt:

Mercy, I am sorry to have to leave you and to cause more trouble in this house. I will send for you if I can. If not, or if you do not wish to come, you will always carry the affection and gratitude of –

Katherine Ryder

Mercy had been alone in the house with the doctor all afternoon. The downstairs girl was on her day off, and the outdoor man had taken the drag to the carriage repairers.

Tutt looked about at the modern, spacious home. Was there no cook?

'There was, but she left a few weeks ago and has not been replaced. I have had sole charge of the kitchen arrangements since then. I prepared his tray, and brought it to him.'

'I see. Why did the cook leave?'

She hesitated. 'It was over Alice.' Tears appeared on the lightly crumpled skin below Mercy's eyes. 'I think it was superstition; she did not think it right that he should be ready to perform such a thing on his own child. Though in the end it was Doctor Maugham who did it.'

'Did what?'

'The post mortem examination.'

'Alice was the Ryders' child, then?'

'Three years old. We buried her last month.'

In times to come, Oswald Tutt never could recall what he had been doing, what matters if any had claimed his attention, just before the carrier entered his office. It was like passing from sleep to reality, or conversely re-entering a dreaded and familiar bad dream.

It was only when the house was secured, and she was gone, that he gave any deeper thought to what Mercy Meadows had told him. Her first reaction had implied suicide. But that morning the doctor had battled for his life against his assailant. Would he then pause in the middle of writing up his notes to go calmly across that threshold, voluntarily? That he had suffered some catastrophic but natural illness seemed equally unlikely. Tutt, the only designated 'detective' officer serving the city borough of Burlas, was oppressed by the formlessness of his task.

He waited in the lane for the men he had sent for. He was sure of one thing only: if he had not failed in his duty five years before, the good doctor would be alive still. However, it would not serve, this continual going over past mistakes. His first object now must be to find Katherine Ryder.

He removed his hat to fan himself, and a massive raindrop fell on his baldness. It had been the hottest day of the year; this was the start of the expected thunderstorm. During the previous night there had been another. He had been kept awake, listening.

PART 2

BEGINNING FIVE
YEARS EARLIER

4

It seems clear to me now that there was a critical period in my life, with its starting point to be found on a railway train one day in the summer of 1865. Perhaps everyone looks back to such a moment, but I think not. I rather think that there are many worthy and contented people who never enter their other lives, who are never forced so far into themselves that they enter a strange country, and on balance I pity them though there are few of them I find I want to know. I think I subscribe to the dreary philosophy that it is suffering of one kind or another that makes us interesting. Not that I believe in any duty to suffer or virtue in mere endurance, but we must suffer in order fully to live, surely. Or can others deny it? I have always been afraid that the truths of my world were personal fancies only, and so am often afraid to speak my mind when it most matters.

Well, it is poignant now to see in my mind's eye the girl – myself – in the railway carriage. I feel for her, I understand her; and if I could speak to her, as I should wish to do, she would not understand me. She would be frightened: 'That cannot be all I am to become; I know I am to be better, to be something truly fine, I know not how!' It could not be explained the way it is. I want to comfort her and be her friend, but I may not. She must live the years.

This beginning is already slower than I meant it to be. To cut the prologue short: did you not spend your childhood and youth longing for something to *happen*? Do you still? I do not.

It was the morning through train from London to Burlas. My Aunt Julia and I were returning from a visit to my brother and his family. I thought myself a woman fully formed and ready to brave real life – of which I understood little, but I could sense it ready to happen soon. In my way I was actively engineering my future, and I generally succeeded in those things I set out to do, a case in point having been the matter of falling in love with Henry Ryder. I watched the country and had deep thoughts. Certainly, I was satisfied in a pure way that is unaware of itself, until it is too late. The most interesting thing to me in that train, on that day, was the package of lace in my bag, destined for a ball gown. That was destiny. Destiny must be what you wanted, coming to pass.

There were a number of stops but only one other person entered the compartment. Aunt Julia was asleep by my side and barely stirred as we halted at Critchley. A young man climbed aboard. Of course I need not describe him; it was William Evenden. As I have said on oath once, which should be enough but perhaps is not, it *was* our first meeting.

I have said there was no-one else in the carriage and so, as he bore all the normal trappings of respectability, he ought to have taken the seat diagonally opposite, just by the door through which he had entered, as far away from me as possible. Instead he looked around very deliberately and, in spite of the jolting of the train as it departed the station, which put him in peril of landing in Aunt Julia's lap or my own, he came over and sat in the window seat directly facing mine.

Now, a question. It seems that almost every work of fiction put before the public in recent times is concerned in one way or another with what Woman, in general or in particular, is to do. Not only do the novels never produce a satisfactory answer; they do not properly finish the sentence. Only ask the army of women readers and they will say in unison that the real, urgent question they face every day is this: What is Woman to do *when a man looks at her?*

It is of little use that in practice there is not the least choice in the matter. When a man looks at her, what a woman must do, with no alternative given, is pretend to be more stupid than the stupidest beast. She must pretend to be unaware. Unless she really is stupid she cannot *look* unaware, so unless she really is stupid she must look silly. It is for the cruel enjoyment of all this that men look at women, or look at them in that especially problematic way (for there are more discreet and therefore considerate ways of looking, which women themselves have perfected).

He looked at me. While he did so, I had time to feel annoyed and foolish, and further time to think about the nonsense of it all so I had the additional annoyance of having to stifle a smile that might be misinterpreted. Full grown as I was, such trivial matters were not yet completely dull to me. His look was cool though, and as it stayed on me a little too long it seemed to be more through forgetfulness than interest. These details, you will know, are significant in their own right and not at all because of my feelings in the matter. The whole business just described lasted only seconds, ending as, with a sigh of something like annoyance, he pulled a newspaper from his portmanteau and began to read.

I had a book with which I tried to occupy myself, a favourite I knew well enough to savour the phrases slowly, the sweep of the story being no longer new. Other aspects of the journey vied for my attention, though the author under study helped to condition my impressions. The countryside became more like home: the meadows more blue-green, the stone more grey, the watercourses more untidy brown. My aunt slept on heavily, her forehead twitching with imaginable fragments of dreams.

The man opposite read with more attention. He was dark-featured. I wonder if those looks each of us finds attractive, in the abstract, bear any relation at all to the looks we eventually love. Dark hair and eyes *had* always seemed essential for a hero. Perhaps it was for that very reason that, when the time came, Henry's yellow and blue had so startled and bewitched me.

I pictured Henry, and I thought about him, which was nowadays a pleasure to me. Then I noticed that the man's newspaper was our own city's *Burlas Gazette*, a weekly publication of liberal intent, struggling to reflect the cultural and political thought of the region – or to conjure, where it found none. The first edition had appeared barely a year previously (and the last was to see the light only a year after these events).

For some moments I tried to confirm the date of the issue, though from the unfamiliar appearance of the outside pages I was sure that it must be the current one, which would have first been on sale that very morning and which in eagerness from a special cause I had been intending to purchase at the station on our arrival home. I was hampered by the movement of the carriage and must have craned my neck forward a little. In the next instant the paper was crisply folded and offered to me by the gentleman, who now bore a mocking look of strained tolerance.

There then followed a dialogue quite without words but perfectly comprehensible. Embarrassed, naturally, I tried to indicate apology and a wish to decline his offer. He indicated his intentions were friendly and genuine, and that he had no further use for the paper. I glanced towards my aunt, whose shoulder rested on mine and who might be wakened by my reaching forward or turning the pages. He looked from me to her and back again, then turned his head ever so slightly to the side and raised his eyebrows. Accepting this challenge, I gently shifted the weight of my relation away from me; she made no sound. We both watched her for a second to be sure, but then I could not forbear from joining with him in a triumphant smile as I accepted the *Gazette* from his hand. So from antagonistic strangers we had become conspiratorial children. Indeed you must remember that Mr Evenden and I were both still very young.

I was soon engrossed in my new reading matter, and the remaining portion of the journey passed quickly. As we slowed at Burlas I lingered before finally closing the pages. Aunt Julia stirred by instinct and clearly believed she had been only 'resting her eyes'. I looked up at length to return the paper to its owner, to find his eyes again resting upon me. This time the look was of perfect ease of spirit, but no less a problem. Feigning ignorance and feeling foolish, I busied myself gathering our few belongings (the trunk had travelled in the van).

Our fellow traveller descended first and handed out our bags before helping us down to the platform. I could see my father moving through the crowd towards us and turned to say a brief 'thank-you'. As I did so, a large man came up quickly behind and passed close by me, almost pushing, and another man similarly passed on the other side.

'William Evenden?' asked the first.

Coming up at that moment, my father also cheerfully enquired, 'Evenden?'

Mr Evenden looked curiously at all three and said 'Yes' to none of them in particular. The second man, the silent one, who I now saw to be in the police uniform, took hold of one of his wrists and, to the astonishment of a few passers-by who had turned to look, began with stiff and nervous movement to put him in handcuffs.

The large man said, 'I am arresting you for the wilful murder of John Herbert Evenden. The warrant is in my hands. Excuse me, miss,' he added, turning and touching his hat to me.

For a fraction of a second more I thought that Mr Evenden looked at me, though without any describable expression at all – and I, I suppose, at him, the same.

5

Something had happened, then, something to be remembered always, and I thought obscurely that I ought to be pleased – that, perhaps, I was. In my life so far, it could only be compared with the moment when I was six years old and Aunt Julia, then a relative stranger, told me tearfully that my mother had gone to heaven. Although I believed that she would no doubt return with a present in time, I must have sensed more than I could understand because I have always remembered with unnatural vividness the beading on my aunt's bodice, the thick plait of her hair falling over her shoulder, the pattern of the carpet and the care and indecision with which she personally supervised the selection of the clothes I was to wear that day, much reference being made to the state of the sky outside.

What should have been the unfolding drama at the station was similarly overlaid with an infinity of peripheral impressions. I still faced Mr Evenden while my father spoke with him and the other two men, but what I most remember is only that the handcuffs looked very heavy and clumsy and out of place. My father through his legal practice was clearly known to Mr Tutt, whom he identified as the larger man. Mr Tutt's dress was ordinary, but he was evidently a policeman too. Father explained to Mr Tutt that he did not know the young man personally but that Mr Evenden senior was a client, and offered his services in any way required.

'Please, Mr James, could you call on my parents and explain that – something – may have befallen my brother?' said Mr Evenden.

'Oh, they know that, sir, and that we were looking for you,' said Mr Tutt.

'In that case, thank you, but there is nothing for now – except my bag is still on the train. Could someone take it home for me?'

'Which carriage were you in?' asked Father, looking round.

'Here.' I spoke up, glad of something to do. 'He was with us.' And I went back for the portmanteau myself. I noticed the *Gazette* he had left on the seat. It would not be right at such a juncture to take it – I must buy my own. I jumped down from the carriage again and held the bag out but Mr Tutt took it from me.

'We must keep this with the prisoner for now. It will be released for collection as soon as possible.'

Then they were gone, quickly hidden from our sight by the backs of curious onlookers who turned as they passed. The crowd slowly settled down to a pretence of normality, though there remained an unusual hush just around us and strangers would look in our direction then, when I caught their eye, look away or glance down idly at my hem or Father's shoes.

Father recovered first to check our bags and the box which the porter wheeled up. My aunt recovered her voice, reminding me all the more forcefully of that earlier day, when she had first impinged on my childhood consciousness. She seemed not to have changed in the fifteen intervening years. It was not, I thought as I watched her face without greatly attending her words, that she seemed so young to me now, but that I remembered her as falsely old before. I think that in that moment came the germ of realisation that she had been a young woman when she took over my care.

'Goodness gracious!' she said. 'Do you know I believe I must have dozed a little. To think I hardly noticed him! Did you notice him, Katherine? All but murdered in our slumber! The times we live in! Is it safe now? Are you all right, Katherine? You know, there is really nothing to worry about now, thank goodness. It is all right, Thomas, no need to fret. It is true we were for a short time alone with him in a closed carriage, but we are unharmed, thanks be to God! And the box seems to be safe and sound too.' This as she tugged the straps to make sure, disregarding the porter's stony look.

'Did William Evenden join you at Millbank?' asked Father.

'No, Critchley,' I answered, enjoying the elaborate play of

23

Father's eyebrows as I did so. 'Aunt, you had a good sleep. I think London exhausted you.'

'Well! You must be right. London is overpowering, but all thought of it flies off with this!'

'Did you have any conversation or exchange of words with the young man?'

'Let us look for a cab while I tell you.' (This to the evident relief of the porter.) 'Yes – That is, no – No, come to think of it, I don't think he spoke until just now.'

'Did he seem agitated, Kitty?'

'Not exactly. There was something about him. Arrogant is not quite the word. But I am sure that he cannot be guilty of any such thing as they charge.'

'You will not be a star witness for the defence at that rate, I am afraid.'

'We are not witnesses, are we, Thomas?'

'You never know, Julia. You certainly cannot be compelled by the defence.'

'But there must be a mistake, mustn't there, Father – if you know these people?' I asked. 'I have heard you talk about the Evendens as your clients, but not on the criminal side.'

'Very droll, my dear. Frederick Evenden, of course, is a fine gentleman and a good man. I do not know the boys *so* well. It seems poor John is dead. Mrs Evenden is an invalid – this might kill her too.'

'Will a doctor be with her?'

'How your mind runs on! She has always been attended by Doctor Hyam.'

'It was a kind thought,' my aunt said to me. 'And Henry would do as well for her or better.'

'Tell us about the sons,' I said. 'Are they the only children?'

'Yes. John is the elder. And I recall he went to live in Critchley about six months ago, to be near some powerful relation whose estate he was to help manage. William means to make his way as an artist, an uncertain living at best. Still, his father at least was philosophical about it.'

'An artist! That explains the odd way he looked at me.'

'Now that will not do, Kitty. You know why men will look at you.'

Later, in the cab taking us home, Aunt Julia began again to speculate on the danger to which unwittingly we might ourselves have been exposed.

'What do you really think, professionally, Thomas, of that young William person? Could he have murdered us, both at once?'

'It is no part of my profession to consider hypothetical cases. Even if he killed his brother, murder usually has a cause, generally one of long standing. He was the younger brother, so John stood between him and an inheritance – a very large one, if the Critchley relation is taken into account. I ought not to reveal that, of course, but it is common knowledge. And I do not think the brothers were all that fond of each other. Now, even if he killed John, and for a reason, he would have no such reason to kill you.'

'All the same it is horrible to think of,' said Aunt Julia quietly. We had all three by now had time to think and to feel somewhat more shaken than at first.

'Yes, quite horrible. I must admit that I do not like to dwell too much on the thought of him looking at Katherine in an odd way. I like it even less than I like any other young man doing so. The thought of his arrogance is unpleasant too.'

'I said not arrogant, and that I thought he was innocent.'

'Thank you, my dear. You bring us back to the evidence. We must not presume his guilt. Those poor people, altogether! What could be worse? And which is worse – the death of one son or the suspicion that the other is the killer? I hope you two can settle in at home without me. I had meant to spend today with my womenfolk, but now I think my present duty lies with Mr and Mrs Evenden.'

He was excused, but there was still time, before the cab deposited my aunt and myself at home, for me to ask, 'What kind of artist is Mr William?'

'What kind?' echoed my aunt, momentarily puzzled. 'Yes, Thomas. What *kind* of artist is the young fellow?'

'No kind, no artist at all as yet, I believe, but he wants to be. He

25

has gone so far as sitting a year's classes at Burlas College of Art, and a few sessions in one of the private schools in London, when the family spared him. I don't know if he went to the extreme lengths of learning anything. I think I recall he led the protests here, agitating for classes "from life".'

Aunt Julia clucked.

'So,' I pursued, 'he could, say, be a copyist for the tourist market?'

'I think he shares the fashionable passion for travel but – no, I think not.'

'Oh, and even less, follow the decorative school?'

'No, you are right; little chance of that.'

'Fine landscapes, or poignant incident, then – to the taste of rich buyers? Or would even that be too much tainted with "trade"?'

'We may be maligning the man, but I fear you are right there also. It is to be art for art's sake, if at all. As I say, he is not begun.'

'And a second son!' said Julia. 'Leaving only one question: does he mean to starve, or sponge?'

'A second son no longer, though,' said Father, following which there was an interval of silence. He added, 'His father was hoping to persuade him to delay, and qualify for a profession, meanwhile; but I was not aware of any decision having been reached. I had the impression that the boy would get his way in the end, if the mother allowed. She usually has the final say.'

We reached home, and took our belongings inside, upon which Father immediately left us. My aunt and I spent the rest of the day in comfortable gossip, sorting and re-sorting the goods from London, until we had the day's events fully in proportion and could face the future all the more bravely, knowing the stuff of which we were made.

'Whatever we do, it will get about somehow, you know – our adventure,' Aunt said. 'Henry Ryder will be among the first to hear of it. You know how some folk prattle on to their doctors. It will make him think of you.' This thought had already occurred to me, though I said nothing.

6

Before long, it was generally known that grand old Mr Evenden's elder son had been murdered by the younger one, and with the latter being certain to hang the house was utterly fallen. (It was even spoken of in Burlas as a blow against the landed interest, and less complacently as a likely cause for agitators to provoke riotousness.)

I confess.

I confess that merely on account of the speed, certainty and universality with which the guilt of William Evenden was decided, I would have taken any opportunity to challenge it. Going against every comfortable assumption was an intellectual habit with me.

By dinner time on the very day of Mr Evenden's arrest and our return from London I had further privileged information from my father who had returned from Evenden Hall. At that stage even I would have acknowledged that the chances were remote of anyone, let alone me, reversing the expected verdict.

I think my father found Evenden Hall that day to be a rather appalling place, and his duties there in advising Mr Frederick Evenden most depressing to his spirits. My father did not see Mrs Evenden, he said. She was shut away with her physician; but the oppressive sense of her grief and self-torture dominated the household. All rooms had been curtained at the first news of the tragedy, and Father's consultations with Mr Evenden were conducted in the glow from a single lamp, in low clandestine voices.

Mr Tutt, the police detective inspector whom I later saw at the station, had called at the Hall that morning to convey the news of John's death, which he had had himself from Critchley by telegraph. On the basis of what he was told there he had returned to Burlas and the station in the hope, which proved well-founded, of intercepting Mr William.

Mr Tutt returned to the Hall again in the afternoon while Father was there, bringing with him a constable who had travelled up from Critchley. Thus news of the principal evidence against William was conveyed to my father.

By dint of harassing him with questions over dinner, I in my turn obtained most of the information, which anyway was soon to be commonly known.

William had left home for Critchley the previous evening, intending to call on his brother and patch up some quarrel. John had offended at their last meeting by taking a high-handed attitude to various alleged shortcomings in the younger brother's general conduct. William for his part thought that John should cut short his time at Critchley and return home, where he was particularly wanted by his ever-ailing mother. This was partly with a view to William himself then being free to follow his own inclination to travel abroad. The full picture of the antagonism between the two was more diffuse and obscure. Father said that over the years Mr Evenden had been wont to remark, with amused indulgence, the divergent characters of his sons.

John's body was discovered in the cottage he had taken at Critchley by the day servant from the village first thing in the morning. She had entered by the front door to which she had the key. The corpse was in the principal room, the skull crushed by furious blows. Furnishings were in disarray, some of them broken. John's bed had not been slept in. The servant ran off to fetch help, locking the front door again behind her. She returned with others perhaps twenty minutes later, to be met at the front gate by a neighbour who asked what was the matter. On being told John Evenden was dead, he said: 'Oh no. I did worry, for I thought I saw someone watching the place last evening, and I heard something in the night, but just now I saw him leave the house in a hurry. He was

28

climbing over the little wall at the back when I saw him, setting off through the wood.'

All then re-entered the house, and found the body and everything as before. They formed the impression that few if any goods had been taken, conspicuous valuables being still in place. There were no signs of forced entry. The back door was locked, but the key was not in its usual place on the shelf – was not to be found, in fact. Moreover, the servant said that her master usually left the back door bolted on the inside at night, but they could all see the bolt was not pulled across. Someone had left by the back door, locking it behind him and taking the key. A couple of men then ran out into the wood a little way, but not a soul could be found, and no sign of one neither.

'I am afraid,' my father said to my aunt and myself at dinner, 'the obvious explanation is that William and John failed to resolve their differences. The discussion on the contrary turned into an argument culminating in murder. For some reason, William remained hidden overnight in the house – perhaps in a stupor himself from drink or blows – and then heard the servant find John's body and heard her leave the house again. Realising that a party of justice would return very soon he made his escape, hoping that if he re-locked the door behind him no-one would know by how little they had missed him. He *was* seen by the neighbour who, though, mistook him for his brother and thought all well.'

We wondered, of course, what account William could possibly give of events. Father said, 'I know only that he has denied the charge, and wisely asked to see me before saying anything more. I have arranged to visit him in the gaol tomorrow morning. I have some things to take to him from his home. His bag, which you will remember, Kitty, evidently contained nothing of significance. Mr Tutt returned it to the family this afternoon and at my suggestion a few extra clothes, books and usual comforts were put into it.'

I had indeed noted that the now familiar portmanteau was standing on our hall table, waiting to be taken to the prisoner.

'Will Mr and Mrs Evenden not be visiting him, though?' I asked.

'Mr Evenden at least might go, even if his wife is too ill.'

Father paused and looked awkward. 'Well, Kitty, they are quite devastated by the news of John's death. You cannot imagine. I don't really believe Mrs Evenden is ill so much – not more than she is generally – but she cannot face up to it.'

'Father! I know the evidence seems strong to us, but are you really saying that they believe their own son to be guilty, without hearing him?'

'I think Frederick Evenden wants to believe him innocent. I suspect that secretly William was his favourite. It is different with the mother, though. John was the only star in the sky, there. Her world must have ended. There is nothing to stop her putting the blame in the familiar quarter. She may be the invalid, but I have always found that where decisions are required she takes the lead. Frederick Evenden is rather like a hurt child himself just now. He cannot help his own son, in his present state.'

'But how can he not go to him, especially if he believes him to be innocent? You would come to me, no matter how guilty you thought me!'

'Yes, I would, and I think in the end he will go, but not yet. And, though he wants to think that William could not do it, as he said to me at one point, "When we are young, we all have moments of such terrible anger, only circumstance determines which of us does murder in a moment like that." I think that is an exaggeration, but it is true that in murder of all crimes, the previous character of the defendant is very little to the point.'

'William's character is good, then?' Aunt Julia asked.

'Well, from what I have heard, it is far from criminal – but not perfect.'

'All in all, Thomas, it seems that as his attorney and defender your cause is hopeless.'

'Even if true, that would not concern me in the least, Julia. He must be defended, and I will do my best if he chooses to have me.'

'Father,' I said, 'I wager by this time tomorrow, once you have begun your work in earnest, you will be saying that the charge is ill-laid and unjust.'

'Do you think you know me so well? Perhaps so. But for this one,

Kitty, I must say I wish I was still young. It will be less easy to see this case as sport. Frederick Evenden is more than an ordinary client; he is practically a friend.'

My aunt retired first. Later, Father and I left the drawing room together. In the hall Father stopped, and abruptly said: 'There is something here that will interest you.' He went across to Mr William Evenden's bag and took out a compact roll sketchbook which he handed to me.

Clearly he meant I should examine the contents, though I was surprised at the invitation to do what seemed a trespass. On the first page was an attractive portrait – skilful enough, as far as I could judge – of the face of a woman of middle years, in gentle repose. She was very handsome, with something of a smile around the eyes and lips.

'Goodness! Somehow I never pictured Mrs Evenden like that.'

'And you are right. That, I am told, is Miss Dorothea Bowlby.'

'Oh.' I tried to remember where I had heard the name. It was associated in my mind, in some way, with desirable things.

Father said, 'She has a name – when she is named politely – as a patroness of the arts, in a small way. Has strange folk round at parties till all hours. She thinks our Burlas is Paris – "the which," as they say, "it i'n't." '

I could tell that most of the rest of the book was still clean, but on turning one more page found a much fainter sketch, more hesitantly drawn. It was a few seconds before I took in that this was because it had been done on the moving train, it being a picture of me. I was seen in full length, sitting as I had been in the carriage, the lines mainly chosen to convey my pose, and a concentration about the brows – the scowl my aunt always tried to amend in me – as I read the newspaper which I was holding. The artist had scribbled some notes at the side: *Girl in train – provincial ingénue. Dress and hat ribbons blue. Sweet face. Age 18?*

'I didn't know, Father!'

'You are always oblivious when reading, you know.'

After a pause I muttered in some disgust: 'Sweet! Age *eighteen!*'

31

Father took the book back from me with a little smile. 'Well, I thought you ought to know. Are you upset?'

'Not really. It's a little odd, though.'

'You mustn't mind. Now, I am for bed.'

We lingered again at the top of the stairs, whispering. I had remembered some amusing story of his baby grandson's doings during my visit at my brother's. Father was reminded by this of something similar from Jeffrey's early childhood, which was bound to be especially interesting to me as I had no memories of my brother as a child, he being ten years my senior.

'I am afraid I remember his first years more clearly than yours – it is always that way with the firstborn, you know,' said my father. 'And when you were small, your poor mother was so often ill. But I do remember when I first held you, I thought, "There is no cause to worry about this lady. This one is given us to be treasured and enjoyed." And so it has always proved.'

This was more sentiment than we were used to, and I think no more was said but we kissed each other on the forehead in the old way as we parted for the night. It had been a full day, but I had no sense then of the well-habituated pattern of my life being under threat. I was even unaware of what it was that could be lost, and I am struggling to understand now when I have the deepest sense of its absence.

On entering my room, however, the room where I had always slept, I knelt. It was no commendable fervour of prayer: no, I was trying to recapture the perspective of a six-year-old; and I did reflect how remarkably fortunate I was, that all matters had always been so contrived as to keep me from suffering.

7

Father left early next morning to pursue his important business at the gaol and elsewhere. While he was gone we heard a visitor arrive. When we learned who was below, my aunt asked me to do the honours alone.

At my entrance he stood, boyish, serious, and rapidly colouring. A lock of hair fell upon his forehead. One really did seem to detect a kind of magic in the yellowness of those curls. For the first time in my life the thought ran through my head that one might put one's arms round a man for no reason other than the simple pleasure of it. Such an idea – the strength of it, at least – is perhaps contingent upon the perception of an equal and complementary one being held by the object . . . I could not for a moment step forward and offer my hand as would have been natural, but I had to speak. We had passed the longest permissible, though wonderful, interlude in smiling silently at each other.

'Doctor Ryder, how good of you to call.'

'Miss James, I was passing and I wondered – that is, I hope that you are quite well after your trip?'

'Quite well, thank you. Aunt Julia is quite well also, and my brother and his family are all quite well, and on our return we found my father very well too.'

As he followed my indication to be seated, he dared so much as to give me a look from under his lashes, asking me plainly though not very earnestly to stop teasing. I could if I tried remember and recount a good deal more, all to the same effect. Given the characters and circumstances of each, it had to be a very proper courtship, with love declared for the time being very obliquely indeed. Just as poignant to me as the vision of Katherine James on the train is the thought of Henry Ryder, perfect as he was that day, with the girl who should have made him happy.

We had guessed rightly that he would hear about the incident at the station and it was brought into his conversation with me very soon. I was glad to feel his concern for me in his questions about it. I sought to intrigue him with hints of the information I had obtained from my father.

'If the younger brother is innocent, I am sure that Mr James will win the rightful acquittal,' he said.

'But things look very black, don't you think?'

'Yes, but with no positive proof. There is a morbid fascination in these matters, one cannot deny! You have said that nothing in his behaviour gave a clue, but I wonder – '

He had paused, his eyes narrowed. 'What is it?' I asked.

'It could be an interesting test of theories, regarding the manifestation of abnormal moral development – perversion, you know. Of course, I have never met the fellow, nor any of the family. Tell me, did you by chance note anything unusual – asymmetric, contorted or malformed – about his features?'

I smiled. 'Doctor Ryder, even the enforced proximity of a railway carriage does not allow for examination of cranial zones and "bumps", if that is what you mean!'

He smiled also. 'I realise that. The science to which you refer enjoys some currency, but remains substantially untried and in my view is likely to prove inherently unreliable. On the other hand, does not common sense itself teach us that the language of the face, which derives both from innate breeding and habitual mental states, must bear some relation to ineradicable leanings of character?'

'As you say, it is almost a commonplace. But you think, then, that study of the face can be made to reveal who among us is capable of the most abhorrent crimes?'

'In that phrase, "the most abhorrent", you have the salient point, indeed. If it could be identified, I believe the distinguishing characteristic would be very particular, and probably of the type categorised as brutish, or atavistic.'

He now looked at me expectantly, so I reflected as he wished. 'No,' I had to say, though with deliberation. 'It is true I would not describe his as a face showing perfectly elevated refinement.' I looked at Henry's while I said it and I thought he blushed again. 'But, no, at the time I did not notice anything more particular.'

'Ah, well.' His disappointment was evidently not intense. 'The court must decide. Have you not wondered, though, whether in this case a guilty verdict, even if there be guilt, can serve any humane purpose? The victim's family will only suffer the more for it.'

'You think it better for a murderer to escape justice?'

'The courts can never cover the land with justice. A man is murdered, and it is lawyers' justice. What of all the other wrongs, all the suffering, for which the law has no remedy?'

'And,' another argument struck me, 'if a man kills his brother in temper one may expect a measure of punishment to be self-inflicted.'

'If it *was* in temper, and no more wicked than that. But of course the matter should be investigated and tried, even if the particular good is not apparent. If a killer can be identified, it would be a dereliction to hold back from him his exact deserts. Miss James, do *you* think he is guilty?'

I thought again. 'At first I said not. I do not know. Now I consider it poor taste in myself to use the matter as a source of gossip and speculation. It is too much the parlour game, and these are very serious matters, especially for my father.'

'Those are excellent sentiments and I am propertly rebuked,' he said.

'Not you! It is I who have been touched by the events, and should show more sense.'

'Oh, Miss James, no-one has more sense, more sense of right, than you, I believe, and it is typical that you rebuke yourself rather than others more deserving of it.'

I liked that, though momentarily it cost me a measure of self-possession. Aunt Julia entered and much of the same talk as before, on the subject of the Evendens, was immediately repeated. As saintly as Henry thought me, and I him, and as much as each was inspired to be all good in the sight of the other, I have to say that neither of us protested.

The subject was indeed entirely and irresistibly absorbing, but each of us brought our own special interest. My aunt's was in what 'the talk' would be. I mean nothing disparaging (and I hope nothing in my account thus far has conveyed anything but respect for my aunt's good sense and intelligence).

'What I never can understand,' she said, 'whenever there is such a crime among prominent people as opposed to the more ordinary kind, is the way it is regarded as somehow different. Everyone is determined, I suppose, either to excuse him and condemn the common herd for their interest, or to blame him, *not* for doing murder but for "letting the side down"! Now, I take a no doubt simple and wrong-headed view: individual wickedness is individual wickedness, high or low. Can you help me there, now, Doctor Ryder?'

Henry looked up sharply and a little nervously, though I think with experience he was learning how to 'take' my aunt.

'Hm, I think,' he said, 'you are of course entirely right and the attitudes you describe are wrong. However, I can understand them, as stemming from a natural fear.'

'*Fear?* How so?'

'Well – the rabble may be roused too easily, or so those with most at stake always think. The Evenden crime will be talked of and cried up, I have no doubt, as a sign of the general moral unfitness of the leading orders of society. Never mind other signs, such as the pestilential conditions suffered by most of the tenantry –' He paused and smiled, a little abashed. 'Of course, I have some understanding also of how prejudice, even futile and nonsensical, can be felt against those enjoying evident privileges in life. It is easy to grow bitter unless one is careful.'

'But you yourself are highly privileged,' contended my aunt.

'You have the privileges of talent and worth, and naturally you find that they are coming to be recognised and rewarded.'

Henry stammered, looking stiff and awkward at such talk about himself.

'At least,' I said, 'the times we live in are advanced to that extent: that natural talent may be rewarded. Are you not glad?'

'I am bound, am I not, to say that I am of course grateful?' Though he looked if anything resentful.

'But you wish that such sweet reason was extended to other fields,' I concluded.

There was a pause before he said, 'I do not hold with every idea that is *called* advanced. While I do not believe in any contrived or artificial order, I do believe in the natural one. As a medical man I must always uphold that.'

He looked, I thought, somewhat defiant and uncomfortable. I reflected that he was never so awkward when alone with me; the presence of others always caused it. I chose to take his remark lightly and I laughed.

Father joined us shortly thereafter with something strained and inattentive in his look, though he stayed for some chat.

'What did William Evenden say?' asked Julia eventually – the question that was in all our minds.

'That he did not kill his brother.' He stared at his shoes, then looked up with a smile. 'Ryder, I am delighted to see you as always. Who is sick this time?'

'I think, sir, that this is the healthiest house I ever encountered. Perhaps I may take some of this beneficial atmosphere and spread it around where it is needed.'

'By all means. Bottle or bag it up, as much as you can use. I hope there will never be a falling off in the parish's need for doctoring, though, for your sake.'

'I have no fear of that.'

'I know you could do with fewer poor people sick, and more rich ones,' contended my father.

'Sadly, people of any degree need the doctor. Though I dare to suggest it is only the rich who cannot live without a lawyer.'

'Oh, yes. But I tell you, when the poor have lawyers, the world will tremble! And it may be no bad thing, if the rich are then sent scurrying to the doctor a little more. I see Kitty smiles wicked radical approval. Well, it used to be radical in my day. I lose touch. Are you a socialist now, Kitty?'

My aunt gasped at the word. It was associated so thoroughly with truly shocking ideas and activities, in the personal sphere, and fell within the category of sounds a young lady ought not even to recognise.

'Well,' Father went on, 'I have enough work as it is. I must go to my study. No, don't get up.'

He left us but I shortly made it my business to follow him, on the pretext of taking him some refreshment from our coffee tray. I sat by his desk and rested my arms and chin on his papers, staring him out for a moment.

'Did young William have nothing useful to say?' I asked.

Father looked away, sighed and fidgeted. 'He said that he did not kill his brother. That, at the time his brother was killed, he was still in Burlas. He caught the early *morning* train to Critchley, got no reply to his knock, front or back, at his brother's home though he had wired the night before, and in a temper came away back here straight away.'

'But his own father says he went the night before! Oh, I see; he says he left home then spent the night somewhere *in* Burlas. But where – and why? Don't look at me like that. Since I am a *socialist* you must think me lost anyway!'

'He will not say where he passed the night.' I felt my eyes widening. Father went on, 'It's useless as a defence. But why should he bother to tell such a feeble lie?'

'He has you, as I knew he would – as they always do,' I said.

I was satisfied to leave him with this and rejoin my guest, who was making his first attempts to leave.

'Surely,' Aunt Julia was protesting, 'no-one can be so desperate as to need you so quickly, or if they are you would certainly be too late anyway.'

This induced in me, unbidden, comical visions of patients in such a dilemma. The humour faded as I remembered the fate of John Evenden and the newspaper accounts of the shooting of poor Mr Lincoln, still fresh in my mind. I opened my mouth to join in my aunt's polite protestations then stopped in that stupefied way that happens when one has behaved like an idiot but has suddenly regained one's senses.

Henry asked, 'Is something the matter?'

'Stay a few minutes,' I said peremptorily. 'I must talk to Father.'

My knees almost trembled as I walked again to the study.

'Father, I think that William Evenden's story must be true.'

'Why do you say so?' His tone was even, half-amused; I recall his exact look!

'Because he had with him a copy of the *Burlas Gazette* which he could only have obtained here, that morning.'

'There was no newspaper with his things.'

'No.' I moaned the word in self-accusation. 'I left it on the train – when I fetched his bag. But I saw it!'

'Can you be sure which issue it was?'

'I read it, Father. Don't you see? With everything, I haven't even bought a copy of my own yet. But I read it, and you *know* what was in it. He gave it to me!'

Fully understanding, Father stared at me now, then said quietly, 'And drew a picture.' I sensed that he was pleased but he was much more serious than I would have believed. 'Kitty, it is very likely that you will be a useful witness, if you consent to take the stand. I must take further instructions this afternoon.'

I fairly ran back to the parlour.

'Wonderful news. I am to be a witness! Witness for the defence!'

My aunt shook her head sadly and muttered, 'Oh, dear, dear, dear.'

Henry caught my hands and a small something of my immoderate glee and expressed himself 'very pleased' for me. It was all of a piece with the morning's excitement that, when we finally parted, our eyes met as he said:

'I have stayed too long. It is hard to leave this house where wonderful things happen.'

8

My intervention caused my father some doubt as to whether he should continue to act for William Evenden as solicitor. The issue remained uncertain for a period, but the Crown expressed no objection and the Evendens, father and son, prevailed on him to continue. Father impressed on me that the defence had no power nor right to compel attendance of a witness, and that I must not be influenced by any consideration of his position. This, though he well knew my decision was made from the first, and unalterable.

He, with one of his partners present, took a careful statement from me at his office. In those surroundings and with a measure of ceremony, I strove to recall the small details which had acquired a seeming incongruity of importance. I had a sudden oppressive sense of the gravity of the matter. I heard my voice become low and hoarse, and had the greatest difficulty raising my eyes from my lap, aware of them both watching me.

At the end Father said only, 'You must remember and speak up on the day.'

I was also interviewed, at my home and my convenience, by Mr Tutt. His questioning was neither lengthy nor oppressive; plainly I could say nothing of material assistance to him, not being able to attest to anything such as a prominent blood stain on the accused's person nor evident turmoil of terror and remorse in his demeanour. Mr Tutt was quite respectful in his language, but nevertheless it was a most discomfiting exchange. Afterwards I reasoned that this must be because I had never before had the truth of my words weighed so transparently in a person's mind. Of course, it was his duty to doubt; and he did not *know* me. I was ashamed to reflect that a small part of my unease stemmed from being quizzed with authority by a person of that kind. He did not drop his aitches – but rather sounded them a mite too much.

My father could not be persuaded to discuss the further progress of the case with me at all. We learned – Aunt Julia and I – that inquiries for the prosecution continued under the diligent direction of Mr Tutt. One would have thought the primary evidence sufficient, but still he sought more. As my aunt had said, the case was 'somehow different'; there would be excessively high attention paid and disputation over every detail. Mr Tutt must have been aware of this. Many of his efforts centred on Critchley. He was said to be seeking a witness or accomplice: it appeared that the neighbour did *not* think the person he saw watching the cottage on the night of the murder was the accused. Now 'it was a frock-coat or skirt in the bushes' was the rumour. This mystery person was sometimes referred to confidently as the 'look-out', but while he or she remained undiscovered it helped what I could not but think of as *my* side – the defence. Altogether Mr Tutt became for a period a well-known figure in the press and elsewhere; for many it was perhaps the first time they had heard of the existence and purpose of the new detective police.

Though the Critchley witness proved elusive we learned that a mystery lady had come forward for the defence, and later that it was Miss Dorothea Bowlby. However, as with everything else, we learned this not from my father but from the common gossip. Our front parlour was in heavy use at that time. The ladies, to judge by their accusatory looks, were disappointed at the poverty of intelligence they obtained from us. Aunt Julia said to me once that she did not know but that she was more pleased than sorry. The Crown case was everywhere agreed to be strong, and some claimed to know that Mrs Evenden herself had damned her younger son – though it was also said that she kept to her bed and spoke to no-one.

The case was fully committed in early course, William Evenden being sent for trial 'for the wilful murder, otherwise the killing and slaying, of John Herbert Evenden, with malice aforethought'.

Once, when Father was leaving the house for the gaol, I asked him to tell his client from me that I was sure he would be proved innocent.

'No,' he said, taking his hat from me, unsmiling. 'There can be no messages of any kind between you.'

I tried to laugh but he would have none of it.

'Then tell me,' I said, 'is it true that Mrs Evenden already thinks him guilty?'

'I have not the slightest idea.'

'How is she?'

'An invalid, as ever she was.'

'How is Mr Evenden?'

'Well, considering.'

'How is Mr William?'

'He has youth and good health and an expensive silk to come from Middle Temple all the way to this coarse and dirty place, on his behalf. He can have no complaints.'

'Well then, and how are you, Father?'

'Thank you, my dear, I continue to prosper, for which I and all mine must be ever thankful to He who watches over all things.'

I received a letter from my brother Jeffrey in London. After family news, it shortly went on to urge the need to preserve our dignity and respectability at all costs, as a duty owed to ourselves but more particularly to our parents, to Mother's memory and to Father, who had 'laboured to bring us up in righteousness, though the dear man *is*, I grant, possessed of an unfortunate loose and careless manner, which however I contend is mere surface affectation. In you he sees the image of her, and any hurt you do to your reputation he would feel accordingly as an insult to her and a fresh wound to himself.' I thought the letter arrogant and shallow of spirit, but I showed it to no-one.

Henry Ryder called on us as often as propriety would allow. This was increasingly often. Propriety, now, would have been offended considerably had Doctor Ryder been found looking at any woman other than Miss James. What this meant to *me* cannot be conveyed, more than the honour and vanity gratified. We talked of anything, and looked our admiration at each other. To receive those looks seemed not self-regarding but nourishing to the soul. I began to think that I was my true self only with him. I was proud of him, of his goodness and simplicity, with all his cleverness. I thought that certainly no-one else had ever possessed such qualities in combination. I could watch him talk until I lost the sense of what he was saying, and then enjoy the awkwardness of silence, knowing that with a smile at the end of it I had the power to transport him. I wanted the future, hungrily, but it seemed also that the hunger itself could be fed upon for ever – almost.

One day I heard him arrive and met him in the hall, but he would not take my hand. He had been in a house where there was typhus and no place to wash, and asked to be directed to the scullery. I led him down the stairs myself. Our scullery was pleasant and airy, and that day a little sunlight filtered through the two panes high in the wall onto the scrubbed table. He removed his jacket, having asked my pardon, and rolled up his sleeves. Then he asked me to open the tap of water, and I did so, watching as he let a cold quantity of it run down over his arms and hands.

'Was it very sad – in the house with the sickness?' I asked.

For a moment he did not answer. Then he said, 'Sad enough, I dare say. One is dead, and the youngest and oldest will succumb. Three entire families are almost all of them in the eruptive stage, those still sensible being nevertheless fevered and in pain. What is worst, is that it is unnecessary. Everyone knows, now, the measures that would expel the contagion. Yet the authorities with the necessary powers refuse to act.'

'And what measures, then, would *you* prescribe?'

He paused again, I think as one almost surprised that interest should be shown by me, in whom it was pointless, when he had been unable to make others listen. He knew of my sympathy, though, and that I had once been a day pupil at an academy – with the nonconformist girls, though not of their faith. In his diffidence, he answered as to an examination question, though not without feeling.

'It is rightly called the poor man's disease. It does not require precise understanding, of germ or any other theory. The mechanism by which the contagion spreads is in truth not known, but whatever the means, we know that it transmits most freely where there is overcrowding and squalor, and seldom progresses beyond the limits of those conditions. Yet argument continues. I fear I no longer believe that men are actually so stupid that understanding is beyond them. The council has belatedly adopted the Local Government Act, and I find that *five years* ago some who are now my colleagues supplied them with a report and the most simple of proposals. It would require the paving of earth back yards, and piping of a minimum of water, so they could be cleaned of – pardon me – the ordure; secondarily, a programme to replace privy middens with closets and rubble sewers with clay, and build new housing to reduce the crowding and in time replace the worst blocks and tenements. Oh, and the provision of public baths and wash-houses.'

'Little enough,' I gently smiled.

'But it can be done, and is not – none of it. The size of the Health Committee has even been reduced because "its duties are so light"!'

He had taken a bottle from his bag and poured a trickle of brown liquid from it over his hands, then scrubbed them roughly.

'They argue that there must be liberty – that interference is wrong,' I said. 'They believe there is a divine relationship between low rates and high morals. They do not understand morality, so they attend to the rates. One could forgive the ignorance if they were not so obstinate in making a virtue of it.'

'Perhaps,' he said. 'I know only that conditions destructive of human life are suffered to continue.'

Dried again, he sought and received of me permission to leave off his outer garment, folded inside-out as it was, until he should depart and so be able to air it again. One did not know, as he repeated, the means of transmission of the typhus contagion. He then at last gave me his hand and held mine for a moment.

'I hope it does not sting,' he said with a little laugh.

'No, but it is cold! Does that liquid sting you?'

'No,' he said, dropping my hand with apparent reluctance, 'not really.'

We stayed then, talking in the scullery which, despite the noise of coming and going through the open door to the kitchen, was oddly intimate.

'Well, Miss James, you will shortly become very famous for a little while. Shall you enjoy that?'

It seemed for the moment a trivial matter, following our more earnest exchange. 'I am afraid that I may not be able to answer the questions properly,' I said. 'I ought not to care about making a fool of myself, but the evidence is important – it should be done right.'

'I have no doubt that it will.'

'Doctor Ryder, will it displease you – my being famous for a day?'

'No, never!' he said immediately – perhaps too immediately for he went on: 'Of course womankind is more properly and advantageously seen shielded from the full glare of the public gaze. Where the cause is justice, though, the general rule must give way. Only your fame, in truth, should be of a different quality altogether.'

I laughed awkwardly, because even he did not know all that must come out in my evidence. 'It could not be for anything good. I do not heal the sick, or fight poverty and ignorance.'

'You have a way of dispelling the foolishness from me, even when you are fooling. And if I was a proper worthy and clever fellow, instead of a dull provincial bumpkin, I could say something quite poetical about sicknesses of the heart and the soul.'

The days passed. Mr Vaux, the expensive silk and fit defender, arrived in Burlas in due course and lodged at the White Hart, as did Mr Johnson, his learned friend representing the Crown. In the bustling person of the Queen rested the retributive soul of her people.

When the judge arrived, Aunt Julia and I walked to the end of Long Wall to see the parade. He was an unremarkable small man, who looked neither to right nor left as, buried in red robes and white wig, he shuffled awkwardly behind the much grander and taller sheriff, who carried off *his* sword and feathers with a flourish.

The day was fixed; the trial 'came on' at the Burlas Summer Assizes. The courthouse in Burlas was the ancient castle itself. I knew the place, without having ever happened to go to a trial in progress. The central castle keep had been rebuilt, the interior rooms panelled with oak. The courtroom was octagonal, narrow, but very high. The upper parts of the walls were almost entirely glazed with old-fashioned diamond glass, so that the occupants were lit from above with a dusty, yellow light. In the summer, when it became stifling, black-cloaked old men would shuffle through the midst of the proceedings and open some of the topmost lights by means of heavy poles thirty feet or more in length, which they bore upright before them. (These contrivances had been introduced following an incident in the old days, when the corrupted air in crowded courts, with their long sittings, meant one must literally tempt Fate to attend. The presiding judge at Burlas had once been told that the windows could only be opened by a man climbing onto the roof. The judge had famously ordered that the windows be shattered forthwith.) In darker weather similar contraptions lit the great candles – no gas, still – many of which tipped and dripped on those below, to supplement the little lights on the desks of the lawyers.

Seating arrangements were disposed to separate the players vertically, there being too little space to do so in the horizontal plane. Highest of all, on a virtual throne accessed from a hidden and private corridor, sat the judge, sometimes kept company by the sheriff, who, with no duties other than ceremonial, invariably snoozed in his chair behind. A little lower sat the jury, and opposite them the public in the tiny raked gallery. Immediately beneath the judge, so that he could be alerted by a hissed command or a poking finger if His Lordship chose to lean forward, sat the clerk. He bobbed and twisted all day, exchanging whispers and papers with his master. Opposite and level with the clerk, but otherwise somewhat isolated, sat the defendant in the dock, usually with gaolers. The witness box was in an intermediate position between the judge and jury, reached by a few steps. In the pit were ranged the lawyers, counsel to the front, solicitors and clerks behind so that their attention could be discreetly sought by the 'briefs' or, though with greater difficulty, the defendant.

In showing me all this as a curiosity, Father had in the past explained the above features. Once, when I was quite a small child, he had taken me through the back corridors and down through the very rock, it seemed, to the whitewashed dungeons which, with new solid doors and locks, did service as cells for the days when trials were on. (The accused would be brought here from the gaol across the city, in the heavy barred black wagon that rattled so mournfully through the early morning streets.) I had been powerfully impressed then when an officer in the cells told me how, after a man was sentenced to hang, he would be dragged back down from the court, unable to support himself, crying for his mother and cursing his accusers.

I had to wait almost two days to give my evidence, during which time I must stay in the precincts of the court, but was forbidden to sit in on the proceedings or discuss them in any way. On the first day it rained and I sat for long hours in the large antechamber. In the morning there was a throng, a *mêlée* of red and blue bags, criers, bailiffs, hangers-on, witnesses and mere spectators. We were silenced by a shout at which we must all stand and bow as the insignificant man in red robes walked through. Then, with the start of business, the swearing-in of the jury and the scrambling for position in the gallery (all out of my sight), the crowd thinned. Then, ushers and officials with little to do, but that with an air of importance, talked together as those who do nothing but talk to the same people day after day often do. It seemed I became all nerves. The high walls and whispering tones deadened everything else.

My aunt walked restlessly to and fro and stopped to talk to me sometimes. I heard names called and witnesses appeared from other shadowy corners, and walked quickly into the court: Mr

Tutt, looking smaller and less confident now in his dark clothes; Florence Driver, whom I guessed to be John Evenden's Critchley housemaid; then two who must have been among the others in the house that morning. The neighbour, Derby Ferris, spotter of movements in bushes and identifier of the defendant making his escape over the back fence, was red-faced and glowering – nervous like myself, perhaps.

Towards the end of the afternoon I raised my head at the noise of approaching footsteps. Seeing Henry Ryder, his face lit by a smile, I could have cried at being so relieved from the boredom and tension. I told him what little I knew. At that time, almost anyone in the city could have told him more. At least it was clear to me that the evidence was going at something near the slower of Father's two extreme estimates, and I certainly would not be called that day. Henry said that he could arrange matters so as to be present throughout the following day, but asked if I objected. I urged him to attend if he wished, then for a few moments questioned myself privately, whether in fact I would rather he stayed away. There were points of my evidence which I should have explained to him, if that would have been proper – Father had now laid so many repeated injunctions on me that I was not sure. I was, however, clear in my own mind that Henry's presence could not deter me from giving the answers that I should. If there would then be any awkwardness, then through it there would also be – I must certainly hope it – unfailing support from him. We meandered together across the stone flags for some moments, and on parting he pressed my hand with such gentle encouragement, and showed in his eyes such confidence in me, I was glad of my decision – not just about his attendance at the trial.

'I am not a child any more,' I thought, 'and therefore I am ready to marry. I have chosen the best of men – if he will choose me. Let tomorrow be over with, I hope that I can be happy forever.'

When Father took us home and dined with us that evening I wondered if he and my aunt noticed my new gravity, but we were each of us preoccupied in different ways. Now that the trial was at last begun, Father did not return to his study and work after the meal, but brought a volume of his favourite light reading – Campbell's *Lives of the Lord Chancellors*, what else? – and sat with us, before retiring early.

The second day was fine and dry. Before he went into court, Father told me that I might walk in the castle grounds, but not beyond, provided that after luncheon I would stay ready as before. As the crowd again cleared and I walked towards the sunshine I heard the call for Mr Frederick Evenden. I was at that moment approaching a well-built but elderly man, who sat resting his hands on his cane and at first only shook his head at the call. Someone discreetly drew near to him and spoke.

'Yes, yes,' he snapped. 'All right.'

As he rose he saw me. I was clearly his inferior, and much more than that his junior in years. His pain was too visible, and at the same time too clearly beyond my understanding, for all I had turned the case over in my mind and prided myself on my sensitivity to its tragic aspects. I knew that he was forced to speak for the prosecution, to explain the animosity between his sons, and the circumstances of William's departure for Critchley. As I moved to walk on he called to me sharply, as at a fresh insult:

'You must not leave! You must stay!'

'Oh, I am not leaving. Not leaving,' I stammered. 'I shall be here this afternoon.' Then I went as fast as was decent, away from him out into the air.

At first I could not think how he had recognised me, unless someone had pointed me out to him. Or, I realised, he could have seen the drawing in his son's sketchbook as he and my father had gone through the contents of the portmanteau, on the day after the murder. As I registered the thought, and looked about me, I found that the path I was following around the ruined ramparts would soon converge with one being taken by another lady.

She wore a striking green outfit but the face was thoughtful, mobile and wise. It was the very book again, the face that had been drawn with such care and sympathy. I was at last seeing the celebrated Miss Bowlby. We had both stopped, and she seemed to guess at my identity also. Perhaps *she* had been permitted to visit him. Perhaps the story was all told in my own staring eyes before I remembered to remove them from her face. In a brief gesture her shoulders rose and fell, and she turned without a word, and walked away so that our paths need not cross. As I looked after her she turned to look again at me and, not incommoded at being discovered at this, did look at me fully before continuing on her way, when I saw her give the least shake of her head. I was puzzled and thought that she might have been laughing at me.

There was no solace in the peaceful green walks among the massive stones. The sense of unreality, and still of threat, was now acutely upon me. I only hoped that composure and some order to my thoughts would come. The city below seemed to sleep, but I knew otherwise. The citizens who could not be at the castle that day, hundreds and thousands of them, went about with half a mind on their business, and half on the early editions. They wanted drama. Could they be blamed for it? It was what I had always wanted myself. They wanted the truth, but the ghoulish detail, not the indigestible whole. Justice they wanted, the breaking of the villain, the odious fratricide. They wanted a hanging – the feet dragging back to the dungeon and the cry of 'Mother!'

9

'Miss James, do you identify the defendant as the man who joined the train at Critchley? Look at the defendant, please.'

I had crossed the courtroom, climbed the steps, taken the witness stand, and repeated the oath, without mishap. The perspective now was strange. Close to was the judge, looking detached and bored, busy with constant pencil notemaking, pausing only to tear a piece of paper into careful strips ('Should he not let someone else do that for him?' I found myself thinking). Mr Vaux, the defence counsel, appeared far away and below. There was, I thought, nowhere else I might safely look. The jurymen beside me and the public in the gallery opposite, including my aunt and Henry Ryder, were all watching me. I was aware of my father, seated behind Mr Vaux, taking his own diligent notes but probably more agitated on my behalf than I was myself. I remembered his advice that I should speak up.

It was fortunate that the identity of my fellow-passenger on the train was not in dispute. Obedient to Mr Vaux's request, I looked briefly in the direction of the dock but in those first moments of my evidence my mind was subject to a stress such that I saw only a figure in space, another pair of eyes watching me. I cleared my throat and spoke as clearly as I could, addressing the unresponsive profile of the judge.

'Yes. That is the man.'

'My lord,' Mr Vaux also addressed the judge, 'there is a circumstance of which you and my learned friend are aware but which must be laid clearly before the jury.' The judge grunted. Mr

Vaux turned to me with what was meant, no doubt, for a smile of reassurance, but which was rather repulsive in its suddenness. 'Miss James, you are in fact, are you not, daughter of Mr Thomas James, who sits behind me and who in this matter acts as solicitor to the defendant?'

'I am.'

'Is it within your knowledge that Mr James has been family solicitor to the Evendens for many years?'

'Yes.'

'Now, Miss James, we must be clear on one point, and before you answer my next question I urge you to pause and reflect, and to study once again, if you would, the face of my client in the dock. In all the years that your father has acted for the family in that capacity, have you ever, to the best of your knowledge and recollection, met or been in any way acquainted with any member of the Evenden household? In particular, had you ever met William Evenden, my client, before the moment just described when he entered your railway carriage?' His tone had risen during this speech, until 'railway carr–i–*age*' was declaimed with an oratorical flourish.

Mentally I asked my father why the law must *be* so. Why must the pleaders make so much of everything, and in doing so take every care calculated to mortify and overmaster everyone else? I could only look again at my father's client. He looked back at me evenly, then just perceptibly rolled his eyes away from my gaze in a gesture of impatience. I remembered the expressiveness of that face, as demonstrated in our exchange in the train. I looked back at Mr Vaux, and paused to gather my thoughts.

'Except on the train on the day in question, I never met any member of the Evenden family.' Then I stumbled: 'Oh, except – I think I saw Mr Frederick Evenden outside the court this morning.' I picked up the thread once more. 'I am certain that I never met William Evenden before. There has never been any interchange between us, before or since that day. We are in effect strangers.'

Below me, Mr Vaux twisted and looked up like a cat receiving drops of cream. 'Thank you, Miss James, for the admirable clarity and precision of that reply. You are – in effect – *strangers!*'

He allowed the resonance of the word to die away a little. His pause, however, only prompted the judge to remark drily:

'I do not think you need be so anxious on this point, Mr Vaux. After all, it is not likely in the normal course that there would have been any exchanges between the Evendens and the James *family*.'

'Quite so, my lord. Now, Miss James, you must know that it has been alleged in this courtroom that at the point when my client entered your railway carriage, he was in full flight from the scene of a most bloody and horrible murder; that he had himself perpetrated that act; that he had cowered, hidden, while he heard others discovering the battered body of his own brother; and that he had then made his escape as best he could and was uncertain whether and how closely he was at that very moment being pursued – '

'My lord.' Mr Johnson bobbed up and spoke wearily. 'The evidence has been presented but not with such luridity, such meretriciousness – '

'That is, that must be, the substance of what is alleged against my client,' answered Mr Vaux.

'I agree,' drawled the judge. 'You have conveyed the substance. I am sure that it was nothing Miss James could not have deduced for herself. What is the question, Mr Vaux?'

'Miss James, as you are a stranger, an objective witness, it would help the court – '

Mr Johnson interrupted again. 'My lord, I object to the term.'

'Oh, come,' snapped Mr Vaux. 'To *what* term?'

'The reference to this as an objective witness. It is either meaningless, or too obscure. Does he mean that she exists, as an object in the real world, or exists merely in order to object?'

'I can answer, my lord, if I may?' said Mr Vaux.

'If you can do so briefly.'

(Laughter.)

'I use the term in the sense of *objektiv*; this witness will give evidence based on facts and observation, not coloured by emotion or attachment.'

'Does that content you, Mr Johnson?'

'My lord, I fear not. I cannot say that that descriptive term, applied to its object, will not be disputed, therefore it should not be introduced unsupported by my over-learned friend.'

'I will assist, once more!' cried Mr Vaux. 'I am content to discount "objective" for the objection.' (More laughter – a little uncertain; the audience humouring the players, not humoured by them.) 'Miss James, please describe for us the demeanour of my client – observed by you, a stranger – as he entered the railway train?'

I waited, but it seemed I was to be allowed to speak. Now, at last, the matter: the *events*. I spoke with care. 'He – William Evenden – entered the carriage. He had a bag with him. He sat down, in a manner quite careless. He seemed a little thoughtful. Irritated, perhaps. That was all.'

'His demeanour consistent pehaps with having travelled some way to pay a visit, only to receive no answer to his knock?'

'My lord!' bobbed Mr Johnson once more.

The judge coughed meaningfully at Mr Vaux, who continued: 'My client, one supposes, gave a conventional greeting of some kind?'

'No, he did not. In fact, I thought him a little rude. But nothing out of the ordinary.' I wondered if I miscalculated in offering this, but I was after all on oath, and I thought I saw Father smile.

The cat had received a small kick, but strove to pretend otherwise.

'Ah well. That is regrettable. But a little rudeness is no crime. Em. Though directed towards a young lady like yourself, one would think it ought to be! Heh, heh.'

I awaited the next question, and at that moment first caught sight of Henry's face in the crowd. It bore an amused expression, and was turned towards the dock.

'Kindly continue, Mr Vaux. This is a serious matter,' mumbled the judge.

'Miss James, what do you remember the defendant to have done next?'

'He took a newspaper from his bag and read, for some time.'

'You are quite sure that it was in his bag – not held in his hand as it might be if he had just picked it up from the station at Critchley?'

'I am quite sure that it was in his bag, and it was that day's new edition of the *Burlas Gazette* which at that hour could only have been obtained in Burlas – '

'Thank you, Miss James, that is known to the jury. The actual newspaper is lost. Did you have an opportunity to study it more closely, to have it confirmed that it was what you thought?'

'Yes. When he had finished with it, he offered it to me to read and I took it. I noted the edition particularly and I read it with interest.'

'Did you see the defendant then take out a sketchbook and take a likeness of you?'

'I did not see that, but I have seen the drawing since.'

'Thank you. So has the court. Making allowances for the movement of the train, it is a pretty good likeness. The error in the artist's note of your probable age is of course understandable and quite forgivable. The court knows that you have full capacity, as a witness.' He had picked up the sketchbook and was waving it around as he spoke. Now he put it down again. 'You will appreciate that it is of critical importance to establish the actual edition. The court has been supplied with copies. Can you, now, remember any particular item from your reading?'

'There was a report on the peace settlement in the United States of America. And there was a new account of Mr Lincoln's funeral, sent by a Burlas gentleman whose name I cannot remember.'

'Yes. Anything more particular still? Mr Vaux probed confidently.

'Yes. Something very particular. I wanted to read an item, under the name of Vengate, which I had been given to understand would be published in that morning's edition.'

'And it is there, on the second page. What was your interest in that?' Mr Vaux knew what was due: cream.

The moment had come, a moment I had dreaded yet also, in truth, in some way desired. 'I wrote it,' I said. 'I am Vengate.'

There was something of a stir. After a few seconds I tried looking up. The worst is over, at any rate, I thought. I saw Henry. His mouth was 'hanging open', exactly in the manner I had believed confined to fiction. I wished I could read his innermost reaction, but I could not. My attention was recalled by the judge. He was roused at last, and looking at me.

'Miss James, you say you yourself *wrote* this?'

'Yes, my lord.'

'You practise the trade of journalism?'

'Not practise; this was the first piece of mine accepted for publication.'

'Well. Of course, ladies *do* on occasion express opinions on matters external to the domestic realm. There are examples of ladies doing so, and doing it well, and in print even so far as passing undetected by the device of a masculine pen-name.'

'My lord, I selected a name which was anonymous, but neutral as to –'

'What? Oh yes, I see. And I note that the piece did appear, as you said. It also makes reference to the American War, with the supposed lesson, or paradox, being in essence – let me see, now – yes, that we in England might have something to learn now from the colonists?'

'From the Americans – well, yes.'

'Thank you, Miss James.' His lordship contented himself with an eloquent pause. 'Hmm. Mr Vaux, pray continue.'

But there was very little more that Mr Vaux, evidently satisfied, needed me to say. The point was made: simply, that in travelling back to Burlas, William Evenden had in his possession a newspaper which must have been obtained earlier the same day, *in* Burlas. The defender soon sat down and Mr Johnson got to his feet. During my evidence, I had become half-aware that he fixed the jury with an unswerving, sceptical eye: a neat trick, I thought. Now he dealt with me shortly.

'Miss James, the prosecution accepts that the accused handed you a newspaper on the train, and that the newspaper could only have been obtained in Burlas that morning. Yet it was in Critchley. Do you know how it got there?'

'No. But I can only think it was brought on the early train.'

'Quite. Do you know who brought it?'

'No.'

'Could it have been anyone?'

'It could, but it was in the possession of William Evenden, in his bag.'

'Now, you have come forward from a disinterested motive, so let us be objective. Do you know when he put it there?'

'No.'

'It could have been on Critchley station?'

'Possibly.'

'In fact, had he seen it on Critchley station, someone seeking an alibi could have realised its significance, and seized an opportunity. Would be very stupid not to, in fact?'

'Thank you, Mr Johnson. That is not for this witness to say,' said the judge.

'Miss James, you described the accused's behaviour. He could be said – correct me if I am wrong – to have been rude, quiet, preoccupied?'

'But not to any extraordinary degree – '

'Thank you.' Mr Johnson, with a look to the jury which said that too much time had been spent on this witness, sat down.

Mr Vaux rose again.

'Miss James, on the day in question, did my client betray the smallest sign of being frightened?'

'None whatsoever.'

'Petrified?'

'No.'

'Tormented?'

'Certainly not.'

'When you first heard the accusation against him, how were you affected thereby?'

'My feelings were of astonishment and disbelief.'

'Thank you.'

My ordeal was over, and had proved supportable. As I passed and glanced at the dock, I formed the impression that the defendant showed no fear, even then; it was probable, therefore, that he was one adept at concealing signs of weakness.

10

Mr Johnson's summation of his case to the jury began as I left the well of the court. Outside, I made my way to the door of the public gallery. An official stood guard there, whose business was to allow no disturbance to the proceedings. I could not be admitted until there was a further break. Mr Johnson's voice could be heard, but I could not make out the words.

'I doubt you'll find a place now anyway, miss,' said the usher in a hushed tone as we waited.

'My friends were trying to save me one.'

'You're one of the witnesses, aren't you? I take it they've finished with you, or you can't go in, you know.'

'Yes, they've finished with all the witnesses.'

'Oh good. Progress at last, eh? We'll maybe be done by tea-time after all.'

'The jury may take some time,' I said.

'They should have the villain in with them, I always think, and open his heart to peep inside,' commented the usher.

Immediately, a shuffling within indicated that Mr Johnson had already resumed his seat. The door to the gallery was opened to let me through. I learned later that in the intervening time Mr Johnson had stated his case briefly, with an exaggerated appearance of confidence as to the outcome. The defendant had a motive, both in the inheritance and the immediate ill will between himself and his brother. He had declared his intention to be at his brother's home at the time of the murder. He had left the scene hurriedly, and by the back way, after the murder. He had joined the train, where he had behaved in a distracted and rude manner, though he had subsequently tried to appear more nonchalant. He had taken care to record the fact that a lady had been with him, reading a copy of that morning's paper, which he had passed to her. Once apprehended, he had claimed that, in spite of his declared intention, he had not travelled to Critchley the previous night at all. As to the other defence witnesses: the jury must form their own opinion of Miss Bowlby but he – Mr Johnson – would suggest that, at the very least, she was clearly unreliable as the supposed mainstay of the defence *alibi*; Miss James was a dupe.

Mr Vaux was rising to answer this as I entered. I looked for my aunt and Henry Ryder. They had taken care to occupy between them enough space on one of the bench seats for three. Seeing me, they made room for me to sit at the end next to my aunt. Once settled, though she by her example tried to suggest that I should fix my attention on the counsel for the defence, I could concentrate on nothing – nor even breathe, I thought – until one matter was resolved. Ignoring my sense of her disapproval, and ignoring also the looks of the several curious spectators who, wearied by the legal discourse, had turned to stare at my entrance, I leaned forward and turned to catch Henry's eye. At first he kept his profile to me and my heart sank, but still I waited and hoped for a look from him that would answer my fears; then thankfully he showed himself also prepared to stand up to the public gaze. He bestowed on me a smile, and a nod. It was enough; all was not lost. I gave my attention to the lesser matter of Mr Vaux's speech – a mere matter of someone else's life or death.

Mr Vaux had begun with conventional remarks on the jury's duty. Counsel for the Crown had tried to make out a case, of sorts. He had set out a story; 'a fable, tacked on to fragments of circumstance. There is no proof. There is a profusion of holes.'

Then Mr Vaux summarised the prosecution's 'fable', and at greater length than his learned friend had done; but I believe the effect was very different. Perhaps Mr Vaux was not the buffoon I had thought him; he was after all a man of great reputation, procured by my father whose experience and judgment were sound. Or perhaps he was one of those fortunate people, usually found in the highest rank in my experience, whose foolishness, though genuine, unfailingly secures an advantageous result. Mr Johnson had presented a small, round, solid tale and Mr Vaux did indeed reduce it to fragments. Partly this was by his characteristic hesitations, groping for descriptive phrases, appearing to lose track of where a particular conclusion found its root in the available evidence.

He then dwelt at still greater length on the defence case. He reminded the jury that William Evenden himself was barred from taking the witness stand, but in these enlightened times one who stood charged with a felony was allowed to obtain the services of one learned in the law, to make answer on his behalf. 'Here we have a man, scarcely more than a youth, of great promise. He makes no grand claims for himself, only that he has never contemplated committing any crime and never wished harm to anyone.' I noted the defendant sat expressionless and wondered, could he have put his own case, what difference of delivery there would have been. 'We candidly admit the quarrel with his brother over his brother's stay at Critchley and the share of filial duty at home, with an invalid mother, which consequently fell to the accused. He wanted to travel abroad and so was anxious to speak about these matters again with his brother. He told his parents he was travelling there on the evening of the murder but, with half an idea in his mind, sent to his brother saying he would come on the evening *or* by the first train the next day. That note has never been found.

'The idea in his mind was that he would like to call first on, and seek the counsel of, his friend Miss Bowlby. It was a friendship of which his parents disapproved, hence the deception. He did call on Miss Bowlby. While they talked, he drew her portrait – here it is. He realised he had missed his train. You may think that was always likely. He slept that night on the sofa in Miss Bowlby's house. Meanwhile, miles away, his brother was murdered.

'And who supports the truth of this? None other than Miss Bowlby herself. That a young artist whom she had befriended and

61

encouraged should spend the night at her house is a fact that, in the normal course, would have remained utterly private between the two of them. But when William Evenden was accused of this ghastly crime, she came forward to tell the truth. In doing so she has been publicly attacked in this court, as she knew that she would be. Miss Bowlby's conduct and principles in general are, no doubt, open to criticism and may be condemned by many. All that you are required to judge, in relation to her, is the truth of her testimony. In judging that matter, gentlemen, I suggest you consider that in giving it she had nothing to gain, and everything to lose that a woman can lose. I say she told the truth. For you, it is enough that she raises a doubt.

'Gentlemen, I contend that you need no more proof of the desperation of the Crown's attempt to convict my client than the fact that, having failed to discover the identity of their mysterious person in the bushes (whom they most deviously persist in calling "the accomplice or witness") – having failed in that, my learned friend put it to Miss Bowlby that she herself had been present, acting in concert with Mr Evenden! That is the level of their reasoning! "We seek a female, and lo here is one! Let us say that it was she!" Miss Bowlby herself called it ridiculous and I need say no more about it, I am sure.

'What more is needed to acquit William Evenden? Nothing. Yet there is more. Members of the jury, you will need little reminding of the testimony of the witness who was most recently before you: Miss Katherine James. Miss James was a stranger to the defendant, caught up by chance in these events. Her evidence is transparently honest and impartial: an "ingénue" indeed, provincial or not. It is most important and valuable because of that, and also because Miss James was the only person able to study closely the supposedly escaping murderer. How did she find my client? She found him to be a very ordinary young man, a little impolite but nothing out of the ordinary; sadly, in these times, that *is* nothing out of the ordinary. And she found him to be in possession of a newspaper which she was most anxious to read, because she had been unable to obtain it, because no-one could have obtained it who had not been in Burlas that morning – in Burlas, *not* in Critchley. And she was particularly sure of the issue because she had herself written an article which appeared in print therein. My learned friend tried to dismiss the significance of all this. It cannot be dismissed. A man's life is at stake. Miss James's testimony stands like a beacon: clear, bright, sure, immovable. I think no-one who was in this courtroom today will ever forget that.' I reflected that he was probably right, and groaned inwardly. 'And remember that she too had something to lose, something of no little importance to a young lady who dares to take up her pen and write of things that many would consider to be outside the proper territory of the female mind: her anonymity.

'The Crown must resort to claiming that she was duped and tricked into this: the defendant is presumed to have had the good fortune to light on an already-abandoned copy of this brand-new newspaper, and the presence of mind to encourage his fellow passenger to accept it from him – even his sketch of her reading is claimed to be part of this stratagem. But what stratagem, gentlemen? This carefully planted piece of evidence was simply, thoughtlessly, left on the train by the defendant. Not the action of a desperate, devious trickster, you may think. And of course you are right. William Evenden is no such thing. He is a young man who has suffered the tragedy of having a brother murdered, and the misfortune of having been, at the time, somewhere he should not have been. He called at his brother's house and obtained no answer, front or back, unaware that a party of neighbours had gone to fetch the police, that his brother's body lay within. Irritated and angry, understandably, he went away and caught the next train home.

'John Evenden, we know, was murdered the night before. He was already dead when William arrived in Critchley that morning. He had prepared himself to retire before the fatal assault. Some sound of the assault at night reached the neighbour's ears. His bed was not slept in; his body when discovered was stiff and cold. So far as William is concerned, that is what happened; there is no shred of evidence otherwise. Yet you are asked to believe that he has lied, on oath, and that another lady of fine perception and understanding has been mysteriously duped into volunteering evidence which confirms his story. My learned friend requires you to believe that this young man killed his own brother, against his nature and against nature itself, then for some reason remained hidden in the house through the long hours of night, before coolly setting off for home, locking the door behind him. This cannot even be believed, and is so far from being proven as to be a fairy tale.

'We all deplore the killing of John Evenden, a blameless man. But until the murderer is found, we must bear our human ignorance, not rush into fatal error ourselves. Otherwise, we only compound the evil that has befallen. We all remember with sympathy the evidence given by Mr Frederick Evenden, the unhappy father, called by the Crown to tell us of the petty squabble between his two beloved sons. How much more eloquently he spoke of his belief in the good character of each, his grief that they should both have become victims in this affair, victims of an unknown assassin. Members of the jury, remit half of this tragedy. Restore, to the only son of the house of Evenden still living, the freedom and reputation he should never have lost.'

Mr Vaux sat down. By the end of this speech, I had of course become convinced that he was not a genuine fool. His little peculiarities were for effect only, and made more impressive the way in which, at last, he commanded attention with the intensity of his argument and the power of his eloquence. Yet something had jarred, in my own mind at least, in the last moments of his address. It was true that his client had left his belongings on the train, to help me and my aunt down to the platform; but he had left the newspaper together with his other things, probably intending to pick them all up himself the next moment. It was not he who had been so careless with the critical piece of evidence; it was I.

However, it was now the judge's turn to address the jury. The facts which he had to recite, as to the suspicious sights and sounds of the night, the discovery of the body, the lack of evidence of a robbery, the sighting of the defendant near the house, the missing back door key, the evidence of an existing quarrel, and the conflict

as to where the defendant was at the precise time of the murder –
all was already over-familiar to me. How much more so must it be
to the jury; but the jurymen attended his words, I saw, with
particular care. All that they had heard up to then had burdened
them, but the judge carried real authority; they looked to him for
help, trustingly.

He indicated that it was not really so difficult. They had heard a
lot of talk. One could mull over the details of it, turn it this way or
that, enjoy even a little laughter here and there. It was the Crown
that must work, and convince them of the defendant's guilt. If they
were so convinced, they must not shrink from finding accordingly,
in justice, in the face of the crime that had taken place. But
otherwise – nothing.

He led them through the evidence, but the nub was the
credibility of the defendant himself, and of Miss Bowlby. If
Evenden had spent the night there, as she claimed, he had
deceived his parents. He could not give his own account on oath;
he was also protected from having it challenged on oath. Miss
Bowlby was . . . He went through the criticisms; she was someone
with whom they may not care to have a son of theirs be acquainted.
'The question is, is it really certain they are both lying in what they
tell you now? Might it not be the truth?'

Then there was me. After the others, I seemed to come as light
relief. The judge paused and smiled. 'Miss James: some would say,
an unusual young woman. But in her capacity as witness to these
events, you may think, in agreement with the learned counsel for
the defence, most impressive: "clear, bright, sure, immovable".'
Aunt Julia dug me in the ribs. That one would stick. 'Yes,
undoubtedly. But significant? The prosecution suggests the whole
business of the newpaper is simply not significant. You have heard
the arguments on that score and it is for you to decide. Certainly it
was right for the defence to bring this evidence before you, if on any
view it could raise a doubt as to the version of events on which the
Crown seeks to rely.'

A judge always took one side or another, my father said; always.
It may be more or less easy to tell which. I sensed the approach of

the crisis: the turning point. I noticed the defendant's hands were busy sketching the scene. Those hands might be stilled forever. But I thought I detected, in the judge's prevarications, the twitches of his nose, a tendency to twitch the noose, by a degree, away from Mr William's neck.

There were remarks as to their duty and the method they must follow in bringing in a verdict, then the jury were 'sent out', with more ceremony, and the swearing of an oath by the bailiff who would guard their chamber. After they had shuffled out, the judge stood, his clerk ordering us all to rise, and we bowed him out too. Then, as always on the judge's departure, there was a murmuring moment of relaxation, easing of limbs among the public, shrugs and philosophy exchanged between rival counsel and attorneys. While the gaolers waited ready to take him back to the cells, William Evenden leaned forward and calmly shook the upstretched hands of Mr Vaux and my father.

'That's gentlemanly of him,' commented a woman in front of me.

'Counts for nothing, if you're bred up to it,' countered a man I took for her husband.

'I think he might get the not guilty, though, don't you?'

'Yes, maybe. The lawyer's daughter did her job all right.'

'Hush! She's standing behind.'

'What then? I've said nothing. Though *some* lies have been told, I'm sure.'

'Not if the defence is right; it's just a mistake.'

'No, I mean it's certain no-one slept on any *so-fah* that night!'

'Oh, you are bad!'

'What of *they*? Nobs or no.'

Most took the opportunity offered to leave for a time the close confinement of the courtroom. Henry, Julia and I paused in the lobby and Father joined us. Then we all walked a little outside, where people of all degrees stood in knots, within range of the call if the jury should return quickly. The afternoon air was soft and pleasant. My aunt shifted a little to enjoy the view. Henry, with an adjustment to his hat, and a further smile at me, politely went with her.

'Father,' I said. 'What Mr Vaux implied about Mr Evenden leaving the newspaper on the train, so that it could not have been a ploy, was not quite right. Remember, I fetched his things from the carriage and it was I who left the newspaper behind.'

'I know, but I think the way he did it was permissible. He was responding to a piece of speculation by the other side. Johnson fell down before, really, in not questioning you about it. The judge had your statement, and steered clear in his address. It does not rank as forensic licence or excess, and it will be all one if we get the verdict.'

'I think you said yourself, Father, this is not a game.'

'Oh!' He looked at me comically, beginning to relax already. 'It is my beacon. Clear, bright, thingummy, immovable. Well, in any event, I hope our side is well enough ahead, though you never can tell with juries, shut away without meat, drink or candle. But you have been most patient with me these past weeks and I will tell you one thing in confidence now, for what it is worth. When I first conveyed to my young client *your* account of the loan of the *Gazette* and its significance he looked at me curiously and said: "She must be very clever." My thought at that moment was, "Perhaps you are even more." '

I paused, taken aback by his cool smile. Then I said, 'Father, I know that my aunt always thought you should have forbidden me to submit my article to the *Gazette*. Are you sorry now that it has come out, in the way I gave my evidence? Jeffrey wrote to me, to say that I should think of the family name, and be careful.'

'Kitty, I think we neither of us have any cause to be ashamed. We must not start to think of regrets because of a little gossip that will soon die down. But I take it someone of our acquaintance may have had a shock. Has he said anything?'

'No. I think that it will be all right.'

'I think you should be talking to him, and I should be going inside to find Vaux.'

'Father! One thing I missed. How did the Crown explain that

William Evenden was supposed to have spent all night with the body before escaping?'

'He probably needed to clean and tidy himself, maybe remove any evidence like the note that really did say he was arriving that evening. He may have washed and dried parts of his clothing, even destroyed them – that can take a lot of time. He could even have taken one of his brother's shirts; they were the same build, and had many items indistinguishable. If he was scared, he may have meant only to wait until the middle of the night, but fallen asleep. Once you start guessing, it's quite easy to work something up. He should have faked a robbery while he was there, of course, but you can't think of everything. I must go.'

As he turned to re-enter the castle a man came up to us and accosted him. One could not call him ill-natured; his face belied that, seeming that of a child mistakenly overlaid with the worn flesh of an adult. I saw that he was a man of the cloth. He spoke with a kind of weary accusation.

'Sir, you can have no objection to speaking with me now; besides which, as you saw, I was not called – '

I heard my father answer as he started to walk away, 'Of course I have no objection, but I fear I have very little time. Shall we walk in together?'

They did so, my father touching his hat to Henry who approached at that moment.

I was quiet and awkward, hoping he would speak first, but he would not. After all, I thought, he knew that I read. He knew even that I wrote; we had composed a short skit together, once. The approach to the editor of the *Gazette* had been different; of course, in my heart I had known that it was, and known immodest satisfaction on first seeing my words in print. Still, to me, the dramatic events immediately succeeding had cast the business in a very ordinary light by comparison. How would it be viewed by Henry Ryder, though?

'Doctor Ryder, I owe you an apology,' I said at last. 'I know the fact that I have written for a newspaper came as a shock to you, and I should have told you of it before now. I know you may disapprove, and you may at least have wished that I had been more open with you.'

Considering his face then I thought he wished I had chosen not to mention the matter, though it was surely a thing on which his opinion must be resolved and acknowledged if – well, if my hopes were not entirely misplaced.

With whatever brave restraint, he spoke as follows: 'But Miss James, this is nonsense, of course! I own that I was surprised at first, but not on reflection, knowing the sincerity and soundness of your views and motives in everything. You had every right to keep your secret – until faced with another's need for you to reveal it.'

'It should not have been a secret from anyone who – who had any interest in what I do.'

'I beg you not to trouble yourself. If only – ' but there he broke off, sighing.

'What?' I asked nervously. He should say, perhaps: if only he had the right to guide my conduct.

He looked at the ground. 'I was thinking, if only I had your way with words!'

There was a murmur of surprise and hurried movement all around. These jurymen would not endure privation. They had signalled their readiness.

11

After the scramble on the part of everyone for vantage-ground in the gallery, the shuffling was still dying away as the jurymen re-entered their benches opposite. Just too late, I remembered another of my father's sayings: that you can predict the verdict from the demeanour of the jury before it is given. The signs are not obvious, but if it is to be guilty then in the main the twelve will not meet the eyes of the accused as they take their seats. If they have decided to free him, though, at least some of them will turn and glance quickly at him, as to confirm something in their own minds.

By the time I thought to test this theory, the jurors were mostly already seated. Among the last few to take their places, I thought at least one looked sidelong toward the back of the court before giving attention to the clerk who stood in his place waiting patiently. The defendant himself looked unswervingly ahead. My aunt, I saw, was perhaps trying some mystical theory of her own, eyes tight shut.

The clerk remained standing and invited the foreman to rise also. The defendant was got to his feet by the gaolers. The clerk waited for complete silence, then when he could certainly have heard a pin, had one been let fall, he fastened a stern look on the foreman as he asked, 'How say you, gentlemen of the jury? Guilty or not guilty?'

The shifty-looking spokesman for the twelve at once sputtered, hasty but clear, 'Not guilty!'

After the attenuated play of argument and the jury's own deliberations, there was a feeling in the air that the verdict also should have been more drawn-out, but there it was; it had been spoken and could not be recalled.

Around us in the gallery half-stifled shouts of approval, or of the converse disbelief, were heard, and one or two sounds of hissing. Behind us someone stood and started to clump out at once with undue noise; I turned and saw the retreating form of Mr Frederick Evenden. All remaining were presently commanded to stand to attention as the judge departed the courtroom for the last time. Below, my father looked satisfied; he spoke with Mr Vaux, then both acknowledged the quiet congratulations of the lawyers for the Crown, only thereafter turning to their client. He had climbed over the front of the dock, which was irregular, but after a capital trial such scenes are less frowned upon, provided always they are in the absence of the judge. He, William Evenden, was clasped in the arms of his father who had made such haste downstairs. The clerk stood with his back to all this, tidying the judge's desk. He carefully folded away the square of black cloth, ready for another day.

My aunt and Henry Ryder and I made our way through the departing crowd to the downstairs doorway into the court. We wondered if we would be allowed in, but no-one seemed concerned to stop us. The scene was a little quieter by the time we entered, Mr Johnson and his assistants having left and Mr Vaux being in the process of taking leave of my father. I walked forward at once, meaning to give my own congratulations to William Evenden. The hisses had stung me, and although at that moment of victory he might not apprehend the harm done by the false accusation once made against him, it would be as well if as many as possible showed openly that they believed there was now 'no stain'. As I walked across to where he stood with his father, I thought I saw a warning look in my father's eye, but he was still caught up with the effusive Mr Vaux, and could do nothing to intercept me.

William Evenden – as well he might – took my hand warmly. Mr Frederick Evenden even kissed it.

'Mr Evenden,' said I, addressing the son, 'I wanted only to give my congratulations to you, but of course no other outcome was possible. It is a shame the case was ever brought. I mean – of course – it is the greatest shame that there was ever cause for it – ' I was concerned lest I had upset Mr Frederick Evenden, but neither he nor his son, who spoke first, betrayed any adverse sign at my words.

'Miss James, how can I ever thank you? There is but one thing, which I hope will be of some satisfaction to you. Since one moment in the trial will live in my memory – ' he lowered his voice to a more confidential tone, 'I will study to improve my manners.'

I blushed. 'I am sorry, but – '

'You were on oath.' Then he looked up, his attention caught by something behind me. I turned and, though she was veiled, recognised Dorothea Bowlby in the doorway. Seeing the little crowd of us standing thus, she paused for a second then went away. William Evenden still looked after her.

Mr Evenden senior looked from him to me and back. 'Your resolution is broken as soon as it is made, of course,' he growled.

His son replied, 'If not for her, I might have hanged.'

'If not for her you might have saved John!'

I was made uncomfortable by their words, and began to stammer some excuse to go.

The old man protested. 'No! Miss James, *I* have yet to thank you. And I think I startled you this morning – overwrought, you know, with everything. But how has old James kept you hidden away from us all these years? You must visit us – if only we had people up to our place more – but you know, my wife is ill – '

My father was now at last trying gently to interrupt, but Mr Vaux succeeded in greeting me first. He thanked me with excessive pleasantries. It had been 'a rare perfect cameo of examination and response, discomposing an assembled case: a minor gem,' though he said it himself. 'Especially gratifying to make the judge sit up like that; that is always the key, when playing these tactics. I hope to see him in the Mess tonight; you can be sure I'll mention it. I shall say that he must become attuned to the modern world, to the glories of political and social observation, as expressed by either sex. May I, in the spirit of intellectual generosity, offer an observation of my own? It is too often, now, forgotten that in this country "emancipation" was also achieved at the cost of some suffering. My own family suffered very materially, from the abolition of slavery. One does not always have to look so far from home to find matters of fit inspiration. My dear James, I was saying, the battle turned when His Lordship questioned your daughter in that friendly way, don't you think?'

'Around then, I thought we had won him over. I knew at least that we would not have a Muirhouse summation.'

'What? "Gentlemen, I suppose you have no doubt? I have none." Ha, ha! Yes, the old days, dear me!'

A gaoler then returned with William Evenden's bag of belongings. This reminded the owner, who leaned up over the dock to retrieve from its narrow shelf another of his sketchbooks and a prodigious number of pencils.

'See!' he laughed. 'They would not allow me a knife for sharpening, so I had to keep a good supply. Miss James, I will show you the one I am best pleased with.'

He leafed quickly back through the pages, then placed the book in my hands open at a picture of Mr Tutt on the witness stand. He had captured exactly the policeman's air of slightly awed, conscientious stolidity. 'Oh! A little unkind,' but I had to smile.

'Excessively kind, I think – in the circumstances,' he replied.

Glancing up to be sure he did not object, I turned the pages, disclosing sketches of other players in the trial, some barely a line, others more detailed. One of his father he seemed to have given up. But there was an amusing back view of the lawyers' benches, showing them in various attitudes, lolling, in consultation, and my father in quarter profile, his head bent characteristically in listening concentration. There was a whole page of faces of the little man, the judge; and one of his clerk, captured nodding in three-quarters slumber. Father, who, with Mr Evenden, was looking over my shoulder, particularly laughed at that.

Next came a drawing of Miss Bowlby, at which I paused deliberately, as being a better course than moving on too quickly. Again it was a nice portrait, and I was sure he had drawn her often.

She stood upright, in profile, her face and eyes grave and steady. I thought she could model as a martyr. There was silence and I moved on to a picture of myself. It is hardest to judge pictures of oneself – one must always be thinking a little too much 'how do I look?' and not 'how does it look?' I saw myself inclining forward a little – perhaps answering the judge's questions. At the margin was written 'Age 21', ringed several times.

'It was almost ruined,' said the artist, seeing the page I had reached. 'When you said you were Vengate, if I had not dropped my pencil, I think I would have added a magic wand and sprite's wings.'

'Father, do you mean to say you had not told Mr Evenden about that?'

'We had other things to talk about. I daresay I did not happen to mention it. Kitty, excuse us one moment.'

I returned the open book to the hands of its owner and withdrew a few yards while the three of them talked business. I could not see where my aunt and Henry had got to, but as I was looking round I came face to face with Mr – or Inspector – Tutt, who came in to gather up the police papers and exhibits.

'Miss James,' he said stiffly enough.

Had the case gone against 'our side' I would have felt hatred against him, almost certainly. As it was I noted the air he perpetually bore, of being somehow sad and honest and unlucky, which urged a measure of magnanimity. If he had been wrong – I remained of course convinced that he had – I thought it was only through too strong a fear of error: a need to believe himself always utterly right.

'Mr Tutt,' I said, 'though you have prosecuted your case against an innocent man, I have admired your efforts in the cause of justice.'

'I am relieved, miss, I am not to be pilloried in the press.' There was a pause as I could think of no reply, then he went on in a softer tone. 'One only puts matters forward. Then it is for the court. Everyone did their job. Proof is a difficult thing. A very difficult thing. Especially, I may say, when the likes of me dares to interfere with the likes of such a family. When else would we get a Queen's own Counsel, on a special retainer I'm sure, and two days' jawing before the jury, on a matter of common crime? When you dare to put a young English gentleman in the dock. I must have been forgetting myself. We are here to keep the peace, not *infringe* the liberties of freeborn Englishmen. Whatever next, eh?'

I smiled and made no answer, disconcerted by his speech.

'Yet they want someone to be got, too, some monster, out of my hat perhaps, for hanging,' he went on. 'For evil was done. No doubt. Be glad *you* did not see it, miss.' Resentment was again rising in his voice, but it was checked. 'But it is all well. I believe you told only the truth as you saw it. I do not think you party to any conspiracy; it is still possible there was a conspiracy and you were part of it without knowing.'

The casual and it seemed malicious suggestion induced in me a wave of anxious revulsion; the words were more horrifying because, still, so patently sincere. I protested, 'Inspector, I really believe that if you think calmly, the plain truth lies all another way.'

'Oh yes?'

Meanwhile, unseen by either of us, William Evenden himself had approached, and whether or not he had heard anything he had probably seen that I was being subjected to some plea in justification.

'Inspector,' he announced, 'allow me to present you with a small souvenir of a day I shall never forget. Accept this in the spirit in which it is given, and you will oblige me.' If any ambiguity was intended, it was disguised. He presented Mr Tutt with a piece of paper, through which I discerned the outline of the pencil sketch of the inspector giving his evidence. Mr Tutt took it, looked at it, and put it up in his pocket. He then put on his hat, took up his box of papers, and without a word – but with a nod at me which I felt bound to return – he made to leave. I watched him go, still unsettled by the strength of his belief that justice had miscarried – and the implication in what he thought of me and what I had done. I saw that he was intercepted at the door to the court by the same earnest clergyman who had earlier been anxious to speak with my father.

To Mr Tutt, too, he protested: 'Sir, why was I not called?'

Mr Tutt led him away, saying, 'Sir, you were not called because you had no evidence . . .'

Rousing myself, I asked, 'May I ask for a keepsake of my examination too?' On looking round though I found that young Mr Evenden had his back to me and seemed not to hear. I did not press the matter.

I caught the sound of his father, taking his arm, and speaking into his ear. 'We must go home now and face it. Then it may not be so bad, you know.'

I stood unattended for a minute, contemplating the timber vaults above, thinking soberly of everything they witnessed from day to day: half-audible exchanges and incomplete segments of truth or deceit. Surely I, in my minor part, had come through unscathed; was it not merely the acute suspense and excitement that had left me feeling sullied, and denied my expected measure of satisfaction? Mr Tutt with his bitterness, or Mr William Evenden with his proud *sang-froid*: in a moment of self-centredness I considered that one or the other had wronged me, in a way that, however small, could never be righted.

As we rode home, Father expressed himself satisfied that it had been a fair trial and, he was pretty sure, the right result.

'Is that all?' laughed Julia. 'Your client bore himself well under it all.'

'Yes, I suppose he did. The times I saw him beforehand, too. When no-one believed in him, another type of fellow might have given up. He's not quite what I expected – though I often had the impression that he was angry, with *all* of us.'

'Oh, surely not! He looked the most careless person in the place, and charming at the end,' said my aunt.

'I know. But, well, his older brother John was always favoured, and more respected. In that situation, one can expect someone to get into scrapes, and be proud of finding his own way out of them.

Perhaps not to this extent, but the second child will always be an oddity, a rebel.'

'I have an older brother,' I put in, 'and I do not rebel.'

'Not much,' muttered Julia. 'Anyway, you meet with so little resistance.'

'Aunt! You should be sharp more often. It suits you better than you know.'

'Oh,' she sighed, 'I do know, but I am afraid I might never stop if I once got started. A woman should be soft and so I strive to be. I am long reconciled to being counted an old maid, but not an eccentric old maid.'

'Father, can you not see my aunt standing in court, in Mr Johnson's place, and making a much better job of it?'

'Oh, Kitty, it's as well for young Evenden she did not. She would have seen him hang, all right.'

Once home, the day drew to a close with a reascending ordinariness, except once, when I went to pull across the curtains in the front room. I disturbed a man whose face was pressed against the pane, watching us! The man was as startled, momentarily, as I. He jumped back across the railings and rejoined a group, men and women, on the pavement, but from there they all stood equably and stared. No cry had escaped me, and I decided to make no comment, as it would only upset Father, but drew the curtains as thoroughly as possible. They were quite respectably dressed, too. It was my first experience of such fame, or infamy.

12

Some two weeks later I stood before my father, desolated, as he pronounced that I had 'never been guilty of a worse error of judgment.'

'I did not consider there to be grounds for objection. I did not think that *you* would object,' I said.

'It is my fault. You have always been one to go ahead without thinking, and I believed no harm would come of it. But – can you tell me – what are we to do now?'

'Surely, we – you will not do anything!'

'I must write, and put him off somehow. Probably with the truth: you acted without guidance, and without permission. It will be hard enough, in every way. Oh, Kitty.'

I must explain that throughout the summer we had been planning to hold a supper party, which as a family joke was referred to as my *début* among Burlas society hostesses. The date now approached.

He held before him one of the replies to my invitations. From William Evenden, it had of courtesy been addressed to him. I had not read it, but had gathered that it was an acceptance, which constituted the difficulty. My father was proposing to forbid his attendance!

'No! Father, you would do yourself too much harm with the family; you must not. What does it matter what people think? If they want to shun him, and us, so much the worse for them! He has been proved innocent. That was your work. Do you not believe in it, yourself?'

'His guilt or innocence is neither here nor there. I mean, as far as *this* is concerned. It may be that no-one will ever know for sure, but I don't care about that. Did you not think him too far above our circle? That alone should have stopped you.'

'I dare say, without the trial, it would have. But I thought he might now be glad of friends – any friends. That's what I thought you would understand.'

'You were deluded. You may know yourself better, in time. I see now the allure, for one of your nature. A man of good family, falsely accused – and you thought no further. You think only of the charm: of yourself!'

'Perhaps.' I was now close to tears; that is, tears were already formed, but I was close to losing mastery of my voice, and I paused to regain it. 'But I have told you what my motives were. You have never accused me of lying before. I still do not understand your objection.'

Father made a sound of astonishment and despair, and no more for several seconds.

'No,' he then said, with averted eyes and a calmness that stung more than blazing anger ever had. 'I do not think you false. But neither did I ever think you stupid – before. How can you not understand what is patent to the world? He may be no different from a thousand other such men, or any other such man, in general. But too much has come out. Perhaps he can rebuild his life, but it must be elsewhere if so, for some years at least. He certainly should take himself far from anyone he sincerely wishes well. This is such an ordinary man: a privileged dabbler, petulant and deceitful with his family; he stares at young girls – What is it? Isn't Ryder good enough for you?'

'This has nothing to do with Henry! How could you say such a thing to me? I do not compare them in the least, and you know that Henry is good enough for me – more than.'

Father looked up sharply. 'Then you should have thought of him too. Evenden is now known everywhere as a dissolute, at best, who openly has affairs. Our rank is not so high nor so low that we may ignore a consideration such as that. My God, I suppose you asked her too!'

'Of course not! Besides, *I* know nothing of any affair!' Really, I added to myself, I have only the most foggy apprehension of what an 'affair' is. 'You are too hard.'

I saw that the shade of sympathy moved him at that point. 'Leave me now, please, Kitty.'

'Father, *please* do not write, not yet. Wait at least. If you still think it must be done, then I will do it.'

'Certainly not! I must. Now go and wash your face.'

Then, as I left the study, I found that Henry was being admitted to the hall. To be discovered by him in that condition, completing a misery already overwhelming, was a circumstance that now came merely with the pall of the almost inevitable. He said nothing in the presence of the maid, but once seated in the parlour asked: 'Miss James, whatever is the matter?'

'Nothing.' I shook my head. 'An argument with Father.'

The room, the best we had to show, looked stale in the morning light, as if the drapes and furnishings would crumble at the touch. In silence, as the two of us shifted on our chairs, even the faint crackle of material was unbearable to me. My vision blurred.

'Are there many more cases of the typhus?' I asked.

'Always a few. The main fear with the approach of autumn is the cholera. Typhus will always kill in greater numbers – '

'But it slaughters with discrimination.'

'Exactly so.' I sensed him look at me a little wonderingly. 'I believe that Burlas has been fortunate in the past, to avoid the outbreaks of Asiatic cholera. There must be every hope it will remain so.'

'No, Doctor Ryder. It is probably another matter on which we are simply behind the times, and it will catch up with us.'

After a further pause, he rose. 'I see that I have chosen the wrong moment to call. My apologies.'

'No, please! I do not want you to go.' It was the truth: I wanted him to stay, but to behave differently.

'No,' he insisted, with a considerate smile. That brand of

consideration, all his own, I already viewed on occasion as something of a paradox; it could be so much the opposite of what was wanted.

I detained him with a few more words. 'I should have told you, and you may disapprove. I have asked William Evenden to the party.'

'Oh.' He was clearly very much surprised. 'I – I quite understand. Your father and aunt approve?' Speechless, I motioned with a hand in the direction of the study. 'Oh – I see. Well, I do not think my opinion ought to matter in it – '

'It matters to me!' I said outright.

He reddened, and his answer, though sincere, was hesitant. 'Then, nothing else does. Do you need to hear me say that, turn yourself which way you can, I cannot find it in me to criticise you? Not your heart – Katherine.'

Then, immediately, he was gone. His words counted for much. I wished he had said more. 'He should speak now,' I thought. 'What is to stop him? When he saw that I had been crying, he wanted to take me in his arms. Oh, so he ought, indeed!' I shivered with fear of I knew not what, though I told myself it was the dispute with Father. Conflicts of such a kind were unknown in our house.

He had said he could not find it in him to criticise, but what did he really think of my conduct? We thought alike in so many things *removed* from each other's actual everyday dispositions and behaviour. Was it possible though that in my person I was some kind of moral monster? I really had not thought anything wrong in inviting William Evenden at the time; in truth I had acted hastily and shrunk from thinking about it too closely at all. The minute I perceived my father's wrath I had understood whence it sprang and wondered how I could have been so foolish. I seemed to have a gross lack of some quality everyone thought natural to young females: a something of docility and judgment. Would Henry not be revolted by this? I remembered, groaning, one scene when he had been assisting with certain of our plans, and we were consulting the new Beeton's, at which he had scoffed. What had he said? That 'a woman should manage her household well, but not with any obvious scientific zeal. The author is a strange creature; she cannot understand that the chief womanly skills are instincts given by nature, if nature be not too much interfered with.'

The convulsions subsided, but the surroundings of home fretted me. Aunt was on her visits, but might return at any time. I must be gone before she did. 'I need,' I said to myself with feeble self-reproach, 'activity, a long walk.'

It seemed impossible that the security of the love my family bore me could be so shaken, so carelessly. Father had looked at me as if he disliked me. In the future, I prayed, Henry would be all to me; but today would never be undone. It may appear that my feelings were exaggerated and ridiculous, but thus they were. No doubt, through my youth, I had been too little chastised and exposed to pain, and was ill-equipped to withstand the least tremor in my serene world.

So I readied myself and left the house with a determined rapid step, almost colliding with a gentleman who stood back and raised his hat to me. My momentum had carried me away before I remembered what was familiar about him: I had seen him twice briefly during the incident-filled final day of the Evenden trial. He was the funny importunate clergyman. However, I did not then stop to wonder what business had brought him back to my father's door after a fortnight's interval, as I might have done had I been less agitated.

I chose the shortest way to the solitude of open country, and then a strenuous path to rob me of breath. I was frustrated when it turned downhill again. This moorland was no wild, inaccessible place; it was just itself, still, and I wished myself far away in the fantasy landscape it had stood for in my girlhood.

I could, I knew, with little difficulty walk all the way to Evenden Hall. I knew where it was now, though I had never been there. I could face him, myself, with everything that had happened and withdraw my invitation, and go back and tell Father and Henry. But it was not possible. That was a part that might have been played by the romantic girl, whose image was now degraded. 'I will never go anywhere, I will never be anywhere but this.' I rejoined the main path, the haunt of genteel family promenades on Sundays, and turned towards home.

Two or three twists however revealed the startling sight of someone lying at full stretch on a heather bank a few yards ahead. I checked. My imagination began to revive already. Could fate be smiling on me? No; it was no promise but a challenge. If I could pass by, why then indeed a spell might be cast. It would confirm my new resolve, to hold my maiden cup with more sensible care, and not chase fancies. The William Evenden that I 'knew', so far, was little other than a creature of pure fancy.

I trod softly by. There was something bizarre in the sensation of passing so close to a man in such an attitude. To have seen him today of all days! Well, I had not disturbed him, and it being none of my affair I would make my way home . . .

'Can it be you, Vengate old fellow?' came the voice behind me.

I started; I was almost *frightened*. Hating to recognise this, I determined to overcome it and did so at once.

'Why, Mr Evenden, did you not know?' I answered turning. 'Poor Vengate had to flee the country, pursued by his victims and detractors. This is only daft Miss James.'

13

He pulled on his coat as he strolled to join me on the path. 'Alas, "poor" Vengate indeed. I noticed, of course, that he had fallen silent.'

I looked past him to where sundry artist's materials lay in the heather. 'What do you find to record, here?' I asked. He may think it a dull question, but he did not know what thoughts had been mine the last hour.

'What do you find to write?'

'Oh, that is much easier. I can make it all up from inside my head.'

'I do something of that kind too. Only my head is sometimes empty, as now. Do you mean that you have abandoned writing because of the trial? That would make it my fault. When I saw your second piece, I hoped it would not be so.'

For one further column had appeared, and under the identical pseudonym, though it could no longer serve any purpose other than convention. That had been my last. The truth was I was uncomfortable at my identity being known, and I suspected despite his protestations that Henry Ryder disliked it also.

'It is not because I am known now,' I said. 'I'm sure I could endure that, if I had the desire. But my stock of good ideas has proved very limited.'

'No! You repudiate what you wrote?'

'If you mean the last piece, no, never. But that merely stated a kind of personal conviction gained from experience. I mean, I am out of clever arguments.'

'It was not "merely" anything. It was rather courageous, coming just then, when every eye would be on you. On such a subject too.'

'But a touch eccentric – Vengate's major fault, according to some.'

'To say the trial procedure is laboured and capricious by turns, and a life should not hang on it? I believe you are right.'

'Thank you, but I think your advocacy will be discounted, as your evidence was barred, on the grounds that you had – shall we say? – an interest. You seem anyway to forget that Vengate's second note covered two subjects; there was also the important matter of sanitary provision, the need for a borough surveyor and medical officer of health.'

'Oh, yes. Seriously,' he went on after a pause and a faint grimace, 'I retain a friendly feeling towards old Vengate, though for me he has been a little *too* clever, with an incipient tendency to preach, to which I never submit gracefully. As for when he was unmasked – well, I am forever in his debt.'

At the best of times, receiving compliments can put me, for some reason, into a state of mental weariness. Compliments will mistime and misdirect themselves even at the moment of delivery. That day, after Father's words, I was made particularly uneasy by these kind phrasings in the mouth of Mr Evenden. I managed a smile. 'He only did what he ought, and what lay in his path to do. Someone is coming.' Voices could be heard lower down the valley. 'And I must go.'

'Yes, you must not be seen with me.'

I had been turning to go, but looked back uncertainly at that. He seemed to understand after a moment that I did not know whether to be hurt.

'No,' he said, 'I know you would never care about such a thing. It is true nevertheless, and in both our interests for the present.'

The voices sounded much closer. It was to be hoped that we would neither of us be recognised, and I prepared to be nonchalant. 'Well, it is too late,' I whispered.

'Not so.' I felt my wrist gripped through the sleeve of my dress and, in surprised unresistance, was pulled after him as with long strides he climbed the bank. I understood his purpose, and in seconds we were hidden behind an overhanging tangle of rock and shrub twenty feet above the path. He had let go my arm, and it seemed that by agreement we were to pretend he had never taken it, though so decided had been his action that I retained the sensation of his impress for some time.

We peered through natural spy-holes, a few feet apart. The interlopers were in view: a young man and woman. From her smart appearance she was in service, on an hour's snatched leave. The spot where we had been standing was hidden by the shoulders of a low hill from most of the rest of the path. As they reached it, the young man stopped and caught his companion's hand.

'Come on, now, a kiss!' he urged.

'Kiss an ugly brute like you!' she laughed.

'Yes, you old witch, come on!'

And, there below us, they did begin to kiss with familiar affection, kisses long and short, and intermixed with laughter and insult, oath and endearment. It seemed every image that day was calculated to work on me. Though I found the scene moving in its simplicity, and intriguing, my nerves had now been pulled taut on every side. My blood sang; I had little power to act. I knew my situation to be both mortifying and comical. The lovers might not move from such a congenial spot for some time.

Looking up at length I found William Evenden's eyes upon me. He made a small gesture of helplessness. He had only meant that we should hide for a moment, to continue our conversation. There were more grunts and laughter from below and, though sensible that to give way would be literally disastrous, I sensed the intoxication of childish laughter within me also. Worse, I detected an echoing thought in the gleam in Mr Evenden's eye. I turned from him and pressed against the rock until, with slow breaths, I was calm again.

When I looked again he was biting his lip and, as he watched first the couple below and then the open hillside round about, I read in his face that he feared his efforts might yet misfire, should they decide to make use of this very hiding place themselves. I did not consider what need they would have to do so, in my dull innocence. Just then the girl decided she had had enough and gruffly insisted they must go back or she would be late and in trouble. Her young man protested but she was already away and he could only drag along after, wiping a hand over his face.

It was yet barely safe to speak when William said, 'A vision of Arcadia.'

I laughed through my blushes, and two tears started out, which I brushed aside. He must think them tears of laughter, as perhaps they were.

'May they be as happy when they *are* old and ugly,' he went on.

Still I said nothing. It was for him now to explain why he had detained me; my sense was that he detained me yet, for some purpose.

He spoke again. 'I know you would not care what people thought, if you were in the right; you have proved it more than once.'

'As much as to say I think myself always right and others always wrong.'

'Well, we have something in common. Thank you for asking me to your home. If you knew when the note arrived, the scene it found, and the foolish need I had of a friendly word at that moment – It is most kind of all your family. I have sent my thanks to your father. Then I thought he may have counted on a polite refusal!'

'Not at all,' I said. Could he detect my confusion?

'I am puzzled as to how, after all these years of living so close, and your father visiting us regularly, you and I have never met before.'

'It is not so strange, just as His Honour the judge said. Father believes in keeping his business affairs separate from our family life.'

'Then I am doubly grateful to him for breaking his rule now.'

'It is – There is no such conflict in my case, you see.'

'Ah –' There was a pause. 'That is, I think, another of Miss James's precise and informative answers.'

I watched a wagtail on the stones. If that was all he had wanted to say, he must find a way, a careless pleasantry, allowing us to part, without awkwardness. It should be in his repertoire. The foolish bird described a rough circle, alternately bobbing and stopping, before finally starting away in dipping flight down the valley; my eyes followed until the tiny creature vanished for good. There was a movement beside me, a shadow, and close warmth against my face. I accepted this as it might be the restorative energy of the sun. The touch was past, I had a glimpse of eyes, monstrous near, black, and still, and was dazzled by the true sun before I comprehended I had been kissed.

'Do you forgive me?'

The question of forgiveness was oddly irrelevant to my feelings in the matter. He had acted *without preamble,* just as one might stroke a cat! 'You have no right to ask. I will not say. Why do you behave so?'

'Because in that moment you seemed to me quite without life, without light and shade. So I tried a first brushstroke, to see the effect.'

My anger was real, but too small and slow-growing. *This* pretty conceit was arrogance. 'It is you who should be the writer, having such a way with words.' The hackneyed phrase carried an echo of Henry, that he would not catch.

Or did he? 'And because soon, in every sense, it will be too late for both of us,' he said. 'Therefore I put off again my sincere resolution about my manners. I wondered if your pen had fallen silent because the engagement had already been announced but we had missed it somehow. In one way, I hope it *is* his fault and not mine.'

'It is no-one's fault; it is entirely my choice. And what do you know of that?'

'You mean the engagement is now in being?'

'No – '

'Well, everyone knows about it anyway. Your father is more pleased than I suspect you even believe. If the doctor has not spoken, perhaps he is cleverer than I thought. A man like that ought to be wary of marrying you.' He paused. 'He is too good for you, you see.'

My anger was of a satisfying degree now. Had the scene with the maidservant raised in him ideas of tricks that could be played on social inferiors? Making every allowance for the fact he had suffered much, still he was insufferable. I could only exclaim wordlessly. Yet, before him, that conventional expression of outraged virtue seemed a measure of retreat.

Turning away, he went on in an even tone. 'I mean of course that the honest way you face life will be too much for him. He does not have a speck of animosity in his soul, but that leaves him also without the grain of special sensitivity, or – no, I doubt not that he is sensitive – consideration, perhaps: sensitivity in another's behalf; it is a rare enough quality, and he might be wanting sufficient of it to understand you.'

I almost laughed. A more misconceived assessment of Henry was not possible, and what he was trying to say about me was incomprehensible. 'You have had small opportunity to observe; how have you reached these conclusions?'

'Oh, one hears this and that. And sitting on trial for one's life, watching all the faces, you would be surprised what an outcast feeling it is. So one's mind wanders, and I thought I saw visions! He is scarcely your inferior in beauty, of course, especially about the head. It is an exquisite pairing.'

The thought of him in the dock, so occupied, brought back to me Father's remark about him being angry with all of us. Were all his queer manners the signature of a rage within himself? Out loud I said: 'And all from hearing this and that?'

He gave a smile, not matched in his eyes, and I was then sure that it had been in his mind to say, *And from your kiss*. Oh, I thought, you hold no glamour for me. That he had been falsely accused reflected no merit on him, even if it had made him a cause to be espoused. I had told my father I did not compare him with Henry and up to then indeed I had not; but now I did, and the contrast was stark. He was dark, 'handsome', but I saw now that his lips and nose were too large, and his brow too low for true nobility (speaking of mere aesthetics, which so dominated *his* view of everything). My anger threatened to dissolve into detached speculation. I took it up once more.

'Then tell me another thing,' I said. 'That day in the train, why did you stare so rudely?'

'Because I was on the run for my life; I did not know what I was doing.'

'I am not joking; pray do not joke with me. I wish to know, again, why you behave so?'

'Do you mean me myself or disreputable men in general?'

'Would the answer be different in either case?'

'Oh, you interrogate harder than Tutt. Well, now, let me think. But, like the best, most devious of inquisitors, you ask only questions to which you already know the true answer. If a man, with cares, but nothing on his conscience, sees something which strikes him, which he would like not to forget in an instant, what is he to do?'

'He need not stare, when it makes the woman, his object, uncomfortable.'

'Clandestine looking is not very manly.'

'You would rather cause pain to a stranger than compromise your supposed manliness, which is to say your infantile self-conceit. And your objection to clandestine behaviour was forgotten when you took my portrait.'

'You would have seen me taking it quite openly, had you looked up even once in half an hour.'

'That was rude in me, I suppose!'

'No,' he then said. 'I have already accepted the charge of rudeness. I am giving only the explanation you asked for. And, in spite of my words, I have spoken honestly before now when I said the memory of it shames and pains me. I can add only this, which is important to a true understanding though also not to my own credit: it has always been one consideration in my conduct, whether I was likely to be found out or not. I have stolen apples in my time, I confess. Though it has been salutary, in recent days, this realisation of how much of a secret life I had built up: the contents of a sketchbook, disgraceful conduct towards pretty girls in trains – '

I was appalled to think that he might go on to allude to Miss Bowlby, but he did not.

' – Anyway,there it is. I have been thoroughly exposed. All such duality or duplicity is of course alien to a crusader for the greater good such as yourself. Though I remark that here you are, still listening to me in a place of deliberate concealment, and you will never tell anyone; or – ' he saw that I was about to protest, ' – you will omit to explain why you should have run away precisely ten minutes ago.'

I was effectively, though I felt unfairly, silenced by that. When at length I spoke again it was in a quieter tone. 'It is the having been exposed that is your crime in the eyes of the world. Will you go abroad now?'

'Oh, yes. It is miraculous the way all objections to that have dissolved. It will be well for everyone, including even one or two for whose welfare I *do* care. I am fixing for Paris first, then Italy.'

'How carelessly you say it! I thought just now it was ignoble for one in your position – before you knew of your brother's death, I mean – to speak of having cares. And even with everything that has happened, it has fallen out well for you, as things almost always will. To see Paris and Italy! I count myself the most fortunate of people, and even I could not dream of such a thing. As for other orders of society, all those you may affect to despise because they dared to be interested in you, just think of the lives they lead, here in Burlas!'

'Why should you not dream of it?' he mildly urged. 'You could go abroad if you wished.'

'You know I could not. I am not one of those women who may do such things. Perhaps if I *was* a serious writer, if I thought it possible so to justify myself – but that is not the case, and I do not complain. You, though, are free and it will not even matter should you have no talent.'

'I have never been free here. Now, I am not free to stay.'

'Am I free to go?' I asked. He looked at me and I continued, 'I mean, to go home, now?'

His face showed genuine surprise, and displeasure. 'Did you think –? You must forgive me. Nothing in your manner indicated – '

He broke off, and formally offered his hand to help me down the slope, which was likely to be more slippery and dirty than the ascent. I held back.

'No; it will be better for me to make my own way.'

He shrugged and scrambled down to the path. I waited until he turned his back. He could think that I was snubbing him; I did not care. He could not conceive the problems caused by a slight behindhandedness in laundering and mending at home, and how vital it could be on some days to keep one single dress from being torn or muddied. I looked round carefully then scooped my skirts up high with both arms and descended in a few long jumps.

'Well, goodbye, Mr Evenden.'

He turned and was surprised at the hand I now offered, but he took it briefly.

'If fate does determine my return to this country one day,' he said, 'it would be amusing, don't you think, for us to meet and compare notes on how we have fared?'

'Yes, and instructive. But I do not believe in fate.'

'Not believe in it! Do you often take this walk?'

'Quite often.'

'So do I. Yet we never met until today. I do not know at this moment if it is cruel or kind, but I certainly believe in fate! Goodbye, Miss James.'

I left him and walked quickly down to the Water Lane stile. It was only there that I recollected myself; for some time I had actually forgotten about the business of the invitation and his acceptance. It occurs to me now worth remarking on considerations that did not enter my head at that time – as striking signs of the girl I was then. I did not think that he might have murdered me; I did not think that he might have done more than kiss me.

14

I retraced my steps down Water Lane – which as yet meant nothing to me – and through the familiar streets to my home. There, I found my aunt returned and my father gone. From my aunt's manner, it was clear that he had not said anything to her of our quarrel and its cause. The problem remained, but I was no longer crushed by it. Not that I felt myself possessed of new strength; the interview with William Evenden had been in its way as dispiriting as the earlier one with Father. My new quiescence was in fact a mystery. I carried on my various duties, in company with my aunt, with fortitude – indeed, I believe, better than usual.

When Father returned late in the afternoon we greeted each other much the same as ever, and I prepared and gave him his cup of tea. I took up my needlework, and some ordinary conversation was contrived between us. He wanted to show that though his mind was not changed he felt kindly toward me. This I understood; I wanted to show the same to him, but whether I had the purity of spirit required –? He related his partner Skipton's pleasure at being invited to the supper party; then that the Molsworthys were buying up the old Basset house ('There will be no stopping her highness,' said my aunt). Striving for my part to find subject-matter, I thought to ask about his clergyman visitor earlier in the day; I was about to do so when I remembered the answer was likely to relate to the Evenden trial. Though this idea raised in me some genuine curiosity, it caused me to abort my question rather than risk having that name mentioned again between us for the present.

But soon after he left us for his regular private hour in his study.

He might be writing to the Evendens now, if he has not already done so, I thought. We heard the door-bell, and the sound of it being answered. Later Father called me, bellowing through the walls, not bothering to rise from his chair or send – again as was his habit.

'What is it, Father?' I asked as I entered.

He looked at me. Then he indicated a paper in front of him. 'Do you know what this is?'

My breath caught as I recognised the notepaper from Evenden Hall, but 'No,' I answered.

'You had better read it then. I should say, I had not finished composing my own letter to them when it arrived.'

It was a second letter from William Evenden to my father, now marked 'P.P.C.' – *pour prendre congé.* It began with an apology for following so soon after the first:–

> *. . . As I believe you know, I am much occupied with preparations for going abroad. I now discover that a visit to London to further matters in connection with this is indispensable. After all, I must miss what will be, I am sure, a delightful evening, but the pleasure and honour at the invitation remain. It may be that we shall not now meet before I leave the country. You will know my sincere hopes for the continued health and happiness of you and your family. In lasting gratitude for your services, I am,* etc.

I kept my eyes on the page, as if still reading, while my thoughts ran on. The briefest recap of a certain passage in our picturesque encounter convinced me that the writer had divined my predicament in full.

'Well, this is a lucky chance, is it not?' I said.

'So much so that, I am afraid, I cannot help wondering if you had a hand in it. You form ideas and act so impetuously, I can conceive of you, after this morning, forming as desperate a counter-plan.'

'Have you been speaking with Mr Tutt? He thinks William Evenden and I are co-conspirators too. I did not engineer this, though.'

'I apologise. But you were so upset this morning, and yet so calm this evening.'

'I went for a long walk, and had a lot to reflect upon.'

'Then I am sincerely glad at the effect. You should learn not to take things so hard. If you never made mistakes, Kitty, you would be much duller than you are. I will go so far as to say you may err again – rarely, I know, but you may.'

I forced a smile. Mr William would be amused at the traps being sprung for the 'honest way' I faced life.

'He shows good feeling in his note.'

'Really?' said Father. 'I thought it rather stiff.'

'Well, I am glad at the way things have turned out. I think I am quite glad after all not to be seeing William Evenden again.'

I hoped the thoroughness with which I thus sought to dispose of the history of that day was not so obvious as to put suspicions of the truth, or something like the truth, whatever it was, into Father's head. Aware of what I must withhold from him, the very ease of the deceit shamed me. All the same, I rejoiced.

His next words arrested me, however. 'Kitty, I shall write to his father, just the same, to explain everything that has happened.'

'But whatever for? There is no need now, surely!'

'He must know that William was invited here. He has a right to know that I was intending to withdraw the invitation, and I must explain why, as honestly as I can. If he is hurt by that, and wishes to dispense with my services for the future, so be it. But I do not think I could face him otherwise. It would be hypocritical.'

'But you will simply upset and confuse him. He is not the kind of man to understand such motives. We have not curried favour with the invitation; he simply bore us all possible goodwill before, and now he will think nothing of the matter, if only you will leave it be. I can understand that you considered yourself bound to accept responsibility for my fault in acting, but now that the action is to have no consequence after all, you are being too nice, really you are, and I cannot bear that you should hurt yourself so!'

'You have convinced me the more of what I must do, and if we are to argue again it will only cause pain. It is out of your hands

95

now, Kitty. I have truly forgiven you. Believe me, it is not a cause for such worry, either way.'

I was dismissed. Before the end of the evening, however, the difficulty was resolved, to my great relief – and Henry was the agent. He called before the dinner-hour, on the pretext of returning a book as he was passing. My aunt begged to be excused on urgent business with the cook. Still standing, as if about to go, he spoke to me gently.

'I hope you are in better spirits?'

'Much better, thank you. William Evenden has declined my invitation after all.'

'Good. I mean, for you and your father.'

'Only Father still means to write to Mr Frederick Evenden, and explain that he was going to forbid William from coming. I wish he would not. But I cannot argue the matter any more.' I sighed. 'I am sorry to bore you with my foolishness.'

His only answer was a shake of the head and a smile of benign amusement. With the lamps lit, the surroundings which in the morning had repelled me now offered perfect repose. Then he reached and took my hand from my side, pulled it to his breast and pressed it, in a gesture very close to simple leave-taking, but in fact much more. His hand was strong, though the fingers were pale and delicate.

'Go, Mr Ryder, or I shall cry again!' I said.

'Well,' he said, clearing a huskiness of his own. 'I should not leave without a brief word to your father. No, I can find my way.'

He turned for the door. Not hearing it open, I looked up after a further minute. He had turned again, and fixed a queer sombre, distracted look on the air somewhere to one side of me. I began to form the words 'What is it?' – but he was gone in an instant, leaving me to ponder this and other puzzles in his character, and to wonder where I stood with him.

Stirring myself some time later to go out into the hall, I heard voices through the door of Father's study. Though I had no wish to hear the actual words, I sat un-ladylike on the bottom stair, hugging my shoulders against the draught. Only one phrase I thought I caught, in Henry's voice: '. . . how much it will pain her. . .'. I sat thus, alone, for a long quarter-hour or more. Eventually Henry came out alone and, not seeing me in the gloom, stood taking up his hat and gloves from the table.

'Good night,' I said, and when in surprise he looked around I stood.

He took one step towards me. 'Good night. I think I may have changed his mind.'

I wanted to hold him then and press him to me, but again held back. *Another has kissed me today, and yet you never have*, was part of my thought.

'Well, good night,' he said, and let himself out into the evening.

Father emerged to find me standing on the stair. He stood too, still I mean, keeping up a quizzical mild regard on me like in one of our old games. At length he looked away, thrust his hands in his pockets, and whistled a single low note a few times as he wandered back into the study, holding the door ajar with one crooked elbow. I walked in, and waited, while he sat leaning back to examine the ceiling.

When he spoke it was on a seemingly unrelated topic. 'I had a most interesting discussion today with Mr Fowler, you know.'

'Mr Fowler?'

'Hmn. Oh, pardon me, you do not know him. He is a young clergyman – well, to my reckoning young! – with the Critchley living. And here in this awesome machine-driven city we think we know all about sin, and that life in the country must be so pleasant and sweet – ! Most interesting. I would recount it all for you – ' (I began to be impatient) ' – but you would be astonished how much of it concerned matters not suited to gently reared young females! Certain of the consequences of poverty and ignorance – ' He paused, shaking his head.

This was not his normal style of talk and I responded only: 'I am sure.'

'He had news – about the Evenden murder,' he said, now looking directly at me once more.

A vague and distant alarm started in me, I knew not why; but it was as if some guilt of my own lay in peril of being exposed. 'Oh?'

'You will remember, I dare say, that at the trial there was some discussion to no purpose of something allegedly seen in the bushes outside John Evenden's cottage on the night before – or rather of – the murder?'

'Oh, yes, I remember that. Mr Ferris's supposed skirt or frock-coat: the "look-out" – '

'A frightened feral rustling was rather how it first emerged, I must say. Well, Fowler, it seems, was always most keen to get to the bottom of that. You see there was a – an unfortunate kind of woman, shall we say, who frequented Critchley. The kind whose fate and fortune is everyone's knowledge – that is something of the difference from the situation here in town – but no-one's concern. Fowler always considered it part of his duty, however, to take an interest in her, though thus far he had discerned no good effect. The fact is he has not seen her since that night.'

'Oh. What did the police think of that?'

'The local police thought very little of it. She often moved about or lay low, to avoid being taken up, you know. Our Mr Tutt, though, was a different matter. Mr Fowler managed to enthuse him with his own fear, that the woman might have been terrorised into fleeing, or even killed, because of something she had seen.'

'Of course Mr Tutt would believe that! You know his prejudice is an obsession: he dislikes William Evenden so much, and is so *afraid* to consider that he may have dropped on the wrong man – he would welcome any evidence, even such preposterous talk of a second murder!'

'Now, wait, wait, Kitty. The indigent woman's hovel was located, and found to have been burnt to the ground. And even so, after all his inquiries, Mr Tutt told Mr Fowler that there was nothing that could properly be raised in the trial. We should never be too hasty to see obsession and prejudice in the actions of others.'

There was a passage of silence before he spoke again.

'Mr Fowler himself still had difficulty adopting such philosophic acceptance. He was so concerned about this woman, for whom no other soul would care a jot, he managed, through my agency, to secure an interview with William Evenden before the trial, which I witnessed. He wanted to hear for himself if the defendant knew anything of her fate. My young client was of no service to him whatsoever except in giving him the benefit of a notable quantity of vitriol, an anti-clericalist diatribe. After the trial, Mr Fowler still tried to press the matter with me. Like many, he was convinced that a man's lawyer always knows the whole truth about him. I had to disappoint him of course. I *thought* that was the end of the matter.'

I looked up. My father was ogling me teasingly. 'You said he came with new information?'

'Yes. He came up to Burlas today on purpose to see Mr Tutt, and then he came along to tell me as well. He has only recently heard something new – clergymen are among those shielded from certain kinds of gossip. An acquittal always invites malicious rumours. The morning after the murder the woman in question was seen by some men from a nearby hamlet. They were crossing a bridge on their way to work in the fields, and she caused them much amusement being up to one of her daft antics, wading fully clothed in the river, singing they thought – singing "murder!" and – so it is now rumoured – "Will!" '

My father recounted it so matter-of-factly! I struggled to make sense of it. 'It cannot be? Or why did it not come out long ago?'

'So it sometimes goes. It is interesting. But remember some such talk was bound to follow. Mr Fowler has been unable himself to identify the actual witnesses. Mr Tutt says he will make further efforts, though Evenden has been cleared. He is not optimistic; he says he always found much reluctance among the locals to come forward because of Evenden's close links with the big family there. And it will be only hearsay, unless he can find the woman who must now be deemed long gone, if not drowned indeed.' Father shrugged, smiling. 'So it will remain; and all the talk round Critchley now, Fowler says, is that William Evenden did kill his brother though the Burlas jury acquitted him.'

I found myself turning in silence to leave the room, though what I had thought to be my main business on entering it had still not been broached between us. Father seemed to understand and followed me out into the hallway once more.

'He is an interesting young man, in his way, this hero-doctor of yours. Will you have him?' he said.

'Father!' I scolded.

'Well, you will be pleased to know he has persuaded me to let sleeping dogs lie. I am too old for valorous adventuring, after all. Frederick Evenden shall not be further upset, by *my* hand.'

I kissed him absently. 'Father, was I in error – to give my evidence?'

'You told the truth – the whole truth – didn't you?'

'As I knew it. Do you think the talk in Critchley is only malice?'

'It may well be. Will you accept my direction in one thing, at any rate? Do not distress yourself further. That which is done properly, is done justly. He was declared not guilty, is leaving the country, and there is no second body to be found, unless it be a poor low drunkwoman, her troubles ended by her own hand. It *is* a form of error to keep our eyes wilfully fixed on the offending aspects of life in the gross, as it were.'

I may have looked unconvinced, thinking unhappily of certain words: *You will never tell*; or, *you will omit to mention* . . .

My father continued more reflectively: 'I have lived too much in the law though, and with getting old, one can become *too* understanding of things, accept any number of compromises, only caring if the form is right. Do not grow old like me, Kitty. Keep some feeling in your soul. For you, it is a question of justice. For me, it is all a game of proof. Like the Evenden trial now. I said that it was the right outcome, but I meant the Crown had not earned victory. I can still doff my hat to the philanderer William, quite easy within myself that he might have murdered his brother. After all, someone did, and as a rational man I accept both the possibility that he did and the possibility that he did not. But I am sure justice would have been stained, had the verdict gone against him on that evidence. It rejoices me, that you see things differently. Do not ever study the law, for goodness' sake. Now, are we going up?'

15

I began to be troubled by dreams all on a theme: of having miscarried or misunderstood some great responsibility, put on me unawares, through forgetfulness of some elusive thing. These dreams left me irritated, fortunately with no foresight that they would recur through a period of years. Their first appearance at this juncture may well be attributed to the coincidence of the disturbance of the trial with preparations for the supper party, which involved remembrance, naturally, of a great number of mutually dependent details.

I was developing an almost wholly new idea of myself and my significance in the world. Before the trial I had made, I now saw, so much of my own importance. But my cleverness, my testament, had come to appear a very small part of a picture which was still barely clear to me!

Destiny had once been a piece of lace; signifying my prodigious self-will. My desire for the perpetual honour of Henry's declared love – for marriage, let it be said – now had less of wilfulness, more of conformity about it. Henry Ryder must ask for my hand. Seeing me in my supper party finery would be his fate. For I knew that the attachment was complete; it must be acknowledged. My sensibility of the lack of the required, merely formal, gesture was become urgent. Thus is every woman, perhaps, when 'desperate to land the catch', and perhaps it would be correct to see the Katherine of those days in just such a mundane and humble light.

What of 'Vengate' and my other vanities? It was all very well to have the heart and stomach of a king if one could have them not only without the body of a woman but without the sensibilities of one, those female sensibilities that magnify every discovered error and self-humiliation. Adult independence I now thought on wryly as a fine but perilous place for a woman. After the briefest spell there I was ready for the intellectual protection of marriage. Besides all which, what else could I do or crave, doting on one man so completely as I did? What else but spend the long hours sewing tiny stitches, attaching the real lace to my best silk like the wise women of old casting charms, the way women have always tried to make their destiny.

That is a suitably confused account of a most confused mental state, a state of super-agitation which is certainly the reason why my memories of the evening party when it finally came are episodic but still vivid. Let me say at once: Henry made no proposal of marriage that night.

Instead I remember a lady asking fervently, 'Is *he* here?' She was partly twitting me, but looking around with genuine eagerness. 'I mean, of course, the young Mr Evenden whose life you saved!'

'Of course he is not,' interjected my aunt who happily was at my side. 'And Kitty did no such thing, but only her duty.'

I remember furthermore that Mrs Skipton talked to me a good deal and embarrassed me by being so plainly impressed at meeting Henry in person. She talked all in the same tone on many subjects, firstly of the new chocolate factory: 'It will be wonderful for the people, also, to get a bar of nourishment so cheaply, won't it, Doctor Ryder? Especially the poor children. One lives long, and sees improvement everywhere, with good will.' Yet it seemed the next moment she was decrying with horror the riots that had been feared and plotted, in the rough courts and taverns, for the day of the hanging that would not now be taking place after all.

'Yes,' said her husband. 'It is known Calcraft the hangman's nerves are susceptible, and he can be terrorised into making a good savage show of it, if the crowd demands.'

'They would have been especially keen,' said Mrs Skipton, 'because it was a "gentleman". I daresay it *could* have been worse, had he been from one of the factory masters' families! Thank goodness it was all avoided.'

'It may have been our last chance of a public hanging in Burlas, my dear,' said Mr Skipton. 'The Royal Commission looks to be set on recommending private executions. Some are angry at the change. They say it is edifying.'

'They mean, an entertainment,' I shuddered. 'It should never be that.'

'Just what I was saying, Kitty dear,' said Mrs Skipton, who had known me since childhood and regarded my opinions with indulgence accordingly. 'Though I am afraid that I don't go as far as you on the question in general. Mr Skipton showed me the article.'

'I know that I went very *far*,' I smiled. 'I do not expect many to go with me.'

'No.' Mr Skipton was sanguine. 'The Commission will hope to stop that debate. It is bad enough that we have ticket-of-leave men. There must always be some crimes that are capital.'

'Of course there must,' said Henry, 'though if anything could ever have convinced me otherwise, it would have been Miss James's eloquence. But sadly such high sentiments cannot be afforded by the ordinary mass of folk, who must live, work and thrive as best they can in the world as it is. The world with its foulnesses and unpleasant necessities.'

Until that moment, he had never referred to the content of my writing. With what consciousness I listened to him, therefore, may be guessed. Of course, I cared, more than I would ever deliberately show, that my opinions had if not agreement then at least respect.

'To return to the more generally significant kind of improvements,' he went on. 'It's true, I confess, that I found the arguments in that part of the piece more practical, and still more persuasive.'

'Hardly surprising,' I said. 'They were your own!'

'Certainly not. *All* your own. I share your sentiments, but not your skill in advocacy. There I found a rare combination of the noblest ideals with a true grasp of necessary measures.'

'You may be gallant, Doctor, but I believe you,' said Mr

Skipton. 'Because I do not think you would be so bold as to bring up the need for a medical officer of health in Burlas, yourself. Your own name is already mentioned as a candidate.'

'I am far too inexperienced! And I fear we verge on the discourtesy of talking politics before the ladies.'

Between such talk, and my supervisory duties in ensuring the evening passed smoothly, there was little opportunity for reflection. At one point, however, I recall being left for a moment before the table set with all the best dishes we had been able to devise. My eye fell on the centre-piece display of fruit: a late and unexpected donation. I would not of course be carrying out my threat, jokingly made to my father, that I would tell the guests, after they had eaten, that the berries came from Evenden Hall, with the compliments of Mr William. In truth it had been a pretty desperate sort of joke on my part, flustered at the appearance of the gift. I had been trying for days to put out of my mind my father's cheerful assertion, that 'all the talk is now that he did it'. I picked up a plum and considered it, and forced myself to recall my evidence and its scrupulous accuracy. Indeed it was not even the case that the man had been so very rude as had been asserted. Reconsidering, my principal recollection was of someone who had been quite easy and pleasant, only not obsequious. My first thought had been that he was innocent. I would trust that. I bit indecorously on the plum, as if it were the embodied ripe fruit of Inspector Tutt's horrid suspicions.

My final memory is of two former schoolfriends of mine announcing a closing *tableau* in my honour as hostess. They presented themselves as Justice (with her scales), and Hygeia (with her saucer and 'serpent'), together holding up the sword against the evils facing humanity. It was hailed as an apt and enlivening diversion.

I do not recall if I slept well, or at all, that night, but I know that I thought myself in excellent looks the next morning when Henry paid an expected call.

I sat almost oblivious through our opening pleasantries and a good deal further, through a silence longer than in any earlier, nicely awkward, encounter of ours. I felt that I 'knew' what was to happen, and did not, or so I thought, need to attend to it greatly. But at length the silence became most noticeable. How could he be got to speak? Well, he *would* speak, of that I remained both sure and determined. If he could be made to look once upon me again, by my coughing and shifting a little . . .

He did not seem to notice. After all, I began to think nervously, what was this fancied inevitability of events, this power of mere expectancy? We all lived so close to our own passions, too ignorant of others'.

I reached my hand gently towards his. At that very instant, he snatched his up, in readiness for some gesture of impatience with his own inarticulacy. It was all in the same instant; he saw my movement, and my hand was clasped within his; but he looked upon it abstractedly, and after a short interval I thought myself no further forward! Then, he spoke.

'Miss James, you will wonder at me.' He put a comical inflexion on the phrase: wonder *at* me, though his tone was otherwise far from light. 'I am full of matters very weighty, which I must discuss with you, you see. But I am utterly unskilled in the language of this, let alone the true interpretation of my sensations – '

'Doctor Ryder,' I said, 'please speak openly, and do not be afraid.'

'I – Thank you!' Indeed he looked on me then, with the light of profoundest gratitude on his features. 'I came to Burlas, you know, with rational anxiety, but with such ideas of the work before me! I cannot speak of that, either, but you understand. You ought also to understand, I think, that it is not really fine stuff, not any of it. I try to follow those who are more far-seeing than I, than most men, and dream that perhaps one day, if I am spared so long, it might be given me to lead in one corner of the great field. I have made very little money, almost none. But now there is this new business, this question of happiness, or unhappiness, as something abstract, which grows and grows upon me – '

A pause settled upon us again. 'This did not feature in your plans?' I probed.

'I never thought of it in my life before,' he said quite flatly. 'Yet I find the position thus. Certainly, I – *You* know, you have so kindly and sweetly shown that you know, often. That I – love you – is certain. Though I cannot say since when, it is become as fixed and plain a thing as – as – a demonstration exhibit!'

We both laughed shortly, the sound quickly strangled as we now waited, both of us wondering, it seemed, what would come next. *Oh, but he loves me!*

He went on. 'I was saying, I make very little money. My prospects are uncertain. I have been very fortunate, kindly used, and honoured since I began my practice. Nevertheless, I am not well connected. And there is more. I consider myself to have some right to my plans and dreams, in those areas where I have laboured to qualify, equip and prepare myself. But I *have* felt myself to be wrong in pursuing this other notion, being unfitted and ignorant.' I remember he looked away at this point. 'One is so conscious of how fragile and temporary this life is, and all the good things it seems to promise! We have less right to involve others in grand plans, when everything can be ended so suddenly, or when one can be struck down and disempowered, without the strength to continue, and made destitute – ' I thought what sad histories he must have been witness to, but he laughed shortly: 'Oh, I should not say I have *never* thought of it. In my student days, I fancied sometimes a future in which I might find a mate; I pictured a homely thing of saintly disposition, probably poor and perhaps simple, happy to share in toil and drudgery. In fancying thus, I was an imbecile myself, for I did not ever consider the mysteries of my own heart, and where that might take me! I am ashamed to present myself to you, in such unreadiness and confusion, but waiting, and considering, seem not to improve my abilities, nor my position. On the other hand, last night I knew, the way you looked and the kind way everyone spoke to me; it was all too far on for the alternative – for me to give up. So, I pray you will excuse my speech.'

He appeared to be finished, or in some way exhausted, yet we remained in uncertainty. My hand was retained in his hand, and myself reflected in the blue of his earnest eyes – and I knew what a contrast I made, with every allowance for modesty, with his fancied 'mate'.

'Doctor Ryder,' I said. 'You speak as one with no right, if I understand you. You say that your prospects are uncertain, but you must know your reputation stands in their stead. Why should I, on such grounds, spurn an approach regarded by my friends and family, in anticipation – and again you must know it – as something most fortunate and conducive to my happiness? When, even in the face of concern or opposition – and, yes, or drudgery or hardship – I would still welcome it!'

'Miss James, what are you saying?'

'That I will marry you, if you will but kiss me.'

Others may think the whole exchange thus reported to have been a little odd, and I was troubled at the time by a sense that I had at some point done him a disservice, but in the moment of our embrace I *knew* that no two people were ever made happier by a morning's work. The ecstasy in his heart was told unmistakably in the press of his lips. My joy was such that I must even disguise it, I judged, rather than exhibit a nature that might be considered sensual.

'No-one ever teased me, until I met you,' he said. 'Shall you always do so?'

'Oh, always,' I replied, 'I vow.' It was like so much else, easily said, not thinking that the littlest promise can be made difficult to keep, through time and durance.

16

Mr Frederick Evenden invited us, Henry and me, to tea at Evenden Hall. He presided in his drawing room, offering us repeated congratulations and thoughts on the happiness of setting out on the blessed state together. Mrs Evenden's excuses were relayed; she was too ill to see anyone. William was by then gone abroad. I had been relieved by that information, having had an uncomfortable premonition of the kind of cool study he would have made of the two of us together.

'Are you acquainted with Hyam, our physician?' Mr Evenden asked Henry at length.

'We have met once or twice. And his reputation is, of course – '

'Yes, the best of men.' Mr Evenden considered his tea cup for a while. 'He is thinking of retirement, you know.'

'Really?' said Henry, carefully. 'I had not heard that.'

'Yes. A few of us are getting up a subscription, for his pension. You know, he comes here every week, at least once a week.'

'He must already have found a successor?' I asked.

'No, no. He has only a few patients left – old ones like us, my dear – and we all insist upon our freedom of choice. Well, Ryder, you will gather I have heard good things about you, and Hyam's been asking for me too, good soul. You might think it wearisome, to take on Mrs Evenden and myself, but would you consider it?'

Henry stammered to the effect that, of course, it would be a great honour, a great responsibility, for one so new in both the neighbourhood and his profession. It was fixed, and Henry would arrange to discuss with Doctor Hyam the details of 'the case'.

At leave-taking Mr Evenden escorted us out to his carriage which was to take us home. 'Miss James,' he said, keeping my hand in his, 'Ryder has won my custom on merit, but I am especially glad. You know how highly I regard your father. And your own goodness has been beyond price.'

'No.' I shook my head. 'You are too – '

'No, please. But if I should blunder in, to pay a call on you one day, just pretend you don't mind; I won't stay long. And don't mind that I won't invite you back here. You've seen now what it's like, and it won't get better in my lifetime.'

Later, as Henry and I sat back in the deep upholstered recess of the carriage, he said, 'This could change everything.'

I knew what he meant. This could not only improve his prospects; it could change their direction entirely. Where the Evendens went others, scarcely less prominent, would follow.

'Are you afraid of becoming another poodle like Hyam?' I asked.

He laughed. 'There are worse things. He was – is – still a good doctor.' He paused, then said aloud my exact thought, but somehow it chilled me a little to discover that we calculated so alike. He said, 'Thank the Lord, the son is gone abroad, probably for good. That makes it easier. The Evenden patronage might be a very dubious benefit just now, if he were included in it!'

In Evenden Hall I had seen the portrait of John, prominently displayed, and had cast on it some careful shy looks when opportunity allowed. The two brothers were alike but distinct, John the elder having a steadier, broader brow if the picture did not lie. The remembrance of the brutal and fatal hurts to his head came to me. The house contained a real and present tragedy. In the warm close privacy of the Evendens' carriage I fingered a yellow lock that lay within reach.

'You are mine,' I murmured.

'Yes,' he said. 'I am yours.' Then with a quick sigh he looked at me. 'I know what they will say. They will say that by marrying you I have got your aunt's money and your influence with old Mr Evenden.'

'Neither is so very much.'

'It will get more in the telling.' But his ardour the next moment was stronger than ever.

My aunt had bought the house in Water Lane for us, in a quick and irresistible piece of generosity. She had always had her 'funds'; this was, as she put it, merely a part of my inheritance in advance – a major part. Henry was overwhelmed but, as he recovered, delighted, as soon we both were, with the project of its fitting out ready for our occupation. It was to be his place of business as well as our home; meanwhile he must still work from his old lodgings. He laboured harder than before so that I missed his attendance on me and longed for the day of my wedding. The furnishing and *décor* were left largely in my hands. He deferred to me through an excessive sensitive consciousness of my supposed more cultivated taste.

It was on a day when my aunt and I were together at 'the Lane', in some curtain or canopy connection, that she made a speech both peculiar and typical.

'Anyone can see you are very happy, my dear,' she said, 'but if you had any doubts I hope you would be open, knowing me as you do, and my constitution as to delicacy or temper. These days, the promise of matrimony should not be unbreakable, by social form any more than by law. You may well think I am silly to raise this, who have no experience of marriage – Henry is, I really believe, the kindest, truest and most loving person you will ever meet, but even that may not alter the fact, if it is actually inadvisable for you to marry him. I can tell you this, because at least you are the sort to be brave enough to call a halt, if necessary.'

'Aunt Julia,' I said in some confusion, 'I am not going to stop the wedding now!'

'All I am saying is that I hope, if my example has taught you anything, it is that the position of a single woman need carry no shame, and can serve as well as any. You know that most of what is mine will be yours, one way and another; you need not be dependent. That is all.'

I assured her that I was not offended but that her concerns were groundless, of course. What was most remarkable was that she had had time to formulate such a considered argument. My aunt had taken charge of numerous practical arrangements as both Henry and I had proved incapable. Seeing that I would never do anything on the matter unprompted, my aunt finally decided the servant question, arranging for us a cook-housekeeper to begin with: Mrs Annesley. This business of becoming the mistress of the house was to me rather terrific, more overpowering than any thoughts of being a wife as such.

It was arranged by letter that my brother Jeffrey would bring his family for a visit and be present at the ceremony. Otherwise, it would be quiet; Henry's mother wrote that she would forgo the journey and be content with an early visit from us. I looked forward to the latter, since she lived at Scarborough and it was many years since my last sight of the sea. I looked forward to nonsensical things such as the intangible freedoms allowed a married woman as to dress and behaviour; but did not (*surely* that is only natural?) contemplate too closely the true nature of mature and marital responsibility.

On the eve of my wedding day my sister-in-law Amelia sat counselling me with determined dutifulness.

'So at first it is best, and shows most modesty, if you allow your husband to indicate everything that is to happen, only being ready, pliant, and quiet. You need do very little, in fact, except of course –' She swallowed, and hastily described the extent of the compliance required of me, at which I first appreciated that she had been speaking of specific relations not, as I had half-understood, merely general ones. I was a little astonished, a little amused, and a little affronted to be addressed thus by a woman I secretly despised (of course: it is the way with those females with whom older brothers become entangled). She assured me that I would suffer only a small hurt; thereafter, no great matter at all. It was coarse, that was unavoidable, but, 'it must be thought of as a holy duty owed, and gladly given, as you love your husband.' I thought very little of that.

So we were married, and afterwards with our little crowd we

111

feasted at home – Father's home – before a hired carriage arrived to take Henry and me to our new domain.

Next morning I rose as mistress of Water Lane, and found all in order. I dressed in my own new bedchamber and left all straight there. Descending, I found that my husband had not yet risen, and then was momentarily startled by the unfamiliar tones of the hall clock, chiming nine. Mrs Annesley had been and gone as promised, and dishes had been left on the warm plate of the kitchen range. I moved the just-steaming kettle over the fire, and carried the other things through to the dining room. Place settings had already been laid out, from the china and silver stacked in the dresser – all still seeming to me more like a scene on stage than any part of *my* effects. Henry soon joined me and we breakfasted alone together for the first time.

As to Amelia's concerns, I took the opportunity of such rare privacy and leisure to seek conference with my husband. It seemed to me only appropriate to consult his medical knowledge, as to whether certain persisting strange sensations of soreness, swelling and tenderness were cause for alarm. He assured me they were a normal and temporary consequence of the first abrasive contact. The organisation of my system was perfection, its functioning he judged healthy. He made clear his disinclination for further discussion, making a somewhat careful and delicate explanation. This part of marriage relations we could not enter as partners, 'with that equal, instinctive understanding that is generally so delightful. The area of brute feeling and reaction is opened to men but, thankfully, not to women. It has sometimes been observed in the lowest order of women but that is uncertain, being so indistinguishable from the most obnoxious knowing artifice. Within marriage, the only care required is that the necessary male function should not sully the spiritual bond. The carnal act takes place on your material being only. The danger of any neurotic reflection is that the woman's feminine essence is coarsened and damaged.'

He spoke as clearly and respectfully as his professional reputation would have led one to expect, therefore I endeavoured to accept his explanation. At the close of the meal we embraced. It is true a hypersensitive critic might have judged it coarse in me that I noted his start of puzzlement, and chose to show him that I did. For I told him with a smile that it was true I was not wearing stays; I had found it impossible to manage them without a maid. I suggested, to his blushing agreement, that until we were established with one, *he* might help! He went to spend what remained of the little holiday with his *Lancet* and his "B.M.J.", in the study-*cum*-consulting room of which he was so proud. I sat in my parlour also ostensibly reading, but daydreaming much of the time.

17

Henry's training meant he viewed the hospital as a potential cradle of the 'new scientific approach'. He wished to take over from Doctor Hyam at the Burlas Infirmary – as a governor. I was in need of useful occupation, so I too began to take an interest in the Infirmary.

It was a simple matter to secure for myself an accompanied 'inspection' of the institution; Doctor Maugham took me through every part one morning, in the company of other ladies, including Mrs Molsworthy.

'We must show our active concern,' she murmured to me following our introduction, 'in ensuring an effective economy is maintained in the application of the voluntary funds. Such extensive calls are made on them.'

It was my first encounter with her. She indicated that she would show me by example her method of giving sympathy and advice where necessary, to those patients whose misfortunes were attributable to ignorance or low habits, in a dignified, not overbearing manner.

Doctor Maugham's care that we should not remain long in the vicinity of any possible seat of infection sometimes frustrated her efforts in the latter object. I had been anxious about my ability to withstand the unwholesome disgusts which I anticipated having to witness. In the event, it was nothing worse than could be seen on certain streets of the city, and I was relieved to consider myself quickly accustomed if not hardened to all that assailed our senses.

Certain scenes were indeed pathetic, particularly individuals whose gaze seemed to tell of loss of hope. And oh, even now, I thought – when I had determined to put behind me all the doubts and abstractedness belonging to my past as a single girl – how suddenly and completely was I struck with the thought of a poor lost creature, mocked and wandering. In the age of comfort, reason, compassion and science, there remained those so unimaginably circumstanced as to be friendless and discarded, and trackless! For Mr Tutt had now reportedly abandoned his search for the lost witness in Critchley. Police inquiries into the foul murder of John Evenden were ended in shame and failure.

As the visit drew to a close, a turn in the grounds was suggested to refresh ourselves, during which Doctor Maugham favoured me with some particular attentions, making a complimentary reference to my connection with a professional colleague, claiming on that account to be especially curious to know what were my impressions of the tour.

'One cannot but be affected by such misery,' I said. 'But it is some comfort to know that the patients are more fortunate than others, in that here they are receiving such care as gives them a prospect of recovery. I cannot judge as to the medical care, therefore I accept what I have heard of it, which is all favourable. As to the nursing – '

'Ah, yes!' The doctor anticipated me with a smile. 'The vexed issue of nursing reforms. We supervise our women closely, and I hope you detected *here* no strong drink on the breath, nor lack of adequate discipline.'

'No, indeed. However I was interested to hear from one that her wage is three shillings a week, less than half what even the mills would pay – '

'They are lodged also.'

'Yes, in the basement all together, except those in the cots between the wards – with two or three jugs and basins, and sharing the patients' food and laundry.'

'Really, I don't know what you would suggest, Mrs Ryder,' said Mrs Molsworthy. 'I have spoken to them often, and find some possessed of surprising merit, for their humble station. They are very sensible that it is a step *up* for them, which is an addition to the moral service the Infirmary provides. Should we pay more, and so attract to this work the kind of girl who *could* stay at home without danger?'

'Doctor Maugham spoke of the "vexed question"; I believe he knows the alternative.'

'I believe we all do,' he said, 'and that it is one expensive of time and money cannot be denied – '

'Conservative of life, though? A properly trained and educated nursing staff offers each doctor assistance upon which he may rely, to implement the most rigorous or delicate régimes and treatments. At present they are fitted only to warehouse the sick like so much perishable merchandise – '

'That may be the theory,' said Mrs Molsworthy.

'And it is well supported,' Doctor Maugham conceded. 'I cannot state my own judgment on the matter; it is a question for the governors as a whole. The speed of our developing understanding is such that there are many measures both possible and known to be likely to be conservative of life – as you put it – in the short run. One cannot proceed without judgment. Suppose there was scope, in the town's production of surplus wealth, for some collective measure. Should we choose nursing reforms, or more new tenements? As a doctor, I know the general ineffectiveness of treating symptoms locally, when the opportunity exists to address the originating cause.'

'It is difficult to move the Council. The governors of the Infirmary can act when they will,' I said.

'I gave only one example of judgment, and perhaps a bad one. We do what we can, as far as new treatments go. I wish we could do more. You will forgive me for saying that I cannot help but view nursing reform – part of which, I maintain, we have implemented – as an advance, but not a *medical* advance, as such. In the public mind, however, it is become something of a fetich, which in itself is not helpful.'

Had breeding and manners not constrained him, I was sure he would have specified, among the unhelpful public, women like myself. Mrs Molsworthy was now determined to have the last word.

'As you have very fairly said, Doctor Maugham, it is a matter for the governors acting as a whole. You, Mrs Ryder, will of course have every chance to influence the issue. Have you heard, Doctor – I hope I do not touch on a sensitive point – how young Doctor Ryder has been favoured? He is consulted at Evenden Hall, now, by poor Mrs Evenden. Hyam was her physician. For a mere surgeon-apothecary to take his place says a great deal for his reputation, does it not?'

'In the cause of medicine there is no mean rivalry, madam. I know you would not imply as much. Young Ryder may count on the goodwill and assistance of his colleagues whenever necessary. That phrase you used might be applied to one of my vintage; these days it is considered outmoded. Mrs Ryder will tell you, I am sure: her husband has the Edinburgh training, the finest available at present.'

'Oh, indeed?'

The visit, and the entire exchange, were of course reported later for Henry's benefit and amusement. I omitted to mention only a final exchange I had with Doctor Maugham, when he took me privately aside. At first it seemed he was only anxious to ensure no lingering impression of professional jealousy remained with me. He spoke to me with surprising earnestness of his admiration at the labours and skills of Henry. 'Such men are needed,' he said. 'But we need them also to be preserved, as bright stars in the making. Only the most robust can expect to survive unscathed an indefinite period of intense medical crusading, while very young. As his partner in life now your part is most important. For an ambitious man, an early marriage can be a disaster – or it can arm him with the support that ensures eventual triumph. Doctor Ryder some-times appears to have more energy than strength. I know, now that we have met, that you have the skill and perception to take care of him as required, and will not let him drive himself too hard!'

I noted his strictures well; it would be too dreadful to think that I might have caused harm to Henry's health or prospects by

117

marrying him. I suspected that the marriage, though his heart's desire, might never have taken place, or never so soon, without my active calculation, so my sense of responsibility was secretly doubled on that account.

Subsequently, I had an opportunity to test the influence Mrs Molsworthy so insinuatingly ascribed to me, when Mr Frederick Evenden himself carried his promise into effect and called on me. My first thought was how I should acquit myself as hostess, under such aristocratic notice. My household had by then already expanded to include a man to see to the horse and the garden, and a girl to assist Mrs Annesley. Both were day servants, and the girl in particular still somewhat 'rough at the edges', giving me an awkward appreciation of my responsibility for training her. My second thought was that I must be subtle, and not seem to presume too much on the acquaintance, if I was indeed to try any politics of any kind. Henry had already once said, perhaps intending some warning to me, that he had 'learned more and more how important it is to proceed on all matters, in such a way as not to make enemies.'

Therefore I sat with Mr Evenden and invited his news of himself, of Mrs Evenden, and of William. His interest lay only in speaking of the latter; his enthusiasm on *that* subject irritated me. I thought the good man's taste dull, to be lavishing so much affection now on his clever, sarcastic surviving son who, on the best interpretation, had behaved badly and shown no remorse.

'Yes, he writes. He is well – very well! And full of himself, as they say. He likes it. Only I wish he would move on from Venice – it's a malodorous place.'

He suddenly wagged his finger at me animatedly. 'I liked that little Venetian tune, you know.' (I had been prevailed upon to play for a little on our poor upright piano to entertain him during our earlier wait for refreshments, though I was always an unwilling exponent, and the 'Italian airs' as lacking in authenticity as such confections generally are.) 'Will described to me the scene on the Grand Canal –'

I stifled a sigh – he could not have noticed it – but he interrupted himself: 'I hope you do not mind my speaking of him so much. Only I associate his deliverance with you, you know, so I cannot help it. Everywhere else, it is a barred name.' I knew he meant, with his wife. 'It eases me to talk of him. You know I miss him – very much.'

He went on to recount the full epistolatory travelogue. I was patient, though I wished William Evenden and his trial to be an incident lodged in the past. When one is only just past girlhood anything that reminds one of it is repulsive. And that event had brought me such an embarrassment of notice! However it was clear that Mr Evenden clung to the fact of the acquittal, as if alone it promised the delayed result of lives magically unblighted, and as he spoke of his son his eyes shone with happy imaginings of his personal posterity.

'. . . He really does have quite the painter's eye, you know, for description. As well as in the little pictures he puts in with the script, of course, but on thin paper with the writing showing through, they are nothing. He does so well though. It makes me afraid he will stay in Venice too long. He admits he should be spending his time now in study, but cannot hold back the commissions from the English colony, as well as even the native nobility.' He laughed coldly again, with an uncertain look under his brows at me. 'He writes, *My misfortune may be my fortune.*'

'Oh, of course,' I said, with too much quickness and meaning. 'At a distance the scandal will be attractive, to them. The man who was tried for murdering his brother!'

'Ye-es. At a distance. Indeed.'

'I am sorry! I am stupid!'

'No, no. You are honest, and innocent. We owe our lives to that.'

'I wish you would not say or – or think so.' I went on after a pause, 'I do think, since William is doing well, you could spend less care now in thinking of him, and more on yourself. I believe – Doctor Ryder thinks so. You had your wounds too, and they must be healed.'

He waved a hand before his face. 'Oh well, my dear. No doubt you will have children. In time.'

I smiled and blushed. 'There is no doubt I will.'

He caught himself up all at once. 'What? Can it be?' (I nodded.) 'Then banish me! Keep aged misery away! Well!' He fairly bounced in his chair. 'Tell me, is there anything I can do?'

'Perhaps I do have a favour to ask. Has anyone spoken to you on the matter of a nurses' home and school for the Infirmary?'

He looked vague. 'Now – perhaps they have. But not to any purpose, I believe. I have not heard Ryder's name in connection with it, or I might have paid more attention. He does not have much to do with the Infirmary, does he?'

'He – Oh, he is an enthusiast for improvements of all kinds. There are many conditional commitments already, it seems. But it needs a push, and all the governors and directors to be got in one mind, at one time. Henry knows the details.'

'I see. Well, tell your Henry to speak to me about it. I was expecting a request bearing more on your own little wishes and fancies at such a time.'

'I have all I need. I do not think you could help me find a new servant! It is my one headache – but not urgent.'

'You are right. Not my field!'

We were interrupted, as it happened, by my still-raw girl. A lad from 'up town' was in the waiting room, and making her nervous. He was afraid the doctor might be gone too long for him. A mother was suddenly taken very poorly. She had the address.

'Has Frank gone home?' I asked.

'Yes, miss.' She would call me that. 'I could try calling on him, to go the message.'

Mr Evenden, however, rose to go. Henry would be at that hour with Mrs Evenden. He would go home immediately, and see that the doctor was sent on to his next call. 'The humble have as much right to succour, in their hour of need.'

As a final postscript to my Infirmary visit, Henry informed me some little while thereafter that he, the 'surgeon-apothecary', had been summoned to the Molsworthy house, in his professional capacity. I could discern that it was becoming the fashion to consult him, though I rather hesitated to put the matter before him in such terms even in jest. Still aflutter myself with new perceptions of the world and its workings, and so full in love with my husband, I was sure that the ladies now searching him out to attend to their families were drawn by more than his professional standing and skill. His person and manner must be to the liking of any woman – perhaps even Mrs Molsworthy. No, I could never share with Henry the cause of my smile as I pictured *her* lying back on the cushion. Would her sluggish pulse quicken at the steady touch of him? Would she exaggerate her symptoms of enervation, while actually thinking – what?

18

Doctor Maugham's talk of my responsibility to care for Henry, to be alert to physical and nervous dangers and to secure his welfare when he might neglect it himself, preyed on my mind greatly. This too at a period when I looked back curiously on my motivation for marrying.

Before marriage, one scarcely sees beyond it; for the woman it is somehow the end and object of everything. She knows that she will exist thereafter, but she perhaps assumes it will be in a different form, just as the law maintains, even with different blood in the veins and perceptions in mind. That does not happen; she wakes – I awoke – every day the same. And so sometimes I must be thinking: 'What *was* my purpose in doing this?' There were, of course, any number of happy part-answers to hand! Yet also among them less comfortable whispers. I had become most determined to secure an immediate engagement just at the point when confidence in my own independent judgment and direction was most rattled. The trial and my subsequent doubts, the novel sensation of being scrutinised minutely, the mortifying speculations of both Mr Tutt and William Evenden as to my inward nature – had I been *driven* to abandon the 'miss' who was subjected to that?

In one sense, Henry was a perfectly inhuman blank, for he lacked the normal person's petty curiosities, foibles, and personal self-indulgences. Yet he had his own peculiarities of character. I was acquiring a sympathetic sense for what made him uncertain or afraid, quickly knowing this in him before he did himself. Mr

Evenden had achieved the needed push in the matter of nursing at the Infirmary, helped by Henry's briefings on the doubts of the directors and their respective weaknesses. But Henry seemed to battle throughout a kind of curious loathness in the matter.

My dilemma was whether in encouraging the scheme I was truly acting for him, or to gratify myself. The end result would establish him more securely as a figure of consequence in society. He would be delivered from much material uncertainty. More importantly, he would be delivered from any remaining serious doubt, I thought, that his labour and zeal would be of value in the world. For one of my husband's stamp that must be worth everything. So I encouraged him, as much as I could, to persevere with the campaign for reform.

Henry returned late one evening to find me still up. He stood before the embers of the late spring fire. On the mantel-shelf was a papier-mâché beaker of spills, and he fastidiously pinched off the burnt ends as he spoke.

'I think it is done at last,' he said. 'They have the majority for the meeting tomorrow. Old Evenden had a crowd around tonight. Sir John Vickers, Molsworthy and Treves. They want me to go on the board of the Infirmary.'

'Oh, well done!'

'I am to have special responsibility for the appointment of a new matron, and the nursing generally.' His smile was a little rueful and he did not meet my eye. 'It is not exactly the field I imagined for myself.'

'But one likely to yield lasting dividends, and the opportunity for further advance in scientific treatment – have you not said?'

He looked up almost startled. 'Oh, yes, eventually. Of course, I am glad.' I am sure his hesitancy, though clear as day, was unapparent to Henry himself.

This then was the type of vibrative event that could shake *his* mechanism out of true. I remembered the way he had phrased his proposal of marriage, as if driven to it too soon; I had been a disruption of his plans. So had the first beneficence of Frederick Evenden. Chance events, even happy ones, were upsetting to him.

123

Therefore I urged him, gently, to explain to me something of his chosen field.

'Oh, but you are tired, and should be in bed.'

'I promise you, not in the least. Is it too difficult for me to comprehend?'

'It is rather that, as you know, I am so poor at making explanations.' He continued to stare a little gloomily, but at length he went on. 'It is true, my main idea is not a simple one, but not in the sense you were meaning. These days of intelligence – the natural sciences – all has grown up apart from my discipline. Medicine must be brought within the new scientific order. The great advances have been in establishing wholly new and separate areas: vaccination, anaesthesia, even the sanitary laws . . . All the rest of medical practice, though, all that has always been, remains untouched. In so far as there is any science in medicine it is in the aspect of description – which is excellent, yes, but without deduction, with no understanding of process.'

'What further understanding of process would you seek?'

He sighed and thought for a moment for a way to clarify his meaning. 'You see, I am taught to observe a diseased patient, to see his body as a wondrous phenomenon, given by the unseen hand all the elements of perfection.' It was curious to find that he shaped his own hand in the air between us to frame his thought, and his look rested somewhere on my person – but as on a diagram not fully understood. He went on, 'I must by instinct find what is to be adjusted to recover the state of harmony. The antiphlogistic principle is all: give aperients, apply leeches or bleed where indicated, then a poor liquid diet. All *action* is left to nature.'

'Oh, come, that is not all!'

'No, we poison, following the *vade mecum* to restrict to a dose less than fatal in itself. My point is that all such practice is not and never has been understood. It is, however, the distillation of centuries' wisdom of honourable men. Therefore, a special method is required, now, to make a science of it!'

'You require to find a – method?'

124

'Experimentation. It is what we must all learn together. Responsible experimentation.'

Seated and now almost unnoticed by him in his passion, I started inwardly. I believed I had understood him. Certainly I did not share the common superstitions that would be aroused abroad by injudicious talk of experiments, but still the word made me shudder.

After abstracted pacing he returned to his pose by the fire, leaning a little away from where I was sitting.

'Never say that you are poor at making explanations,' I murmured. 'Beside your belief in yourself, I think my talent a facile and graceless thing.'

His shoulders moved, a sigh and a shrug. My husband was an impossibly fine, impossibly delicate machine. I would ache from handling him. Too good for me, had someone said? For anyone, perhaps.

The following morning a letter came for me. It was in its way astonishing, being from Miss Dorothea Bowlby. She wrote, she acknowledged at once, as someone with whom I was not formally acquainted, and apologised if that was deemed an intrusion. She had been given to understand that I stood in need of a good servant. She had an excellent maid who wished now for a new position in a larger household and, though sorry to lose her, she would do what she could to further this ambition in consideration of the affection she had for her. If I had no interest in taking up the matter, no reply was necessary and no offence would be taken. If I wished to speak to her and to her maid, then the briefest message appointing a time for them to call would suffice, without obligation of course.

I put the letter down. For two minutes I considered what to do. I knew that I must raise it with Henry. I had no serious concern about taking on a new maid; we had discussed it fully and in his solicitousness for me he was more anxious than I that the step be taken as soon as possible. The question was whether we should seek any dealings at all, even of this kind, with Miss Bowlby? On the one hand we should not fear gossip if it did not touch his or my own virtue and rectitude. On the other, there might be those with whom his reputation was just newly, and valuably, established who would disparage any connection with a name so scandalous. I was very intrigued at the prospect of meeting her though.

I cleared my throat. 'Henry, I have had the most curious letter, and I don't know what I should do.'

'Why, what is it?' He raised his eyes only momentarily from his own correspondence.

'It is from Miss Bowlby, of all people.' I rushed on in a casual tone, thinking that he would not want me to reply, might in fact, unfairly, want me never to have received the letter, or to have kept its existence hidden from him. 'It seems she may be able to help us to a new servant.'

There was a pause. He grunted, 'And?'

'Should I reply?'

'Yes, yes, of course.'

The days that followed were all gratifying excitement, with much praise of Henry in particular after his performance at the public meeting. Of course he was very little at home, but I was quite satisfied that the uncertainty being past he was more robust and happy-looking.

Then came the day when Miss Bowlby herself was sitting in my drawing room. I studied her costume: the dark green which so suited her, of a fullness between a crinoline and a bustle, but with a heavier more elegant drape than either. An easy elasticity showed in all her parts, yet each move was also measured. She looked at me and smiled.

'Oh,' she said, in response to some opening pleasantry of mine, 'why is that?'

Why? Why had I 'so wanted' to meet her?

'Well, I – ' I began. 'One has heard so much about you.' Her brows narrowed a half-amused fraction and I hurried on, flushed, before she could ask, What, pray? 'I mean, you seem to know so many interesting people.' I stopped abruptly. What a thing to have said, when our only common acquaintance was the defendant in a murder trial, reputedly her lover!

'Do I?' Dorothea Bowlby's slow smile broadened by a single notch. 'I suppose I do. I am interested in people; I dare say that it amounts to the same thing – don't you think?'

My own more unruly features broke startled into a laugh. 'Yes,' I said. 'I think it does.'

'I admit that I am not above putting myself out to gain the acquaintance of those who are more clever and talented than I can ever be. Such company is my passion, and I indulge. Otherwise, I have no-one to think of but myself, and that is dull stuff!' Again the little smile which might be invitation, challenge or insult.

Under her gaze I found myself glancing down to check the state of my hands, my dress. 'I have envied you,' I said.

'I enjoy a modest sufficiency of most things considered desirable, but I take it you do not refer to that. As to my reputation, that was got by deliberate planning and execution – by *work*.' The smile. 'Do you envy me my reputation, Mrs Ryder?'

I shook my head, and smiled too.

'Oh!' Even her exclamation was measured. 'I *do* see what they admire in you.' Before I could form the inquiry as to what, and who, she went on, 'Well, what matters to me is that I enjoy the company of my friends. They are not all wild, or geniuses, really, you know, but they are all interesting to me. Yet – perhaps you have found this too – there is something not quite genuine in Burlas people. I don't mean any fault in them at all, but as if it is something in the air. We see Manchester and Sheffield, and take a kind of model of rabble-rousing. And for conversation and culture, we try to create some synthetic essence of London and Edinburgh, a whiff from the express trains, perhaps. But sometimes,' she dropped her voice to a whisper, 'it is too amusingly like charades!'

I murmured, 'I thought the notion of living a kind of pretended life was unique to me.'

'Oh *that*,' she said easily. 'That, I am sure, is universal.'

Was there any warning in my breast that I would come to regret this quickly adopted habit of opening to her so readily my private thoughts and ideas? She brought the talk on to the nursing reform, for she evidently knew of my interest and Henry's involvement in the Infirmary scheme.

'A most admirable *coup*,' she said. 'One hears so much of doctors, and especially young ones, not wanting the new arrangements.'

'There can be no grounds for opposition.'

'If it were merely a question of health and sanitation, no. But above all it is a question of power: power and women, combined. Oh, my! To have at one's elbow, suddenly, a woman of equal, or superior, social origin; to have women about with trained intelligence – There are grounds to fear what your husband will bring about. I do not say, of course, that in *our* Infirmary there is any of that.' She spoke with sly amusement.

'Of what?'

'Scandals that the ladies love to flutter about. Unspeakable forms of experimentation, under the cloak of privacy, and chloroform. It is said the doctors want to keep the new nurses at bay, for fear they will be found out!' She laughed outright now. 'More seriously, had I been younger, I might have thought to train as a matron. You do not know what it is, to be one of the surplus millions of women!'

'I am grateful to you for writing to me,' I said, bringing the subject back to the business of our meeting. 'But I am most curious as to how you knew I was in need of a new servant?'

'Yes,' she said. 'It is true I am quite cut off, and know nothing of respectable polite Burlas society.' I blushed again. 'But there is a great deal of the other sort. And while Burlas may not speak to me, I hear news from the far corners of the globe, and gossip will take the most roundabout route, if the direct is blocked. I am sure that you can guess.'

I could, but it seemed incredible. Mr Frederick Evenden would have included anything, willy-nilly, in his letter to his son, certainly. But then, for the son to repeat such particular details, in a letter back across the sea, from *him*, to *her*? My imagination dwelled for a moment in the unknown landscape of such a letter. In what tone would I have been introduced? *'Little Mrs Ryder, already with child – you know, Miss James as was – who sat in her papa's parlour in her blue ribbons, and eulogised "poor sweet Mr Lincoln and the darling blacks".'*

In due course we sent for her maid, Mercy Meadows, to join us from the kitchen. I liked her. She seemed clean, tidy and unafraid, outside and in. My aunt was to christen her 'Mercy Baptist' because that was what she was. As I talked quietly with her in the presence of her mistress, I already congratulated myself on my acuity. Then I caught myself up. Mercy had after all simply been dropped in my lap by Providence in the most fortuitous way possible; there was no merit in that.

It was agreed that she would take up a position as senior upstairs servant, and in time have oversight of the care of the baby as well as being my own maid, though much of the practical work might be undertaken by the other girl. Miss Bowlby took care to send her out of the room again before taking her leave.

'I would like to invite you to my home, Mrs Ryder, one day when it is quiet, of course – just you and me. But no doubt, you cannot contemplate new friends and exertions.'

Moved by her considerate phrasing, I demurred. 'You are wrong. I would be delighted.'

'Good. I have added a lady journalist to my stock of interesting acquaintance.'

'Who? Oh, no. No, not I.'

'You are not a lady, not a journalist, or you do not after all wish to be acquainted with me?'

The task now before me, of recounting Miss Bowlby's visit and its outcome to Henry, was not entirely easy. I was in a different part of the house when I thought I heard him enter. He did not seek me out at once as expected so I went to look for him. I snatched nervously at the consulting room door to see if he was there.

The scene within the room caused me first to raise my hand to my mouth, in mirth it must be said. Henry sat at his desk, his coat, cravat and shirt were quite open and much of his chest exposed to view! A stethoscope dangled from his ears, he having dropped the end-piece in his confusion at my sudden entrance.

I stared and blushed, and began, 'I am sorry – '

'Katherine!' he interrupted. 'This of all rooms surely you should knock before entering, and wait! Suppose I had been examining a patient?'

'Yes, I know. I am sorry. What were you doing?'

He began to re-order his attire before answering. 'It is a new instrument. I was merely testing its efficacy on myself.'

'No worse experiments?' I tried to tease.

'For experiments to be worse,' he said testily, 'they must be bad. In fact they are beneficial and one should not, even as a joke, continue such false notions.'

'Oh, quite so. Did you find all well with your heart, my dear? I hope it is not altered toward me.'

'All quite well until I was so startled.'

I chose to laugh at that. Then I said, 'Henry, you would not put your health in danger? You have been working very hard. Perhaps you should rest more.'

'What?' he exclaimed. 'So recently made your husband, must I already be buried in swaddling? If you care for my equanimity do not ever make any ridiculous fuss, if you please.'

He had restored his proper appearance, a little redness still remaining in both our visages, I suspect.

'I was anxious to find you because I have some news,' I said. 'I have found a new maid who will answer our requirements perfectly. Her name is Mercy Meadows. She is very experienced and her character seems excellent.'

Henry obliged with a look of approval.

'And she and her mistress are clearly on the best of terms; there is nothing behind Miss Bowlby wanting to give her up.'

'Miss *Bowlby*? Not Dorothea Bowlby?'

'Yes. Remember, I told you she had written.'

'I am certain you did not.'

'My dear, I did, though perhaps you were not listening.'

We both stared at each other for a moment.

'Do you mean she was here?' my husband said in a suppressed voice.

'Yes. And I have agreed now to call on her. I hope you do not mind.'

He stared a further minute. 'I cannot stop you, I take it. And mind? How should I? You have a much superior understanding, I know, of intellectual society and what it winks at.'

'But I know the objections, and of course you can stop me if you mind in the least!' I protested; but I went on quickly, 'If I am to see her, I will ensure it is done discreetly.'

'Of course. It is not as if we could present her to anyone! See whomever you judge fit, my love. I would not on any account deny you that freedom.'

19

I was in terror at my 'condition'. My mother's health had been ruined and her early death determined by a difficult childbirth. There were many other women I could name, many I knew well, whose bodily vigour had been wrecked by either a single disastrous childbed or a series of unrelenting, debilitating episodes. There was another new acquaintance, Bella Treves, with two surviving children from (Henry himself told me, through compressed lips indicating his horror and disapproval) sixteen *accouchements*. Though our circumstances could never be alike, I looked on the pathetic lady with a kind of superstitious horror, in my heightened sensitivity seeing her physical and even intellectual fragility as a personal portent of evil or bad fortune.

Be in no doubt, I knew that my fear betokened a lack of righteousness, the moral counterpart to my bodily deformity. For my relations with my husband had done nothing to dispel my sense of my own physical disharmony with Nature. I did not at all comprehend what was to happen to me, and thought it certain that a child could not be born out of me. I believed that my husband knew this, and that his moments of despair were camouflaged with false cheerfulness for my benefit. Once only, collapsing in unrestrained weeping, I tried to reveal to him the state of my 'knowledge' as to the abstractedness I detected in him. He regarded me as one would the victim of a dangerous insanity; and even as he held me and tried to restore me to my feet I sensed a clammy lightness in his touch where it should have been firm and eager, a horrifying repugnance in him, at *me*! I did not speak of my fears again, but lived somehow through those months with a lack of faith in the quality of communication between us. It was a strange experience, which I thought at times was close to sending me mad indeed.

I am a coward who knows the fear that hardens the soul. I did not ever confide, not fully; I tried with Henry, then recoiled, and I could not with my other loved ones. But two people had come into my daily round with whom I began to feel at least more safe than with anyone else. They were Dorothea Bowlby and Mercy Meadows.

With Mercy's arrival the house ceased to be 'new'. It became at last a home. She was not proud or sanctimonious; she behaved as if she were picking up a pattern already worked. She did not point to where things were wrong, only saw to putting them right. After one week, even Henry commented that it was as if she had lived with us always.

It was the same with her attitude to my condition. It began to be referred to between us quite naturally, like a conversation that had been carried on intermittently for years. I was indescribably relieved.

'They have good light flannel in Fuller's now,' she would say. 'So I'll get five yards, if you don't mind, and do a dozen vests and what nots. I have a pattern much better than their made-up ones; *their* armholes are too tight and the wrapover is skimpy.' As if it was a need of which I had spoken. 'If you wish to wear your grey tomorrow, I'll get on and let this dress out again too.'

It was soon apparent that with her sense and knowledge, and Henry's direction, an additional monthly nurse would not be needed when my time drew near. When it did, without instruction she lined and quilted the berceaunette, and put ready in it the small clothes, napkins, cloths and other necessary items.

Miss Bowlby, true to her word, invited me at the coffee hour in early course – though she served me a light herbal infusion while taking coffee herself.

'You see, I know a little of your needs,' she said. 'Though I am not of course as expert as you will be yourself. Please let me know where I go wrong, or if there is anything I can help to provide.'

'I am not expert at anything,' I said. 'I drink coffee; is that wrong?'

'Oh, I have only read something on the dietary needs of expectant women. If you and your husband judge most of these ideas nonsense, no doubt you are right! You look to be in perfect health.'

I envied the freedom with which she used such practical terms as 'expectant women'.

We began to exchange visits regularly, and became 'Dolly' and 'Kitty' in no time. My aunt and father knew that we had become acquainted, though probably not to what extent. Henry knew how often I saw her, but he chose not to react when I dropped her name in conversation. Sometimes indeed this raised a sense in me of something akin to annoyance, but I shook myself out of such unreasonableness, perhaps because his attitude suited me quite well. No-one approved of her, but no-one would voice disapproval openly, to my face.

Now, I think of all the reasons why such a rapid development of intimacy was so extraordinary. There was the possible peril to my own or Henry's good standing – though no ill effects accrued at that time. The unpleasant misunderstanding that had already resulted, at the very first, because of Henry's initial alarm – I wonder why on earth that did not cause me to hold back. Above or encompassing all was the mysterious but definite nature of her continuing connection with William Evenden. He, his history, and our respective opinions of both, were all subjects which then, of course, could not be mentioned between Dolly and me. With all these indications to the contrary, all I can say is that she was my most valued and understanding friend. The unease of spirit begun in me with the trial was soothed and forgotten in her company, though the very opposite may have been expected.

Her continued interest in Mercy was genuine. Sometimes I imagined them as an unseparated pair, enfolding and watching me. If Dolly wanted, I would send for Mercy then leave them alone for a while. I wanted them to know that I had no fears of what Mercy might report. Once, I returned to find them still together, as was not unusual. Mercy stood immediately though I indicated there was no need. She looked at Dolly, then excused herself anyway.

'Yes, we were talking about you,' Dolly said, skilfully covering the trace of awkwardness. 'How much we are both getting to like you, and how we can look after you better.'

'Did you expect not to like me?' I joked, as I sat and pulled cushions around myself.

'Well –' she began. Then she stopped and leaned over to put another cushion behind my head, and touched my cheek with her forefinger. 'Anyway, we do.'

On that or perhaps another occasion, she wondered aloud if I would have a boy or a girl, and initiated some general talk about the coming event.

'I wish I knew what *was* going to happen,' I said.

'Oh, no. I would *never* wish to know the future, and spoil the pleasure!'

'No, I mean, there are things that can be known, but I do not even know –'

'Really?' she said quite pleasantly, unperturbed. 'You should have said. I have books and pamphlets, I am sure – but what am I saying! You can surely find something in your husband's library. Is he busy now?'

I looked at her then, wide-eyed. 'He is out.' I swallowed. Why had it never occurred to me? I called myself an educated woman. 'Shall we go to the consulting room?'

Once there, I moved to the bookcase, watched by her. I scanned the spines of his textbooks until my eyes lit on the *Manual of Obstetrics*. I took it down uncertainly; my understanding even of terms was hazy, so that I was unsure if it was what was wanted. I held it out for Dolly to see.

'Yes,' she said, coming over. 'Well, that is – it will do! Let us see.'

Under her gaze I rested the heavy book momentarily on Henry's desk and leafed through a few pages.

'Oh, my goodness!' I breathed, seeing a diagram of the female form, in cross-section.

'Yes, no doubt it will be dry and turgid, in the way of these medical men – Oh! Pardon me, of course!' Dolly closed the volume and bore it back to my parlour for me, preceding me as we walked. 'This work is rather old now, but I believe still the most thorough. A book may be respectable, though its author commands no respect.'

'How do you mean?'

We settled ourselves on the parlour chairs again, as she went on, 'I mean the author of our manual here. Do you not recall the name? Perhaps you are too young. He is an utter Luddite, if it is not stretching the term too far to apply it to such a noble profession. He was foremost among those, years ago, who contended that it was against nature to offer women any amelioration of the pains of confinement. To bolster his argument, he claimed that chloroform was known to induce "the excitement of the sexual passion", and involuntary acts and language accordingly. All very well, he implied, in Paris or Edinburgh, but an Englishwoman would willingly endure the last extremity of physical pain, in preference!' She laughed. 'That lecture was widely circulated, you may imagine, among those of us concerned with the advancement of the rights of women. His case was in time fatally undermined, of course, when the dear Queen plumped for chloroform.'

After we had both finished laughing, and praising Her Majesty immoderately, I said, 'You are remarkable, Dolly. How do you know so much, about everything?'

'Oh, but I am a very stupid woman, my dear, not learned or trained for anything. I suppose I have found things out because, situated as I am, no-one can stop me. Boredom is the one thing that I hate.'

When she left, I took up the book, and was still absorbed when Henry entered much later.

'Hello, my dear, what are you reading?' He added, with gentle admonition, 'You should sit back, and rest your feet on the stool.'

'I know. It's this.' I held it up awkwardly for him to see, inevitably perhaps seeming to thrust it at him; I was not only embarrassed to mention it, but unsure of the pronunciation. 'I hope you don't mind my borrowing it; I shall return it shortly.'

'No,' he said quite quietly. 'No, of course not. How could you think *me* so antediluvian? Or rather who could have made you think it?'

I did not reply directly, but after a pause I went on, 'Much of the text is too complicated, and defeats me. All the same it is rather wonderful to sit here, feeling our baby move, and see the diagrams at the same time.'

'Yes, of course. But I really would not advise you to look any further. You will only alarm yourself. At this stage, the utero-spinal system is under such stress, nervous excitement is easily aroused and factors tending towards it – even contemplation of the wonderful – should be avoided.'

'I promise you, Henry, nothing in the *book* has alarmed me: rather the opposite – even the plates showing all the instruments. What has always concerned me is my ignorance of what I must do –'

'*Kay!*' It was the name he gave me now, from all the notes exchanged before the wedding, signed only with initials. 'Kay, please, my dear. *I* can see only too well that you have already excited your imagination too much. You have such a beautiful, but lively mind! I must ask you to let me put this away now. Really – it is not very suitable – is it?' He took the book from my reluctant but unresisting hands, then he pressed my shoulders up and against the chair-back, and kissed my forehead. He spoke low, his breath warm in my hair: 'Most wonderful of all is this learning about each other! You set me such lessons; consider they may be beyond my poor skill and understanding. Do not *so* often, if you please, test my ability to accommodate your more unusual attitudes. I become anxious about you; so go more gently.' He stood upright. 'You know I love and admire your passion for learning. Learn about me, too.'

I watched him leave the room with the *opus* of Tyler Smith safe in his arms. The thought which came, again, into my mind was: 'You think that I am going to die.' Then, 'You have not kissed my *lips* for weeks.' I burned also to think how much I had been trying to make everything easy and unburdensome for him, and how I must still be failing in that. When I had expressed open concern about *his* health, I remembered, it had served only to irritate him.

I could easily have consulted his library again when he was from home, but never did, from both a dislike of such covert behaviour and a recoiling apprehension at the works themselves, once the first wave of enthusiasm was over. This meant I also must avoid recurrence of the same subject with Dolly, who otherwise could have helped me certainly. I had no wish to open to her the details of what had passed between me and my husband. When she mentioned it I indicated lightly that my concerns were at an end.

Then came a day when I sent Frank to find his master. Mercy fetched me some water then began to help me up the stairs, her manner the pattern of the ordinary everyday. We had only reached the half-landing when Henry himself entered below. He stopped suddenly, seeing us. I had almost schooled myself against panic, under Mercy's influence, but the sight of his upturned face put ice in my heart. Unguarded for a moment, he looked grey and fearful.

'It is not time?' he asked.

'Yes. Did you not pass Frank?'

'No – Thank you, Mercy, I will take her. See to that list I prepared, will you?'

'Yes, Doctor.'

Henry was beside me, his arm at my back and his head bent, watching my tread on the stair.

It is not done, I know, to write of what followed. There is the matter of delicacy, of course, and if I had been outside the room I could have given a proper account of anxious listening faces, perhaps of prayers being offered and sins repented. Unfortunately, I was not made delicate, and moreover I *experienced* the event itself. There is also, however, an artistic difficulty. I have heard it said that it would need the language of angels to describe the lives of women more closely than has been attempted in literature. The

138

language not of angels, I would say, but of animals, did we but know it. The beasts' tongue may have more strong, plastic beauty, more sorrow and delight, than our dreams.

My Henry was a good doctor; he could even have been a great one. I was never his patient, though. What he saw was his wife, and what in others was an accepted phenomenon was, in me, grotesque. Afterwards, I thought I understood this. At the time, I took his coldness, hesitancy and passionate impatience as confirmation of his fear on *my* behalf. So I tried to cling to him and beg his mercy, and so his disgust must have been greater as he fought the evidence of his senses, that the natural beast he had to deal with was his sweet, pure and dear one. In absolute terms, my time was easy; Henry had put ready the chloroform equipment in case of excessive pain or difficulty, but did not use it.

The baby lay limp and lifeless at first, and it was with a kind of frozen calm that I watched Henry rubbing her with his hands dipped in brandy, with an agitated rhythm, until on an instant redness suffused the blue of her skin and she cried.

Mercy cleaned me. With her skilled hands she eased my breasts into a state of readiness, and put the feeble little lips to suck. Then the doctor – so he seemed, then, 'the doctor' – stood over me, blushing and confused, and Mercy withdrew. He was watching the baby. I touched his brow. Still he watched the baby but he seized my hand and kissed it. I knew it was the tenderness within that made him frightened and cruel, cruel in effect but not in intent, and I could not speak. I looked afresh into eyes which were as trusting, open and free of guile as his infant daughter's, now patterned always on my brain.

PART 3

16th AUGUST 1870

20

Henry Ryder's death was reported in the newspapers of the 16th August. In Burlas itself in that era there had become established two rival daily newspapers and fierce competition ensured the fullest possible coverage. The reports caused locally, in the true sense, 'a sensation'. The alarm, excitement, and possessive interest were palpable, wherever people gathered in twos or threes: in shops, works, offices, in the street and on the omnibus.

It was easily the greatest event since – well, since the Evenden trial at least. From that, indeed, it merely obtained an added lustre, since there, reported in conjunction with Ryder's sudden demise, was the news that William Evenden was seriously ill with gunshot wounds, being the last patient to have been treated by the doctor who, witnesses reported, had explained that Mr Evenden's injury was accidentally self-inflicted during an attempted assault on himself. Nor, with plentiful room allowed on the front pages, did the reports, any of them, scruple to remind readers in detail that, five years before, the same William Evenden had been tried and acquitted for the murder of his brother John, a crime which remained unsolved, following which Evenden had been for some years absent abroad . . .

The morning's newspapers lay on Oswald Tutt's desk. In that immediate aftermath, the reports had not yet made the connection with the Evenden witness 'Miss James'. But many would have, and Tutt grimly acknowledged to himself that the talk would be spreading like oil on water. Beneath his solid exterior he battled, as usual, with unhelpful, fevered and illogical self-accusation. He should have nailed Evenden somehow, five years ago; failing that, he should have predicted some harm to the good man who became the husband of that pert little miss. At the time, though, he too had been sure that she was innocent – a mere sideshow. There had been nothing to warn him of any continuing connection with Evenden, not until the doctor himself had confirmed it on the moor and that was only hours before his death, when it seemed Evenden had done his worst and was powerless to do more. Until then, as far as Tutt was concerned, there had been nothing to contradict the words, as he could still almost hear them: 'They were, in effect, *strangers!*'

While Tutt was in many ways an enemy to himself there were parts of his personal philosophy helpful in a crisis. It must seem that the whole world outside his office was buzzing with the Ryder business but he knew that, mysterious or otherwise, spectacular deaths are, were, always have been, actually ten a penny. He knew that, outside Burlas, Ryder's was not so notable and would be eclipsed. It was exactly one week since the papers had reported the execution of the Denham murderer, perhaps the century's most notorious: John Owen, killer of one man, three women and three children. Even the hanging was exceptional for its shocking qualities. Owen had roundly cursed the clergy attending him and, unrepentant, cried: 'I am only sorry that I did not shoot Superintendent Dunham and a —— Justice of the Peace that once sentenced me as well!' No-one (certainly not Oswald Tutt) could have read those accounts, so recently, without some agitation of spirit, upon which fresh scandal and outrage must resonate with a more awesome quality and raise primitive, subrational but distinct fears of new-generated evil abroad . . .

So, what progress? Mrs Ryder still had not been traced. By some typical garbling process the newspapers all had her down as 'too distressed to speak to anyone'; goodness only knew what they would have made of the truth, that she had flitted. Miss Bowlby also had left town suddenly with no forwarding address. Finding them both was a priority.

Evenden, according to the papers, 'hovered between life and

144

death'. That was old news. He lay under guard at the Infirmary, recovering his strength speedily, like the devil. Tutt had taken a formal statement from him there that morning, in the presence of both county and city justices (jurisdiction over the two incidents, the shooting and the poisoning, separately or combined, being uncertain, and everyone always so touchy on etiquette where Their Worships were concerned). He fingered his copy of the statement again, determined to re-read it. His mind, though, still ran on the awakened memories of the John Evenden murder. Case closed – unsolved.

This new supposed science of detective policing – how could anyone honourable find satisfaction in such a field, when there would *always* be unsolved crimes? They haunted him. He, Tutt, could not forget that for every crime there was a human villain. Then he thought that he should perhaps improve his filing system. Failure to obtain conviction was not always the same as unsolved. 'Failure to obtain conviction' – no, too unwieldy. Not unsolved, but – unpunished.

It must be remembered that fear was the key to Tutt: fear of failure, above all. William Evenden's acquittal had been an actual failure and, worse, the seed of fear of future ones.

He picked up Evenden's statement.

. . . Yesterday, the fifteenth day of August in the year of our Lord 1870, I was visited in the morning at my home, Evenden Hall, in the County of ——, by Mr Henry Ryder of Water Lane, Burlas. Mr Ryder is a doctor of medicine, and known to me in that capacity and otherwise.

Ryder's visit was of some fifteen or twenty minutes' duration, in the course of which he showed himself heated and angry, accusing me of having injured his interest, specifically of plotting to abduct his wife and/or committing immoral and adulterous acts with his wife. In the context of the dispute between us, threats were exchanged, being on my part no more than threats but, I now believe, in the disordered state of his mind at the time the threats made by him were serious. I had not known him previously to be possessed of a violent or unstable temperament.

He departed from me at length only upon being warned that he would

145

otherwise be forcibly ejected from my property. A short time afterwards I was
alerted by one of my servants to the fact that Ryder could be seen on the moor,
about half a mile distant, setting watch on my house. This caused
consternation in the household and I walked out intending to speak with him
and urge him to go about his business. I took with me for my own protection
the pistol which is now shown to me as being in the possession of the local
constabulary. I intended no harm to Ryder if I could help it but only to warn
him off if necessary, though the pistol was loaded when I took it up. I am not
in the habit of going armed. I carried the pistol in my coat pocket, not in my
belt as has been alleged.

Tutt had questioned Evenden further about the loaded pistol, but the suspect had refused to say anything more. In fact, a mocking smile had begun to play about his lips as Tutt pressed him. Seeing that, Tutt had shut up, inviting Evenden to proceed with his version. There was, after all, an old saying: give a man enough rope . . .

I took with me also my sketchbook and pencils, as I am often in the habit of
sketching on the moors, and my thought was that I could contrive a more
peaceful interview with Ryder, perhaps, by pretending to happen upon him by
chance in the course of such a pursuit, having in mind the anger that had been
aroused in him. As I crossed the fields separating us he was lost to view. When
I reached the point from which he had been watching, there was also no sign of
him, but there was much cover of scrub and rock around and I thought he
could be hiding. I therefore did not set off home but made my way slowly
across the corner of moorland towards the well-known stile into Water Lane,
which would also be the way to his house. I stopped to listen at intervals and,
though I at first saw nothing, I fancied that I was being followed. Eventually
he did show himself, coming out onto the path some way behind me and
calling on me to halt.

'No,' I replied, indicating a hillside a little way ahead, 'I am going to rest
there. You walk along with me.'

I turned and continued my way. The belief that he followed my footsteps
caused me some unease but I meant not to show it by turning again, rather as
one must show confidence when dealing with a temperamental animal. When
I did turn and sit on the hillside he was again not to be seen. I placed my

sketchbook on my knees and made as if to study the view; in fact, there is there a pleasing half-opened prospect. I heard a rude shout a moment later, close behind me. I stood and turned and was immediately knocked back as by a blow, at which I heard an explosive report. From where I lay I saw Ryder standing some yards away, a gun in his hand.

I knew I was hit, and as Ryder approached I feared the worst, but he seemed to show concern and even surprise at what he had done. 'You are hurt!' he said. 'Yes,' I said, 'and unless you help me now we are both like to die, for you shall hang!'

At this, however, he straightened and gave a laugh. 'I shall not hang,' he said, 'but I shall publish your guilt to the world, and hers. From the outrage you have offered me, everyone shall know now you are a common murderer – you killed your brother, didn't you? She has done me great wrong also, and may die for it!'

Then he bent again and I had some hope, but he only took up my sketchbook, which had been thrown some feet away and was, I saw, splashed with my blood. Holding it away from him, and his gun in the other hand, he began to walk down the hill, abandoning me. I now feared not only for my own life, as I felt the strength leave me, but also for his wife whom he might pursue. It cost me some effort and loss of blood, and time, to reach the pistol in my coat pocket, which was caught underneath me. When I had it in my hand I could not raise myself, but twisting could still make out his back as he strode away. 'Turn, or I shoot!' I called, but he made no sign of hearing me, or else of caring. I aimed as well as I could, my arm resting on the heather, and fired. With such a small weapon, it was a near hopeless shot in the circumstances, and missed its mark, nor did he even note the retort in any fashion but only continued his way. I next recall waking in the Infirmary, in the presence of Ryder and of Inspector Tutt.

Tutt paused in his reading there, his own name acting as a marker. Evenden had covered the disputed shooting most cleverly. He had explained how his own gun came to be discharged and at present, Tutt had to concede, there was no material evidence to challenge any particular in the statement. There had been only the challenge of Ryder's contradictory account.

But now Ryder was dead. Ryder's death must for the present

147

itself be viewed, in Tutt's calculation, as principal evidence in relation to the earlier shooting. It showed the doctor had been meant to die. The doctor had said he had been shot at, but survived. The fact that later someone, somehow, contrived to poison him appeared to corroborate his version and undermine Evenden's. But Tutt knew this to be far from sufficient evidence against anyone!

The detail he most admired in the statement was the insertion of Ryder's alleged reference to the old trial. Pale and prone on the Infirmary bed, speaking slowly, Evenden was nevertheless bold or inventive when he said that. His impulse may have been only to taunt the detective. Ryder may have said in truth in the course of their argument: 'You killed your brother.' Either way, in raising the continuing suspicion himself, had Evenden not to some degree weakened its persuasive power?

Tutt recalled the scene that morning as the statement had been taken. The proceedings had next become still more tense and frustrating. Evenden had equally refused to say more, refused to say whether he had any knowledge of Mrs Ryder and her whereabouts, and refused to explain his statement the previous day that Mrs Ryder was 'safe' and 'innocent'. Tutt himself had then carefully sighed and leafed through the pages his assistant had already written out. It takes a long, weary time to obtain and set down to dictation a written statement, much longer than you would think when reading it; it had by then already been a long morning for all of them, police, suspect, and the justices, one of whom even gaped repeatedly and it seemed incurably. Tutt had deliberately allowed Evenden the impression that it might be over.

Then, as he saw Evenden begin to relax, he had said, 'I have to tell you that Doctor Ryder died yesterday afternoon. The present evidence suggests he was murdered by poisoning. We seek Mrs Ryder in connection with the matter. Now,' he had paused, 'do you wish to say anything more?'

Tutt had bent low over the bed, watching his prisoner's reaction. Evenden had looked up at him steadily, still not wavering. After perhaps half a minute, though, he had closed his eyes, making at first no movement, until Tutt saw the lids flicker and Evenden's jaws move with an ill-concealed swallowing motion. *Are* you surprised, now? thought Tutt. Are you shaken? Are you afraid? Still he waited.

'I wish to add to my statement,' Evenden whispered.

Tutt eased back again in his chair. The police clerk settled a fresh sheet on his portable desk and dipped his pen, then held it poised above the page. Finally Evenden began to speak, and the nib scratched with painful slowness after his words.

I have now been informed that Ryder is dead. I have no knowledge of how or why. Mrs Ryder, for her own reasons, sought sanctuary in my house on the evening of 14th August, and did not return again to her own home. She did not wish to see her husband, was aware that her leaving him thus would injure him, and this caused her pain. From every aspect of her behaviour, as I witnessed it, I would stake my life she was innocent of any other ill-will toward him. I know not what other enemies he may have had.

Mrs Ryder was still at my home at the time of her husband's visit. Upon his departure, arrangements were made for her to leave with another, into whose company I saw her delivered before leaving the house myself. Everything in my statement above is true, but in going after Ryder I had the additional motive of drawing him away from sight of the Hall, so the other person could take her from there in safety. There was no question of her returning first to her home, but rather of going immediately as far from Burlas as possible. She could not have administered poison or otherwise done her husband harm later in the day. When I awoke in the Infirmary, and was asked by Inspector Tutt where Mrs Ryder was, I took his question as confirmation that she had made good her escape from her husband's wrath. I have nothing further to say.

Indeed, further efforts had been to no avail. Tutt had done his best, making plain his poor opinion of the last amendments to the statement, which were furthermore, he goaded, of no value, probably negative value, as evidence for the defence of Mrs Ryder.

'Your opinions, Mr Evenden: who will credit them with anything? It is well known a woman can be strangely unbalanced by the death of a child. Everyone agrees she was distressed.'

149

Evenden stared at the ceiling and would not react.

'Well,' Tutt went on. 'I remember when she saved you from hanging. You do not look fair to repay her in kind, not with that testimony, do you? I dare say you are quite happy to throw this one onto her, if you can. You may choose to criminate each other, or not, as you wish. The poison could have been put in place any time. Then again, however hard you tried, you could be of no help to her, could you? Who, now, would trust your word, on anything? Dear, dear. With a friend such as you, she has no need of enemies!'

Evenden had turned his head on the pillow, and opened his lips. Then he had closed them again, and thereafter his whole expression was closed. Tutt had abandoned that task, for the day.

Now he put down the statement once more and pushed it impatiently across the desk, rubbing his eyes. Meanwhile, there was Ryder himself, under the knife; Doctor Maugham was carrying out the post mortem and had agreed to report directly to Tutt. Tutt moaned through his fists to himself: 'Oh, no. Dear God, the deuced inquest.' He had two more days – until Thursday the 18th – at the most. He must be sure and get somewhere by then! Even before, he must satisfy the Superintendent with frequent reports, for there was the ever-present, scarce-disguised threat of public humiliation: calling in Scotland Yard.

Maugham was one who would always do you a good job at any rate; Tutt knew that from experience. Setting to this grim task, moreover, Tutt had been pleased to sense in him a missionary determination. It did not guarantee any decisive discovery, of course. Maugham had said that he expected 'to clear up the *poison* question very easily'. What had been meant, if anything, by that emphasis? Tutt resolved to ask about it when he met with Maugham the next morning, if the doctor did not volunteer the explanation. He would also ask particularly about the death of Alice, the Ryders' little child. Tutt wrote *Child? Cause of death?* on a piece of paper in front of him. Maugham had carried out the post mortem on her; he would remember anything unusual, Tutt was sure.

There remained Mercy Meadows. 'Mercy Meadows the maid,'

one of his men had trilled, irreverently and predictably, filling in the ledger. Tutt had rebuked him sharply. For now, she was about all he had. A statement had been taken from her. It had been agreed she could stay at a given address: her sister's. Should he arrest her? Or bring her in for questioning again? Tutt recalled her demeanour when the body was discovered. Her responses had not been strange or suspicious in themselves, but as it were sea-misted with calm. Certain facts could not be ignored. She had been alone in the house with the doctor and – for the present let it be assumed – innocently or otherwise had conveyed to him the fatal poison. Pehaps she blamed her master for the death of her little charge? She certainly showed her allegiance to her missing mistress . . .

One of his moustachioed constables entered, giving a single knock as an afterthought once in the room. Tutt scowled up at him and the man scowled back.

''Scuse me, sir,' he said, none too respectfully. 'Miss Bowlby's outside, wanting to talk to you.'

Miss Bowlby! Not yet Mrs Ryder, but the next best thing – and come to *him*?

'*What?*'

The man's face cleared, he gave a kind of sympathetic shrug and exited. Tutt collected himself and followed him quickly. While the door had been held ajar anyone in the outer office would have heard the exchange perfectly.

Tutt blinked. He had been sure that he would know Miss Bowlby again, but it had been five years. Two women were seated among the people in the room. From their bearing neither was very young, and both were moderately veiled. Tutt looked about, but the constable who had announced the arrival was not immediately to be seen. He approached the nearer possibility.

'Ahem. Miss Bowlby?'

The woman lifted her veil, and spoke loudly and with quavering dignity.

'*I* am Mrs Ryder!'

Oswald Tutt fairly stared, at close range, at the wild eyes and haggard features revealed to him.

21

Tutt stood speechless while, at first unnoticed by him, the other lady rose and made leisurely progress across the room to relieve his plight. Upon reaching his side she lifted her veil and at length attracted his attention by her quizzically raised eyebrows.

'Mr Tutt?' She extended a gloved hand. 'I am Dorothea Bowlby. I believe *this* lady,' she indicated the still-seated figure, 'must be Henry Ryder's,' she moved her lips close to his ear and dropped her voice, '*mother.*'

'I am indeed mother of the late *Doctor* Ryder. I have every right to be here, and I know not why this painted jade is suffered to mock me. I have heard some things about her – yes, madam, even in Scarborough!'

Miss Bowlby spoke gently to her. 'Mrs Ryder, do not be so agitated. Allow me to say, I am sincerely –'

'Sir! Will you give me no assistance?' Mrs Ryder interrupted. 'We have not been *properly* introduced. I am Mrs Ryder. I did not catch your name. I was visited last night by a policeman. One single constable, who stayed with me no more than five minutes. However, I am told that it is now the business of the detective police to report how my son died, and to see that he is avenged. Therefore, I have come to wait here.'

His men, and the usual oddments of rough hangers-on and tagrags from the street, listened to her imperious tremolo. Tutt saw in her features now a weak and watery reminder of the doctor's face, but the bloom that had characterised his smooth cheeks became, in her, twin angry spots of red.

One of the constables coughed, and muttered, 'Yes, sir. I was about to tell you Mrs Ryder was here.'

'Thank you,' said Tutt, and paused. 'Thank you. Permit me. I am Inspector Tutt. Ladies, please to enter my office, where we shall be more comfortable, I think.'

He indicated the way. Miss Bowlby waited to let Mrs Ryder sweep ahead of her. Tutt followed them both, pressing the door to behind him, but with no sense of relief. The way to his chair seemed everywhere blocked by skirts and overmantles, the air cut, as the conversation was taken up again, by gloves, ruffs and muffs. Miss Bowlby wore a new-looking plum-and-cream travelling dress. Mrs Ryder had already equipped herself in full mourning, he noted. The outfit was old-fashioned, making the skirts even fuller, and there was an odour of mothballs. The smell was overlaid with Miss Bowlby's perfume.

'Well, Inspector Tutt,' Mrs Ryder went on. 'I know you already have Evenden, but can you be sure this time you will not let him off again? And do you have *her* yet – the other one? You will understand that I could not name her now if I tried – the brazen belwether!'

'She means Kitty, I suppose,' said Miss Bowlby. 'But, Mrs Ryder, you are being unfair on the Inspector. Why talk of him "having" either of them? No-one knows yet how poor Henry died – by his own hand or another's.'

'Ay, and they can try and brush it off as natural causes, his health being always so frail. You both smile even now! Let me tell you, my son is – was – a *gentleman*, as good as any of them, and no-one here is worthy –' She broke down in a sob. '*And remember I am his mother!* If his heart gave out, it was those two, in their mare's nest, killed him as surely as if that man's shot had found its mark and, Inspector, you must agree they should hang for it, whatever?'

Tutt would have spoken, but Miss Bowlby again got in first.

'Mrs Ryder, I have no wish to distress you, I have the greatest sympathy, but I must remind you, if it comes to talk of attacks, and murder – which is not proven – all that is known so far is that Henry shot William and near killed him.'

153

'Do not be so sly! You know my son gave an honest and true account of that. It was a murderer's shot, and meant for *him*.'

'Indeed, that was Henry's account, but I understand William gave a different story.'

Tutt seethed. Was there nothing his men would not blab about to the world in general? He hastened to soothe Mrs Ryder, giving the other woman an impatient look. 'Mrs Ryder, if you have some accommodation in town I think you should go and rest. Let me assure you, every effort –'

'No. Tell me first, does Evenden claim to be the injured party? Could even he be so wicked?'

Tutt caught himself waiting for Miss Bowlby to reply again, but seeing her lips compressed he said, 'Yes, he does.'

Mrs Ryder's thin look fastened on him for uncomfortable seconds, and remained on him while she spoke. 'All I say is, I challenge you to find another soul on earth with a word to say against my son. He was a good man, and good to his mother if that means anything these days – to decent people it does. Contrast *that* with – with –' She turned her look on Miss Bowlby. 'Henry never did wrong. I know my boy!'

Mrs Bowlby said with calm, 'And I know mine!'

There was something shocking in it; the silence between the three reflected that. But Tutt had to admit to a grudging admiration for the way she acknowledged Evenden thus. Mrs Ryder swayed and put her hand out to his arm for support. It was yet another warm day, the room was stuffy, and she was more than nine-tenths buried in her black mountain of clothing.

'I shall leave you for now, Inspector,' she said, scarcely above a whisper. 'I have a room at the White Hart. Only tell me,' she dabbed at her face with a trailing cuff, 'where is my son?'

Tutt hesitated. 'Why – he is dead.'

'Indeed. I am his mother and must bury him. We shall see if she comes out at that! No, she would not dare show herself, being no wife but a damn whoring murderess!' Her voice had thickened dangerously and her grip on his arm tightened.

Tutt moved her towards the door. 'One of my men will go with you, ma'am.'

'When,' she seemed to speak normally again, 'do I get his body?'

'Tomorrow, I expect,' he said. 'Tomorrow.'

He ushered her out, ordering one of his younger and better-presented men to see her to the hotel. Stepping onto the street, the offer of the constable's arm seemed to be taken by her as an affront; she demanded her escort should walk behind her, remarking audibly to herself that she was 'unprotected, even now!' As Tutt watched them go, he thought: God preserve us from grieving women.

Returning to his office, he placed a chair for Miss Bowlby and seated himself at his usual place at his desk. As he spoke, he busied his hands clearing a space among all the papers that lay between them.

'Now, Miss Bowlby. I am glad you are here. I think that you and I may have a lot to talk about.'

'We may. I hope that we can help each other. That is why I have come!' Her smile was suddenly dazzling as she looked straight back at him, as if she planned to enjoy herself.

Tutt wished he had been able to prepare for the interview. 'Five years ago William Evenden claimed you as an alibi without naming you, and you then came forward. This morning he again referred to a mystery "friend". I am correct in assuming that you called on him yesterday, and that it was you who left town in company with Mrs Ry – with Mrs Henry Ryder?'

'Yes, of course. So he would not name me. He will never learn, will he? Shall we call her Kitty? It would save further confusion! I always think of her thus anyway, and I am sure in the circumstances I can speak for her and say she would have no objection.'

Tutt could not think of any either, though the nomenclature discomfited him.

'And do you know, er – Kitty's – present whereabouts?'

'I believe I do.'

'Are you prepared to tell me?'

155

She slid her eyes to the side and softly smacked her lips together before replying. 'Ye-es. First, however, I will speak of another matter, because it may be most important and I do not wish it to be forgotten in what may be your *rush* to lay hands on her.' Her eyes had returned to him and widened mockingly on her last phrase.

Tutt kept himself silent and immobile for a moment, looking back at her, wishing to reassert some degree of control.

'Do you insist?' he said.

'I do.'

'Then – proceed.'

'Well, Inspector, I believe you have an item of my property.'

'What?'

'Oh, no, not that I am in any *great* hurry to have it back, though it was a gift, and I have been getting rather used to having it about. A dear American friend gave it me when I effected an introduction for him – it was nothing, though he was very grateful. I would not have accepted any ordinary gift for it, but it was so unusual, witty yet actually sensible – so *me* somehow, as he said –'

'Miss Bowlby?'

'Pardon! I mean my gun, of course. You know – the little pistol with the pretty white handle?'

'*Your* gun? Well, I don't know – It may have been your property, Miss Bowlby, but it was found in the possession of Mr Evenden, and he committed a serious crime with it.'

'Did he, though? Remember, *he* says there were two guns. The other did the damage. Mine was only used in a rather poor attempt to protect Kitty.'

'I have his statement, and I gather that by some means you have learned its import – I will not ask how. It is only his word. The gun is a rather more solid piece of evidence.'

'Precisely!' Her tone startled him. 'Let me tell you about my little gun, Inspector. It is what people disparagingly call a "new-fangled" thing – it represents progress! It was presented to me, together with this.' She drew a small white box from her reticule, and opened the lid. Inside, it had padded grooves like a jewel case. 'See? One dozen bullets. Now, with one gone, there are eleven. I always kept the gun loaded, in my bag. Terribly dangerous, I know, but I thought that if I was attacked it would be perfectly useless to beg for time to load the thing, which involves *breaking* it, and I find it rather stiff. Now, look.' She took out a bullet and held it up between finger and thumb. 'They are *cartridges*. This part is brass – hollow – it holds the charge of powder. Though the powder is sealed within, it is exploded when the trigger is pulled, by means of a primer charge of fulminate of mercury located here in the rim, which stands a little proud, ready to receive the strike. Once fired the cartridge case separates, and this long, smooth, factory-shaped lead part is the actual projectile, as it were.'

Her enthusiasm irritated him, and he was impatient to find 'Kitty'. 'Yes, Miss Bowlby, I have seen these things, and I know the theory.'

'Already other revolvers have still cleverer firing systems, I am told, but these are such tiny bullets, it remains the only method. Point two two, which means about one-fifth, of an inch – exquisite! You see, Inspector. No dirty powder. No casting lead balls in the kitchen. Protection, in an instant.' She held the bullet up and turned it so the slanting afternoon light caught its brass sheen. 'What you are looking at is, I truly believe, a revolution in the lives of women! Does it not worry you, that we will soon have no need of a police force?' Tutt sighed, and she seemed to recollect herself. 'But none of that is relevant to you just now, of course. Forgive me. What I hope, and what on a mere balance of probabilities is likely, is that Ryder's gun was not so modern.'

'Miss Bowlby, if Doctor Ryder had a gun with him, ancient or modern, it has not been found. I think that we are no further forward.'

'One bullet entered William, and nearly killed him.' She spoke with a tremor of emotion, quickly stilled. 'Henry Ryder says – said – it was a bullet from my gun. William says that it was from Ryder's gun. Now do you follow?' He began to, indeed, and intentionally or not the clever, subtle woman had started the trickle of his self-doubt once more. She pressed on. 'If it was one of these,' she indicated the cartridge still delicately pinched between her gloved fingers, 'it may have been pushed out of shape on impact, but would surely still be recognisable – slim, machine-moulded? Yes? If what you have is a rough-cast ball, then – then William is vindicated.' She added, mercilessly: '*Again.*'

Next she would begin to question him, and he wanted above all to stop that. He found his voice and spoke tonelessly. 'We have no bullet. I saw the doctor remove it from the wound, but I took no note of its precise shape. That would not be normal procedure. I do not know what happened to it. I will check; it may be in the pocket of the coat the doctor was wearing, or in his bag. However, the chances of finding it must be small.' He spread his hands. 'I am afraid I must say again, we are no further forward.'

Miss Bowlby sat motionless for a moment, then sniffed and put the bullet back in its box, and the box in her bag. 'You disappoint me, Inspector. I will not pretend otherwise. Still,' she looked at him with a quick smile once more, 'perhaps your checks will turn up something. We must keep thinking. There is also, of course, the other puzzle. I mean, Henry's death.' She put her head on one side and her finger on her lips, like a schoolboy.

'Yes,' he said. 'That does concern me somewhat. What can you tell me of –?'

There was a sharp knock on the door followed by the entrance of one of his officers, a keen fellow with some wits about him.

'Pardon me, sir,' he said, and began to retreat, seeing Tutt was not alone.

'No, no, Otley,' said Tutt, his gaze not moving from Miss Bowlby's face. 'What have you got for me?'

'Well, sir.' Young Otley advanced a little self-consciously. 'We found the driver that called for Miss Bowlby yesterday. He went to Evenden Hall, waited, and picked up another woman – answers the description – then took them both on but only as far as Frith, where he dropped them in the market square. I went there but there was no trace. Then I thought, the coach still runs through once a week, and I asked and the times tallied. They could have gone to Scotland, or anywhere in between. But then I just thought, they're obviously being a bit foxy, so I thought of the next place they would cross a railway, and found the coach would stop at the station in Dale. It's little more than a halt, but they could pick up the West Coast line. So I telegraphed, and the station master there must want company. He sent back a folio!' With a grin, Otley passed Tutt a sheet of telegraph-paper. 'Descriptions and all. It was just luck, really.'

Tutt read from the telegraph: ' "The ladies stated their ultimate destination as –" '

'Aberystwyth,' Miss Bowlby finished for him. 'I've liked the sound of it ever since reading of the new line through the Welsh mountains. But we were only travelling to Shrewsbury.' She turned and smiled up at Otley. 'It wouldn't have taken you long to work that out, I'm sure. We weren't trying to evade the police – so we thought then – only her husband. Give me pencil and paper, Inspector, and I will set down full directions.' She was supplied with her wants and continued as she wrote: 'It is the house of an old lady cousin of mine – quite deaf, but imperturbable with surprise guests!'

'Thank you, Otley.' Tutt nodded in dismissal. 'You did well. Fetch me Bradshaw, and stand ready to take a telegraph to the Shrewsbury police.' He watched his crestfallen assistant depart.

'How do we know that she is still there?' he asked Miss Bowlby.

'I should think she will be. I think she slept ill last night. She was distracted this morning. So, she did not read the papers as I did, you see.'

'I see.'

'And I brought my copy away with me. I told her that I would be away for a day; I had a plan for a quieter place she could stay, perhaps eventually a position. She was keen for that. She was restless, but I think you will find her there. I would like to send her a message, to prepare her, but I daresay you –'.

'No.'

'Ah, well.'

Otley returned with Bradshaw.

'You must excuse me,' Tutt said to Miss Bowlby. 'I have matters to attend to. However, I must seek your assurance that you will stay in town now. I shall need to see you again soon.'

'Of course.' She rose graciously. 'One more thing: you will think me strange, but I do like occasionally to read the more lurid periodicals – if Henry's account was true, the gun was pressed against William as it fired. Does that not always leave a smear of black powder? William's clothing would show something.'

Tutt spoke now with something like resignation. 'The doctor treated Evenden on the moor –'

'Do not tell me! He had to cut away William's shirt-front, and no-one noticed where that went, either – just like the bullet. I will go. You are going to be very busy, aren't you? You must make an especial search of the area, for the other gun.'

As Tutt walked with her through the outer office, a uniformed man came up. Miss Bowlby hailed him. 'Do you have it?'

The man looked uncertainly at his superior officer.

'When I heard what William had said in his statement,' Miss Bowlby explained, 'I asked if this gentleman would allow me to examine my revolver – I knew I could not take it with me now, without your permission.'

'Well,' Tutt inquired ironically. 'Do you have it?'

The luckless subordinate shuffled, muttered, and produced the weapon. At Miss Bowlby's request, with another pained look at his superior, he broke it open. Miss Bowlby plucked out a little twisted cup of yellow metal.

'As you will no doubt say, we are no further forward. We knew this was here, whoever told the truth. Goodbye for now, Inspector. You may keep this, though it was mine. It is a gift. A *souvenir*!'

She pressed the cartridge case into his hand and walked out quickly into the close afternoon air.

Some moments later Tutt also stepped out into the street. There were a number of bystanders taking their ease, watching the comings and goings, with no particular business there. One couple stood directly facing the office main door, so he had to step round them. The man munched a pie, while he heard the woman say, 'And that's Tutt. He'll be in charge of the investigation.'

160

He tried to ignore them, but felt his sleeve plucked as he made to walk away. Looking round, he faced a tall, rangy old woman with something of a searching look on her face. She was decently if poorly dressed.

'Mr Tutt, is it? God help you,' she said. Then with a deliberate motion, she raised her arm. Tutt flinched before he saw that she was only thrusting a religious tract at him.

'Thank you. I belong to the established church,' he said impatiently, but he took it anyway.

As he walked on she followed him, and he was disconcerted when she began to moan some indistinct lament.

He stopped and turned to face her, at which she ceased her noise and looked innocently at him. He found his instinct urged him to aggression, even violence. She was one of the unavoidable reminders of where the boundary of order stood, always too close, ready to catch him should he stumble. He took extra care to be gentle with her, even as he felt himself reddening.

'Be off home with you now. You are simple.'

She gave a little winsome laugh, still staring at him. 'Merciful Lord Jesus, my saviour in heaven, am I mad again? Do not hurt me, do not hurt me I beg you. I am gone. See?' Then as she turned, she began the same noise again, it must have been unconsciously. Tutt walked away rapidly but, low as the noise was, it penetrated the general hubbub in an irritating fashion, seeming to remain inside his skull and making his reflections more agitated. He looked over his shoulder after a few paces to find her vanished indeed. He crumpled her tract and pushed it into his pocket, where his fingers touched the similarly discarded cartridge case.

Miss Bowlby's presence had stupefied his reasoning processes damnably. How had he forgotten to question her about her own movements, her *rôle*, what she really knew? True, he was tired. Had he imagined the extent to which she had been mistress of the dialogue between them? If it was true, and he believed it was, that they must now look to the shape of bullets, and scraps of cloth, then it was time for a mere honest man to get out of this job.

He must *think*. Most crimes, he reminded himself, were simple sudden acts. If he could only decide on the most basic and obvious explanation for the doctor's death, then he might with hope look for supporting evidence in the most obvious places.

Forget, therefore, Miss Bowlby; forget the child. Ryder's wife had left him for William Evenden and the next day Ryder was dead. Therefore suppose Evenden to have been the primary plotter – a theory Tutt found attractive and repulsive in equal measure, since it was through his own past failing that Evenden had been left at large to do his worst. Say he had planned to poison his rival, which involved an uncertain delay if the poison had been left waiting in the doctor's jar of relish. He must also have had assistance, either from Katherine alone or – to be more certain – Mercy Meadows must have been employed in some way.

Before taking his poison, Ryder had arrived at Evenden Hall, nearly foiling the adulterers' plans to go away together. Evenden, supplied with a gun by his friend Miss Bowlby, of course was tempted to kill Ryder at once. In the struggle he was hurt himself. Waking in the Infirmary, Evenden must have known his revenge was still waiting, and he had said nothing, even when told that Ryder had saved his life! So the doctor had been allowed to go home, and meet his fate.

It was perfectly simple. It did not much matter now whose account of the shooting was correct! Let Miss Bowlby have her theories therefore. It would be merely a good irony if the two men had each simultaneously planned to kill the other! The doctor shot Evenden and failed (and in remorse, returned to save him). Evenden poisoned the doctor and succeeded. Murder! Murder!

Tutt stopped in his tracks and found himself listening now to the myriad ordinary shouts and rattlings of the street. For a second he forgot how to breathe, as his memory called up the keening of the old woman, as penetrative as before but now washed clean and distinct: *Will, is it you? he cried. Murder! Murder!*

With the instincts of the secret neurotic, Tutt knew that if he once questioned the validity of what he had heard, or the mental process by which he only now heard it clearly, he would not be able to act. So he turned and ran back toward the place where he had last seen the old woman. It was two hundred paces back, so absorbed had he been in his conscious calculations, through crowds and along an upward incline. Tutt, his face set, crashed and lumbered and brought forth indignant shouts and stares to which he was oblivious, except when now and then a shout sounded high and wailing like the call of the woman. But each time he jerked round to determine the direction, it resolved itself into something ordinary, not what he was seeking after all.

By the time he saw again the entrance to the police office he had inevitably slowed, his pauses had become more frequent and hopeless and realism had overtaken him. There was no sign of the female. He could not explain to his men what to pursue or why. All he could do was scurry away before any of them came out and saw him. He would continue to Mercy Meadows' sister's as he had planned, for he had very little time before catching his train to Shrewsbury, and a fresh and present murder to solve.

He allowed himself many sighs all the same. In the flesh or by less natural means, somehow she had recalled his failure: the lost witness whose name he alone remembered perhaps: Zillah Dixon. The undistinguished speck, shaken off from her dark corner the night she heard John Evenden's dying cry.

22

Hot smells, cooking and others, spilled out of the cramped houses along with the children as Tutt approached the house in Mary Street. One of his constables was positioned at an intersection, where he could watch the housefront of Mrs Borthwick – Mercy Meadows' sister. Tutt spoke to him briefly. There was a visitor, he learned. A gentleman had arrived on foot.

Tutt went and knocked at the open front door. The lady of the house appeared. She had an infant on her hip and seemed to be gently pushing a tide of something behind her as she closed the door from the back kitchen.

'What is it?' she called, coming out from the shadows, pleasant but wary.

Her dark curls were softer; everything was softer, in fact, and the eyes brighter. She must have been the younger of the sisters. Yet her round cheeks dragged the corners of her mouth down a little, where the spinster Mercy retained a delicate appearance.

'Pardon me, Mrs Borthwick. I am Inspector Tutt, of the Burlas police. Might I speak with Miss Meadows?'

'Mercy is in the parlour,' she indicated. 'Shall I bring you a dish of tea?'

'Thank you, don't trouble. I shall not be long.'

'Just go in, then.' Mrs Borthwick turned back to her kitchen and family. The sound of the exchange, through the thin internal walls, would be sufficient introduction for him.

Tutt left his hat on one of the pegs which jutted from the polished frame of the hall mirror. He tapped on the parlour door and entered. The room was narrow and dark after the brilliant sunshine of the street. Mercy Meadows sat composedly drinking tea with her visitor, lawyer James. Tutt held out his palms to them to forestall their rising on his entrance, then gave the man a brief handshake, showing Miss Meadows that the two already knew one another.

'I am sorry that I have not been to see you personally yet, sir,' Tutt said.

'That is quite all right. It is a sad and also a very strange business, this of my poor son-in-law. I cannot believe he is dead! I know you must have been making what inquiries you may.'

Mr James' tone was quiet and ironic, not unlike that which Tutt had heard him use on numerous occasions in the course of the work in which they were both, in different ways, involved. Tutt derived a certain reassurance from the company of such people: James, and Mercy Meadows. She was in an upright chair with her back to the window, beside the little tea-table. Tutt now took up one of the 'easy' seats near Mr James. Most of the chairs which crowded the oilcloth in the room were draped with rugs or quilts, with here and there unmatched antimacassars perched on top. It was impossible to sit down without pulling and crumpling the careful arrangement, impossible at any rate for one of Tutt's bulk.

'I came,' Mr James went on to explain, 'to see if Mercy had any knowledge of my daughter's whereabouts. It seems she has none. Can you help us?'

'I –' Tutt was inclined to be circumspect. 'I have some information. I hope to have definite news by tonight.'

'I hope you find her soon, safe and well,' murmured Mercy.

'Oh, my information is quite definite as to *that*. I –'

Tutt was taken aback by the effect of his words. Mercy and Mr James exchanged looks and caught their breath as if a veil had fallen. Of course, they might have been worried.

'Of course, I should have said sooner,' he said. 'I am sorry.'

'It was only,' said Mr James, 'that we were talking, that if my son-in-law was murdered – well, who knows what?'

'Who knows what, indeed,' Tutt concurred.

165

'Yet – we were saying – if he was murdered it can only have been by poisoning, from what Mercy tells me, and who would have done that?' mused Mr James.

'You will not be surprised to hear my view, sir,' said Tutt, 'that the most obvious suspect is presently under guard at the Infirmary.'

'On the grounds that he seems to have tried to shoot Henry, and – though in the absence of fresh evidence, and perhaps even then, you could not adduce this – there was once before sufficient to bring a charge of murder against him.'

'You state the matter perfectly, of course, Mr James.'

'William Evenden was once my client.'

'And – do you have an opinion?'

'Of the man? He is clearly a scoundrel, and always was. I have no idea whether he ever killed anyone. The worst I know against him is that he has lured my daughter away somewhere – if that is the truth. You will understand, even there, I am reluctant to believe – without further evidence.'

'I understand.'

'It is difficult to fathom, though, is it not? William may have killed his brother. I have always admitted the possibility. He may have aimed, or wanted to aim, a shot at Henry. Both acts of jealous passion, in hot blood. Poisoning is rather different, and he would have had to set the poison first. Why? To make assurance doubly sure, I suppose. You would agree with me from your experience, though, that someone who clubs a family member to death is not generally regarded as representing a continuing danger to society as a whole? Should he escape justice, I mean.' Mr James took a sip of tea as he watched Tutt for his reply.

'In general, I don't know. I might agree – in general. But we must not expect perfect consistency from our murderers. One in my position must not, anyway. It does not pay to believe anything impossible, until we have the proof.'

'Ah, yes. Proof.'

'I try to have an open mind. Villains are often not normal or predictable in their actions –'

'True.'

'The more serious the crime, the more – well, you know.'

Mercy cleared her throat, almost the first sound she had made. 'Well, Mercy?' Mr James asked.

'If the Inspector is saying Mr Evenden may be insane I – Well, I don't know him well of course, but I have known him, sort of, since years ago. And I have known poor souls – one or two – as have lost their reason. I think Mr Evenden is quite all right in that way.'

There was a pause.

'As it happens, Miss Meadows,' said Tutt, 'I quite agree.'

Tutt was aware that he had little time to spend at the house, but was also sensible of the unexpected bonus of finding Katherine Ryder's father there. 'Mr James,' he went on briskly, 'I must leave shortly, on the matter that I mentioned, and first I wished to speak with Miss Meadows alone –'

'I certainly will not delay you. I shall go –'

'No. That is, thank you, but first – would you assist by staying to answer some questions?'

'Of course, to the best of my ability.'

'Can you then – can either of you, perhaps – tell me if the doctor had recently been in any dispute with anyone in particular? In short, had he made any enemies aside from this sudden conflict with Mr Evenden?'

Mercy and Mr James looked at each other blankly for a moment.

' "Henry Ryder" and "enemies",' Mr James smiled, 'are not terms one would ever normally find juxtaposed –'

'I believe this matter of the Infirmary had weighed much on his mind lately,' Mercy offered.

'Ah yes,' said James. 'But a theoretical dispute, not really *ad personam*. That is, I doubt if the wilder and ignorant accusations of experimentation on patients troubled him nearly so much as the waverings of his colleagues on the hospitalism question generally. And I do not seriously entertain the notion that Maugham or any of them were on bad terms with him personally, as a result.'

Tutt struggled to follow him. 'Doctor Ryder had disputed with Doctor Maugham?'

167

'And others, but only professionally – regarding treatment methods. You may have seen the correspondence in the papers.'

'I shall return to it. You say he was accused of carrying out experiments?' Tutt asked a little queasily.

James smiled again and waved a dismissive hand. 'No, not seriously, by his colleagues. But rumours were spread among the public, playing on their fears; because anyone could see that Henry was scrupulous in recording his methods and results. And if he did not understand anything he would actually admit as much. People are not used to such traits in a doctor; it alarms them. Henry and I used to laugh about it!' James paused suddenly and looked down. 'True,' he said more quietly, 'he did not laugh so much recently.'

Tutt shook his head to clear it of ideas that could shed only darkness at present. 'And – until yesterday – his relations with William Evenden –?'

'Quite cordial, I believe. Mercy?'

'Yes. Certainly.'

'It was even a brave or foolish friendship, some would say; I would not go so far myself. Henry commissioned a painting of Katherine from him, but I do not think it was finished. They only took up with him after Mrs Evenden's death.'

'Ah yes, now,' said Tutt. 'Remind me of something if you will. As I recall, at the time of the Evenden trial, the way it came out was that your daughter and William Evenden did not know each other – were not even so much as acquainted, I think?'

'I am sure you recall it perfectly well. The way it "came out" was, of course, simply the truth of the matter.'

'Forgive me. I only – Well, then, can you assist me? When did they become further acquainted? I mean, they are acquainted now, aren't they? Were there any social meetings, what not, after the trial?'

'I know for a fact they did not meet again for some years. You know he left the country soon after.'

'Thank you. One further matter. What of your daughter's friendship with Miss Bowlby?'

Mercy looked up but said nothing.

168

'Miss Bowlby?' said Mr James. 'Might she be involved?'

'It is only that her name has come up.'

'I scarcely know Miss Bowlby. I did know that Kitty saw her sometimes. She was not underhand, though she knew that I did not approve. Once she became a married woman, of course, she was more free in such matters. And in a way I could understand it.'

'Oh? From all I have heard, your daughter would seem to be a well-brought-up young lady. An adornment to society. What could they have in common?'

'My daughter has a quick mind. And respectable society sometimes has – very little variety. Also, all her life, I suppose I talked to her about my work. She has perhaps a sympathy – a fascination – with outcasts and misfits of all kinds, without being one herself. I can tell you now, I have in the past wondered a little, on no particular evidence, about the nature and extent of Miss Bowlby's influence over my daughter. While I never knew or suspected anything of any *entraînement* in respect of young Evenden, I have wondered whether in its own way this relationship with Miss Bowlby bore something of that character.'

Tutt preferred to turn the English phrase in his mind. 'Outcasts and misfits,' he sighed. 'Myself, now: my fascination is with the way assorted folk *do* fit together. Thank you, sir. Sorry if I have imposed.'

'Good afternoon, Inspector, Mercy. I can see myself out.'

Mr James rose to go and Tutt waited until they heard him call a salutation to Mrs Borthwick, then his steps and shadow passed the window as he walked away from the front door.

'Miss Meadows,' Tutt then said quietly, genuinely curious. 'What do you make of Miss Bowlby?'

Mercy's brow contracted and she looked at her feet, puzzling, for a moment. 'I wouldn't count it against a person that they're deep. They can't help it.'

'Yes?'

'I was for some time in her service.'

'I know.'

'In the matter of opinions, whatever her position and mine, I could never have called her a friend.'

'I see –'

'But, Inspector, I have to say – though it be as a mistress, and a sinner – she was true and kind to me. Her manner is slippery, but from what I know she's straight as a die.'

Tutt raised his eyebrows and pondered. 'Well, that is noble in you, Miss Meadows. However, I really came to talk about your present mistress. Let me put something to you. You recall the scene when we – you and I – discovered the doctor's body yesterday?'

'I do.'

'I think we are all assuming that he was poisoned.' He paused, wanting to place his bait carefully; he would give her an opportunity, if she had acted with anyone, to try to put the responsibility entirely on the other. 'As the person knowing most about what came and went from the kitchen, you could be of very great assistance to the investigation –'

'I have reflected on that,' she said at once. 'I can think of nothing to help you.'

'Did your mistress, or Mr Evenden, or indeed anyone, ever behave in any unusual or unwonted manner, say in the way of being in the kitchen or larder unexpectedly? Were you ever supplied with unusual instructions? Or cautioned in any way – by Mrs Ryder, say – about her husband's relish?'

She looked at him for a moment. 'No.'

He returned her look and fancied she understood his stratagem perfectly.

'You noticed, I think,' he went on, 'that the doctor had been writing something just before his death. Then he had broken off, it seems. He had written, very unevenly, two things: the letter K and the word Alice.'

'Yes.'

'I think it is clear that the break was caused by the poison suddenly taking effect, and the final writing related somehow to the doctor's thoughts on realising that he was dying – perhaps on understanding that he had been murdered. He recalled the two objects of affection – his wife and little child.'

'One would think so, sir.'

'I wish to put to you a slightly different possibility. Suppose he suspected, in that instant, that his wife had poisoned him –' Mercy began to shake her head. 'No, hear me out,' Tutt went on. 'Mercy, you know, I am sure, that a woman's mind can become twisted after the death of a child, not in the straightforward way of losing her wits, but to make her see things wrong. Listen. You know, anyway, that women can be strange even after giving birth without mishap. Nature can be perverse in them, notwithstanding their general character. The law recognises that.'

'I know.'

'You are loyal to your mistress, but perhaps she was not herself.'

'Of course she was not, but –'

'I have something still worse to suggest to you. Doctor Ryder wanted to carry out an examination of Alice's body, though in the end he was persuaded not to. He may have suspected that his wife had hastened Alice's death too.'

'No, no, no, no! Never! *No!*'

'What did you mean – that she was not herself? Was it since the child's death?'

Mercy's head had been held stiff, upright. In answer to his last question she merely bent it down, tense and silent.

'I only ask you to think about it,' said Tutt, rising. 'I must go. I have a train to catch. My man on the corner will get me a cab.'

'Inspector,' she said. 'I gave it him, as I told you. Isn't a servant usually blamed when food is poisoned?'

'I have no evidence against *you* as yet.'

'Then you have no evidence against anyone, it seems to me. But can you spare one more moment?'

He sat down again carefully. 'Certainly. If you have more to tell me, after all.'

'It may mean nothing. But if you find my mistress, and question her in – *that* fashion – she will probably tell you. So perhaps you had better hear it from me first.'

'Yes. Hear what?'

She lowered her eyes and sighed. 'It is about Alice.'

'Oh?'

'You mentioned something may have – hastened her death. Everything in *my* power was done for her, I promise you.'

'I am sure.'

'The doctor tried many preparations in the course of her illness. One in particular, a draught to be used when she was especially faint, I was cautioned not to over-supply however bad she was. But one day I was sure the level in the bottle had gone down a great deal more. It was when we were in rooms at Heysham, for Alice's health; but the doctor had come to visit. When I discovered it, as I thought, I was anxious and I told him about it at once.'

'What happened?'

'At first he seemed alarmed, and angry, and he questioned both me and my mistress. I even thought I might lose my place, but I was more worried over the child. Then he summoned me and told me that he was satisfied she had come to no harm, and the matter was closed.'

'Did you ever notice such a discrepancy again?'

'No. Only at Heysham.'

Tutt reflected silently, then remembered he was indeed pressed for time. 'Thank you, you are most helpful.' He rose again. She went out with him to the hall where he retrieved his hat.

'You said I must ask leave, to go anywhere,' she said. 'There is a revivalist meeting tonight –'

'That will be all right.'

'Thank you.' She stopped, looking past him at the open doorway.

Tutt heard a now-familiar voice.

'Hello, Mercy. How are you, my dear? And Inspector,' as he turned to see again the cream-and-plum check tones, 'I might have known. I suppose you are going. Take my cab, by all means. I may stay for some while, and I can get another one. Then you will have plenty of time.'

'Miss Bowlby?'

'I take it you are after the five-ten? I was going to take it myself, had you not put me on my parole of honour.'

'Yes. Thank you for the cab. As you say, I shall be in good time.' His irritation with these conversational tricks of hers was becoming intense.

'Be gentle with her, won't you?' Her observing eyes held his.

'I do not think,' he answered gruffly, 'that her conduct of herself in the recent past, even what we know of it, has been such as to justify the status of *gentle* woman.'

'Do you not? I myself do not *know* of any impropriety. But I see you wish me to be candid, and I shall be. We speak of my two dearest friends, and you must know that I will be loyal to them unto the end. In the world as it is, Inspector, you and I know that what we believe to be true, and what may be admitted to – while *reputation* drags everywhere on everyone like a shroud – are two different things. I have never had a friend to care for my reputation as I intend to care for theirs.'

Tutt replied firmly, but struggled to keep his voice from rising too far. 'Am I to feel sorry for you, Miss Bowlby? I too have no-one to care for me, and need no-one. I am a respectable man, and have never thought it too great a trial to conduct myself as one. I take it you mean that you have *never* felt bound to tell the truth, where your friends are concerned.'

'You are to understand no such thing, and my past truthfulness is not to the point at present. You are to consider Henry Ryder's death, not John Evenden's. You have nothing against William, if you take out your bitterness over the old case. And you had nothing against him then. He was in my house when his brother was murdered.'

Tutt put on his hat. 'William Evenden is fortunate in your friendship, as always,' he said. 'Thank you for coming to my office today. I will consider your views, taking due account of your admitted partiality. But when you say that I have nothing to show against him, you go too far. There is already quite a bit. Quite a bit!'

'*My* partiality, as you say, is admitted,' she rejoined.

173

He allowed that to stand and took his leave of her and – with a silent but deeper nod, which was returned – of Mercy.

The cab carried him to the station. On alighting there, he queried the charge, which seemed excessive. He was, he discovered, paying Miss Bowlby's fare as well – a small matter which she must have overlooked.

Otley met him with the tickets all ready. The first leg of the journey involved the local train to Sheffield, where they would change. It had just arrived as they reached the platform, and they pressed past the incoming passengers. Tutt was remembering the day he had arrested William Evenden at the same station, off the London train. As the crowd thinned, he could see a figure walking slowly from the end carriage. The engine, noisily going round the other side of the train, caused a flickering dark pattern in the afternoon sunlight to fall on her, filtered through the carriage windows. Clouds of vapour floated between them. She came closer. Her mantle and bonnet bore the signs of having been soaked and dried without the attentions of the smoothing iron.

She stopped before him, and spoke uncertainly. 'Mr Tutt? I was thinking of you. How did you know to come here? *This* time?'

He removed his hat, but could think of no reply.

She spoke again. 'Is it true that my husband is dead?'

'It is,' he said.

She closed her eyes for a moment but stood firm. Otley looked from one to the other in silence.

And –' Her voice weakened *then*, Tutt noted well. 'And – Mr Evenden?'

'He is out of danger, from his wounds at any rate. You heard the news?'

'Yes. The old woman would keep coming in to talk to me, whatever I said. I think she was deaf. Then, "Do you also know Burlas at all, Miss Smith?" she said. Miss Smith,' she smiled apologetically. 'That was what she called me. "Do you know it?" she said. "Listen to this paragraph in the paper!" '

A little self-mockery had been attempted, in her tone. She made

174

to raise a hand to her face, then let it fall. When she spoke again, Tutt thought there was a kind of deadness in it.

'Such a loud voice,' she said wonderingly. 'So very loud!'

PART 4

BEGINNING TWENTY
MONTHS EARLIER

23

Alicina, who lived in a fine old house with gardens all round, claimed she could always hear noises outside. Whenever she went out to play, lured by the calls of happy children, she found no-one on the street but a funny little boy. He was a ragamuffin, so wizened, thin and pale she believed she might see right through him. Indeed his bones could be seen, she thought, tied up together with granny knots inside his skin. At first she would stand apart and watch him, then in time the two began to play together for lack of other companions. They devised a special game, secret unto themselves. In it the boy and Alicina would hunt for material, which the boy would make into a coat. When finished, they said, the coat would have the magic property of making its wearer live forever.

He really did make the coat, and was wearing it always when Alicina saw him. At first it was a bundle of scraps pinned to his shirt, then it became by stages a waistcoat, then a jerkin. It was all made of feathers, dead leaves, tufts of sheep's wool, dirty ends of string, scratchy clumps of heather – even bleached and fragile birds' and rabbits' skulls were woven in with vegetable twine next to a great heavy flap-clapping old boot. With delicate skill he fashioned long roomy sleeves, and in time the skirts of the coat trailed lower and lower until they dragged in the dirt behind him.

In this strange garment of all the colours of the earth he was a sight to see, a fright, of course – but she never said so.

On a certain afternoon in early wintertime the wind cut their cheeks and the two friends lay on a bank watching grimy clouds massing above the earth. The boy with solemn delight said, 'The snow is coming! Will you creep out and away with me to the hills tonight, Alicina?'

The two climbed the hills behind the town, ever higher and colder, until they must bow low before the roaring wind. Alicina held fast to the knotty little hand of the boy, for though he led the way into the maw of the gale, she feared that without her restraint he might blow away altogether. He pulled her upwards toward the final ridge that could be seen against the glowering sky. Then she heaved and hauled on his arm shouting he must not go there. The wind carried her words away out of her throat. She saw him laugh heartily at her but could not make out the sound of him distinct; the noise of the storm was all. He pulled his hand from her grip and left her in the lee of a rock. In the same moment the snow broke over them, she could see no more and fainted with the cold.

One who falls asleep with cold must ordinarily die before she wakes, but Alicina woke in grey early morn to find herself in a round little hole of snow and rock. She pushed out into a calm, white world, and made crunching footsteps upward to the brow of the hill. From there she looked all around. The only feature was a stiff windblown old thorn tree, putting out black fingers against the snow. High in its branches was caught the spreadeagled shape of the magic coat, in one magical piece still. It was as if the boy had become one with the wind and blown away across the face of the land, leaving his coat in the hooks of the tree as he himself whistled through.

Alicina climbed the tree, and with tender care she pulled the coat down, thread by leaf by feather. She put it on herself and walked home . . .

When she said a child was lost on the hill a search was made, but no trace ever found. As no child was ever posted missing, the matter was put down to a feverish dream of hers, since she had ever been a spoilt, lonely and peculiar girl. With a great show of temper she insisted on keeping the heap of dirty, smelly rubbish that she had carried about her that morning, putting it away in a chest with other precious things. She vowed to herself that only when she was a very, very old woman, and ready to die, would she give it up, and then only to a friend who was true.

*

Aside from social notes and household lists, I had written nothing in more than three years, without feeling any lack. I had used to excuse my poor application and attainment in music, drawing and so forth with the rejoinder that I fashioned words instead. Now that I was past any threat of training, mistress of my own household, I needed no such excuse, and wryly told myself that this explained the sudden evaporation of my muse.

I *did* still read though. Even that, truthfully, I did less. I certainly had not developed into the tyro *philosophe* I had once pictured. With my tiny daughter now absorbing most of my attention, I read among other things many of the new, muscular children's books with their fantastical illustrations. Alice was a child who, before she could so much as voice her first 'mamma', liked to hear stories. At any rate, she liked to sit on any warm and welcoming lap and listen to *something*, or have a gentle noise made at her perhaps while she lazed and dreamed her own dreams. She responded, in time, to the commonplace picture board books with their monosyllable tales, but was equally content with chapters from weightier stories, which certainly pleased her mamma more in the recitation. Her father and 'Dee' (Mercy) might cluck at my nonsense, wasting time on works beyond the stage of her understanding. Yet I persevered, usually long after the flaxen head, dewed with sleep, grew heavy on my arm. The only view that could be gained from the low chair through the nursery window – scudding clouds and distant hilltops – became familiar to me that winter.

Then one day I found that a story had lodged in my brain, and, reflecting upon it, knew that it had been taking shape there for a week past. I sat to unravel and understand it and, almost without conscious intention, in an undisturbed hour it was fully written on the page before me, quite as if someone or something had reached inside me and opened a tap.

The story of Alicina and the nameless boy was more fully written out at the time, of course, and, such was my fancy, I copied it in round 'print', and put the pages in a box. When I read them to Alice, then barely two years old, her only concern was to have pictures to accompany the words. For me, this was a problem, but she was at length satisfied with my dozen or so identical drawings of a stick boy in a plain envelope of a coat. These were afterwards put away in the same box with the story, and later augmented by a few more each time she asked to have it read, which she did now and again.

Since the time of Alice's birth our lives had continued on a path that was I suppose entirely predictable and unremarkable. There had been but one matter of terrible sadness: my Aunt Julia, one day before Alice's first birthday, had fallen and injured her foot. She received the best of care but the limb became infected, and within days she was taken from us! I missed her motherly help and companionship, so little prized as she had been during her life. But for that great loss, and anxieties over Alice's health, everything had continued well with us. Henry enjoyed success and favour, and a new field of enthusiasm in his involvement with the nursing and administrative arrangements at the Infirmary. He had been, for him, strangely excited on reading a series of articles in the spring of 'sixty-seven, priding himself (rightly, as it turned out) on being among the first to appreciate the wide application of 'the antiseptic principle'. He was even inspired to tell me anecdotes, a rare thing in him, of his personal memories of the great Syme's reserved and unapproachable assistant consultant, Mr Lister, who collected frogs from the lochs and ponds around Edinburgh, and had been known to be conducting experiments with them on the early stages of inflammation and coagulation of the blood. More feelingly, calling up both our tears, he had whispered that if this light of new understanding had shone but one year earlier, my aunt might have been among those spared.

Even the animation of this new enthusiasm in Henry, however, would be interrupted with spells when it seemed a sense of mean disappointment showed through. I think the disappointment may have been with the nature of the work, implementing the antiseptic principle in the Infirmary. The changes were mundane matters of procedure, but nevertheless requiring to be followed with rigour and precision, so that he must go against his nature again and battle and browbeat the nurses and even his sceptical colleagues. This latest theoretical breakthrough was no single drama elegantly and irrefutably stated; it was a matter of diverse application, continual confusion, refinement and amendment. One could not *see* the lives being saved; but the dry statistics were there.

One day in late January or early February, a message came from Evenden Hall that Henry would be staying there for dinner. It did not surprise me that he returned quite early, but I was startled when he walked in with Mr Frederick Evenden. Henry hoped I had not yet sent for tea, since we would need an extra cup. Mr Evenden begged us not to trouble, he only came to say hello. Tea was ordered, and had just come in – I had asked for the urn and all to make it myself – when Alice rushed in also, being ready for bed, carrying on this of all evenings the box which she had no doubt just chanced upon. 'Magic Tote, Magic Tote,' she chanted ominously.

I tried to urge her to wait for another evening to hear her story, but no child will conspire quietly when it knows that is what its parent most wants it to do.

'What is it, a story?' Mr Evenden was asking her next, pulling her onto his knee. 'Let me read it. Mamma is busy with the hot tea! Oh no, I see, it is a lot of lovely pictures. Did you draw these, Alice?'

Alice was scornful, and put him right. Then he found the story and read it, holding it out with one arm, while Alice lay in the crook of the other, happily squashed every time he had to find a new page. I fumbled with the tea. Mr Evenden finished the story at last, and as Alice slipped to the floor again I noticed him take out a big handkerchief to wipe his face. He was, as may have been indicated, of a fine old breed with an unashamed response to sentiment. All the same, I met Henry's eyes for a moment. Mercy knocked discreetly. Henry carried Alice tenderly up to bed, and after tea Mr Evenden was driven home before the night was far advanced.

'How is Mrs Evenden?' I asked Henry when we were alone.

'Quite the same as ever!'

He was not often even so sharp as that, about anyone, and I looked up.

After a sigh, he spoke again. 'Kay, my dear, you know to keep utterly quiet about anything I say, about my patients, don't you?'

'Of course!' I reached and took his hand.

'Well – as is so often the way, when one of a married couple is a long-standing invalid – it is actually Mr Evenden who is dying.' He glanced up at me. My smile had gone, of course, and I was speechless. 'He has a – oh – some tumorous tissue spreading in his neck. There is nothing that I can do. It will either reach his brain, or choke him. I have explained to him. He has seen your father. Everything has been arranged. There will be full provision for Mrs Evenden, while she lives. He understands everything, but now, beyond that, he chooses not to know. He will not have anything done or said, even to his wife. He will simply go out like a candle.'

We both stared into the flames for a while. 'Has he sent for his son?' I asked.

'I don't know. He may not, because I think there is still some difficulty with Mrs Evenden there.'

'Ah, yes. He would have to explain to her why he had done it, at any rate.'

I was by now used to making compartments in my thoughts, and it was not difficult to keep even such a secret as this. I did think, though, that if Mr Evenden himself were to call again it might be hard to know how to behave. His wish for normality must be respected.

Some two weeks passed, but then he did call, unannounced, in the usual way. He would not have me go to any trouble, he said, but accepted a glass of madeira wine, which we kept in the side cupboard. His glance flickered about, while he talked on family and public matters. With my new knowledge, his illness was plain to me. Frailty sat strangely on such a figure but it was there, and beneath his high soft collar and cravat it was clear his neck was wider than before.

He was not then in the habit of speaking so often of William as he had been at the beginning of our acquaintance, immediately after the trial. It was possible, therefore, for me to say with both lightness and plausibility:

'It is so long since I have heard of Mr William. Where is he now?'

It was easily extracted that he stayed in Florence, in a pension on the Via Rosanna owned by an American couple, the Strand-Carpentiers. Then I listened in chastened mood to a lengthy catalogue of his latest triumphs. I steeled myself to make a farewell when my guest took his leave, trying not to think that I might not see him again. It was true; I did not.

Still I waited a day or two, but in the end it was the very passage of time itself that drove me to my action. I wrote to William Evenden in secret, our first contact since my walk in the country three and a half years before. As near as I recall, the letter was as follows:

I write because I so esteem your father, and am aware of the affection which, you must know, he holds for you above all others. I am breaking a duty of confidence, and make no further explanation, but wish that I could find better words to state the matter. Your father is dying; his time may be very short. He knows this, but I am afraid he may not have disclosed it to you himself. I am very sorry.

I considered remaining anonymous, but thought that I had lost enough of pride. He would have known, within a guess or two, who had written; and I hoped that I could depend on his finer impulses, at least so far as to protect me in this. I also considered urging him to return, but any action must be for his own judgment. All consideration had to be brief. The letter was in the post.

24

Henry's sorrow at the death of Frederick Evenden was pure and becoming. But I knew, though he seemed unaware, that he was anxious once more. It was told me in his every gesture, pause and glance. Change! Mrs Evenden might prefer someone else. Others might follow. It would not harm us seriously; our position was secure. For the threat was in change itself. Nevertheless, I could not stand by and see him afraid in that manner; I must do what little I could.

When I announced to him my intention of calling on Mrs Molsworthy, his look was bright, as I had known it would be. I had never paid her and the other ladies to whom we stood in similar relation quite as much attention as I should, was its message. I knew this and squirmed inwardly that he might think me a snob; I was convinced I was not. I did have a sense of social awkwardness: I had expected my feeling of self-consciousness at the role of doctor's wife to pass soon after my marriage. Before then I had always enjoyed all kinds of society. Somehow it never did pass.

At the regular calling hour I approached the house, the grandest in the town itself. It had been built with railway money by the Bassets in the forties that are *now* called 'hungry'. Set back from the road, and although in one of the healthier localities, twenty years had nevertheless blackened the frontage utterly. With all its glass glittering in the sharp early spring, it resembled nothing so much as a stout widow festooned with jet.

I had remembered my card, and the maid took it, but her

mistress appeared in the hall before she had time to deliver it. Mrs Molsworthy saw me and removed her voluminous wrapper, bundled it and pressed it into her servant's hand behind her back all in one movement.

'My dear Mrs Ryder! What a very great pleasure!' She approached me with both hands outstretched. 'You find me in disarray.' She indicated the principal room, from which she had just come. 'Let us sit in what I call my winter parlour – it is warmer anyway. Carrie!'

The girl took my things, and shortly there was seed cake, and negus, though I was the only visitor. We sat in a small front room, where the fitful sunlight fell. We exchanged some suitable remarks on Mr Evenden's passing.

'I expect he remembered you?' she said. 'It was such an excellent connection, with your father and husband, and then his real condescension with you, the finest prize of course.'

'Yes, indeed, the finest. We have no further expectations.'

'It is unfortunate that there can be no continuance of the social exchange. Poor Mrs Evenden is such a recluse. She will still value Doctor Ryder's attentions, of course. As we all do.'

'It is very kind of you to say so.' I was back in my usual state of intercourse with her, in subtle fashion reminded of the place wherein she would have me stay, complaisant.

Then her face grew animated, startling me again, promising better than the usual gossip.

'And let us *hope* there is no chance for further contact with *him*!'

I looked at her warily. It was not out of the question that Mrs Molsworthy gave credence to the table-knocking craze then so much in vogue, but her tone was most inappropriate to the occasion.

'With – Mr Evenden?' I asked.

'Yes! You *have* heard. I was sure you would have. Have you actually seen him? Or did you hear from the doctor, or Mr James? Does he plan to stay, do you think? It would be too dreadful!'

'I am sorry,' I said, 'to whom do you refer?' Though, of course, in the same instant I was certain of the answer. Strange unseen powers were at work indeed – in my case, the power of guilty knowledge.

'Why, as you said, Mr Evenden. The son. Only he is really here! Our man Howson met Mrs Drake from the Hall's boy at the market this morning. He turned up there yesterday evening, stayed two minutes with his mother, viewed the body then out again! But he ordered his fly not back to the station, but to the White Hart. He must mean to stay for the funeral, though she plainly does not want him near. What do you think of that?'

'I – suppose it is only natural. I think it is a shame, if true, that there should still be bad blood between them.'

'Your charity does you credit, my dear. And no-one could blame you for what you did in the past. I do not presume to question the verdict of the court on that part of his behaviour. I admired your spirit, to be paraded so in public with him, and the likes of that other woman. That is by the by.'

She had stumbled almost, the least amount; she had remembered too late perhaps that I was acquainted still with Dolly. *That*, surely, was known abroad, in such a town. My mind filled with rushing conjectures and thoughts, mostly unpleasant.

She went on. 'Do you care for more seed cake? No? Well. As I *was* saying, you acted nobly then, but this is different again, is it not? Why should he have come? His father is dead, and though he may have had some feeling there he should have reflected that *he* was beyond earthly comfort. If he shows himself at the funeral it will be a humiliation for her. And that is the best motive he can have. He may hope to stay and drive her out – to her grave or elsewhere!'

'Mrs Molsworthy, I do not care to speculate. I know nothing of the matter. I did not know that Mr William was home, until just now.'

'*Such* charity, my dear, really. Normally, of course, I too would shrink from judging anyone of such good family; I do not lose my sense of where I come from. But I must beg some respect for my longer experience in the ways of the world. The dear Lord knows . . .'

There was a pause of some mild confusion, before she rushed on again on a new tack. Had it not been for my inward agitation, I might have warmed to her, in her simple eager animation and glee, as she spoke of *what* interest there would be in the *cortège* the next day, and how she would certainly now make her husband go.

I let her continue, while William's return played in my mind. When Mr Evenden's illness had progressed so rapidly, and when he had then died with no word still from the son, I had allowed myself to believe that if my letter had arrived at all the notice of death would follow in time to forestall any action. At least he would have been prepared for the news. I had suppressed any mental anticipation of this, the worst outcome. Had he made best speed to his father, and arrived at the Hall to see the blinded windows and the stigma on the door?

'Perhaps,' I interrupted Mrs Molsworthy in the midst of some quite other topic, 'he heard that his father was ill, and that was why he hurried home.'

Caught off guard, she paused for a moment.

'No, no,' she said. 'It was so sudden. Poor Mr Evenden. Poor lady!'

As she then showed dangerous signs of beginning a curious study of my face, I made haste to take my leave, as bright and careless as I could contrive. She appeared truly anxious to detain me, but then escorted me herself through the hall. Then as I stayed, readying myself to face the outdoors again and offering yet more inanities to obliterate any earlier suspicious impression, the drawing room door opened.

A little scene was played out in the hall which left me stunned for a moment.

When I looked again at Mrs Molsworthy, our *rôles* were reversed: she was now all gush and pleasantry. Thus was I *brushed* onto the step, still being urged to return often. I scanned the towering black wall then looked her in the face. Out came the sally I had bitten back in the past.

'Your lovely home,' I said smiling, 'always puts me in mind of Her Majesty.'

I walked away in a troubled and bitter depression of spirits. It was a feeble cut, which at that moment she probably did not notice in her relief at seeing the back of me.

It has always been acceptable to walk unaccompanied in Burlas, in almost all areas at any rate. The place has certain airs, but not *that* one. I walked home and by Water Lane I was calmer, yet still my preoccupation was such that I was almost at my house before I saw two figures standing before the gate. My husband was one. Though he had his back to me, a slight turn of the head was enough for me to recognise the other as William Evenden. I slowed, and sighed thankfully as, with a touch on the shoulder of what seemed easy friendship between them, Henry saw him into a waiting fly. The fly turned and came past me. I held my head down and sensed rather than saw the occupant touch his hat to me.

'Did you see who that was, Kay?' Henry greeted me sombrely but beneath his tone I detected an excitement as childlike in its way as Mrs Molsworthy's.

'Yes,' I said. 'I heard in town that he was here.'

Henry thrust out his lower lip. I turned away to enter the house, realising that my voice in turn had revealed more than I would have wished – an impatience I did not care to explain.

'Very well,' I said, to mollify, as he joined me in the hallway. 'Tell me what he wanted.'

Henry shrugged. 'To hear how the old fellow died.'

I stood before the pier-glass. Henry had not detailed the final hours to me. 'How did he?'

'In pain. Asphyxiated.' He looked blank for a moment. 'Quickly enough, though.'

'Did you tell him that?'

'Yes.'

'Did – the old fellow – say anything about William, before he died?'

'No. And I told him that too. At least we know he thought a great deal of him, still, and I said so. I did not say he was a bore about it.'

'I should think not. Did William say why he has come home? You know his mother threw him out last night, they say.'

'I would have guessed as much. I didn't ask why he had come.'

He seemed to think about it for the first time. 'I suppose it wasn't really wise, was it?'

'I don't care as to that. I have something more important to tell you.'

I walked into the drawing room and he stood in the doorway behind me. I believe he would have stood thus forever, ill-concealing the anxious distaste aroused by any display of emotion in me, before he would ask what the matter was.

'I have to go out shortly,' he said.

'It will not take long. You remember the boy you saw, who died? You told me about the injuries on his back, how the carbon had worn into the flesh, and the eruptions it caused?'

'Yes –'

'Remember what you thought of people who broke the law and used boys in that way?'

'Yes.'

'Well, I can name one such respectable household whose mistress is willing to grind down little children to save a few pence! We can do something about it now: we can refuse to have any further dealings with them, if you agree!'

Henry laughed briefly. 'But – who is it, my dear? *Who?*'

'Mrs Molsworthy. I told you I was going to see her; I was there this morning and indeed I am glad to have found her out. She tried to keep it from me but the sweep and – and the tiny little thing, his boy – came into the hallway as I was leaving. You should have seen her face, and the way her maid scurried them out the back and she scurried me out the front!'

I looked at him expectantly. He made a sound, relieved and dismissive. 'You always knew *she* was a hypocrite, surely.'

'Well, can you still continue to serve them?'

He studied me for a pause, as if assessing how long it might be before my normal composure re-asserted itself, and when he spoke it was in a low gentling tone as if to a child.

'You would not have me refuse medical help to anyone as a sanction against their opinions or actions, would you?'

I fidgeted, instantly defeated by his imperviousness.

'I will not go there again, or have her here,' I said.

He then spoke as if considering my proposition, but only for form's sake to show its impracticality. 'We can hardly refuse invitations, and then we must return them sometimes.'

'But, Henry!'

'And how would you help matters anyway? The only way is by example and argument, not being proud and apart.'

'Can I argue with her?'

'Not easily, I grant you. You *did* not say anything?'

'No. That is, not really.'

'Good. The world is not always pleasant. Do you imagine the man we use does not keep a boy, and would not bring him if we dropped a hint?'

'You may be right – but I am so angry with her!'

'Of course you are, and I would expect nothing less of you. But you know, it is thanks to the Molsworthys and the rest that I can treat those, like the boy, who can pay nothing even at the point of death. I must go.' He began to brush his hat with his sleeve. 'I suppose Willian Evenden will show at the funeral tomorrow,' he mused. 'That will be interesting.'

'Mrs Molsworthy says he only came to spite his mother, or drive her to an early grave, to get the money.'

He looked at me abruptly then. 'Ah!'

'What do you mean, "Ah"?'

He turned away with a little laugh as if nervous of explaining. 'I – er – Merely, I think I see the real cause of your displeasure with Mrs Molsworthy. It is that the creature you once nobly stooped to rescue lives still despised, and by such an *ordinary* soul as she!'

Confused, I sighed resentfully. It remained a part of Henry's disingenuousness that he was not tempted to judge or analyse persons and motives. All that had changed was that in my case, and in private between us, he sometimes made such an unflattering essay as this. The special exercise of right in relation to me, the demonstration of possessiveness, should no doubt have pleased me since I did not expect glutinous newly-wed worship all my life – did

I? However, whether I considered his 'insights' just or not, they were always aggravating.

'That is nonsense. But I do think it unfair. A man is innocent until proven guilty.'

'Certainly he is, bright-sure-immovable!' He returned briskly and embraced me, then paused abstractedly. 'I wonder how long William will stay? I hope he does not intend to call here as a regular thing. That *would* be awkward, while I must see his mother so often still.'

'You would not wish to lose her either, of course.'

'I did not say that. I do not imagine "losing" her.'

'I am sorry. Everything is chiming wrongly in me, today. After all, why should he come here again?'

'Why did he come now? I attended his father, and that is the whole reason for his return after all. He spoke very pleasantly to me. He may still feel some sense of obligation to you, besides.'

'Over the trial, you mean?'

'Naturally, over the trial. If he should call, I know I may rely on your judgment to act courteously, but with no trace of encouragement? That would be my advice. Goodbye. I will try not to be late for dinner.'

'If he returns, I shall do no more than is required by good manners, but,' as he began to pull away I seized his arms, 'you do still, don't you, wish the world was different? That we could see and speak with whom we wished, and not see those we despise?'

He pulled free of my grasp and stood upright. 'How can you ask it?' he said very quietly and with even an exaggerated tone of hurt which instantly stung the tears into my eyes. 'Kay, you can be most provoking. It is not your opinions that offend, but this impression you give that you believe my motives so much more venal! Do consider the effect on me of such scenes as this. I try to treat Mrs Evenden and Mrs Molsworthy the same as all my other patients. When I work to achieve practical good, *I* cannot afford the mere impulses that you may indulge. You question me, but may I ask you, do I as your husband not deserve that you respect *my* judgment still?'

193

'Oh, my dear.' I hung on his unbending neck. 'You do! Only I wish it was in my power also to do some of the good you do; that is what troubles me, don't you know it?'

'It is hard to be sure, sometimes. While I am gone then, rest and recover yourself. Perhaps I have neglected you; a course of tonic may be indicated. And – I will not press you – but if you think you may have left an unfortunate impression with Mrs Molsworthy, I would rather you demonstrated some apology to her than to me. I do not like to see you like this, my love.'

I composed myself and we parted formally reconciled, as ever.

25

Burial weather marked the next day – blunt sleeting drizzle. Mr Evenden's relict had given out that she would be withdrawn as ever, and the funeral would be in the proper old form: *no* women. For any gentlemen who cared to follow to the country graveside, hospitality would be furnished afterwards at the Hall, but it would not be vulgar. She could receive no-one. My father, as her agent, would supervise proceedings in her absence. The event would fit the occasion – solemn, businesslike and grim: the qualities least associated with the deceased.

There would be interest in the *cortège*. But little could happen. What little, did. A carriage with a single post-horse waited without the Hall gates. A bare-headed young man descended as the hearse approached along the drive, then, as it passed, he fell in at the head of the straggling, silent procession. The band had no doubt been swollen and encouraged by the tantalising prospect of his presence, as it had been shrunken and discouraged by the spirit of the widow, a hawk-watch that was felt whether it existed at that moment or not. Whether the mime at her gate humiliated her was a matter indeterminable.

Half a mile along the road the horses stopped at the church wicket. The young man stepped smartly ahead of a bearer and took one of the head corners of his father's coffin as it slid down from the hearse. My father made no move. Henry and the others took their lead from him. So Frederick Evenden was laid to rest, his William bearing the rope-weight as the cold, wet darkness closed around him, in a corner where rank and privilege were tried against the graveyard counterpane of equality.

As the service ended, William Evenden was first to walk back to the lane where the empty carriages now stood. All watched him, to see if he would wait to test who among them might shake his hand, but he did not turn or look back, only mounted his brougham and was away before they had made a move. Then they returned to the Hall. There, the wine laid out was meagre, and the message being taken it was barely touched. The mourners mumbled the dry meats and left for their homes. Molsworthy, contractor of child slavers, Treves, heedless progenitor, and the rest of the urban industrialist contingent mixed uneasily with the squirearchy. Between mother and son, they bore themselves as if they were the ones humiliated, but with dignity maintained.

I had a warming late luncheon prepared at home, for Henry, and for Father if he could be persuaded to come. I was pleased to see the two turn onto the front path together. The day's events were talked through by us, with no sighs nor tears, though it rained on outside and I had towelled both their heads.

'The scene at the graveside, now, you would have thought perfect,' said Father, after some description.

I shook my head. 'No. I had him certainly tearing over the hill in a damson-coloured velvet coat and wide-brimmed hat.'

Henry ate his soup and peered narrowly. When Father and I were in this mood any third person, even he, tended to be somewhat excluded.

'Ah, but I have not told you yet: he bears now an eye-patch, and a grotesque claw-hand, which he strives assiduously to keep hidden – so!' said Father.

'Oh, too bad, Father. I saw him myself yesterday, remember.'

'Tsk. Dash it all.'

'We were wondering, Kay and I,' Henry put in, 'why he had come back to England.'

Father shrugged. 'For the funeral. Why else?'

Then he and Henry gave each other weighing looks across the

table. 'But you and I, sir,' said Henry, 'know that he specifically was not invited.'

Father chewed for a while, grunted, then spoke in a low tone for my benefit, overcoming professional reluctance. 'Shortly before, and again immediately after, Mr Evenden died, Henry and I together asked Mrs Evenden if we should telegraph for William. She said no, there was no address, he must read or hear of the notices in the English papers. We said all William's letters were kept to hand by her husband; it would be no matter to trace him. Then she simply forbade us to act. Her husband had no need of his son, and she had no desire to see him. She said she would write to him herself. But we were not sure when, if ever, she would.'

'No letter from her could have brought him,' said Henry. 'He arrived so suspiciously soon afterwards, in the eyes of many. He must have seen the notices, and moreover happened to be on the near continent, for I did not disobey her command.'

'Nor I!'

'I never thought so,' said Henry. 'Perhaps, though, you have an informed view on whether he hopes for some advantage by being here?'

'Mrs Evenden and William both know the will now, and that it is sound,' said Father. 'William called on me yesterday morning at my office. However, he immediately made it clear that he knew he would not get the Hall nor any income from it until his mother died. He only wanted me to know, he said, that I need not concern myself with approaching him in connection with a reading of the will or any such nonsense.'

Henry shook his head, smiling. 'You could broadcast that all over town, they would still think he was here wanting money. Did his father leave him no annuity or advance on his expectations?'

Father shook his head. 'He was to have, until he made a change last year. William has been making his own way for some time. Moreover, Frederick Evenden told me, at the time of the alteration, that it was at William's own request.'

'If only *that* could be made known!' I said.

'Well, I have to say, Kitty, that at the time, though Evenden was

197

proud of his son, I thought I saw a more likely reason. He did not wish to draw on the estate precisely in the eventuality that his mother was left as the paying agent. He has deferred, not renounced, his inheritance. I can understand that.'

'Then why is he here?' asked Henry again, while I listened, keeping silent. 'Why come only for the funeral, and arouse such comment against himself, as he might have known that he would?'

'Frankly, I think he would have been disappointed had he found his reception otherwise than it is. He wished to pay his respects, yes, but beyond that, animosity is its own engine. It needs no motive force. He has a particular animosity to his mother, general animosity to the whole world here. It seems to be a diversion welcomed by everyone. I would not be surprised to see him stay some time. Let his mother fume.'

'It may do her no harm,' said Henry.

I could no longer look them in the face, but staring at my plate said, 'I am sure he had a better motive.' There was silence. I closed my eyes. 'I *know* it!'

Still they said nothing, waiting, while I sat on in my darkness, forming the words of what I must reveal.

'My dear, the same as ever!' There was a clap on my shoulder and my father's laconic voice. 'I thought you quite the woman of the world by now. Good Henry here must be keeping you young.'

I started and looked at them in wonder. Their faces were turned to me now, but their eyes met in amusement, sharing *their* small piece of indulgent and confident observation. They were men, with their version of me sealed and preserved under glass, and my courage failed for the alternative. In all the time that had gone by since the sending of my letter, I had been too deliberately forgetful, and allowed better opportunities to pass unmarked.

'Perhaps,' I said, 'there can be some reconciliation between mother and son. Someone should try it.'

There was a further pause, then simultaneously Henry spluttered and my father threw himself back in his chair with a low whistle, his shoulders heaving.

Over subsequent days it began to appear that William Evenden did mean to stay some while. I heard nothing directly from him, and in that interval nothing from Dolly, nor did I approach either of them. But it was reported that he had moved out of the White Hart and into rented rooms in town. I played with, sang and read to Alice, while my thoughts went round.

One afternoon I took advantage of a break in the weather to walk alone. I went uphill to the stile where the country began, and crossed it, taking the well-known path across the moor. Certainly, it remained my intention to tell Henry that I had broken his confidence and summoned William Evenden; only first, I would try to make something better of my interference.

Yes, a voice hissed in my head. As you will tell him of your meeting with William before you married. After all, where were you at fault there? As you will tell him of your hopes on your wedding day. As you will tell him what you thought of him the day you bore Alice. As you will tell him how fully you comprehend his secret fears and dreams . . .

But this I must tell him, *because* I was at fault.

But *can* you?

I took a small, meandering side-path, to traverse a shallow valley of fields, then up to grassy parkland. I walked round to the front steps of the Hall, climbed them, and pulled at the doorbell. The chime was so distant, I could not hear it.

26

To do right and keep a pure conscience are matters too simple and easy for my mazed brain to follow. Many of the decisive actions in my life I have carried out in the fashion of pulling myself backwards, seeing no course as the good but in full flight from mere passivity. So, now, I half-expected and, frankly, half-hoped to be denied access. Sarah Evenden never saw anyone, by her clear wish. I was suffered to wait, then ushered into the drawing room, a room I recalled well, where I fancied she may never have been. I entered in the belief that after a further spell of solitary reflection I would have her excuses reported to me there.

I stepped into the expansive chamber of old, and recoiled. The drapes were three-quarters pulled across. A lamp burned on a low table. The candles were in their holders but being saved, dusty and unlit. The lamp, with the overstrong fire which leapt in the hearth, produced a dirty quality of light.

A sickroom smell assailed me, of a particular species of richness, wherein the recognised odours mingle with the smell of cleansing and disinfection and medicaments, and are further overlaid with powerful masking unguents.

Mrs Evenden reclined on a divan at the far side of the fire. Her deep mourning was apparent, though it was difficult at the same time to discern whether she was 'dressed' at all. She wore a black fitted jacket with full sleeves, and swathes of black silk fell around her nether parts like skirts and aprons, but rustled with a kind of unattached motion, and I formed the impression that they were an elaborately clumsy contrivance. She herself lay under sheets and blankets, supported on pillows and invalid air-cushions. Similarly, her head was wound in flannel but a black cap was tied round the whole. Her dark eyes glistened in a sallow face which bore the outlines of beauty. Whatever the preferences between the parents and the sons, *she* was the one William favoured in looks.

'I have had myself removed downstairs, now,' she announced. 'For convenience. Come in, Mrs Ryder! I think I know what you want.' Her voice was strong in volume, but forced and ringing, as if no longer naturally emanating from such a frame.

'I think you do not, Mrs Evenden,' I said. 'I hope I find you – tolerably comfortable?'

'I have forgotten what comfort is,' she said. 'But do not be afraid. I do not imagine fancy new doctors being of help. I do not speak of bodily comfort. I accept my condition, and know my advantages; everything is arranged as I like. No-one helps with the discomfort of the spirit!'

'Surely, comforts will be offered, if you –'

'I do not mean religion, either!' she scoffed, as if the word were a trifle. 'That order is to my satisfaction. There is, though, spiritual existence in this life – if you call it life. I *will* have peace when I am dead. It is wanting now.'

'If you harbour bitterness, is that not a religious question?' I asked. 'In fact, Mrs Evenden, you mistake me. I am not here on any matter of my husband's interest. I would not presume –'

'Why not? A good doctor needs a wife busy in his interest. Your husband got his position here thanks to you. I believe you are as busy as most of your kind. Fear not. I like your husband. I like to keep him around me. He is young. He is calm. He is –' she compressed her lips and spat out the words to herself (as I found she did now and again at the end of a speech, to disguise a temporary failure of breath), 'a *blank spot!*'

'I am not here on his behalf. I have business of my own.'

'I do not harbour bitterness, Mrs Ryder. It is heaped upon me, and no-one will pluck it away. Are you finished?'

Earlier in the day, I had chosen an uncertain course. Now, in the murk of the room, pricked with dull light and stabbed with fierce heat, I no longer had any choice but to strike out as best I could.

'Not yet begun,' I said. Though not invited to do so, I brought a low chair close to her and seated myself, not caring that it was in the full glare of the fire. 'Perhaps I may help. I came to speak of your son William.'

'That is the name of a child I once bore. Then, I had my strength. Afterwards, I did not. You, help? I bore two sons, to a foolish man. I first bore my son John. You never knew him. You know only my misfortune. You come laden with more bitterness in your arms. Are you finished?'

'I come only with facts, which if they cannot help must surely interest you. I hold no brief for William either.'

'How very clever you are, Mrs Ryder. Facts are delicious, are they not? I devour them. But there is no nourishment in them –'

'William came back to this country because he knew his father was dying. Only he was too late.'

'– What do you make, for example, of the giant lizards?'

I resisted the urge to look round at the dark corners behind my back. 'Mrs Evenden,' I said, 'did you not hear me? I was in error. I wrote a letter informing William of his father's condition.'

'I heard you perfectly. First, talk of the giant lizards. I love to think of *facts* such as them!'

I was confused into a reply which I hoped might impress her into temporary attention to my purpose. 'I believe – the theory of evolution is not incompatible with a form of Christian belief adapted to the age. I am not competent to judge its scientific validity.'

'You disappoint me! Look at my hands.' She held them up, then jabbed the fingers toward her eyes. 'Look at my face. It is perfectly obvious my ancestors were monkeys. And the strong have dominion, and the weak must be ploughed back – like Frederick. William has my strength. I talk not of monkeys, but of the giant lizards, who left nothing but their bones. They were the rulers, when the earth was still steaming!' Her hands clutched at the silk in her lap, while her legs, and the bedclothes, cast about beneath. 'Wonderful, is it not?' She really showed a gleeful passion at it.

'William stands everywhere accused of coming here only to pain you,' I said. 'That is not true. And he does not have John's blood on his hands. That I also know.' I did not know in that moment why I added that, and in the pause afterwards reminded myself that in the past I too had had my doubts and had rather deliberately argued myself out of them.

She looked at me with a kind of mocking acknowledgement. 'Oh, yes. You are another of her cronies, aren't you? You see, I am not mad. Did your husband tell you I was?'

'No. Did he tell you of my friendship with Miss Bowlby?'

'Oh, no! Oh, my!' she chuckled drily. 'Can you not see him, kneeling before me, pouring out his little heart! Oh, that is funny. No. He did not need to tell me. He does not speak of you.'

'I did not come to speak with you of myself, or Henry, or Miss Bowlby,' I said. I raised my hand to my cheek, against the heat of the fire at my side.

She darted forward with her upper body and seized my wrist. 'Do you think you are in hell?' she asked. 'You have not taken one step of the journey I have gone. Not yet.'

I did not struggle, and spoke steadily: 'Mrs Evenden, why did you agree to see me?'

She leaned back again, holding my arm and hand firmly against her waist, so that I burned while I could not move. Her eyes and mouth became slits.

'For – my – amusement!' she said.

I met her stare for a moment, caring nothing for her, but pity of a searing kind was drawn from me painfully, homage of humiliation; and I and all my concerns were for that instant consigned, as was no doubt her intention, to the order of ignominious trivia.

I turned my face from the fire, which meant from her face also. 'William is all you have left,' I said. 'His faults are – perhaps – your own, I think. Do you have no natural feeling for him?'

'I thought you had children?' she asked, while with bony fingers she still held and kneaded my hand against her hard, beaded bodice.

'I have a daughter.'

'Oh. All the same, you should know better in the matter of what it pleases you to call "feeling", as it applies to a woman who bears a child. William is flesh of my flesh. He broke me. He took my heart and my strength. Before I had him, even with my John, I was still a girl. Think of it! Me, a girl like you. No! Younger, prettier, stronger, more clever and beguiling than you. But no more. When my time came – the torture! And afterwards, nothing but pain.' She broke off, gasping.

'That is never the babe's fault!'

'No. But it is the worst of having children – is it not? – that from the first, from the very moment one gives them existence, they hold all the keys to one's sorrows. You spoke of "feeling". Yes, I suppose I care for him; but if I could, I would *choose* not to have that care. He has always known his power. I have fought him, but did I hurt him? That boy would try me until I gave him the rod, then turn and laugh at *my* tears. Then he would run, and I could not move or follow, and I must hear him go to his father, and make the fool laugh with him too. My John was the only one who still saw the girl his mother was, to the end, because he needed me . . . Then Will wanted to go to Paris, as if no-one knew what would become of him in such a place. He hated me because I saw through him. "Why not let me go," he taunted, "and keep *John* by you?" He saw that I was afraid, that night, though no-one else could have. I know not how John died. I know that it was me Will aimed at, and hit. Now, it does not matter what he means to do. He cannot touch me, since I choose to keep him out. Because all I have left, as you put it, is that right. A mother is without rights for just so long, Mrs Ryder. In time, she wins them back!'

She held me fast, my head being low over the silk 'skirt'. I felt her attention wander from myself and the present. When I could bear the silence no longer I raised my head and recalled her.

'Mrs Evenden, I do not pretend to understand what you have suffered. If William is guilty – not of murder, truly I do not believe that – but of any failing of duty – In fact, Mrs Evenden, even knowing nothing of the pains of you both and the right and wrong, I wonder if unknowing you did not in some way cause the particular form of his flaws, such as they are. That is my thought as a mother, if I dare to put it so. If I had a mother living, I like to think she would be loyal to me in spite of all faults. William may be too proud to ask for your loyalty but I am sure he feels its lack, especially in his present grief.' Baked as I was by the fire I shivered inwardly at her continuing stillness, and my own boldness. I had twisted to look on her unmoving profile, etched in red light, as I spoke.

Suddenly she inhaled sharply and loosed my arm as if it were some object absent-mindedly put down, while she rummaged ineffectually through certain loose papers on the table beside her. Like a cat's forgotten mouse I did not move though I longed to retreat.

Without looking at me or otherwise acknowledging my speech, she held out to me a small key and said, 'Take this to the desk in the corner!'

Standing first and easing my stiffened limbs, I took the key from her parchment fingers. Looking around, I saw in the shadows the article of furniture described and crossed to it.

'Well?'

'Well, open it, of course!'

I folded down the writing surface, revealing the pigeonholes behind and beneath them a row of narrow drawer-fronts, but it seemed I was not to unlock any of them.

'The centre opens out,' she said cryptically.

I tugged awkwardly for a while at a panel in the centre then detecting some movement found that by pulling at an angle the central section of pigeonholes could be swung out on a hinge. The door to a small hidden compartment was thus uncovered and without waiting for further instruction I fitted the key in the lock and opened it. In the gloom I could just make out certain curled papers, old keys and a tin box.

'Bring the tin to me. Close up the rest.'

When I put the key back on her table and the tin into her hands my heart was beating fast. Was I to be entrusted with some gift or letter to her son? I sensed my adventure would be rewarded at last. With a grimace she prised off the lid, then she paused, looking on assorted letters, bills and other documents evidently of assorted age. She sniffed, and turned leisurely to adjust the lamp's position. She pulled out a folded letter and, without opening it, she laughed over it. She seemed to greet it almost as a familiar but not welcome acquaintance. Passing it into my hand, she made an introduction.

'If you think me so unnatural, Mrs Ryder, read this. Read it and know the mark of my loyalty, for no eyes but mine have looked on it before.'

Curious and fearful now I took my place again on the low chair, so as to benefit from the downward-cast light, the only one the room supplied. As I began to unfold the letter she reached and pressed a hand on mine to delay me.

'It will be for you to decide if you share that loyalty. For once you have knowledge, you cannot cast it off!' With a further dry laugh, she lifted her hand.

I read the letter, which was undated.

To Mrs Sarah Evenden,

A woman may address you, I pray God, who knew your son John not well nor as an equal, but as a good and blameless man. Since I heard he had a mother living, and sick, I have sought the strength to do this.

Be comforted. The evil night that robbed you of your earthly comfort wrought changes more amazing, terrible and wonderful.

I am better than I was. Truly I fear God, and love him, but I walk in darkness still that I fear William Evenden more. I was in Burlas and called for his death, but had neither the sense nor the courage then to tell what I knew.

My courage is very sick still. I dare only this much, to put this in your hand and the Lord's. There is a policeman called Tutt who has asked after me. He does not know that I travel with good people now and am much changed and bettered. I will continue as my prayers dictate, and await what comes, for you may show him this if you choose. When discovered for who I am my new life is over, my only life. I must bear all else then, for I was a wicked creature. I should have spoken but my courage failed. I have feared to tell what should be told, and the load is heavier with each day that passes.

Above all I beg mercy of your son, his brother! For as he holds his life precious he must hate the one who has tried, with these words, to put the great debt of her soul in your keeping.

I read it over more than once, wonderingly and with a creeping sense of horror – for all, I told myself repeatedly, that it was mad and uncertain of meaning. I knew what manner of 'gift' this knowledge was that Mrs Evenden now shared with me! At last I returned it to her, wordlessly – but I knew that as she predicted I could never cast it off.

She seemed infused with new vigour.

'Do not think so badly of me. I am in my way proud of him. Look at this –' She rummaged among her things on the table for a fold of fresher writing which she thrust at me. 'Is it not capital?'

She held it steady before me until I was forced to take it.

'Again, read! Read!' she cried with daemonic joviality.

I opened this note too. Still, between the poor light and my stinging eyes, I had to stay near to make out the words.

My dear mother – It occurs to me that you might put the possibility of remarriage from you, in sensibility of my feelings. Pray do not be inhibited. Mr James, for instance, is a good man. Why not marry him? Your loving son.

'He is a fine boy, is he not?' she said, laughing. 'I will keep my other letter secret for his sake. You may do as you choose. Are you finished?'

On the instant I crumpled the note and flung it into the blazing fire. 'Quite finished, thank you,' I said. 'I shall see myself out. And I vow,' I added, now speaking purely on instinct, and addressing her directly, 'I will play no more part in the affairs of your family. You must arrange all matters as you see fit.'

She pulled at the bell rope which had been extended over the back of her headrest. She was laughing still. 'Rather as I thought – but we shall see. It's all right. I have it by heart. I suppose we should not trouble the doctor about your visit here? Such a pleasure to meet you at last!'

I passed the maid in the doorway, and stood stiffly in the hall until my things were brought. As I walked out I was disconcerted by the cold air and the prospect of high clouds everywhere. That foetid sickroom! It was astonishing that Henry allowed her to continue so.

27

An uncertain time later, it may have been a fortnight or ten days, Mr Evenden – William Evenden – paid his call. What passed in the interim is now a blank, but it most likely consisted in the dense repeating pattern of domestic existence. When his presence was announced, of course, it was a stimulus to some renewal of nervous tumult. I had first to settle Alice back with Mercy, in order to go to him.

I opened the parlour door. No, naturally, no sulphurous auras and pendant ferns, nor any monster reptilian, but only a mortal man was there. As mortals waiting to be received will do, he stood at ease before the window, his back to the room and to me. A small parcel wrapped in brown paper and tied round with string had been left, I saw, on one of the chairs, presumably by him.

'Mr Evenden. Please sit down.' This as I did so myself.

He turned. His face bore still the permanent colour of the warm south but I did not perceive any other especial warmth about his presence. He did not immediately obey, nor speak, but crossed to where I sat and took an opened letter from his pocket and gave it to me.

'Thank you,' I said, recognising it as my ill-fated summons.

He sat in a chair opposite. 'I thought you would wish to see to its destruction yourself.'

'Yes,' I said, then standing in my turn placed it on the glowing coals of the fire, taking a poker to press it until it fairly caught alight. I watched the flame shoot up into brief life, remembering the great fire in Mrs Evenden's room and wishing that thoughts could be erased as easily as paper evidence of them.

'Your letter took ten days to reach me,' he said.

'I am sorry. I could not risk the telegraph office.'

'Oh, I meant nothing by it. I am in your debt. It makes no difference after all.'

I remained a moment bending near the fire, one arm resting on the mantel, as he delivered this series of small contradictory statements.

'It would have been better had I not written,' I said.

He did not deny it. 'At any rate,' he said, 'we now have an opportunity to carry our agreement into effect.'

'What?'

I looked at him quickly, truly startled. He looked back with an expression of some wonderment, which may have been for effect.

'You cannot have forgotten, Mrs Ryder,' he said hesitantly. 'It is not so many years ago. We anticipated our lives would take us in different directions, and made a conditional agreement, should we meet again, to exchange our impressions.'

'I – had indeed forgotten,' I said truthfully, resuming my seat, 'from that day to this. I remember now, of course; you are right. But I regret I can render no account ready prepared.'

'I hear you have made a good doctor's wife.'

'I will not ask from whom you heard it.' His father, Dolly, perhaps both. 'I am the wife of a good doctor.'

'So nicely distinguished! What are your flaws?'

'Too numerous to say. But it was a joke. My way of life, my position in the world, does not allow for serious wickedness.'

'Fortunate the one who can say so.'

'You think it dull.'

'I think I have heard nothing on which to judge the matter. Your husband, and your little girl – I hope they make you very happy?'

The dialogue seemed all awry, to be going on so, on a sudden resumption of acquaintance, and all about *me*.

'I – I think I am not prepared to furnish what *you* would think enough to judge,' I said. 'Yes. Very happy.'

'Yes, that is plain. A woman in your position must be very happy.'

'Do not make fun of me, Mr Evenden. You know I am not so shallow as to believe that. I am indeed fortunate, however.'

'I would not dream of making fun, as you call it. I believe seriously that men are sometimes driven to the bad, by some force of nature, because in the absence of male sin the lives of women would entirely lack texture, and grain. You see, you happy women sit there, and smile, and smile, and drive us to it!'

His talk was foolish and *risqué*, but I was grateful that it seemed at least intended now to be general and impersonal.

'Is there not enough grief in the world, that the men must be wicked?' I asked.

'Not in some quarters. The continent swarms with ladies thanking heaven for the release their husbands' imperfections grant them.'

'You judge womankind very harshly.'

'Certainly not! I do not judge them at all. Many of those ladies are my friends. I have learned sympathy for them. But not pity.'

'Do they thank heaven for you, too?'

He shifted in his seat, and laughed a little uneasily, though I did not think it in my power really to succeed in embarrassing him.

'Oh! My dear Vengate,' he said, then paused, looking away as he formed his reply. 'I do sometimes find my – reputation – burdensome. My life history. It doesn't help, knowing that it is my passport, and in part my meal ticket, in the course of life I have chosen. So many of them, especially the women, are so openly fascinated by me.' I raised my eyebrows at that, but saw that there was intended to be some self-mockery in his words, as his eyes widened and he spoke with an increasing undertone of melo-drama. 'To see those eyes, so hungry for new diversion, turned on you – It forced on me the habit of always guarding my true feelings, even when there was nothing to conceal: never being relaxed in company, but always light. Don't you recognise the picture of a confirmed fraud and trickster? I would even see it in myself. Mrs Ryder, the day came when I thought there must in truth be a blot

211

on my past: the real William Evenden lies in a concealed grave, somewhere along the way!'

Since our first ever meeting, I had thought of him, if at all, with some sympathy, or what he might distinguish as pity, because of his history. That had almost been crushed out of me through my recent unwanted glimpse of the true state of his relations with his mother, and by inevitable speculation on the meaning of the letter she kept secret. As complication there was my personal outrage that of all his *undisputed* misdemeanours a mocking reference to my own family name was the worst. Now, as he spoke of his life in the salons of the continent – so alien to all my experience! – I was taken with a renewed rush of understanding, something like fellow-feeling even, at the picture of him trapped, perhaps forever, in pretence. I may have been particularly undefended after his hasty, casual 'my dear' – an appeal whose effect he might have calculated ... It was a tight circle. How much of his behaviour might be trickery, as he even hinted himself?

After some seconds of silence he looked up, as if to gauge my reaction. Whatever he saw in my face encouraged him to hold my gaze as he spoke again.

'You know, since your father's first interview with me all that time ago in Burlas gaol, no-one has asked me straightforwardly: *Did you kill your brother?*'

It was I who looked away first.

'Are you surprised?' I said. 'No answer you could give would please them. By your account, they want the question to attach to you; they do not want an answer to it.'

'Yes,' he said. 'You understand.'

I feared to inquire into the meaning of that, asking only, 'Is that why you remain here in Burlas? Here no-one is in doubt. They are all either for you or against you.'

'Yes, in part. Also, to be among some people, at least, who knew me before it all happened.'

'Do you find yourself restored?'

'I hope to – Oh, but I had forgotten! I was counting you among those I knew before; but I am wrong, of course. Even at our first meeting, when we were mute, John was already dead.'

The recollection seemed a disappointment, and to bring about a duller, briefly more forbidding silence. I thought of my half-seriously accepted duty, seriously imposed by my husband, to be no more than polite to him. So much of seemingly greater weight had intervened. I should see him off, but there remained one question.

'Mr Evenden,' I said. 'Did you have no warning that your father was dead – after my letter?'

'Only the warning in the letter itself. After that, until I reached home, I had no news.' He rose to leave. 'Thank you again for the letter. The accusation it contained was well made.'

'There was no accusation.' My note that I had just heedlessly burned – I tried to recall its words. 'None whatsoever!'

'On the contrary, I assure you. And it found its mark.'

I rose too, yet detained him. 'It is a shame the true motive for your return is not known.'

'I promise you,' he half-laughed, 'I care nothing for that. I should be rather appalled, on this occasion, for you to repeat your heroism, and expose yourself in my defence.'

'You confirm something my father said, though my father did not know *my* position.'

'It is an honourable secret. Mr Ryder's professional reputation would be too much embarrassed if it was known what happened. Fear not.'

We stood with a polite distance between us. I could not think of any secret as honourable: mine were I thought all equally hateful. And that Henry had been brought into it only made things worse, in my view.

'I did try to correct the damage caused by my interference,' I said. 'I called on your mother.'

On the instant I thought I saw her again, in his face.

'What! But she did not *see* you, I take it?'

'Oh, she did. It was – no good, of course. Anyway, she knows.'

213

'I cannot conceive by what right – what you thought to achieve by such a move!'

'As I said, to correct –'

'But, Mrs Ryder, *I* was here, in town. Yet without consulting me, you went to her!'

He made a sudden movement, probably not seeing that by instinct I flinched at it. He turned and walked again to the window, his anger evident in his reluctance to speak further.

'Really, Mr Evenden.' In my unease I spoke somewhat coldly. 'I do not see that you have such a right to be consulted. Mrs Evenden is scarcely more of a stranger to me than you are yourself. I had to correct a false impression, and went to the one by whom it was held.' Still his back was presented to me, and feeling the injustice of my position I was moved to go further. 'I do have reason to believe she is not so uncaring as – as perhaps your habitual relations make her seem. I would urge you to see her again.'

He made an exclamatory sound then turned to speak at last, with obvious effort at control and for all that not gently. 'Mrs Ryder, I would urge *you* of all people, if you please, not to plague me with advice. That I would appreciate – I mean, if we do remain strangers as you say.'

'I think it is a fact of circumstance that we are – almost. And should remain so,' I said hoarsely.

'I take your point,' he said more quietly. 'Well, I shall leave you.'

He made to depart, allowing no chance for me to offer my hand. I therefore turned my back, and rang for the girl. My eye caught the parcel on his chair and I picked it up. His hand was already on the door when he paused.

'You will think my manners unamended, after all,' he said. 'They are. It is you who are the evil influence. That is another joke, by the way. Perhaps I should apologise for all my unseemly levity. I keep forgetting that here in England we have no sense of humour.'

I held the package out to him.

'You have left this,' I said.

He saw it. 'Oh – it is for you. I was working on it when your letter arrived, and finished it here. I think my father was the finer artist.

In his letters, he put down everything, and never tried for effect. In his last, he described something that – Well, I hope you recognise it. Hello, Mercy, how are you?'

Mercy had answered the bell herself, perhaps out of curiosity to see him again. She gave a monosyllable reply to his greeting, and her closed smile, as she handed him his hat, coat and gloves. I turned back toward the fireplace so that she would leave me undisturbed, and I heard him leave the house. I sensed her pause again in the doorway, then she pulled the door to and her footsteps receded.

I opened my parcel. In a small frame, behind glass, done in ink, there to the life was my little spirit bantling boy, breasting the storm. The immortal coat, in exuberant detail of bone, feather and scrap, trailed behind him. By the hand he pulled along Alice/Alicina.

I cried tears of the kind my child could make me cry. When Henry came home I told him that Mr Evenden had called as he had predicted, and showed him the gift. He admired it, and agreed that it should hang in the nursery.

28

William Evenden's sojourn in Burlas became thought of as more indeterminate than temporary. He was not by any means everywhere spurned. There were interesting and new segments of urban 'society' developing in those days, and he could count on arousing the hospitable instincts of many. Among the circle were, as ever, Dolly's variable collection of artists and *emigrés*; it may be wondered what perverse current washed them up at Burlas, but they and others like them were sedulously wafted to places just as unpromising, by the efforts of a network of enthusiastic women, as she herself drily told me. They might be introduced to the radical editor of the *Burlas Star* and his wife, organiser of an improving 'settlement' in one of the poorer areas, and occasional collaborator with Henry and other public health campaigners. The new chief librarian enjoyed such company, as did even the professor of engineering at the Ironworks College, and all the leading lights of the College of Art where William (idly enough, dreaming of running away to the masters on the continent) had once followed courses. Travelling theatre companies and concert performers naturally found their way, or rather were sought out and pulled, into the same gatherings. Even factory owners might infiltrate on occasion, particularly representatives of the older, more secure Nonconformist families, who still kept themselves apart a little, and were as large and liberal in their social and cultural leanings as they were strict and narrow in the domestic sphere. In the evenings, they would meet with self-educated socialist agitators and share visions of a world where men and women would grow in morals and finer emotional responsiveness. In such circles, William Evenden could survive indefinitely, cushioned against the effect of scandal and suspicion.

Molsworthy and his type, by contrast, still represented the public face of the city. Publicly, Burlas took perverse pride in its reputation as the most philistine of all the miraculously conceived, culturally formless northern towns.

As for me, I belonged in the camp of the burgesses. When younger, I had wished that my father, with his cultivated tastes, would help us to move in what I thought of as more exciting circles. He did not care to exert himself in that manner.

'We are not qualified to join the clan,' he said. 'One must be notorious, or decayed aristocracy at least, to merit inclusion among those superior egalitarian beings.'

I had been a lawyer's daughter; now I was a doctor's wife. In both cases I moved among peers, but nevertheless subject to their patronage.

One day I strode into Dolly's own Chinese parlour. There sat Dolly, and there – to my surprise – William Evenden lay before her on the hearth rug, his chin on his hands, his look craning over his shoulder to where Dido the cat snoozed on the small of his back, her complacent answer to the act of usurpation. The circumstance was the likely cause of the intimate laughter heard as I entered; Dolly's maid, on instruction, never bothered announcing a presence.

Dolly waved me to a seat at her side. William's greeting was spoken all but into the carpet.

'For shame, Will,' said Dolly. 'On your feet; never mind Dido!'

'No, not for my sake,' I murmured hastily. 'Let her sleep on.'

'But she will sleep on if she wants, whatever. Come, it is too bad.' With that, Dolly crouched low, and as I watched she gently slid her hands between the cat and its human pillow and lifted Dido onto the floor.

William stood and brushed his hands together. 'You are right,' he said to Dolly. 'She did not stir.'

'Oh, she is only pretending to be asleep.' My friend remained at his feet a moment, giving her cat a reproving prod. 'She is so proud; but she makes herself the more ridiculous, like all such silly females.'

He turned to me then with a slight bow, and our fingers met briefly. I fought to control my breathing, and the colour rising to my face. I was seeing them together for the first time, which besides all else would have disconcerted me. I wondered whether Dolly could have planned it. She had always before (apparently) taken such care to ensure that our meetings were undisturbed. Perhaps he had special privileges, to call on a whim, and stay by her.

'Does Kitty deserve no better apology?' asked Dolly.

'Mrs Ryder deserves anything she wants, in full measure,' he said.

'Then tell him you want an apology, Kitty, and see if he can manage something handsome.'

'Oh, but I don't. Mr Evenden has told me often enough that his manners are excellent. And as I do not doubt his word, on any question, I do not require a demonstration.'

'Once,' he said. 'Once only, I told you. I know they *used* to be bad.' Yet he favoured me with a small smile, as if I had spoken some kindness or flattery.

Having arrived, I felt obliged to stay for a while, and surprisingly the conversation flowed easily between the three of us – perhaps I was the quietest – on all manner of impersonal and unconnected subjects. The atmosphere would have seemed light to any observer, helped by Dolly with her usual stream of new ideas and impressions, offered for examination. While she recounted at length a full issue of a serial novel she was reading, I fell to thinking how quickly I could decently depart. The conundrum prevented me from concentrating on the story, even though Dolly's renditions, however detailed, were never dull, and she did not lose the thread through all William's sarcastic comments and queries.

Still in private confusion, and expressing myself surprised at the time that had passed in their company, I finally made ready to go. Both of them protested.

'Why then,' said William when I insisted, 'we must simply

reconvene this day week. Dolly will have her next episode by then.'
He leaned forward and spoke loudly over the sleeping cat. 'Will
you be of the party, Dido?'

Dido delighted us by starting up, more likely disturbed by a
coincident dream than by his appeal. After looking round, she
leapt onto my lap and rubbed her face against my chin.

'It is done. You are commanded,' said William.

I sought in vain for a form of words, then merely laughed,
trusting he would take the inconclusion as the actual conclusion
that was intended.

'Cat, I am wanted at home,' I said, lifting her, paws dangling,
onto the warm seat as I rose from it. 'Goodbye, Mr Evenden. What
of my manners? I did not know how to direct a note to you, or I
would have thanked you for your gift. It is a complete success.
Have you thought of going into illustration?'

'No,' he said, taking my hand. 'Too early success is fatal. I could
never repeat it.'

I tried to indicate in my look at Dolly that I wished her to see me
out and she took the hint. Out of the room, I spoke freely, if low and
awkwardly.

'Dolly, don't think me ungrateful as I have nothing but liking
and good wishes for Mr Evenden –' Any white lie in that related to
my liking for her, my friend. 'But I think it would be best if he and I
did not meet here, especially by arrangement. I should be in
difficulty with regard to my husband's position – I mean with Mrs
Evenden – and – well, can you understand?'

'My dear, I not only understand,' she pressed both my hands in
hers and tipped a quick, arch look in the direction of the parlour
door, '*I* am entirely of your opinion. It would be folly, and
unnecessary. You need not worry about it happening again. But
come to me soon. Goodbye, my sweet.'

We kissed, and parted.

That evening Henry and I were out at a dinner party. I sat with the
other glimmering ladies after we had withdrawn and wondered
what they would give to know all that I had witnessed at Dolly's.

'I am sure the gentlemen will not be long,' smiled the hostess, who on this occasion was Mrs Molsworthy. I had come along all meekness to her table without a word being required from Henry to make me knuckle under. 'They never can leave us alone, can they?'

'I am always thankful to see them,' said Mrs Treves. 'Not because I cannot bear very well to be without them, but their reappearance is so eloquent of their sobriety and decent sentiment. My mother's tales of heroic drunkenness, in the old days, do haunt me so.'

'In the old days at least people knew to stick at a thing once started,' said Mrs Molsworthy with what was meant for a wicked smile, 'at drink the same as everything else, I am afraid. It is true it tires and depresses me, the way people flit about from one thing to another these days: one idea to another, just like that. We do not even know how to *converse* in the proper form, the way we used to. Oh, but it is true, of course, that the men being civilised and sober makes up for everything!'

Her firm little spinster sister-in-law piped up. 'But my dear, you can only speak of our sort of people. I do not think we can be at all sanguine in the matter of raising up general morals, while the lower orders remain little better than savages.'

'It does not do, though, to speak of such dreary things,' said Mrs Treves, ignoring the look of the previous speaker. 'Arthur was telling me of a book he was reading, which said that certainly in time all classes would learn to be sober, educated and well-fed.'

'Bella is divine and illogical!' expostulated Mrs Molsworthy. 'How could they – *all*?'

'The writer said yes, my dear. They would then be waited on by negroes and Chinese.'

'Ah, I see. Now, Mrs Ryder – oh, you young girls, you are always so *quiet and good* while you wait for your husbands to come back – what do you think about that? Because I remember, I think, your former interest in the negroes. But here they come already, and yes, I think I detect the spark of joy in your eye.'

So, fretting impotently under her attentions, I never did form any statement referring obliquely to chimney-sweeps.

A man who had not been at dinner followed the other gentlemen into the room at that point. He crossed over to Mrs Molsworthy, by whom he was evidently expected. I was struck by something familiar about him and before their greetings were concluded had remembered him. As Mrs Molsworthy prepared to introduce us I saw that he too was momentarily caught off guard by recognition.

'Miss – James?'

'Oh! Yes,' exclaimed our hostess. 'But she has been Mrs Ryder for some time now. My dear Mrs Ryder, though I perceive you may already be acquainted I should introduce you. Most apposite to our conversation, this gentleman has, even this evening, been abroad in the streets working selflessly at his calling, with the fallen women.' She pronounced this evenly with lowered eyes as one would recommend a cure for reeking breath. As she paused I addressed him myself.

'It is Mr Fowler, is it not? What brings you to Burlas?'

His look stayed on me and narrowed quite unselfconsciously. 'What a coincidence this is; I was only now thinking – And you remember *me*! I do not think we were ever introduced before, were we? But they were memorable times. Yes, pardon me, I have been in Burlas a few months, but not for much longer now. The charitable trust dictates, you know –'

Mrs Molsworthy paid close attention and I sensed was not displeased to see her *protégé* distracted by my presence. The interest of our meeting was credited to her, she seemed to feel.

'Oh!' she said, gently upbraiding herself. 'Of course, I should have known! Your time in the living at Critchley – you did once tell me of it, and I forgot. You remember our Mrs Ryder featured prominently – no fault of her own, of course.'

'Of course. I hope Mr James continues well?'

'Thank you, his circumstances are exactly unchanged – unlike yours!'

With a small hesitation then he explained that, after wrestling

221

with his conscience, he had resigned the comfortable living to take up his present work not many months after the trial. 'The events themselves played a part. Not a direct one, but they were the source of some reflections of a personal nature.'

'I can imagine.'

Mrs Molsworthy said, 'Mr Fowler excused himself from dinner with us in order to attend a salvationist meeting this evening. One must not be too nice about doctrinal differences, as he says. These groups with their charismatic lay preachers – it would be an abhorrent indulgence for those of us already with a more properly distinguishing moral sense. But they are known to be a means of rescuing the most unfortunate from the paths of wickedness. Mr Fowler has been working hard for some days to persuade numbers of women, whose trust he has gained, to go along. I hope your noble endeavours had some success, Mr Fowler?'

'Well, a little, yes, as far as that went –'

'Oh, that meeting!' I exclaimed. 'I know someone who was there; perhaps you met her –'

His look was quite excessively astonished. 'You *do?*'

Taken aback, I laughed nervously. 'No, none of your – I mean – my housemaid. I gave her leave to go. Her name is Mercy Meadows.'

'Why, believe it or not, we were introduced! A woman, I thought, though we only had the briefest of speech together, of,' he groped for a word, 'penetrating religious good sense. For a moment I thought you meant –' He pinched the fingers of one hand together and prodded his brow with them, shaking his head. 'No, of course not. That would be ridiculous. Yet Miss Meadows is your employee –!'

There was an awkward pause.

'You are distracted, and rightly so,' said Mrs Molsworthy. 'Coming upon all our frippery and frivolity, after such serious duties. You honour us with your presence. I wish to tell you that we ladies, at any rate, have been having some earnest discussions of our own. We were saying – some of us –' (with a look at her sister-in-law), 'that improvability can be discerned in all classes. With

222

good will, and selfless work such as yours, the most degenerate may be redeemed. It behoves us not to abandon hope for any soul, indeed to hope for the glorification of all, if we wish it for ourselves!'

Mr Fowler shook his head again. 'After what I have seen this evening, madam, I too would believe anything possible – though not through my efforts.' He spoke more quietly and as if to himself though absently looking at me: certainly, as if to no-one *but* me. 'In fact the person in question regarded me with horror, I believe. She has found self-respect and honour, even; and I am one whose only power is to fasten back on her an old identity, an old shame – and I don't know what other terrifying responsibility – It was pitiable. I have long thought of seeing her again, but this I never expected, and I never was in such a quandary!'

Mrs Molsworthy took his arm and drew him away, to introduce him next to Henry on whom as ever she fawned quite shrilly.

As we prepared to leave, however, I had another opportunity and a less observed one to exchange a few words with Mr Fowler.

'Our hostess's talk is always pious and irreproachable. She may be glad of your advice as to action suited to such a person. When her chimneys are cleaned, she may wish to abide by man's, as well as God's, law on little children.'

'Is it so? I thank you. That is something I may do, really. Goodnight, Mrs Ryder. Pray convey my particular regards to Miss Meadows.'

Henry and I rode home, with a rug wrapped around the two of us as the nights were still bitter, and even my warm cloak and fur-trimmed hat small protection. Beneath, my evening dress, though merely in accordance with the fashion, exposed more than I cared to the raw atmosphere. There was a silence between us of that sort married couples at the end of an evening can put down to tiredness, though each knows very well that neither is yet sleepy. He was the only one who had heard my final comment to Mr Fowler, but he passed no remark on it, nor on anything else.

I walked before him into the house, where Mercy immediately took my mantle and hat, and a shiver passed over me. Henry stood behind me. A few words were exchanged, then he walked smartly past me upstairs.

I waited behind to ask Mercy how her prayer meeting had gone, to which she replied that it had been very full, and full of spirit, and she was grateful to have been allowed the time to be present at it.

'Just now I met someone else who was there,' I told her. 'A Mr Fowler, who said you had been introduced to him. Do you remember him?'

'Yes, very clearly. He seemed less impressed than the rest of us with the joyfulness of the occasion; I mean, just at the point when I met him, he was quite preoccupied, which surprised me.'

'Perhaps he sees too many such scenes to be properly impressed any more,' I said with studied idleness.

Mercy began to pick over the fur trim of my hat, and I thought would not after all volunteer more; but then she paused.

'It was not that, I think,' she said firmly, still with her eyes on the hat. 'In fact he said he had recognised someone he once knew, and that he had been quite longing to speak to her. But she had just seen him and shrunk from him. I think he was rather put out by it.'

'Well, he sent you his regards, and said you were a woman of penetrating religious good sense.'

'I cannot think why he should say that!' she responded with a rare spontaneous smile. 'Because he seemed so uneasy, I said that sometimes the wish to know and understand all, especially about the lives of others, is part of the sin of pride.'

'Did you know he was the parson at Critchley, when John Evenden was killed there?' I asked.

'No, I did not.'

'Thank you, Mercy. That will be all for tonight.'

Going up, hurried on by the cold air, I went first to the nursery to see Alice. A child asleep is a sight to effect a strange arrestment of the spirit. Alice had that sweet purity of beauty, the dark curve of her lashes perfect against the round cheek. But I was anxious about her. Her 'delicacy' became more defined with time. She grew very slowly, in spindly fashion; she was always cold to the touch, even in bed, and her bouts of energy had little endurance about them. Her eyes were bright, her mind strong. Like all children, she saw things in a peculiar personal light and reacted comically or passionately. Yet however peculiar she was, I always felt that I understood her!

She was changing, I thought. Her blonde-white curls were straightening and darkening. I caught her in the fold of a dream, moaning and turning, her brows puckered in alarm. She had been thus, alone in the dark. I pressed the covers close and felt her tiny breath. She coughed and turned again.

I went to my own room. A door within it led to the dressing room – actually a little corner passageway shared with Henry, with whose room it also connected.

Seeing Alice reminded me of his reasoning in favour of separate sleeping apartments. It had long been suspected that the danger of fatal termination attached to the practice of infants sharing rooms and even beds with adults was caused by the child's great need for uncorrupted air; in the night adults throw off quantities of carbonic acid in their respiration, and further mephitic gas through the pores of their skin. The common medical advice was thus to ensure children slept in separate and well-aired rooms. Henry believed there was greater similarity than yet understood between the conditions necessary for infant survival and those conducive to adult vigour: crowding during the hours of sleep, when the system was active in its self-reparative functions, was inimical to the health of all. He furthermore concurred with the view that the single marital bedroom could foster habits of deleterious sexual frequency.

Henry, unlike too many other husbands still, was enlightened and considerate. Repeated childbearing, he knew, was a mark of barbarism imposed on womankind. It not only dissipated the woman's health and strength, it robbed her too early of her girlish aspects of physical form and spirit, and was thus an aesthetic affront. On the other hand the ill-effects of unnatural abstinence or desuetude for both parties to a marriage were to be avoided. He made use of widely available medical knowledge, and supplied me with the simple humane apparatus inhibiting conception. The sponge in its dish of liquid had been left discreetly on the washstand in the dressing room. Henry's delicacy of mind was such that his face had blushed scarlet as, some weeks after Alice's birth, he handed me the letter in which he had set out his views, details of the apparatus and instructions!

I shivered again, seeing the dish and its contents, always so cold! Of course with experience the revulsion naturally attending the procedure had become mild and transient.

When ready, I knocked gently for him. In a moment he would softly open the door and come through. Again, with time, though he had said our comprehension here could never be mutual, I had divined that for him such moments approached the sacred, representing powerful abstract confirmation. Had I ever disturbed him in that rare private reverie, then it would have been I who was guilty of the greater violation. Though the merest word or indication at any time would have been enough for him to leave me alone, I had never felt driven to put him off. There was never any necessity for intrusive words, all in accordance with his established habit and natural preference.

29

No, I could not deny to myself that I knew, beyond serious doubt, whom it was that Mr Fowler had seen at the prayer meeting, whose reaction had given him such pause as to make him betray himself to Mercy and to me. This, now, was an immeasurably stronger trail than the enigmatic letter Mrs Evenden had shown me; and my decision to keep the secret of *that* had caused me doubts enough! All it would take would be a word from me to Mr Tutt: that Mr Fowler was in Burlas and had seen the Critchley witness here too. Mr Fowler being already in two minds, distinct pressure from the unwavering policeman would see the information disclosed at once. If Mr Tutt further knew that the witness had approached Mrs Evenden by letter, and the terms she had used – what would his fever of eagerness be to lay hands on her!

But should I drop that word? If Mr Fowler held back, why not I – only because my motives were less clear? I seized on Mercy's dictum about the sin of pride, while I did nothing.

For any woman in my position to approach the *police* on such a matter, confidentially, would require courage and self-possession enough. For me to approach Mr Tutt, on this one, was barely imaginable. Was any duty owed Mr Tutt by me? If I had certain information as to the identity of a felon, I told myself, it might be different. My duty was arguably as much to make disclosure to William himself, but that also I could not contemplate, making it also impossible to confess all to Dolly, who alone might understand me.

As I turned over this delicate argument, my conscience accused me of not *wanting* to discover the truth of John Evenden's fate. It alleged my reluctance was because I had 'stooped to rescue' William – and more besides.

Questions can become so difficult that one can no longer think about them. Besides, in life there are always pressing distractions to hand. In life, the distraction may be in truth more important than the original question.

I have been presenting a false picture, in so far as my daughter Alice has featured very little. This is an account of historical events, causes and consequences; and where in the columns of such would you place a mere child? A child is at most a disturbance within the patterns of causality, not part of them. We regard a child as a mass of potentiality, a conditional being only. An amusing paradox, is it not, the way children themselves are observed to experience the passing moment most fully and fiercely, as if they hold their present of more account than we do our established permanence – or as if their small life is as much to lose! My cynicism is unbecoming, I know.

It was a day in late May or early June. I stood at an upstairs window and watched through heavy, tossing boughs of lilac and honey-suckle. Alice, aged between two-and-a-half and three, was intent: devouring the first of summer, spinning and singing on the grass, making a constant medley of responses to stimuli too refined for adult senses. Henry's voice called as he entered through the garden gate, and she ran to meet him. *Carry me, throw me, whirl me round.* Soon she was gulping, her frame exhausted. *Hold me.* She took an over-long time, in his arms, to recover. He knelt, resigned and patient.

I had often watched the way Henry watched Alice, and the way he examined her, the diets and tonics he tried. By sly unconscious degrees I had mounted a vigil at one remove. I would only turn away when the kindness in his voice and hands, the softness in his eyes, became too painful to witness. After seeing her he would stand in concentration a moment, scarce breathing, his eyes often seeming distended and unseeing. Then I would say something sharp and irrelevant to him to announce my presence. Had our positions been reversed I would have known that *he* was watching me. But with his exceptional capacity for self-absorption he did not, I am sure, suspect that my fears anticipated and matched his own.

On this day we met and kissed in the parlour.

'She seems to grow weaker,' I said.

He sat, pulling off his shoes, and slid his feet into the slippers I had brought and placed ready.

'It is a common fancy of mothers,' he said, 'to think their first-born is not strong. You look too deeply for the signs. See how bright she is today!'

'You watch more closely than I. What do you see?'

Then I sensed that even in asking the question for the first time I had inflicted some hurtful defeat. A bitter understanding came, that he had placed reliance on me to maintain a mental denial.

Shortly thereafter it was agreed that the seaside should be tried. Henry's mother, at Scarborough, was the obvious choice. Alice, Mercy and I went to stay. I had hoped that Henry would come over often, but it was three weeks before he joined us for a Sunday afternoon. He could not leave his practice.

'Think of the expense!' chided his mother. I knew that the expense, now, was nothing, but his awareness of how she might view it was more.

She indulged Alice, but infuriated me by dismissing her grandchild's weakness as merely a repeat of her trials over Henry, with the single difference of my good fortune in having no doctor's bills to meet.

I did not trust my own assessment of Alice's progress, but wrote to Henry with the results of my conferrings with Mercy. The child had rallied, but then had begun to fret for home. The North Sea wind could be inimical. Henry came at the end of the week of that missive to bring us back to Burlas. Another summer was going, or had gone. Everyone approved of Alice's new colour and energy.

I no longer felt at ease in my own home. My anxiety over Alice perhaps gnawed inwards now that others thought the threat deferred. Small household difficulties chafed me, yet I did not move to remedy them. Even having Henry again, his distracted coming and going at all hours, I did not know of pleasure or irritation which was uppermost. His presence or his absence: in both I was taut and – albeit ashamedly – resentful. I even took inexcusable pains to avoid contact with his patients who, of course, must call and pass through the house.

It was while my spirits were in such uncomfortable disarray that an occasion arose for the venting of confused and vehement sentiments: unsatisfactory though, in every respect.

I made an excuse to visit Dolly the earliest day I could, having warned her first as ever. I found her nevertheless thoroughly wrapped up, though on *her* head even the duster was tied with a flourish. All round on the floor were propped canvases, framed or wound in cloths, and wooden chests half-unpacked. Portfolios lay one atop the other on a large desk beside the wall. Dido sat at bay, her eyes occasionally glittering slits, at other times pretending a weary interest in the goldfish in their globe.

'Look, all William's, just arrived from Italy, you might guess!' Dolly said, passing a hand across her brow. 'Come; I have missed you so! Sit, sit. I have been waiting for you, to allow me a break from this.' Her hand moved to her stomach as she panted laughingly, pulling away from the swift embrace.

She was delighted to have me back again after the long absence. She asked for all the news. On the basis of my account, she insisted Alice was healthy, and under the influence of her presence for the while I willed myself to believe it.

'But you –' She made a little growling noise, searching for a word. 'You seem – not sick – but I know, sometimes a homecoming can set the nerves jangling?'

'Yes, you have it. If it is so noticeable, I am sorry. Really I am well. Why is all this *here*?' I asked, looking about me.

'As a favour, of course, what else? The boy claims to have no more space.'

I had seen little of William Evenden's serious artistic work and could not disguise my curiosity which in any case rather gratified her than otherwise; therefore we viewed one or two of the paintings together.

'In some of the works, now,' she said, ' – perhaps he has accepted that his grander ambitions will not be realised and that is why – something more than facility shows through. Something personal and unique to the artist, honestly and unaffectedly revealed: *that* is what I always look for. See that figure in the foreground, looking over his shoulder, as if he would run from us. Will always says he cannot paint the human form; he is all right with a pencil or pen, but with a brush he seems to drag the life out of them.' (I thought that a notable, some would say unfortunate, turn of phrase; Dolly talked on, unheeding.) 'But here, it is almost as if he has turned it to advantage. The figure began as something to give depth, and a less conventional perspective, but it has become in a sense the subject.'

I rebuked myself for having expected to hear ill-considered praise.

'Do you think his success will continue?' I asked.

'Who can say? At present, his work outsells its true value, because of his notoriety. That will not last for ever. But his craft should always be worth something to him.' She now stood. 'Would it shock you too much to see some drawings, that might include studies of the nude?'

Naturally I protested that I was more than equal to the challenge, and she then selected a portfolio and opened it for me on the table. She left me for a while, to take a painting through to the place where she had decided it should hang. I turned over the paper sheets of assorted sizes one by one, unsure if they were in a particular order.

I stopped at the first drawing on any significant scale of the female nude. The practised account of the face, creating an impression so reminiscent of the original, was a repeat of something I had seen four years before. Then there was the figure, not at all unbeautiful, the signs of age less numerous than on the

231

face itself. The familiarity of the artist's touch extended throughout. The drawing was signed and dated. It had not made the journey to Italy and back, even if its folder had.

'There.' At my shoulder was Dolly's voice. 'He can do the human form, can't he?'

'Did you mean me to see this?' I asked.

'I think so.' She shrugged. 'Don't ask me why! Look, there are more –'

'Of course I must ask you why!' I turned sharply. My hand had still been resting on the drawings and several paper sheets were swept aside by my action. They floated unhurried through the air, and landed around us, restraining further movement – an unlikely trap, effectively sprung.

'Kitty,' she said wonderingly, reaching out a hand whose touch I brushed away. 'I purposely asked if you would be shocked.'

'There is a world of difference between the female form drawn from some human model but, I would take it, not intended to represent any individual, and the exhibition, naked, of an actual person!'

'What *difference*?' Dolly was still calm.

'In the face of what people say about you, I have stood by you, and in my heart I have defended you.'

'Did I ask you to? Did I seem to require it in any way?'

'How could you do it? Why permit yourself to be used so?'

'*Why?* Ah!' She rolled her eyes. 'Let me only say that I would *never*,' her voice trembled with brief emphasis, 'allow myself to be, what *I* would judge, "used". But I do apologise to you, my dear. I am become so fond of you, I find you so exceptional in many ways, I was guilty of some forgetfulness. I forget that you are just an ordinary – a delicate little woman after all.'

I sank to the floor and began to gather up the drawings, not looking at them. 'I cannot move for these –'

'Careful with them, Kitty!'

'I am being careful!'

But then I put them down again, and pressed my knuckles into my eyes. With deliberation, Dolly picked up the papers and put them all away, carefully fastening the laces of the portfolio into bows, standing silent with her back to me. I knelt immobile throughout. When finished she turned to me and, placing her hands beneath my elbows, pulled me to my feet. In another moment we were seated together on the sofa. I kept my hands pressed to my face, until the strongest threat of paroxysm had passed.

'There, there,' Dolly said, and I felt her pliant arm winding about my stiff shoulders.

'I may be an ordinary little woman,' I said, 'but I understand – more than you know.'

'I know.'

'I know what relations have been between the two of you. I may not have cared to think or speak of it, is all. I asked – *why*.'

'My dear,' she sighed. 'We are different, you and I. At times the difference is so small it seems almost to disappear. Yet, it is everything. You found contentment; or you think so, which is the same thing. I have never married. I did, almost, once. But I could not do it – it was almost a premonition. I was like a horse, that *cannot* pass a certain point on the road, however well-schooled it is, however much it is coaxed! And, indeed, soon after that the young man died. I myself was very ill, but I recovered. And I learned that, for me, it was a nonsense to carry on *waiting* for a life. The great thing is to live, though it may not be the way others think proper.'

I felt her arm about me still, and my eyes hot and red.

'I do not know,' I said, 'what joy there can be for a woman, even in sincere affection, which I can understand, if there is no hope of the man being open and noble – and total – in his devotion to her.'

'You think marriage is the only thing that love is worth? You know, without meaning any offence, that I view it as another scheme of rights and privileges for the man, and pains and penalties for the woman!'

'Marriage is not what you think it; it is not a mere thing of tying up rights and privileges. It becomes a labour; it is your whole life, your whole duty. However long the marriage, it remains a shining aim – to become something greater than oneself alone.'

'Perhaps it can be, Kitty,' she said. 'But not for me. Say, for example, could I ever be with a husband as I am at this moment, with you? You can tell me. Could you speak with Henry like this?'

'That is not worthy of you! I will not be disloyal to Henry. This relates to you and me, alone, none other.'

'I am glad, at any rate, that there are still some things you think not worthy of me. But are you sure, are you so very sure, Kitty, that this fire in you is fed all by anger with me, and not in part by your disappointment in him?'

'What, in Henry?' I asked.

'No. In William.'

'I hope I *do* judge you and him the same way. I do not hold with double standards,' I said. 'But in one way I think it is worse for the woman: only because, as things stand, women are looked to more to set the standards of behaviour in such matters. That is why I do not like to think of you – It is true, I blame him. For some time now, I suppose I have compared him with his father, and found him wanting.' I looked at her – I had so many doubts about her William that I could not put even into such halting words – but she was not seeing me just then.

'Oh, no-one knows what his father did, or cares – provided only it is kept secret. Would you rather William had not cared for me, but had done as other men do, taking careless loveless pleasures in secret, perpetuating that trade and all that belongs to it, because what else do we expect from a man? But, oh! Never mind, if he but remains *respectable*, and if only women like me would be respectable too, and lie down and die, I suppose –!'

'I would "rather" nothing. I care nothing about it, but only in regard to you! You will keep trying to turn me. In hating the injustice meted to certain of our fellow-women in the name of male freedom, must we also turn from the opposing ideal itself, from the bonding of marriage? I cannot believe that it is so.'

I had been resting my head on her shoulder, as she rocked us both. I looked up at her then.

'Well,' she sighed. 'You are a rational creature. So, I pose, and he takes a drawing, and it is done with clear eyes and affection

234

between us. Yes, and pleasure. And now I am ashamed of myself, because I think at heart I may have intended some of this hurt in letting you see it. Perhaps I am jealous of you.'

'Jealous?'

'After the trial, and you, and all, in a sense he became everyone's, and to that extent he was lost to me; what had been in the beginning was lost. Though I must have relinquished it at some time, regardless.'

'Not altogether,' I said, pressing my cheek to hers.

'Thank you,' she whispered, and she softly repeated the words a few times in the quiet pause that followed. 'Come, let us make a pact – never to be jealous of each other again!'

I could not see what cause I, with my husband and child, had for jealousy but I made no comment. When, finally, I sat up, she held her hand out about my cheek, and said, 'You have the air of my cat waking from sleep! Will said he may call later. You will not stay, I suppose?'

'By no means.'

'But you need not be in a great hurry.'

'I must go. You – you will not speak to him, of what an idiot you made of me?'

'Do not make me think you are still angry. No, you know I never would. To break such a confidence would be to live accursed, I believe. That is no part of my original contract.'

'What original contract?' I asked, thinking it some joke, and glad of it.

She gave me a sidelong look.

'Ay, me! And that was no accidental slip either, I suppose. The playful genie is with me today. So, how do you think I first came to approach you, and offer to supply a new servant, when you were in need of one?'

'Oh, that was clear enough. Old Mr Evenden must have told William, and he mentioned it in a letter to you.'

'Yes. And there may have been some mention of a young lady with – how did he phrase it? – "a peculiar cast of mind", who might value an understanding friend. So he asked a certain old lady to do him the favour and offer the friendship, if it proved acceptable to her; and watch how she fared, on behalf of one who was in her debt but barred from doing so for himself. I am not very clear, am I?'

I had still a smile on my face where I stood, under the charm woven by her a moment before.

She looked at me narrowly. ' – Kitty?'

'Alas, I suspect far too clear,' I heard myself say, with a false lightness that sounded harsh to my ears. 'No, truly I assure you, I am not angry. I am too full of wonder to be angry, I believe. Well, it is quite something. I did always admire your artistry. But to keep up a pretence of friendship for so long –'

'I never kept up any pretence, not for a second. I am your true friend. The first overture was made at the request of another. That is all.'

'Is it? What of your contract? Have my doings been reported fully enough for his taste?' I had aimed at sarcasm but could not keep the tone of revulsion from my voice. Renewed speculation had been released in me, as gradually I took in the possible significance of her revelation.

'Oh, Kitty!' She actually looked amused. 'In the normal course, I may have referred to the young lady – but if you could see the tone of the correspondence, the context, I swear understanding and forgiveness would come at once!'

I took a step away from her, and having once found the power of movement again made haste to be out of the room. In that second I recalled that she too had once been implicated in John Evenden's murder, by some – but there had been no grounds for *that*, had there? She called to me as I reached the door.

'We have both been, and are, your true friends. Do not be so hard on Will!'

'Why must you insist on telling me what I must feel for *him*?' I replied. 'You have no idea what I think or know of him! I must go. I think I have been – defiled.'

She did not try to call me back again, and I hurried away from her house. When I was many streets away, I began to look around. My mind ran on too many things, including here and there what had been revealed of her view of the world, and of men. There was perversity in that too, certainly.

Reaching my home I ran up the stairs to the nursery. My eyes fell at once on my charge, my Alice – being rocked and crooned to sleep in the arms of another. I had entered too violently and disturbed her. She jumped from the knee, wakeful again, and ran to tell all her unintelligible news. I held her, light as air, more spirit than body.

Mercy it was whose lap had been her rest at my entrance, who now patiently waited to give all the care she could. I know only that I turned to her and said something most sharp and unthinking, for what I *was* thinking was that perhaps I had been her sport, also! Very quiet and shocked, she at once left the room.

I could not have explained the thousandth part of that day's meeting with Dolly to Henry, who perhaps at best would have regarded it as the thousandth part of nothing, at the most, a new threat to his vital tranquillity. Equally, over dinner, hours later, all my thoughts and conversation, though he was unaware, could not help but be influenced and shaped still by what had happened. He asked about my doings, as ever, and I had to mention that I had been at Dolly's, and from that in one smooth stream, unpremeditated, I heard from my lips a plausible and false account of what had formed the substance of our talk. I said – which was true though it had not been mentioned that day – that my friend's interest grew ever stronger in the campaigning then prevalent on behalf of fallen women. In my fever I was (I thought) even witty on the contrast of her approach with that of Mrs Molsworthy to the same matter. I said Dolly had sought to arouse my active concern in the particular efforts to influence Parliament, to reverse those measures of control and enforcement then bearing cruelly not only on women of low morals but also on those simply taken as such by unanswerable authority.

'It is being made up into a debate of some importance,' he commented.

'And is one of some difficulty, not least in the challenge it presents to the decent women who have taken it up, don't you

237

agree?' I said, in a tone of detachment. 'On the one hand, they must pretend to ignorance of the class of evil that is both the foundation and object of the Act –'

'I do not think that an insuperable difficulty – for them,' he answered, in the same tone. 'I have no difficulty, you see, in admitting to your clear understanding, which is plainly sufficient for the debate, but based on concerned intelligence. At the fundamental level your spirit could not comprehend, your instinct remains uncorrupted, and revolted.'

My spirit cannot comprehend, I thought. But I am reeling, my husband; and my understanding seems poor, or I am very ignorant – or becoming insane, I think – for I scarcely know what we are talking of. I saw the little smile he gave me and answered in kind.

'I trust,' he went on, 'that your friend shows no signs of being,' he coughed, 'affected in her sensibilities by the contemplation of such matters? You know it can sometimes take the guise of undiscriminating, anti-male censoriousness.'

'Oh, no. Though the cause is now thoroughly entangled in that of the rights of women generally.'

'Yes, which is very curious, and damaging to the prospects of both, I would say.'

After a pause I was moved to pursue him a little further. 'Henry, would further progress of the female sex offend *you*, in principle?'

'Progress is inevitable. The essence of woman is fixed by nature. I am a scientist, and fail to see what logical discussion there can be of such matters, once those facts are admitted.'

The meal being concluded, I walked over to stand behind him, and put my arms around his neck and fell to fondling him, for comfort. He laughed in pretended alarm and humoured me, as he rested his hands on mine, and was good-natured with me. Nevertheless I could not at once forget the new puzzles that secretly beset my mind; neither could I hold them all there clear and distinct. I did not feel so indulgent even toward Henry as I was forced to pretend was the case.

30

No-one thought any more of Mrs Evenden. William's presence was still criticised, and if grounds were cited they might include *inter alia* the insult to her. But no-one thought of her, herself. I did not dwell on the scene in the former drawing room where she lived out her existence, and wished that I could forget it altogether. My father may have seen her once or twice; I do not know. Henry was her only regular visitor. I knew when he was there; we rarely spoke of it.

We spent Christmas as a family, my father also joining us. The dinner was scarce over when a messenger came from the Hall, and Henry left at once. I thought it her act of spite but closed my mouth on any comment. Father and I amused Alice with singing and games while the solstice dark crept over the gloomy outdoors. My father at length began the process of introducing his grand-daughter to the intricacies of the game of spillikins.

When at last I heard my husband's step in our hallway I was ready to be annoyed, subject to anything he might say; Alice had been ready for bed a full hour and had begun to whine for him. At the first sound of him she was up from the floor, scattering the spills. He entered the room, picked her up at her insistence, and then addressed Father and me.

'Sarah Evenden is dead.'

Father pulled a rueful face. 'Great heavens. Poor woman. How?'

'A stroke of paralysis.'

In the pause that followed I thought Alice's heedless prattle sounded suddenly more loud, as if in a newly opened hollow within me.

'She lived on for a few hours,' Henry explained. 'She could not speak, but she got Mrs Drake the housekeeper to understand she must do something. Then Mrs Drake fetched a sealed letter from her own room, and when she offered to show it me Mrs Evenden nodded repeatedly. She had quite some energy!'

I was thinking at once of the writing I had been shown by her, its reference to the murder. A letter – *sealed*?

'And what was the letter?' asked Father.

'It was marked "Instructions in the event of dangerous illness". It seems she had prepared for just such an eventuality, and given it to her woman months ago. There were some household matters, but the principal item was an injunction that her son William was never to be informed as to her state of health, nor sent for until *after* her death. She watched the two of us read it, then again nodded vigorously. On first seeing her I had not been optimistic, and as she was worsening I stayed with her of course until the end. Then I sent a despatch off to William. Where or when it will find him, today, I do not know, but I told the man to try Miss Bowlby's.'

I cleared my throat. 'Yes. That will be right, I expect.'

'I told the housekeeper you would call at the Hall tomorrow morning,' Henry said to Father.

'Thank you. I shall see the staff, or William if he is there by then. If not, I shall leave a letter for him about the arrangements. You may as well know, there is something for you both. She had only a life interest in the estate, of course. She did not have much of her own apart from her jewels, but she has left you a hundred pounds. The rest goes to her niece in the south.'

'Yes, she told me,' said Henry.

I was astonished. 'I knew nothing of it!'

'That was also a few months ago,' said Henry. 'She said expressly that it was for the two of us. She said, "To you for your care and nice manners, and to your wife for her care of you, and because she saved Will's neck." '

'The devil,' was Father's dry reaction. 'She said that?'

'Indeed she did. Then the subject was closed. It was the only time I ever heard his name cross her lips.'

I was seated before the fire, and Alice now had found her way back to me and lay quietly on my lap. She knew that the grown-ups had been forgetting her while they talked, and to postpone bedtime was doing her best not to remind us of her presence. I looked down at the head on my arm and she gave me a sleepy, furtive smile. Distracted, and to hide my agitation, I stroked her pink cheek where the sugar had been scrubbed away and found it warm and soft. It was almost a year, already, since she had lain in the same room, exactly thus, in the arms of Frederick Evenden. It came to me that there were superstitions about sudden death. The life may have been taken in another's stead. This news bore an unearthly quality: I could not grasp that the woman's bitter travails were ended so abruptly. I pitied Sarah Evenden; but I smiled on Alice then, for did she not mean more than all the rest to me? In all reason, I tried to persuade myself, I ought to concern myself with nothing and no-one else.

So it was that William Evenden came into his inheritance. During the interregnum since his father's death he had been considered by many an embarrassment. To have him master of the Hall and lands was a more comfortable arrangement. He was not lauded into his kingdom; in fact it must have been a strange and subdued occasion when he arrived, alone, to take up the reins of office. Few who had been hostile in the past were so transparent as to make immediate overtures of friendship. They readied themselves, however, to do business with him. It was natural, with time, for revulsion to ripen and soften into magnanimity (though the more sternly principled lapsed into honourable silence, and looked down upon the rest).

It seemed everywhere accepted that William's new status called into being a great wilful forgetfulness as to his brother's death. Unanswered questions were dropped. Of course, I wondered if his mother had ever informed him about her strange letter. If not, had he discovered it now? Or had she destroyed it? I heard no news; I had no contact with him, and for some time I had had no contact with Dolly.

The drag had been brought round and I was seeing Henry out onto the path one frosty morning. I put my hands behind my back, beneath my cloak, and twisted them together.

'I had hoped to see more of you, now,' I said.

'How do you mean?' he asked.

'No more visits to Evenden Hall.'

'Others can do with my full attention, and more.' He kissed me 'As husbands and wives go we do quite well, don't we?'

'Yes, indeed.'

He put his bag on the seat, and I was ready to wave, when he came back to me.

'In some ways we *are* better off now, you know,' he said. 'There is less need to be watchful over whom we take up with, and so on. That can profit both of us. We do not need to keep William Evenden at a distance any more, for instance.'

'We never did, deliberately! Are things so bad that you need him? It is not for us to take *him* up, anyway.'

'I do not need him professionally in the least. He is too healthy to be of use.' Henry gave an involuntary, twitching smile to the ground. 'I do not deal in bogus curative regimes, and nor, I suspect, would he.'

'What, then?'

Then he first opened to me his idea, a fancy he had, to commission a painting from young Mr Evenden: a portrait of me, no less. My instinct was to reject the proposal. I tried to suggest to Henry that it would look to others as if we were currying favour with William.

'We no longer need consider Mrs Evenden's feelings, but as we enjoyed her patronage it might seem that we seek our own advantage from the opportune moment, might it not?' I said, privately wondering how it would be viewed by William himself.

I had chosen the wrong argument.

'I am offering to pay for a service,' he said, with an uncomprehending frown. 'There would be no ingratiating motive whatsoever, whatever anyone might say. Though, surely, they wouldn't? I hope not, but damn them if they do, if you will pardon me.'

'I should like to think more on the matter. Let us discuss it this evening.'

'I am afraid that I have already put the proposal to him by letter. I thought you would be pleased.' His voice, consciously or not, conveyed to me a familiar nervous imperative that I should not admit any difficulty which might cast a reflection on his judgment or good taste.

'What does he say?' was all I could ask.

'There has been no reply as yet.'

But it was arranged as Henry wished, since I had nothing more convincing that I could urge openly against it. One day I met Henry and William coming out of Henry's study; I had not known who the visitor was and had thought it another patient.

When he was gone Henry confirmed that they had been discussing the proposal for a painting. William had considered it, his explanation for the delay in his response being 'on account of my recent preoccupation with estate matters'. He was prepared to accept the commission to paint Mrs Ryder, cautioning that portraiture was not his strength, but there would be no obligation on Henry to accept the result if it did not please. If acceptable, the price proposed was little over half what a landscape of similar dimensions would fetch. Henry was more than satisfied.

'I did not send for you to join us, to spare you any confusion of modesty,' he said.

'We cannot be concerned with that, surely,' I said, 'if I am to pose and be painted?'

'Well, no, I suppose not,' he replied. He was looking around the hall, already selecting a place to hang his acquisition. 'It should look very fine!'

'Henry, why didn't you ask him to paint you?'

He laughed and shook his head. 'I do not think we are ready for *that* yet!' Then he saw that I was serious and scowled quizzically back. 'It is all right, I assume, for me to indulge an affectionate fancy. The other would look presumptuous, like vanity, wouldn't it?'

'I thought you did not care what people said.'

He only laughed again. 'I think he was more easily persuaded to agree because it was you. And quite right: the beacon of his good name.'

'Don't. I hope everyone has forgotten that. I am sure he has.'

'He ought not! Speaking of what people say, I assume you will ask your friend Miss Bowlby to come for the sittings. That should be sufficient propriety.'

'Do you think so?' He had no idea that Dolly and I had quarrelled, nor over what matter.

'Oh yes,' he answered. 'This is 1870, and he and she are old news. No-one will make anything of it; and his mother is dead. I confess, every time I think of *that* I feel a kind of release, still.' He shook his head, walking away.

I wrote to Dolly in careful terms, mentioning that her presence was Henry's wish. I found myself surprisingly unagitated by the issue of whether or not our quarrel should now be patched over, though the sense of having been misused, in however subtle a fashion, remained concrete. The initial fault, if such it was, had been William's and he being less of a friend the injury must accordingly be less felt. So argued my sense of fair play. It would not suffer me to hold out strongly against Dolly, while I had yet found no opportunity or courage to accuse William.

The first of the sittings, so called even though I must stand through them, was arranged. I descended, in a costume of maroon silk, in the middle of the day, to my parlour whose curtains were drawn against the sun. Every candle in the house had been assembled and found a stick or stand of some description. Some days previously, betraying perhaps his underlying excitement at the project which I did not share, Henry had suggested the dress. I had agreed shortly. His manner had been hesitant and more than ready to attend to my views, but I had no opinions on what I should wear.

Henry, William and Dolly were waiting when I entered. Henry asked the artist at once if the costume was to his taste.

'Perfectly,' he replied, taking an overshirt from his bag as he regarded me, 'if you are both happy to have the result displayed – remembering that a picture, if it is hung, is on show always, not only during the evening hours.'

'Perhaps it does not meet your idea of what is proper for a provincial *ingénue*,' I said.

Henry laughed, and said to William, 'A doctor should, I think, hold advanced views; especially he cannot share any excessive puritanism or delicacy as to addressing the parts of the human figure.'

'I am not a medical exhibit,' I said.

'Oh, but you are! We all are.'

He and William fell into a short, quiet and halting exchange as to the pose, while Dolly approached me and produced from a parcel a prettily worked cotton bonnet.

'I wondered,' she murmured, 'if this would do for Alice. You know, I have no idea; only I saw it and liked it – '

'Thank you,' I said. 'It will do.' Then I had a clear impression of her awkwardness on anything touching the unfathomable requirements of little girl-creatures, and I smiled. 'How lovely. It will do very well.'

Henry was almost ready to leave us at last, if reluctantly. I saw it with relief; to be again with William and Dolly must be difficult for me, but to have Henry there as well made it more so. As he said a polite farewell to Dolly, however, she detained him.

'Tell me,' she said. 'Doctor Ryder, are you, like many of your profession, including many from whom better was expected, on the side of the sinners in this wretched business of contagious diseases laws?'

I remembered the minor falsehoods I had told him, but my anxiety was not aroused since it was true that she was deeply interested in the subject and the campaigning.

'Though I fear to disappoint you, Miss Bowlby,' he said, 'I am one of those whose arguments you would dismiss as such. Is it such

245

an issue, here? Burlas is not a garrison town and the legislation therefore does not affect us either way.'

'I will forgive you, since it seems you may on that account, misguidedly, have failed to give the issue the reflection it is due. You make insufficient allowance for the strength of fellow feeling between women, and also working men who have wives or daughters who may be caught innocently on the streets – '

'Oh, that is surely exaggerated!'

' – put on the abominable register, forcibly examined with the unspeakable instruments – '

'Miss Bowlby, I must protest.'

Neither of them raised their voices in this altercation, but Henry at this point looked at me and then back at her with a reproving expression: her language was not for mixed company. His look made me blush on everyone's behalf, but it seemed particularly on his and my own. She would not have given a thought to whether a moment was more or less appropriate for the discussion of a moral controversy, merely because it concerned the regulation of immoral behaviour. I, standing already under personal inspection, sensed exactly my husband's recoil even as I was partially mortified by it.

'Oh, so must I *protest*, you see, good sir,' said Dolly lightly. 'But I apologise, and I will promise not to do so again in your house.'

William Evenden had been erecting his easel and selecting other equipment from his bag, and thus evaded any part in the discussion. I wondered if he too thought my mind too fragile for the subject. Henry had more to say, however, and said it with the tone of determined finality that was always unexpected and startling in him.

'Please do not mistake me, ma'am. I have thought well on the matter, and my position will not be altered. I would not sacrifice the rights of the unborn to those of harlots. I have seen the effects of the diseases in question, and support any and all measures of control.'

A short uncomfortable silence followed, in the course of which my confused eye caught that of William. I was astonished to see him smile and wink! Some more amicable exchanges were contrived, to confirm I dare say that here was a party sharing advanced views and this was 1870, and then I found myself alone with my guests – in striving to appear at ease paying almost no heed at first to their conversation.

Dolly too seemed nervous and talked with a greater trace of acerbity than I remembered, rapidly of this and that; then of a lady with whom she and William were mutualy acquainted but who was unknown to me.

'She displays to an extreme degree of openness a truth which I am sure applies to everyone. We all have some internal plane where the love-state is constantly played out. There are only two states, both equally wretched: either bitterness and renunciation – you could call it "death" – or else transporting torment, which you might call "life".'

'Come, now,' said William. 'You have heard of the "happy medium".'

Dolly sniffed with assumed testiness. 'You know I am only repeating your own views. Perhaps there is a state of rapid and constant flux between the other two, as two images can be alternated rapidly in a phantasmagoria, until they seem almost to merge and become a third.'

William studied me. 'You would thus define a happy union.'

'Or an unhappy one,' she said.

Turning at that moment, he made to kiss her hand which lay across her chair back; in doing so he held his own unclean hands out from his sides in appeal, but her knuckle was too swiftly withdrawn. He attended to his painting again, merely enjoining me to 'Stop smiling, if you please, Mrs Ryder.'

I was pleased to discover that I had been smiling: beginning to anticipate the prospect of entertaining times in their company after all, feeling renewed affection for Dolly. One could consider her endlessly, as people did, puzzling her 'peculiarity'. Was it not the case, I thought, that she was only a rarity in being a woman who felt and acted simply as *herself*?

As William and Dolly were leaving, they met my father

unexpectedly on the path, and I was amused by his elaborate courtesy. It transpired he was curious about the painting and had come on purpose to gossip with me about it; he still missed my aunt, I believe. Later I asked what he thought of Miss Bowlby, and he replied that by a trick of the light she had reminded him fleetingly of my mother. 'I thought, furthermore, that though your dear mother would never have placed herself in the way of the same cause for it, she possessed the same quality of courage that, from everything I know of your friend, is *her* best attribute.'

The sittings punctuated the late winter season at irregular intervals. There was a kind of enjoyment to be had from them, for me. The very occasion was flattery, of course; though to have someone's eyes fixed on the point of a jawline or elbow, usually with an expression of journeyman's disgruntlement, is less amusing in fact than in anticipation. From time to time I would remember moreover who this was – perhaps after he had joined in some inconsequential talk – and I would know an uncomfortable inward pause. If only I did not know certain things. Or if only I knew more than I did. Or, indeed, if only his brother yet lived – though the world and even my history would then be different altogether.

Though fitfully troubled by thoughts connected with his presence, my reconciliation with Dolly on the other hand was the more complete, to judge by the unalloyed pleasure that I took again in *her* company. It was a physic that moderated my brooding over everything else: over William Evenden, and over Alice.

At that time Henry had concerns more pressing, from his point of view. A dispute developed, and was taken up by the general public, 'beyond all reason,' as he said. The arguments were fragmented and pointed in contrary directions, and were made in speeches, 'open letters' and rude slogans. The cry was that hospitals were the receptive matter on which infectious agents materialised, were themselves the simple cause of the deaths therein through hospital fever. The complex triumph of antisepsis had thus been touted by its adherents merely to obscure the public's perception of the more simple truth!

Henry was at first disbelieving as well as dismayed, that the nonsense was not only mouthed but repeated in any quarter with approval.

'Of course, infection will flourish among the sick and injured, if not checked!' he cried. 'It will soon be known whether there is a true originating source of sepsis and putrefaction – or none, but only a perpetual presence. *We already know* the best defence against it – and they would tear that down?'

Among the common people, who were the only ones by circumstance required to seek treatment in the Infirmary, there had always been a widespread superstition. Now, the proportion and vehemence of those refusing to enter even in extremity was swollen, in a new raging epidemic of doctor-hatred. Even that could be faced with steadfastness, but more hurtful were the opinions of respected colleagues, all with minds as closed to logic when offered spurious new insight. The defeat of reason in them was clear when it began to be apparent, in the isolation of those like Henry who held out, that this was viewed as a timely reverse for the parvenu Scottish influence that had become so strong, threatening the position of the London Royal Colleges. That the hospitalism argument had itself been put from Edinburgh, by Simpson, was loftily disregarded. We observed and experienced this swift spread of mistrust and innuendo, hoping only that it would, in as fickle a fashion, subside before much damage was done. I was much concerned by the visible wearying and disappointment of my husband under it all. He felt the lessening of public esteem – and rightly since the alteration was beyond his power, and unjustified – but would not wish to admit as much, nor to discover that I knew his particular hurt . . .

'Tell me, Mr Evenden,' I asked one morning as William began the day's work on my portrait, 'is it not absurd and ridiculous for a nobody of a provincial doctor's wife to have her portrait taken? You can speak quite openly, for we must become inured to the talk there will be about it.'

'I ought not to be made to speak openly, against my interest. The doctor and the artist, both, have their business to maintain.'

Dolly had been delayed, he had informed me; for the first time since the painting was begun I found myself alone with him. Smothering a childish impulse to withdraw I instead spoke unguardedly, though shying away from subjects still more personal.

He straightened and went on with more reflection. 'Who would find absurdity in it, provided only it is a wanted thing? I find it absurd that artists are put to work for so many other reasons – I do not usually accept commissions for portraits, but I accepted in this case partly because Doctor Ryder so plainly *wanted* it.'

He did say 'partly'; I recalled Henry's calculation about why he might be tempted but questioned him no more as to that, not directly. He too seemed to have come under the kind of influence that I had always sensed in my husband, who was so good-natured as sometimes to appear even ineffectual, but whose wants and needs and weaknesses could be commandingly absolute.

In allowing myself that moment's fatal reverie, awkwardness had been suffered to intrude since the conversation had lapsed into silence. How long would Dolly be?

'Have you had any further dealings with Mr Tutt, since your mother's death?' I said abruptly. 'I mean since your return to England, that is.'

He stood a moment comparing two brushes that lay in his hand. 'Mr Tutt?'

'I mean,' I went on a trifle hoarsely, 'the inspector of police. If you remember – '

'Pardon me, I know very well who you mean. Is he yet living?'

'I believe so.'

'No, I have had no dealings with him. Why should I?'

He looked up very pointedly on that phrase and our eyes met. Surely, mine must have betrayed more than his; but I would not look away.

'I thought you might have been curious to know if anything more had been discovered, about your poor brother's death.'

I thought I caught a momentary expression, then: difficult to describe, like a chivalric habit, acknowledging a thrust or parry.

'I would hope to be informed of any such news, of course; but I have little faith – and, you must allow, with reason – in Tutt's prospects of solving that mystery. If I could I would choose a different ally for that.'

'Ah, so you would!' I said. 'You have experience in private investigation, and setting spies.'

He had set his brush to the canvas; at that, he withdrew it carefully and stood back. He gently laughed. 'I heard you had taken that wrongly. I am afraid I thought it was forgotten, and rather tended to blame Dolly; I could imagine her mischievous way of putting things. However, I do see my error, and I apologise for the offence.' I merely looked; and he repeated more solemnly, 'I apologise. That you may have thought I – insulted you in some way is mortifying. At that time, especially, you must know I rather sought to honour you above anyone. It seemed a small thing to contrive a friendship between two people, each owed a favour from me. I thought you would be good for each other. Tell me I was not wrong there, at least!'

'You were not wrong in that, but somehow I do not think our friendship a thing for which the credit should be given entirely to you –' He began to protest. I continued, 'I had the impression there was more besides: at the least you presumed to determine or control an aspect of my personal life, without my knowledge. Is it not true, though, that you sought reports of me; and if so, why?'

He stared at the canvas again for some seconds, feinting a few times with the brush, before speaking quietly but more tense than before. 'Must everything in your life have its reasons? If I assure you that mine, if I had any, were trivial and the opposite of malicious, must I say any more?'

'I wish that you would!'

Then he burst out at last; the blaze rose quick and light. 'Then I must ask *you* why? What reason can you expect, or fear? Do you think perhaps I doubted your faith in me? So I wanted to be sure you did not discover or deduce the dreadful truth!'

Of course the quiet after this was terrible; certainly to me it was.

'If – ' I said not very composedly, 'I doubted your innocence, would I be here with you now?'

He looked pale. 'Please forgive me – ' he began.

We heard noises without the room then, a few seconds' warning only that we were to be interrupted. He wheeled away, putting into proper order the palette and brushes he had waved about distractedly. I took a deep breath into my hands and looked upwards, to cool my eyes.

When Dolly entered she began talking at once, dispensing some new entertainment. I was grateful that in those early moments William was able to appear at ease and make an appropriate response. At the same time he enjoined me to keep my head very still which excused me from any requirement to do likewise. I was affected curiously, being made unwillingly complicit with him, just as if his private manner with me had shown improper kindness rather than the opposite.

I recall no details of the conversation immediately following, but that by some means Dolly and William came to be disputing the nature of after-life, and that Alice must have found her way into the room for I remember a pause made her suddenly look round at us, suspicious.

'Children!' exclaimed Dolly. 'They are so unnerving, the way they stare at one so!'

When Alice then turned her gaze on William, he said: 'The butterfly, if he thinks at all, must think himself the ghost of the dead caterpillar, flown up to heaven.'

Alice laughed shyly into my skirts, not at the wit, but at the solemn way he had addressed it particularly to *her*. Then she peered out, and dared to call, 'Where the butterfly?'

William drew paper and pencil from his pocket, and with tantalising look and gesture tempted her to his side, where she was persuaded, to the amusement always engendered by sight of a child's self-importance, to trace her representation of the insect winged in summer's livery. Then he took the pencil, and drew an Alice, with a great net, ready to pounce on her big wobbly butterfly.

'Do you think you will catch it?' he asked.

'He can *fly*,' she explained simply. 'He can get away.'

'Oh, I see. I must remember that.' He dropped his voice to a confidential whisper. 'I needed to escape from a net once, and these two ladies were my wings!'

I looked away. He had gone too far and Alice showed herself dubious and scornful. Shortly afterwards Mercy arrived to locate the little errant, and carried her away.

All had of course seen the portrait in various stages of execution, but a time now came for more solemn appraisal. I pulled my shawl around me as I stepped to his side of the easel, and Dolly drew the curtains open before joining us. I was somewhat numbed still in my effort to consider it for what it was. Dolly had referred to him dragging the life out of his portraits. For a moment as I first studied the picture now I fancied a mortal struggle in progress, whether truly between the artist and myself as his object I could not say. The principal image was simple and unemphatic, as had been I think the intention. But there was an inconsistency between that and a hesitant look about the eyes, confirmed by my hand half-clenched at my waist. All that, at any rate, was something of what *I* saw.

'I admire the effect of – of light and shade,' I commented. 'Is that not what people say about these things?'

'Mm,' said Dolly. 'Or what they more usually say: "something not quite right about the mouth". Perhaps Kitty smiled too much.'

'I must have some discussion with Doctor Ryder,' said William. 'But as it is proceeding at present, I rather think it will not do. I am no painter of portraits.'

As William departed we shook hands, each giving a firmer grip than usual in clandestine token. What he called my faith in him was much less than absolute – whether he suspected it or not – but we were both acknowledging that more private words had been required, for which there might never be afforded another opportunity.

After they had taken their leave and as I was going desultorily round the room, extinguishing candles and putting back order, I found William and Alice's joint production: the picture of her, chasing a butterfly giant. He had torn it from his sketchbook and left it propped on the mantelshelf. Was it really possible that in spite of all my present concerns I could have smiled *too much*, I wondered? If so then it had been only an interlude. The time for smiles was drawing to a close.

31

Henry's preoccupation with public business combined with other circumstances touching still closer to home, and brought about the indefinite postponement of any plan for further work on the portrait. The canvas was meanwhile fetched back to the Hall.

Alice was neither growing nor thriving but weakening again. This time no formal admission of the fact between us was needed. Henry began to talk of the seaside once more, and I murmured that somewhere other than Scarborough should be tried. He responded that hers was not the kind of recuperative case where a full journey south would benefit; rather the fatigue of so much travel was to be avoided at all costs. Furthermore he wanted us to stay within his reach. Nevertheless, he conceded that the west coast was gentler, by repute, on delicate constitutions. It was settled that I would take her to Heysham, after he had spent a half day there himself in reconnoitring the quiet haven and reserving light clean rooms for us. It was not only Alice's poor health but also his professional difficulties that made it an opportune time for us to depart, removing us from an oppressive atmosphere and relieving him of the distracting anguish of the useless contemplation of his child's condition.

As I packed the trunk he brought to me more and stronger medicines than before, each with its label and fastened stopper, and written instructions which he repeated to me carefully as to their use against diverse symptoms and eventualities. By ill luck his speech had to rise in competition against his daughter's lusty protests, in the next room, at the modest restrictions Mercy was proposing on the number of dolls to join the party. My hand shook as I took the bottles from him. His own hand then was placed on my shoulder and he assured me that he would visit us as often as he could.

I placed each bottle in its wallet with its instructions and then rolled each again in flannel articles. My head bent to this task, I muttered breathlessly:

'What *is* the matter with her?'

Henry spoke tonelessly and without hesitation. 'It is a non-specific disorder. She is of a fragile constitution, and requires excessive protection and strengthening to withstand the normal shocks and invasions of young life. If you were another patient's mother, I might find some more impressive and hopeful terminology, but that is all I know, and all that anyone else could find I am sure.'

Time and again the memory of Heysham returns to me. When I see a small child making delighted secret dancing, intruded upon by observation, then Alice is with me again; and so also, inseparable, is my fear, a thing pitching into hollow emptiness. Earth shows no mark of her passing so brightly. I look everywhere, for a lingering shadow.

Alice was affectionate and clinging with both Mercy and me. In my memory, she ran alone but once in our time there.

I had walked with her up the path beside the church, which leads on to the place they call the 'Viking Chapel'. It is a ruin on the seaward face of a knoll. Before it the grass slopes and breaks down to a deserted cove, open to the spreading sands beyond, the sea, and the setting sun. To the side lie flat regular stones in which unearthly deeply hollowed shapes of men are to be seen. These are said to be the opened graves of ancient Norse adventurers, come here to the end of their world. I stood considering them, the hollows filled now with black water, my face to the sea breeze, Alice's hand in mine. I stood thus until I sensed that she was watching me with an equivalent serious understanding, and I turned my head to meet her look. We stayed, face to face, above and below, until she was satisfied. She loosed my hand, but only after a further pause did she drop her unwavering gaze at last. She turned and ran from me, I fancied with a silent farewell in her heart. She ran to the left, where the ground dips and then rises again. In a moment she was over and gone from sight. I followed quickly to the brow of the rise. There the illusion of an enclosed kingdom is lost; there is a prospect of the coast to the south. Alice was standing waiting. After a pause she took my hand once more to plod away back home.

She was too young to prattle of heaven in the knowing way that children, marked for death, are wont to do in books. Yet she was trying to impart a truth; she knew a strange passage lay ahead and had courage for it.

The progress in her health was uncertain. She gained colour again, but this time it bleached away each night. Imperceptibly at first, she grew more and more tired. Mercy and I barely spoke to each other save when necessary, but we behaved with ever more kindness and indulgence toward the child.

At the month's end Henry arrived for his regular weekly visit to find his daughter lying in bed scarcely marking even his entrance. I left him examining her. When I came upon him later his face was white and set.

'Henry, she must go home,' I said.

He would not look at me, but nodded. A moment later he shocked me. Without warning he began to examine me closely and with intensity like anger, almost, as to the use I had made of his medicines and how I had interpreted his instructions. I answered with something like grievance in my voice, saying that he must refer to Mercy, who had been in charge of most of the administration.

'What!' he exclaimed. 'I entrusted you with the responsibility. *This* was not something to be left to a servant!'

'Henry, calm yourself. You know she is more competent in such matters then anyone, and would give her life for the child.'

After a moment's pacing before me, he acknowledged the truth of my point, and offered a perfunctory apology before making an abrupt exit from the room. The wonder of it was, to me, that he should be so much more afraid than either Alice or I. For that was what I had seen: the fear in my husband.

I had shared in the decision to return home but when it came to packing again and readying ourselves for the journey I was beset with lassitude and reluctance. The already half-familiar common-place views from each little window held me, and my movements were disorganised and slow. I could not say that my thoughts were elsewhere: I had lost the inclination to follow my destiny.

Such was my state of mind (the day after the discussion with Henry described above) as I tried to sort Alice's and my clothes into the trunk, when Mercy came to say my husband wanted my presence in the next room. Though her composure never wavered she looked troubled, I thought; I felt a sensation of panic and reminded myself forcefully that Alice was with me, on her cot, therefore no change in her condition could be the cause.

Mercy returned with me into the little day room. Henry was standing looking serious and uncomfortable, blinking rather at a medicine bottle which he held in one hand, and at the instructions accompanying it which paper he held in the other. I assumed we were to be informed of revisions to those instructions.

But he said, 'Mercy has brought me this. Do you recognise it?'

I looked instead at him, and briefly at Mercy, not understanding. I did recognise the bottle. Like most of those we had brought it had been prepared by him and labelled simply with a brief code, referring to the details written separately.

'Of course.'

'And you know what it says here: only to be given when she is at her most low, a maximum of ten drops in warm water, twice a day?'

'Yes – '

'Are you sure the advice has been followed strictly? Since you delegated control of the drugs to Mercy is it possible that between you, with insufficient consultation, you have used too much?'

'No. We have used it very little, and – ' I looked again, puzzled, towards Mercy, 'always with consultation.'

Alice called from the other side of the door and both I and Mercy turned our heads by instinct. Henry spoke with more emphatic insistence: 'So she also maintains. Mercy, you may attend to my daughter now.' He waited until the door was closed behind her then put the bottle actually in my hand. 'Look. Can you recall how this compares with the level remaining a few days ago?'

I held it upright, against the light from the window. 'But – this is astonishing! Even if we had been giving double doses – which I swear is not possible with the care we took – so much could not have been used!'

He retrieved the medicine from me gently and turned to put it away. As his back was presented to me he said very quietly and evenly, 'Would you still entrust so much to her?'

'Are you suggesting – ? My God! Alice!'

I was ready to run, that second, to the child and perhaps do some violence to Mercy, though still not through conviction of her guilt – rather as a reaction to the incomprehensible. Henry restrained me.

'Do not be so alarmed. Surely you must be mistaken in your estimate of what was used? Think again. Or was there an accidental spillage, that you have forgotten?'

'I know indeed there must be some explanation, but I can think of none, really – oh, Henry!'

His tone in response was impatient rather than soothing, though his words were some comfort: 'Well, I can assure you Alice's present condition is not at all consistent with any excessive administration of this particular mixture – '

'Are you sure? What is it? What would the symptoms be? What if we start to find them in her, now?'

'There would have been signs by now. I will not tell you what, because in your present state you would certainly start imagining things. But whatever the explanation, I cannot simply let this pass. Go through to Alice, and send Mercy in here to me again.'

'What will you do?'

'That all depends.'

I turned at the door. 'I do not think Alice could bear to lose her; just – now – that would be cruel.'

He grunted, 'I know.'

He and Mercy were cloistered for half an hour. I did not hear raised voices in that time but when she emerged her face was tear-stained.

Henry being then satisfied, the subject was not suffered to be mentioned again, whatever suspicions he may have retained regarding myself or my maid, even assuming they would concern nothing more than carelessness. It was troubling indeed, but many things were troubling at that time, and as he accompanied us on the sorry sombre journey home it jostled in my thoughts with other forebodings.

I have indicated that I had lost the taste or desire for continuing with any regular activity. That was not allowable. In Burlas it was expected that life should go on as usual. I must leave Alice's side over and over again; the time when life seeps from a child is still time in which it is compellable on the mother to go forth and labour and meet and talk.

Had there been pain I can only think I must have smothered her at once. Such a fading away is thought of as a kindliness in death. It is awful though, the way the life goes. Make fast the door and shutters, and the body; give it breath and warmth; the extinguisher sidles through and runs away past all restraint.

Out in the world there was a name on everyone's lips, voiced with bemused admiration and anxiety. Bismarck and his machines and systems would claim the earth while we slept, it was said. I knew that as nothing to fear. It was nothing beside the power that could steal a child in the very face of a love so strong.

I sensed Henry as suffering equally but differently. For him, too, the coming loss eclipsed all other trouble, but then the other troubles, which for him were close and continuing, did not cease to be but became all part of the same evil; so it seemed written in his bearing.

'Must the Infirmary close?' I asked him once, being in a dull and stupid frame of mind. I knew that there had been an utter collapse in receipts and contributions, and had been hearing talk.

'Good God, no! It will never close; and the nurses shall be paid.' He rested his head in his hands. 'I would I had gone to hell before I ever heard of it, or them.'

He told me that two patients had died that day, after being operated on by Doctor Maugham the week before. Examining the staff, he had found that Doctor Maugham had neglected certain basic elements of antisepsis procedure and shown himself complacent before the assistants, 'stating that the view now was that the degree of care required had been overstated; new understanding means the practice can be refined down to what is necessary – when his omissions negated the value of every prescribed step he *did* think proper – !'

On another day Dolly came and spoke kindly to me. As soon as she was gone I wandered unthinkingly until I was back with Alice again. She slept. I stroked her head until she woke; it was past time to see rest as hopeful. She lay wide-eyed and silent. I asked if she would take some milk. She nodded, and I helped her to a few sips then sat holding her hand. She was looking at the picture of the boy in the magic coat. I took it down and assisted her to hold it for a while. Her lips pressed in a cypher of a smile and her dull eyes flickered over it.

Dolly's talk had gone unheeded. She was my greatest, sometimes it seemed my only, only *true* friend, but even she could be so unsatisfactory. She always had new enthusiasms, such as poor France, whose danger (for she was one of the many for whom the coming 'War of Surprises' was to be nothing of the kind) she could hardly bear to think of now, nor hear and read of all opinion being for Germany. I had not listened, but the echoes of her words still sounded confusedly in my head. She said 'Will' had asked after me; he had seen me in the street but I had not recognised him.

Alice had fallen asleep again with her eyes part-open. I closed them in a grim gesture, and replaced and straightened the picture on its nail.

On another night she fell asleep in that way, and the sleep-breaths deepened in stages. I sent for Henry and he watched and saw as I did. Now, at last, he did nothing. Her breaths were slow, and so heavy, to shake the tiny frame! It seemed they were not hers. Always after a minute of lifelessness the next came, dragging out the long night. Then, when the next did not come, my darling had died. If any God was skulking in the room I made no appeal to him. How can a zero, an emptiness, make appeal?

Henry was insistent that a post mortem be done. I respected this sign of his love and care. What, they would say, for a mere child? Yes, though young lives are cheap and the registers blind to the slaying of thousands, for her. He wanted to carry out the examination himself, which would be further matter for comment among the ignorant and superstitious. Doctor Maugham came and spoke privately with him, and Henry agreed that he might perform it in his stead. I cared not at first. I was finished with her, and she with me.

The examination showed, Henry reported, nothing untoward; and a quiet burial took place at the municipal cemetery, new, sanitary and spacious. The world shrank a little. Even Mrs Annesley left, for her own garbled reasons, all but unnoticed. Mercy closed the nursery and took over the kitchen.

My poor father came to see me more frequently than at any other time. His sympathy was the strongest and the least use; it forced him to match me in silent contemplation, hour for hour.

One time though, the little he had said – of other matters, trying I dare say to rouse me – left my thoughts meandering fearfully. I knew very little about Alice's specific illness, for children die and that must be accepted without presuming to understand what the physician knows. I knew not what potions I had administered nor against what faults in the organism. The little corpse had been opened and examined without my intervention; the examination had shown 'nothing untoward', but Henry had insisted upon it –

My father had been talking about Henry and the allegations that he had carried out 'experiments' on his patients; it was wild talk which if anything had served to bring his colleagues back to their senses, and to his defence. My awareness of these developments was vague, through having been away at Heysham and otherwise absorbed with Alice. I wondered if there had been anything in his treatment of our child that he would not care to have to defend before his peers? Was that why he sought the reassurance of the autopsy, and why the discrepancy in the medicine used on her, at Heysham, had been first investigated then dropped by him with so little fuss?

I told myself I must be mad; I knew I travelled close to that state. I was so lacking in a normal sense of who I was, and what therefore befitted me, that I felt unashamed of such thoughts. If I was ashamed of anything then it was of the way I put the thoughts from me utterly, out of a remaining care for my mental integrity.

Dolly was much occupied with leagues and petitions. Still she visited whenever she could. She hinted at some more personal preoccupation, saying once that she was 'probably doing too much'. I concluded that my grief discomfited her.

Then William Evenden called to express his sympathy. He did the best thing, though the most painful, which was to speak of his small memories of Alice. He said he had thought her not strong but had hoped she would live. He said she had been very beautiful.

As he sat on in silence I thought that his response was of the type one would supposedly call 'well-bred', and if so it was no bad thing. For the first time I could believe with my father that his guilt or innocence was of no consequence. In this instance he wished to do good. I had devised a private sport for myself, exercising a genius now revealed in me for the *instant* detection of false sympathy.

In token of all which, I merely said, 'Your father was also a kind man.'

'My father wished to be a friend to *you*, Mrs Ryder. I think that is all we had in common.'

I shook my head, suffused with alien coolness. 'I am sorry to tell you that I have not always been as you think I am. What happened long ago does not matter. There had to be a trial. It was properly done and I told the truth – '

The reverie continued in my head, as to the things that matter and the vastly greater proportion that do not. I had no idea how I

263

may have affected him nor how long the silence continued in the room.

'Mrs Ryder, I believe you wish to be alone and for that reason only I will go, at once. I would say, with whatever force I can: if any thing appears in which I may be of service, no matter what, I could not count it any trouble; rather I should be glad, always glad and grateful. I hope you understand.'

And he did make to leave, with alacrity. By his words he could not have understood what I had said; but his sudden haste seemed to show the contrary, that he was stung – or alarmed.

'Please, Mr Evenden!' Then I stopped.

He looked up. 'Pardon me?'

I found a smile for him. 'The – the portrait! I would hazard it is not likely ever to be finished. I am sorry for your wasted efforts.'

He frowned, puzzled, for a moment; then his face cleared. 'I shall certainly refrain from reminding Doctor Ryder of it, since I take it that is your wish. But there is no limit of time. It may yet be finished one day, perhaps when my skill is more equal to it. Good-bye, Mrs Ryder.'

Henry at this time continued going about his duties, pale, pinched and diligent. I thought also that he apprehended danger in my acute suffering, or rather the deadness of my sensibilities in many ways. Certainly he regarded me more often and more closely than had been his wont. If I had calculated that William Evenden might react promptly or suddenly to the hints I had chosen to give him of my suspicions, I was wrong; he did not. What was in store for me was quite unexpected: my husband's reaction to the visit.

When Henry came home that afternoon he tasked me, 'Mercy says you received William Evenden this morning. Is it true?'

Of course I had no reason to deny it but my answer, being weighted with my own reflections on the significance of the few words exchanged, was slow.

He pressed me further. 'What occasioned his visit?'

Again I had to think for a moment. 'He – he called to express his condolences.'

At this there was a pause which I took to mark the closure of the subject. We were in the consulting room and I stood while he sat. Without enthusiasm I recalled household duties and turned.

'Just a moment.'

Henry rose and passed me, and closed the door to ensure privacy. Then he returned to face me. When he spoke his tone was indeed gentle, even exaggeratedly or falsely so I thought.

'There is a most painful compunction on me. I must insist that you never question me as to why it is so. If you are innocent – surely you are! – it is best you should remain so, utterly. Only listen now, and answer faithfully; and if you answer as I expect there shall be silence and forgetfulness. It shall be as if no such thing ever required to be asked! You look puzzled and anxious; I only hope you have understood. Has that – gentleman – ever sought any – any shred of improper or criminal conversation with – with my wife?'

. . . Puzzled? Anxious? Was I 'puzzled and anxious'? 'How can this be?' I murmured.

'Katherine, my injunction was clear, you must not ask that. Answer, please, at once; you see the importance of answering me, your husband, at once and clearly!'

'How can this be?' I repeated – I fear several times. 'You say when I have answered it will be as if you never asked, but how can anything ever be the same, since you have used such – ' for a second I heard a little laugh, my own, 'such terms to me? Improper or criminal conversation! Ah, my God!'

'Kay, I cannot blame you for this; I feel it too. But if the pain is to be excised you have to answer –'

'I told you. He came to express sympathy. He was very proper. I thought for once he spoke most properly, and he was sincere.'

Henry's face worked a little. 'Then, he has never . . . I asked, if there had ever –'

I remembered what he had asked. I pictured the entire history of my acquaintance with William Evenden. 'Never – with your wife.'

Once more but with a deal more animation I made to leave; but he held my arm, loosing it at once and speaking in the same voice of conscious gentleness as at first.

'My dear, it is over; and let it be as I said. There is no supportable alternative. I cannot suffer you to remain in this state, at any rate.'

'Oh. What will you do?'

'You probably know, I have been concerned that you are – perhaps – becoming unwell. You have undergone a trial, and now this dangerous agitation – caused by me, I know – It is high time I stopped neglecting you – you, of all people. I shall examine you, if I may; and I anticipate that a draught will be called for to soothe the nerves, together with a period, hopefully short, of absolute rest and confinement. Come, I will assist you.' And he reached toward the first fastening, at the back of my neck.

I took a step away.

'Please,' he continued, 'after all the difficulties I too have endured, allow me to assuage this concern in the way I think best. For once I ask you to concede to me the authority of both a doctor and a husband!'

Still I would not present my back to him, while I wondered what authority or power I might ever have to call on. It seemed unbearably unjust. 'I am not yet a lunatic, to have my faculties and freedoms questioned like this!'

'Did I say you were?' His gentleness was minutely breached; I saw his impatience, his true anxiety that there might be something in me that could not be subdued. It made me afraid too. I had thought of madness, but I had not till then been afraid of it. He said with the new edge in his speech, 'Would I press you, or force you? You know I would not. Though I might wonder what can be the cause of this resistance. Why do you fear to be examined?'

While I mutely stared I seemed to hear again Dolly, arguing with him on behalf of women suspected of immorality and 'forcibly examined . . .'. I fled the room. He did not try to stop me, nor did he seek me out.

We met at dinner like the ghosts of strangers. At the close of the repast while we remained alone together at the table he said, 'You know I was thinking only of your welfare.'

I responded, 'You know I have never betrayed you.'

He nodded as if wishing to believe a formal reconciliation had been achieved. He escorted me to the drawing room. Leaving me there, he returned shortly as Mercy was serving coffee. He stood waiting for her to finish. Looking at him, I was struck by how reduced and etched with trouble he was. It was so marked I was ashamed not to have seen it before, realising that he had been first to see a degree of change in me.

When Mercy was gone he crossed to me and drew a small stoppered phial from his pocket.

'It is merely a mild opiate,' he said. 'Taken at this hour it will not inhibit your daily activity in any way; but it will calm your responses and promote sleep and nervous repair. I strongly advise you to take it.'

'Will it satisfy you?'

'It will greatly ease my mind.'

I looked at it in his hand for a few seconds, then took and unstoppered it and swallowed quickly. With swiftness also he took back the tell-tale vessel and returned it to his pocket. Within minutes my eyes and limbs grew heavy.

I excused myself early and climbed the stair; but as I was readying myself for bed he came into my room. I looked at him curiously. He at first said nothing, and as by a mechanical instinct I rose and went to the dressing room, but what I looked for was not there. I returned to sit beside my husband on the bed. His eyes had been lowered; they turned to me as I reached him.

'Henry, do you wish to talk?'

He shook his head. He touched me.

'But I – ' I looked back toward the dressing room.

'Are you afraid to bear another child? You need not be.'

'I am not afraid. But I am not ready – I still think of Alice. And you see how tired I am!'

He sat on beside me, holding me. When he pressed me I pulled away, merely to express my feeling which was becoming too difficult to explain, with my thickened tongue and thoughts out of focus. It was hard to recall even why the day had been so full and strange, or whether I felt kind or bitter towards him at that moment.

He looked and sounded pleading. 'My dear, I – we – *cannot* be childless!' He stroked my cheek. 'These morbid obsessions with death are very common. Believe me, they must be indulged only so far. If they persist, the humane course is to excise them, with resolute action, or they poison the constitution. There will be permanent impairment! So, let us – comfort each other!'

My limbs became more heavy and my thoughts still more imprisoning and torpid. He knelt beside me now, clasping my waist, and I stroked his bent head, the rich yellow curls.

'I am very tired,' I said again.

'I too.' His voice was muffled, and I felt a sigh rise within him.

After a moment he stood and took my hands, pulling. He kissed me, gentle and persistent. All the urgings and caresses of ardour and affection, of hand and mouth, of which I had lived always in utter want, were now cast on me. I was shepherded as he wished.

Only then, as if on this occasion driven to seek still greater assurance of his dominion, did he utter his reproaches. His words by then flowed over me, half meaningless. Some I recall, as his voice resounded harsh and urgent in my ear. He said that I had made him what he was, therefore it was not for me to decree now that his efforts be all wasted. He was quite vehement, swearing that it should not all be for nothing! As he had never addressed me before at such a moment, and never at any time with such bitter emotion, and myself having never had so acute an appreciation of my helplessness in the world, I fell insensible, quite choked with sorrow, actually craving the refuge of unreason if that might come.

I had such dreams, that when I woke I did not trust my final memories of Henry's words and manner. I thought I had seen him prone on the floor beside my bed, struggling for strength and breath, and then half-rising and staggering to the door. When his eyes caught mine, by some words and gestures (that I could not recall these made me sure it had been a dream), he forbade me to follow him. But had I willed it I could not have moved; I was returned to the heart of sleepy chaos at once.

32

'My dear Kitty, I am alarmed at your looks today.' Dolly was to the point as ever. 'Your eyes are positively hollow. Will you not take the air with me, and then promise to rest this afternoon?'

'It is looks, merely. I think that I have taken a summer cold. My eyes are too sore for the sunshine outside, but I promise you I do rest a great deal. Henry insists upon it.'

'He is sure that it is a cold?'

'Yes. Also, he gave me something last night to settle my nerves, and that has left me a little heavy. I shall not take it again. He does not approve of using such aids too much, in any event.'

'I am sure he is very sound, as to that.' She paused for some moments, then said with very insistent mildness, 'You and your husband must depend upon each other.'

I sat forward with my arms folded and examined my toes to avoid the level gaze aimed always at me. There was a clock ticking and the sound of birdsong outside. I could hear Dolly's very stillness, watching me.

'He says that I am morbidly obsessed – that I must not be indulged –' I pressed a hand over my eyes, unable to continue.

Her voice was calm, sonorous, like solemn music.

'You must find a way to be yourself, you know. That is the way for a brave soul, though you think that you are noble now. You must find a way to be yourself, or you will end by hating him. Female devotion is an act of the greatest love, but it bears within itself the seeds of hate. Always. Always.'

The stillness settled again between us. I was the next to speak.

'You do not know how terribly he can be hurt.'

'That is why it is you who must be brave. You know that you must, or destroy yourself inwardly, which is only another way of hurting him – and a meaner one. And if you, with all your ardour, ever came to hate someone, I think that I for one could not bear to see it.'

'You do not understand. Sometimes there is no choice. But I shall never stop loving him. How could you understand that, after all?'

After a pause, I spoke again. 'I am sorry. I was wrong to say that; I did not mean to be hurtful.'

'I have eyes which see, Kitty,' she said. 'I cannot close my eyes. It has always been my curse!'

I reached across and fastened my hand on one of hers. She turned hers palm upwards and examined mine, stroking the fingers.

'I hear from Will that he called on you recently. One word, my dear, in spite of what I have just been saying: *careful*!'

My hand as of its own volition drew back from her grasp. 'Don't be silly, Dolly. I have never been in any danger from Mr Evenden.'

That the very name had so startled me was of course a residue from the day before: the unspeakable implications in what Henry had said. Now came this unaccountable tone, from *her*! Yet so uncivil were my rabble thoughts, after the night's torrent of dreams and visions, I found it in me also to wonder what he might have told her of our interview. I had intimated that my faith in him had not always been unwavering. In what respect, after all, should I be 'careful'?

She frowned to herself. 'Perhaps I sense some looming danger to the pair of you. I was appointed, remember – I do not want to open old sores – to watch over you. These days it seems I don't know which friend to watch over for the best.'

'If you wish to be released from your appointment you must apply to him, not me.'

'Yes. Yes, indeed, I think it is time for me finally to have done with him, now.'

It seemed I had no use in those days for any notion of being careful, for though she may have expected me to ask her what she meant I did not do so. Instead I affected (without difficulty) a weary stupidity, and deflected her talk back to a principal object of interest to her: the war, or more particularly the prospect of a new republic. I wondered that such a woman of the world (beside whom I was generally to be counted *naïve*) could really see so much hope for mankind in the expedient footwork of a few clever men, for all they had ringing cries, expressed moreover in French.

Henry heard from me that Dolly had called with but a pursing of lips, eloquent of his displeasure.

'Should I not have received her, do you think?' I asked with, I fear, unbecoming irony.

'Oh, I mean no such thing. However I do believe her company is of that irritating, invigorating quality not likely to be of benefit to you, constitutionally, just now.'

My recollection of the order of days and weeks after Alice's death, especially after the day of William's visit and its after-effects, is uncertain, and there must be whole passages lost entirely. I have often puzzled over whether my wish for insanity was granted in some measure. I submitted to my husband's advice in continuing a nightly *régime* of the nerve tonic, for lack of any impulse to resist nor grounds to argue. How far my derangement extended I cannot tell. The worst of it was the blindness that affected me at the time, and persists now looking back in relation *to* that time.

I used to visit Alice's grave, in the new cemetery, and be curiously offended at knowing that our family plot was there reserved now. The 'family' for the present was limited to Henry and myself, and who knew if any more would ever bear us company out of this world. My other family – as it must now be regarded – had another place, familiar of old, in a different part of town entirely: a noxious, crowded burial place, Henry said. There lay my mother and aunt, and there my father would lie.

My husband was correct that death had completed its hold on my imagination. If I imagined death as having any residence it was Evenden Hall. There the incubus rested, complacent, ordering human destiny. Was it not there that Sarah Evenden had promised me a journey into hell? Her child first brushed against me, as I

271

happened to lie in his path, five years before; and he had trailed the invisible stain across me. Perhaps there had been real blood on his hands. Now, not only John but also his father and mother lay in the bleak country churchyard, and the last of the line had returned to sit alone in the house of death.

To prove itself undeviating and unimpressionable, the same chance had now abused and stolen my child. I had shared every smallest tremor in her great soul; each had sent a signal as on a taut wire anchored about my heart. My heart lay strangled among dark tendrils rampant.

One day as I sat (as often, unoccupied), Henry recounted to me certain reports of the British Association meeting at Liverpool. There had been multiple new assaults on the theory of the spontaneous generation of life, led by Mr Huxley, and a paper by Doctor Child 'On Protoplasm and the Germ Theories'. He explained it all in a manner sardonic, as of one now justified rather than satisfied; he made a comment that it was all 'a little late in the day'.

I sat pondering a moment, absorbing what he had said with no attempt at judgment.

'I should like to know,' I heard myself saying, 'what were the treatments applied to Alice, and what were the reasons for them.'

Grim, soft-spoken (the combination which was becoming so terribly familiar in his manner of address to me), he said: 'You do not trust me?'

'I trust you utterly. But I wish to know. Was there, for example, any experimental aspect to your prescriptions?'

He paused, somehow expressing a sense of great injury and self-restraint. 'What do you think I have to tell you?' he asked.

Then, without waiting for my reply, he walked away into his consulting room. I followed and watched as with rapid, disjointed motion he pulled open the little top drawer of his desk and took out a key, crossed to a cabinet and unlocked it.

'Here, as you know,' he indicated the shelves, 'is my dispensary. Most of these are toxic to some degree – the best we can do generally is little more than selective and experimental sanctioning against the human system. In the past, Katherine, you urged me to explain my beliefs; you showed yourself willing to understand and support me, always. Now, just when the whole world turns against me, you ask a question – I know it was not your intention, but nevertheless – which shows you too understand nothing! Naturally, in the face of disease everything we do should be regarded in a sense as an experiment, with scepticism. We remain so far from matching the enemy's powers. It will not be in my time, but *at the least* understanding must somehow be shared, with someone, for it to be passed on – '

He stopped with a sigh and pulled open a drawer at the base of the cabinet. A ledger lay within, together with his father's old pistol (a sentimental possession brought back with us from Scarborough the year before). He took out the book and put it in my hands, together with the key.

'In there,' he said, 'you will find a full account of everything that has left these shelves, and the observable effects. Make yourself comfortable, if you wish, and leave all as you find it. I trust *you*.'

He was ready to leave me there, while I scanned the array of bottles and packets.

'Henry,' I said. 'You know I could never understand on my own. I am sorry if you think I mistrusted you, or that you hoped I could help, when I cannot.'

I put the unopened ledger and the key back in his hands. He put the book away and was about to close the cabinet doors when I spoke again.

'Is it time for my medicine, dear?'

He paused. 'It is rather early.'

'Nevertheless – I feel the need of it.'

He took down a bottle. Seeing another with a familiar label nearby, I indicated.

'That is what we gave to Alice – remember, when Mercy thought too much had gone? It has been replenished?'

'Yes. I supply it to other patients.'

On his desk he used a glass funnel to pour an exact quantity of my own draught into a marked phial. I took it at once. After putting everything away, and the key back in the desk as before, he sat heavily in his chair, staring before him. I moved to his side and knelt there, resting my forehead against his arm.

He began to talk of what he could have tried with Alice: blisters and purgatives, shocks and poisons with the effects described in the last detail. 'And nobody would have breathed a word of opposition!'

I pressed against him and for the only time we wept together for the loss of our joy.

Yet still his feelings were different, though he felt as deeply as I. His grief had an urgent, fearful quality, revealed to me alone, frequently in the night. I am ashamed to own that those appeals drove me from him in spirit, more than anything else, though it was gratifying at least to be acknowledged in the marital bedroom, under the cloak of night, to be needed, even if that need was voiced in terms of demand and reproach.

I have said my memory of the order of days is uncertain; much more so is that of the nights which were often disturbed with vivid nightmares.

Once I dreamed I was wandering cold and unhappy, looking for Alice whose weak and despairing sobs I could hear. Mercy had abandoned her somewhere and plainly her heart was breaking, but I could not find her. She needed medicine; without it she would die. I could hear the sound of her fading, and became frantic in my searches –

'No!'

The cry was sudden and compelling, and I wailed too for after it Alice was silent, and I would never find her.

'No!' came the voice, and something grasped me; my arms were pinioned. This was William Evenden, I knew, carrying me away; he knew no restraint, that was clear . . . Now a dog clawed at my hand.

'Kay, stop!'

It was Henry, holding me to him. I was awake, gasping as if near drowned and as wet, with clammy perspiration.

'Give it to me.' He spoke with great firmness; now his familiar voice seemed to assure me of safety and homecoming.

He took something from my hand, then a lamp was lit. We were in the consulting room, at who knew what hour of the night. I was in my night-gown. I looked about to see all as normal, save that the doors of the dispensing cabinet hung open. Henry stood before me in his night-shirt.

'What has happened?' I asked him.

At once I saw relief in his pose; I must have alarmed him dreadfully.

'Only a dream,' he said. 'Thank God, I was awake and heard you leave your room, and I followed you. I hoped not to have to wake you, because of the shock; but when you came in here – '

'Why? What was I doing? I thought I was looking for – '

'What?'

'Nothing. I cannot remember.'

He groaned and shook his head. Then he showed me what was in his hand, what he had wrested from me: a small bottle with on its label the emphatic red ink reserved, I knew, for the strongest poisons.

'Whatever it was, it was not this. Let one pure drop of this touch your lips, you would be dead before you could cry out!'

And so it came that on another night I found myself again alone, hurrying through the dark under the open sky, away from my home – but no.

No, I have said truly that my memories are disordered, but in more rational review I know that there were other events leading up to my departure. I will recount them all as they may have been experienced by a fully reasoning mind.

After Henry had displayed to me that sovereign poison, and secured it again in its proper place, he led me, both of us trembling, back to bed. In my room he hesitated.

'After what has happened, I fear to leave you,' he said.

'You will stay?'

'No. No, I think a more effective course – ' He turned the key, locking the door. 'With unconscious wandering, very often the sufferer will return to bed calmly if obstructed in some common-place way rather than by forceful intervention. The shock of waking can also be avoided,' he explained. 'In sleep, I do not think you would take the less usual route, through my room; and if you do I will likely be disturbed.'

He bade me good-night and, taking the key away with him, retired through the connecting passage to his own room. After the alarm just suffered I welcomed his precautions. Nevertheless, I could not settle again to sleep at once, though I huddled beneath the covers remembering the exact terms of my dream down to the moment of being shaken into my senses by him. It may have been two or more hours later that I was driven to rise and go to him.

By his breathing and his form as he lay curled he had succeeded in sleeping; but with some part of his mind still alert, he stirred at my entrance. At my first word he started up, looking at me solicitously.

'Henry,' I said, placing my candle on the table beside his bed and kneeling there. 'Henry, I have had the most terrible thought!' I was crying. 'Please tell me truthfully – I will not be angry – have I ever walked like that before?'

'Not so far as I know. I am sure it is the effect of your nervous exhaustion and, of course, a minor consequence of the tonic draught.'

'I too am sure. But, Henry, I dreamed I was fetching medicine, for Alice – Oh, tell me, have you ever drugged me in secret? When you came to Heysham I know I was very low in spirits, and you seemed angry. I thought perhaps I could have had such a wild dream, and wrongly made Alice take something – !'

He sat up fully and seized my heaving shoulders. 'Kay, I am appalled! You know I would never do such a thing! I told you I was utterly satisfied that Alice received nothing but the proper attention. There never was anything to show otherwise!'

'Do you promise it? I thought it could so easily be disguised, in wine, or coffee – '

'I do promise it. And I take nothing amiss in your saying such things. My poor dear; you are not yourself.'

That would be too easy a thing to say: that I was 'not myself'. It was I and no-one else who, when Henry was out of the house, found again the key to his cabinet, and took down and fondled, wonderingly, the various glass receptacles. In particular, I ranged on the table before me three, and considered them: that containing the draught of unrestful dreams now supplied to me each night; that which I had been seeking in my dream – the medicine to overcome Alice's faintness; and the smallest bottle with its few pure drops of death. So close had I been to joining her in a sleep without dreams.

William Evenden had been in my dream and I thought I knew why. If I knew for sure that he had killed, what I would want to know from him would be something more awful than any question of remorse or dread of retribution: I would ask where in oneself one discovers that well of authority, of power, to overthrow the very sanctity of life, to slay a close and loved companion? For I knew that if any action of mine, or of my husband's, had in truth harmed Alice, I would wish to avenge her even to that degree. Meantime I remained ignorant and powerless. I had enough cunning to have noted precisely the positions of the medicines, and I returned them leaving no trace of my studies.

I hoped without real hope to be made well. Each evening I took my medicine. Each night Henry locked my door and took the key away. I would go to bed and wait for his return, or not. Once I dreamed that my room was furnished only with a coffin, a coffin with a lock and key. I woke to find him holding me.

Each morning too he came in quietly, before Mercy's hour to rouse me, and turned the key in the door, leaving it in its accustomed position.

One night Henry and I ascended together to our rest. Having locked my door and seen me readying myself for bed he left me, expressing himself more tired than usual. I then managed, alone, to re-fasten my dress, and wait for utter quiet in the house. After more than an hour of silence I started to move. I had not been out of the house for many days. I turned to my bureau and with great care took a sheaf of paper from an inner compartment: twenty-five pounds. Then I wrote a note to Mercy and left it on the bed, folding the cover down to hold it. I put the money in a purse, adding on

277

reflection a few jewels from the dresser. I do not care to analyse why I did these things; they were not planned. I believe I wished to escape for a while the contemplation of something I had done, or simply to escape a house now so devoid of happiness, without even the echo of past joys. Finally, treading softly, I went through the connecting passage. As my eyes grew accustomed to the gloom I contemplated the form of my husband again. This time his sleep was deep and unbroken.

I recalled how that evening, as ever, he had supervised my taking of the draught of medicine. When I returned the phial to him he had gone at once to dispose of it. He had not seen me take up a cup from the tray, but I remembered my own small disgust as I watched the drool from my mouth fall into it. Then I had poured his coffee. So I had confirmed it: it could be so easily disguised.

Yet as I watched him now turn and mutter to his pillow, I was sure he had never done such a thing. I trusted he would take no harm from it; given his own pallor and agitation of late, would he not benefit as much as I? We could both for a time be spared the fever of his attentions.

Passing through the hall I took my mantle and bonnet. I paused beside the door to the consulting room, and I was half ready to go in and take the physic of which I had earlier abstained; but in some horror at the thought of broaching again the sanctum of the dispensary, I found within me the motive to resist.

The next moment, I was walking up the lane.

My steps never hurried or slackened. For I told myself I was merely walking, for a little solace. A voice within counterargued: what had I written to Mercy? Never mind, I would return in a short while and recover the note before she could see it. No-one would know. (Yet I would know.) Perhaps this was the first of many such secret midnight rambles!

I had reached the stile. I need go no further . . . But I had crossed it. The truth, now: I knew that not for anything would I turn back. Before so much as leaving my room I had calculated that the stage would pass through Frith the next day, that I was not likely to be sought *there* before I had boarded it and made my escape secure; that a summer night in the open would be discomfort sweetly tuned to my temper. Still I thought of my escapade as a mere retreat, wherever I might go. Anywhere. The sea. Somewhere.

Here I – my present, reasoning self – must intrude to deal with the question of shame. To recognise it as I ought would mean for much of my account up to now, *and all the remainder*, to lie as a passage of silence. Therefore, to reach the point which I have identified as my conclusion I must do injustice to it: after this one brief exposition, turn my face from the question of shame or justification.

Why did I not proceed to that door where I might beg refuge and always be admitted, no matter what my sin? The answer lies in this matter of shame. I could desert my home and husband and still face my father. I could face him with what I saw as my loss of faith, even. If any man could withstand such news and love the sinner, not merely in duty and theory but with heart and soul, it was he. Yet, to own all that *and to seek his help* – for all that could not be owned without such a request implicit – that was beyond me. Out on the blackening shoulder of the moor, alone, I did not feel the painful *presence* of shame. Now, and I hold to my resolve, the rest shall be silence.

I began to stumble as I struggled to keep to the path in the dark. No moon nor stars had come, after a brilliant day, which was curious. I perspired though in the heavy night air. Before very long I reached a point where a light could be seen. I knew it and was grateful for it and made my way downhill more confidently, though losing the light in the declivity. While I cast about in the dark shallow valley, a growl of thunder sounded.

To the extent I could have been said to have any spirit left, it was unaffected either by the sound or by the struggle to climb the rise. My feet met easier ground, signalling the edge of the parkland around Evenden Hall. I almost came to grief in a boundary ditch but it was dry. Then I saw the light again, this time much nearer. I was thankful that the servants had been so negligent as to leave one window uncurtained, shining out to guide poor travellers.

I made my way to the trees bordering the avenue. As I walked beneath them there was another roll of thunder, and the hissing rain gliding over the land caught up with me, drenching all below and myself too, without discrimination.

The avenue led to the park gates, which stood open and gave on to the road from Burlas to Frith. Emerging, I turned towards Frith.

It was for the most part a featureless route but I walked for a while with sheltering trees and rhododendrons rising higher than the wall to my right. The rain drummed on the road about me, raising spatters of mud. That my very skin was wetted I took as benediction; and if I could continue thus without thinking I did not fear the journey or the night.

I heard a faint jingling variation in the noise and turned to see a carriage – by its lights through the rain I discerned it – turn in through the gates. A dazzling flash and near-simultaneous deafening thunderclap sent the horses cantering out of sight and I heard the coachman's cries to them receding. I myself turned back towards my road, though blinking and blind for a moment and reflecting but briefly, as the explosive blast resounded yet to the very marrow of my bones, that death might be striking at me even now.

Away from the influence of the trees was a vivid light around the full horizon by which I could make my way. By degrees I gained, then passed, the low weatherbeaten church and the graveyard. Some way ahead my next landmark would be the toll bar of the turnpike trust (the nearest one remaining to Burlas, the irresistible demands of whose commerce had uprooted the others). Frequent thunderbolts circled at varying distances.

The plateau was not entirely a plain; valleys had been worn through by numberless small streams. After one sharp fall and rise in the road, finding myself by a milestone, I crossed to it to rest. Immediately on this cessation of action the rain's noise in my ears increased, and I was chilled for the first time and suddenly. I bent and with stiffening fingers sought out and traced the markings in the stone.

Three miles to Frith.

33

To shield my face for a short while from the downpour I remained bent, resting with both hands pressed down upon the milestone. In seconds, the wetness that had been on my shoulders extended over the whole of my back, my mantle and dress being no defence. My front was already soaked Now at last I began to wonder at the reality of my situation. I knew that I could continue and complete my journey, but that it was not being made easy for me. And I *must* find warm lodging at Frith, or else . . .

I remained thus while two more close flashes of lightning and thunderclaps passed, then a sequence of lights and rolls running together at a greater distance. A small sound escaped me as runnels of water made their way down my neck and inside my bodice.

All at once, a voice close behind me cried: 'Who's there?'

The chill that I had been feeling was as nothing to the freezing of all summoned courage effected by such a shock. I knew the distinct and tangible fear that the voice was inside my skull: that my last resource, my reason, had left me entirely. Then I apprehended that there was a different quality to the light now dimly shining. I managed to turn, not without another gasp.

A lamp was suspended in the air a few feet away. Its light made everything behind it black. The voice – and, impossible then to understand, it was familiar – came once more.

'I wish that you would come over here and pinch me, for I am having the most peculiar dream!'

Instead I sat on my stone and shook my head against the lamplight.

'How on earth did you find me?'

William Evenden lowered his lantern and approached.

'Well, I will tell you,' he said, speaking firmly so as to sound clear through the rain. 'But not before you are better protected from this. Here – ' He gave me the lantern to hold, while he began to remove the good rain cape from his back.

Slow to grasp his intention, too amazed by his manner as well as by his being there, I made a late protest. 'No, we shall go our different ways in a moment.'

'How so? Since evidently you *must* return with me?'

He was crouched a little now, and the light caught both our faces.

'No,' I said clearly with cold lips. 'Not you, nor anyone else, can tell me what I must do.'

We remained unblinking for a moment.

'No,' he said then. 'I see that. But this – tableau – is farcical.' He held his hand out to the rain; a very near thunderclap seemed to answer and amuse him. 'So at least consent to put this on, while I tell of this dream of mine; and I may end by begging some account of yours.'

'It will make no difference; I am soaked to the skin.'

'It will help. And even without it, my dress is more rational than yours. Come, we must have better justice.'

I suffered him then to fasten the cape about my neck, and it kept further cold replenishings from me.

'Thank you,' I said, though knowing what strange protection it was, to be with him. I cared for almost nothing, but I wished he had not appeared; I could hardly believe he had. When I studied him he showed no sign that anything extraordinary was taking place. The scene itself was a stranger to reason, or one or other of us must be.

I said, 'Speak if you can – did Macbeth say?'

'To the witch! Bravo.' (Small wonder if he like my husband perceived me now as someone to be watched and humoured.) 'Yes, I can.' He remained on his haunches, regarding me close. I looked ahead through the small circle of light into the rushing gloom

282

beyond. Even so near his voice was ringing, to rise above the noise of the storm or to fix my attention. 'I am flesh and blood. And what am I to make of this? There was I, almost at my home, having had an evening's pleasure though not too much to drink, I hope – or was it a rogue vintage? No, I was already one quarter asleep, is the most that can be said. A thunderflash startled the horses. But it was as if only *afterwards* I saw – what it was I surely could not have seen, in such a compressed instant of brilliance. I blundered to myself; the image remained burned on my brain. But it could not really – surely! – have been *she*? Standing on the road outside my gate, half-turned – so vivid – but quite impossible.'

He paused. I held still, and he went on.

'I went inside, dismissed the servants for the night, still in quite a fog about it. My reverie led me to thinking that perhaps, of all women, your circumstances – And then I thought, what had brought you to my door –'

'No!'

'Oh, metaphorically, I mean. I believe in fate, remember; though I recall that you do not.' Still the ringing tone, something both cautious and skilful, compelling. 'And in fact it was that very single thought – *fate* – that lodged in my mind and, having once settled, I knew, would not let me rest, however improbable my vision, until I had investigated further. So I made haste at last to equip myself – would you believe, with hands that trembled – as you see; and so I set out again into this night.'

There he stopped, and waited. For perhaps a minute I believed I could withstand his silence and frustrate him. Yet who, falling, can forbear from clutching, grasping?

'And such a night,' I murmured.

'What? Yes. Such a night!' There was again a brief silence. 'I almost gave up,' he went on more softly, 'when I got as far as the church finding no sign. But I think my poor brain was by then too dull to decide on abandonment all at once. So I trudged on a little, and a little. And even so, I never saw anything, but there was – just a *noise* at the side of the road! And tell me *now* that you do not believe in fate!'

Not to look round at him cost me a suppressed shiver. 'Oh, I believe in good and evil chances,' I said.

'Then, by good fortune I have found you and my quest tonight was virtue, not folly,' he answered sombrely. 'You may speak or not, on the road, as you wish, but now you must return with me.'

He had risen, and held his arm in a burlesque of chivalry before me.

I rose too and stood aside, not taking the arm he offered.

'I thought we had agreed that you could not command me,' I said. He took one step towards me which I matched at once with one back. 'Not long ago I dreamed of *you*,' I warned hastily. 'It was a nightmare.'

Looking at him I thought his eyes narrowed; he made no further move.

'If you must know my story,' I went on, 'it is short and not fantastical. A woman bolting is notable perhaps, but not so rare as all that. I do not wish it to be your affair, or anyone's but my own, and so I bid you – good night.'

I was struggling with the fastening of his cape which I wore. He merely watched for a moment. Then he said, as if it were idly, 'I will not accept it back from you. If I can bend your will in nothing else, can I not persuade you to accept the loan of it a little longer?'

So much darkness in my soul; yet he was ridiculing me.

'Do you promise then not to dispute with me further?' I said.

'With the quibble that we have not had the least part of a dispute this night – all right, I promise! I would offer the lamp, too, but I think,' he spread his hands, and cast his eyes about, 'that, alone, you would be safer unlit.'

'I will not be *frightened* from my purpose, of which I assure you the most – most desperate part is achieved –'

'Desperate? Why, what have *you* done?'

'Very little, so you may go in peace. Good night.'

I walked away along the road, where the rebounding rods of water shone before me still in the yellow light from his lamp. There was no further protest and my ears were soon insulated by the blanket of natural sound. Wildly I thought it just as well that, of all

284

acquaintance who might have come across me that night in such a chancing manner, I had met the one most exceptionally endowed with black unshockability.

After walking some hundred yards I stopped. The raindrops bouncing on the road shone as at first, and when I halted the limit to which I could see them also held steady. I turned and addressed the lamp which hung in the air.

'What does this mean? I thought that you had given your word.'

The answer came. 'I do not command you. I do not seek to argue with you. I am merely exercising the same freedom as yourself.'

I was still more peremptory. 'Why?'

'For my own reasons.'

I stood awhile perplexed, attempting to stare down the mesmerising light.

'If they depend on concern for me, you have none,' I then said. 'If you follow, it will be a dull pursuit. I wish to be alone.'

I turned and walked on, commanding my steps to be firm. The next halt came after a shorter interval. I did not turn again but spoke over my shoulder.

'Can you be serious, sir? How far will you go?'

'I find that I am serious,' he called. 'As to the distance, you know better yourself. At least to Frith, I imagine. You have some idea of a plan, perhaps? Say, to change your name, and go as a governess! Does the stage run tomorrow? . . . She will not say. I will be silent if she wishes. It will be fitting for us to pass another journey together as strangers.'

'God help me. What am I to do?'

I do not know if William Evenden heard those last words of mine; he did not acknowledge them. After a minute I began to retrace my steps, passing where he stood with his light. This time he turned to walk beside me.

We went some way in silence. At a certain point my steps slowed but I was only made aware of it through noticing that he, watching me, was slowing too. I hesitated then whether to hurry on or stop. We were by the church and the graveyard flanked the road;

headstones meant one thing only to me then, though hers was miles away. We stood for some seconds in that great emptiness, yet also near to his father and mother, and brother. He held the light up patiently; his profile was set.

I spoke with a small voice. 'What is it?'

'I am cold,' he said, 'and wet.'

We resumed the journey. The brunt of the storm had seemed over, but as his face (and at the same moment mine) returned to the front a startling bolt shot down merely feet from us. I gave an unconscious jolt – as I sensed that he surely must have also – but walked on. A little while thereafter I heard him speak.

'I wonder if we might guess which of us the thunderbolt will strike? I think by rights it should be you, since I have committed no sin this night, but rather an heroic kind of thing – so *I* would claim. But then, I am the taller.'

I made no reply. Neither of us spoke again until we stood level with the last pair of avenue trees, facing his home. There I stopped, and so did he. On turning into the gates he had shaded his lamp. The last spots of rain were falling and I spoke low into the new quiet.

'It would have been futile and undignified to have tried to outrun you.'

'I know. I do apologise.'

I looked away, momentarily, in the direction of my home. Then I turned back to face the dark, but nevertheless populated, building.

'Do you have some idea – of what to do now?'

He offered a hand. I had been clasping the cloak tight about me till then, but I dropped my hold and reached out. Our fists, fastening, were cold so as to be numb to fine shades of feeling. He led me with a soft tread to the corner of the house, thence to a long window which opened at his careful turn of the handle. Perhaps this had been the route of his earlier exit. When we were inside he stepped behind me and re-closed and bolted the window.

'Wait,' he whispered, and walked away a few steps. He took candles from the cold summer mantelpiece and lit them from his lantern, then used one in turn to light a lamp on a table in the room's centre. I watched pools of light spread about what had, in her latter days, been the court and entire living quarters of Sarah Evenden. It had, of course, changed, been cleaned and brightened once more, since my interview with her; that had seemed almost forgotten, but the memory of it returned to me now.

William came and stood before me. I was not insensible of the fact that there was, in merely practical terms, an awkward situation between us and that I was its originating cause and dependent on him for navigation out of it. My feelings toward *him* at that moment were not paramount, but such as they were they veered between obligation and alarm.

His voice was low and even. 'You will be made warm and dry. You will rest, and eat. If you decide to continue your journey in the morning, you will be helped on your way.' He paused. 'So far as it is in my power, none shall know – or at most one or two who must and who can be trusted. Do you agree to all this?'

Speech was now but a necessary burden to me. 'I am obliged to you –'

'Poppycock. I brought you here, in effect.'

He moved back to the side of the fireplace where he extended a screen, then he looked back and motioned me to approach and take up position behind it. I moved in obedience to his gesture. He caught me by the elbow as I drew level with him, and with his other hand he pulled a chair behind the screen. I was conscious of the degree of my tiredness for the first time.

'Wait,' he said once more. Hidden thus, I did not see but heard him leave the room. He returned bearing a dry greatcoat, which he gave to me. 'Take off your wet things and put this on,' he said. 'I'll ring to find if any of the servants are still up.'

He disappeared and I heard him walk to the other side of the room. I stood and went through the motions required to remove his cape, my clinging mantle, and my hat, all of which I put on the back of the chair. I then eased the greatcoat over my shoulders, feeling its satisfying weight as if it would press the very moisture and cold – and apprehension – out of me, and I put my arms through

287

the sleeves before resuming my seat. Shortly afterwards, I heard a low cough from William and he paced unhurried back to the centre of the room. I stiffened, and pressed a hand to my face. I heard the door open and someone enter.

'Yes, Mr Evenden?' It was a man's voice.

'Oh, Craig. I wondered if anyone was still up.'

'I was only waiting for the noise of the storm to pass, sir. I am sorry, I had thought you were long upstairs.'

'Yes, well, as you see I have been out – ah –' the voice was laconic, 'in ill-advised pursuit of artistic effect!'

'Can I get you anything?'

'Is anyone else still about?'

'No –'

'Then could you please have a fire lit in my room?'

'I will see to it. Will there be anything else, sir?'

'Yes. I'm afraid you must get Mrs Drake's boy up, and tell him to stand ready in the kitchen to take a letter into town for me.'

'At this hour?' Craig's tone was aggrieved.

'He can take the pony. It is dry now, and he will be back before half past one.' William affected a fine carelessness. 'He can lie in bed tomorrow, and have a sovereign for his tin.'

'Oh, he'll go, but I'll not have any lying in of the morning. I'll make the fire in your room first, and fetch you your dressing gown.'

'No, I do not need it and I would rather not be disturbed again; and *I* am not to be roused in the morning. I shall come to the kitchen with the letter shortly, if the boy will wait there.'

'Very well. Good night, sir.'

'Good night.'

There followed the sound of Craig leaving, a few seconds of silence, then William came round the end of the screen and stood before me again.

'Are not those things wet also?' He had seen the bottom of my dress showing still beneath the coat. He was shadowed, the light being behind him.

'This will do, thank you. And it will be easier to pass off, if I am discovered.'

288

'Very true,' he quickly acknowledged. 'Well, we must wait a while. If you are comfortable you had better stay there, in case my instructions are disregarded. I shall write my letter.'

'Very well.'

I watched him walk away. He took a light to the writing-table (I remembered it!) which in its place by the wall was visible from my seat. With a blank page before him he paused, then began writing and continued with few hesitations. When he had concluded he sealed the missive in an envelope and addressed it. Watching him was a matter of sufficent interest to occupy what remained of initiating power in me. It must, I knew, be a letter connected with my situation and fate, but I was not inclined to inquire or discover more. The position I was now in was far from anything predicted or planned and it was a matter of near total indifference to me what would follow. My detachment was in its nature almost scientific.

He put the finished letter in his pocket and passed a further minute tapping his fingers on the table. Then he said:

'I shall see how things stand.'

He rose and extinguished all lights bar one, and left the room. After some minutes he returned and offered me his hand, drawing me to my feet. He placed the wet outer garments over his free arm, snuffed the remaining candle, and led me out of the room.

Dimmed lights in the hall indicated cavernous openings in all directions. We crossed it and climbed the stair. I was hindered by my heavily soaked hems the swishings of which, penned by the greatcoat, echoed over-loudly. However we gained the door which I perceived to be our object without other alarm, and entered the room, wherein I found myself softly laughing.

William turned the key in the lock behind us and seeing it, hearing that sound, was like being wakened sharply after days and nights of sleep. He moved away leaving the key in the door. There was a new fire still climbing and strengthening in the grate. I crossed and knelt before it and added fuel.

There was another door to the room and by this he went out, returning with a man's long night-shirt and hose, which, with a dressing gown underneath and towels besides, he draped over a chair arm before the fire. At the unsummoned thought of him readying himself for bed I again laughed aloud, but silenced myself shortly.

'The best that I can do, I am afraid,' he said. Then he sat on the edge of the chair, bending towards me. 'There are two doors, as you see. That one is locked, and here is the key to the other.' He gave it me. 'It leads to the dressing room, and thence to a room I have turned into a kind of store and studio, where I can sleep.' He went on without pause. 'I shall go there now. Lock the door behind me, and then you must at once get out of those things and into something dry. I pray you have not already done your health mischief by this. I will see this letter is dispatched, and return with some supper for you. When you hear three knocks on the connecting door you will know that it is me.'

As he was regarding me with some concern I was again required to speak.

'Go. You need not worry; I am not so fragile as you believe.'

He answered only with a thoroughgoing look recalling old 'bad manners'. How little he had aged indeed, beside me. He left and I locked the door as instructed.

When the three knocks came I was able to answer in a presentable state, in the circumstances. The night-shirt almost reached my ankles, the dressing-gown was commodious and, tightly belted, gave the impression of a skirt. My hair hung down, but I had brushed it back as neat and flatly as may be with a man's hairbrush. My own clothes were spread before the fire. He entered with a look, I thought, of approval. He too was re-clothed, more conventionally. He bore a tray with a bottle of wine and a single goblet, a plate piled with several kinds of meats, assorted small loaves of bread and a knife.

'Lock the door,' he said, his hands being full.

We settled together on the rug, he pouring wine while I cut the bread; then he drank a little from the bottle.

'Mr Evenden,' I said, 'the glass has two sides, at least, I believe.'

'So it does. I thank you.' He took his next mouthful of wine from the glass, then exclaimed (though all our exchanges were in a tone cautiously muffled still from the natural), 'Ah! You thought it poisoned?'

'I do not think I am yet so much of a problem to you.'

He shrugged. 'Not even so much of a problem as to steal my appetite, I assure you.' He ate, indeed, with vital relish.

Bizarre to relate, I too found that I had an appetite; I would say even that meat and drink never tasted so good. Towards the end of the meal, catching his eye upon me, I knew a moment's self-consciousness, a further sign of my revival of reason.

'Would this,' I asked, spreading my arms a little, 'make a study for a narrative painting – say, "The Fallen Woman"?'

He laughed. 'No! Have you ever, knowingly, *seen* a fallen woman? No, but a study for – something – I don't know –'

I looked at the fire. 'But in the eyes of the world, having done what I have done, it might as well have been anything!'

'Not in your own eyes, or those of your friends. I have it: "The Woman Reborn"!'

' "The Woman Reborn",' I echoed, musingly. 'You could show it in Paris, perhaps. It would not be well regarded in Burlas.'

He laughed again. Then with a rapid gesture he reached out to take my chin and turn it an inch. I gave a start, as if my blood drained through his touch.

'You are afraid,' he said. 'Of me?'

The fire was past its zenith, the logs collapsing in little falls.

'No. I fear nothing that you can do.' I sighed. 'To be born again, to discover all anew – what a terrible thing.'

We sat on in silence, until at length he said, 'Good night to you, Mrs Ryder.'

I turned then to see him rise and go to the door. There he paused, as merely waiting for my salutation or considering a further, less abrupt valediction of his own. I saw him, with his fire-shadow leaping beyond; and I felt my self-created homelessness like an ocean all around.

34

'On the road you spoke of a virtuous quest,' I said. 'But you kissed me once, remember.'

That was what I said, and all that I meant. Yet it sounded different, by some accident, no doubt through my weariness and the imaginings that had been crowding me, and by one of those mischances so unlikely as to become (for certain fated souls) inevitable. So my halting voice sounded across to him as follows:

'. . . You killed – ' and in the hesitation I saw that his aspect barely changed but was charged with quick attentiveness, '– *kissed* me once, remember.'

Afraid or not, in part I wished to descry no reaction, and not to have him return to my side. He did turn. He stepped forward, halving the space between us before he halted and mused aloud.

'Virtue! The word always puts me in mind of Heracles. Do you know the story that in his youth he was approached by two beautiful maidens, Vice and Virtue? Each urged him to go with her through life, the one promising him ease and happiness, the other offering hardship, sorrow, labour and renown. He vowed to follow the path of virtue, and did so always. But he committed a great crime in the eyes of men – he killed his own family – because that was his fate. He followed the hard path, and in the end there was atonement.'

It was a wry speech, but his voice was earnest. I dropped my gaze again to the fire and spoke hoarsely.

'Heracles, indeed! And your life is not one of ease?'

'In allegory, things are not what they seem. I do not illustrate my own life, but that virtue may mean something different from what is cantingly assumed. Yes, I kissed you once. The strange thing is, that I should now find myself trying to resist you!'

'Resist,' I said, 'by all means. Do not be false to yourself.'

He approached softly until I sensed him looking down on me.

'I must be false to myself, since I am a divided soul. All this night I have been driven by my desire to perform a pure labour in your service. Yet in truth I wish, I long – to put it bluntly – to profit by it.' He half-knelt behind me, and I felt a hand on my shoulder. 'What did your heart intend, by your reminder?'

'My heart is as nothing. You must listen to your own.'

'I hear only argument.'

Yet he was patient as he waited; and there was a kind of peace in the room, though my head throbbed with his different notion of virtue and atonement. Had I not suffered? And did I seek now the hard or the easy path? Did he speak of his own great crime?

I turned to face him. With one or two hesitant movements we came together in an embrace. It was gentle, long – and mutual.

'And this is *not* your heart?' he murmured. 'If this passion is truly all negative – For myself I wish it were otherwise!'

'Then pretend, if you wish. I could not reproach you.'

Pretending, or pretending pretence, we continued.

'Surely we will not bid our good nights, now?' he asked.

'I have come to your house, eaten your food, drunk your wine, and more. My betrayal of my husband, and of myself, is already complete.'

'I forbid you to think in that way!'

'Can you stop my thought?'

He stopped my mouth, and held my head as if to spirit the grief away. He did not leave, but caressed each part of me into union in measured, full degree. It was no seduction or ravishment. I was passive and pliant, but my mind shared with his in instructing each step and affirming it.

Then I put my arms round his neck and rested my eyes in the curve of his shoulder. My lashes were wet. He pulled away to look at me.

293

'Say that I did not hurt you!' he said.

I made to reassure him. 'On the contrary, I promise you I felt nothing!' which was in some sense the truth, for his behaviour had been in no wise invasive or brutal. However, across his face flashed a delighted look of old giving some inkling of my innocent error.

' "Pretend if you wish"!' he repeated, with irony. 'You make all pretence impossible!'

He talked on, of art and beauty, angels, gods and goddesses. I wished that I was a goddess, a happy antique bather, with no concern that her single dress, caked with mud, must be put on in a few short hours for a journey into the unknown. I called him an unlikely faun, and so found that such a scene could be material even for a joke! That was the least expected revelation of the night, and we smiled together; so unschooled and ignorant did I seem.

The fire in the grate grew cold and we lay close together for warmth. The talk died and I believe we drifted together into sleep when, with his hand resting across my throat, I heard again the long-dead tones of my aunt, crisp as ever:

All but murdered in our slumber!

I awoke; I had slept for a single second. Beside me William breathed evenly, not stirring. What did it make a man, if he had killed another human creature? Murderer, yes – what besides? He had no cause to kill again, but suppose one given to him; suppose him to understand that from the next break of day the rest of my life was a burden to me? Not that I thought to seek any service of that kind, but the speculation fed on itself feverishly, in my startlement and in the dark.

I took hold of his hand, cradling the fingers, and eased it from my neck. He sighed and moved the arm about me. I raised myself a little and my lips felt for his ear.

'Did you kill your brother?' I whispered.

He lay still. I stroked his hair and kissed his cheek. I put my head again on the pillow. His arm drew back from me and he turned on to his back.

Then I heard him speak: 'I knew that you would wonder, and be the one to ask. There is that cleverness about you – and those ferreting eyes!' I felt him turn to me again, and raise himself on his elbow to lie above me; now he stroked my hair. 'Well, I killed my mother. So she always told me, and it came to pass.'

'So did I. Kill mine. No-one ever thought to fasten the guilt upon me.'

'You were a fortunate child, then.'

'Are you angry with me, so you refuse to answer?'

There was silence, though his finger moved over my face.

I spoke again. 'You made Dolly report to you about me, because you wanted to know if I suspected you.'

'That is not true.' He put his face against mine, so that I could feel his smile. 'I did it, as you know, because from the moment we met I have worshipped you.'

He turned away at once. I reached out to him.

'Do not be angry,' I said. 'It is only that, tonight, I do not care what you are, what you have done, or what you might do.'

'I know,' he said.

Despite the unease in his last words it was he who was first to fall back into sleep. Unconsciousness stalked me more warily, casting me to and fro on the border of dreams and wondering. There was a series of approaches to rest, when my thoughts turned to visions propelling me back each time to awareness of myself and the breathing man beside me in the dark, and the rest of the unsuspecting slumbering household spreading above, around, beneath where I lay.

I was entering a room where I found myself behind a chair on which sat the motionless figure of my aunt. My heart turned with the joy and relief of meeting her again, but also with fear of seeing a dead person quicken. I moved in relation to her, as if I were being pulled round in a circle always facing the chair in which she sat, or as if that seat itself slowly turned on its own. My mouth opened in torment that was the more profound for being silent, as I saw first the marble skin of her face appear, then her glazed eye, and shrank from the next sight which I knew would be the child clasped to her breast.

295

Next, after an interval of staring into darkness, I was in the gallary in the courtroom once more, amid the uproar at the conclusion of William's trial. From the dock he looked up at me in triumph. His hands could not be seen where he throttled twin snakes down below the barrier. In a moment, I knew, one hand would reach out, notwithstanding the distance, to seize my chin in a strong grip between thumb and forefinger.

Then I stood where I had never been, but in a place I recognised: before the cottage at Critchley where John Evenden had died. A man whom I identified as Mr Tutt, the detective police officer, took my hand. He led me down the path towards the door of the cottage. As we reached it, I pulled back.

'Come, now, Miss James,' he remonstrated.

'No,' I tried to explain. 'I am the doctor's wife!'

'Is it so?' he asked with smiling insolence, and proceeded to open the door.

Lastly, of what I still remember, I was again in the room with my aunt, continuing to circle round her or, transfixed, watching her turn. At length I saw her full face, grim and unanimated, and the burden in her arms was revealed. The 'child' was a miniature figure of my husband, unclothed, or draped all in white – somehow, I could not tell.

At the next wakening I felt again the warm life at my side. By chance, William moved a little in sleep at that moment. Remembering again where I was and all that had passed, one thing struck me for the first time as more strange than all the rest: in all of that night not once had he troubled to question or seek *my* motives for the step I had taken – so extreme as it was!

The birds were awake, and daylight entered through cracks, long before I found oblivion.

35

I woke, unrested, and it was with a pang that I found myself alone. I acknowledged then that William for long had been the pattern of my desire; though a few short hours before I had listened in silence to his regret that it was not so.

I rose and set about clothing myself in my dried raiment. I was not concerned as to my present position and prospects, immediate or otherwise, but operated once more under the inchoate impulse that had driven me from my home the previous evening. There was a fresh urgency and strength to it, in my awareness of the pulse in me that beat for William – still not knowing what wrong he had done, or could do. I knew for sure that he would never, could never bring himself to answer the question I had put so woundingly.

As for the man whom I had called husband, and regarded as such until the last second before my betrayal, I thought I must have a heart that loved him still – and my dear child. Only I seemed to have no heart, as I busied myself in the strange room. A mere chill cavity had housed itself in me.

I am discredited utterly with any reader, of no matter what persuasion, for stating the truth: that while yet married to one who never dishonoured me I was both repelled by him and sensible of the attractions of another. Set aside my actions, the contents of my mind alone are damning. What is to be done? Why was I so tested – only, being female, to learn *not* to know myself?

I was indeed sick, recognising the banality – on any proper view – of what had been uncovered in me. I have expressed it thus: the pattern of my desire. I cannot elaborate. Such feeling never allows for just and true description. If I tried to be particular even as to the sight, the sense of him, to me, I would seem to recreate such another pathetic monster, ill-composed of select details, as is too familiar in works of *fiction*. All those over-particularised automata I now think to be ill-judged monuments to real loves or longings. From this, my true account, I believe little more can be known than that one man had yellow curls and the other was dark; and that is meant.

I opened the curtains and shutters a fraction and settled to wait beside the now unwarming grate. I heard a knock on the dressing room door and kept silent and still. The key turned gently in the lock and William entered.

I perceived that to him my present habit and manner might be deemed incongruous: demure and forbidding. He spoke with some measure of gravity, though merely asking if I was well. I answered him.

'I must leave now, by some means without damage to your interest, if I am to catch the coach at Frith. Last night, you mentioned – ' I was curiously shy to ask an open favour. 'Can you assist me on my way there?'

'I can do better. Dolly will be here shortly in answer to my note. I trust her to respond precisely to instructions which are mysterious, urgent and secret. She will be ready to accompany you so far as may be helpful – to stay with you, if you will allow.'

'I am more grateful than I can say. But I rather think I should go alone. This business should not touch my friends; I do not consider that either of you have any share in my crime. Certainly she does not.'

'I believe you do not yourself, unaided, have the first idea of where to go or what to do. Do you imagine that I could desert you now, after last night – and even without that, after you stood by me?'

I could no longer meet his eyes. 'As you know, I have doubted you.'

'But you have not judged.'

A welter of thoughts was quelled, before I murmured, 'I cannot allow you to be identified with my – It would not be just –'

'For God's sake, Katherine, we are not counting out some dole of obligation here!'

After that small explosion the room resounded, principally with the echo of my name: Katherine. Always before he had addressed me as Mrs Ryder, or long before as Miss James, and but once or twice Vengate. A degree of formality had been preserved between us long after it was natural. So now I was sensibly moved, hearing my given name on his lips for the first time. I answered him something. I cannot remember what, but in the course of it I deliberately named him too: William.

He reconnoitred the stairs and passageways, then I was hurriedly spirited back to the drawing room. The screen was positioned as before, and at a knock I hid. Miss Bowlby was announced. She entered; the servant was dismissed. I revealed myself.

William explained to her the full purport of his note of the previous night: '. . . Katherine must be helped to leave, and to stay in safety somewhere away from Burlas for a while.' His explanation hung flat in the air as something unnecessary. She looked at me, as I reddened, throughout; and I knew that, whatever his letter had left unsaid, she took in everything: my dress, everything.

'Now, let us say Katherine has just arrived on foot and been summoned in by us.' He crossed to open the French-style door onto the terrace. 'We must order something – some refreshment.'

He was about to pull the bell-rope when there was another knock followed by the quick entrance of Craig. Seeing me, he gave his message in a dry and insinuating tone.

'Doctor Ryder is here, sir, and asking to speak with you.'

William barely looked at him. 'Just show him into the library,' he said, with discernible emphasis on the first word.

With a grimace Craig went out. William and I looked at each other.

Dolly made her first sound, quietly. 'Well. What did you expect?'

299

William came across to me, so that we could all three converse in whispers. 'Do you wish to see him?' he asked me.

'No! – Yet I believe I must.'

'No,' he said. 'Say not what you must, but – ' and his voice became *very* low, breaking almost, with a sensibility that left its impression upon me in just such a half-disbelieved instant as he had described seeing me by thunderflash a few hours before, '– what you *will* do!'

To that, I found I could say nothing.

'Well, it is simple enough. A few moments later, and he would have missed you. It shall be as if he had,' he said.

He was ready to move when Dolly's voice arrested the pair of us. 'Kitty, I have asked nothing. Answer me just this: has Henry ever given you cause, that you should fear him?'

Still for a moment I was silent. It seemed my frame was ready to give way at last under its load. Watching me so closely William cupped his hands about my head.

'My God!' he said. 'Then his life is forfeit!'

That strengthened me. For a sharp second I looked my pity and contempt back at him. 'It would be a more friendly act to kill me, I think. My husband never gave anyone cause!'

The truth of each word may have stunned him momentarily. Then William turned and left us.

Dolly, as if it were the most natural thing in the world, took my hand and led me across to the closed double doors which connected the drawing room with the library. There we stood, bending close to the keyhole. I strained to hear, and to endure what I heard.

When I first heard the voice of my husband he spoke not with deference, but in a tone that recalled something of past deference uttered in that house.

'My wife is missing.'

'Oh. Since when?' William must be duplicitous, though his answer was a question not a lie.

'Her bed was not slept in last night.'

'And why have you come to me?'

'Merely because, I regret to say, someone recently told me, or warned me, that you –'

He said something more, of which the clear sense was lost in a low, quiet delivery; similarly, William's immediate brief answer was no more, to us, than a single questioning tone, but it perhaps prompted Henry to raise his voice once more so that we heard his next words:

'Improper and immoral, as regards another man's wife.'

Dolly's hand tensed on my shoulder. I looked and saw sudden frustration and annoyance in her face quickly smoothed over when she caught my eye. I had not the leisure to puzzle over her.

William spoke again. 'May I ask from whom you heard this?'

'I will not say. Is it true?'

'I will not say! Besides I must first ponder what can be meant by it: improper *and* immoral! Can there be any help for a spontaneous mental response, Doctor? And if not, can anyone be blamed for such? Are we not judged by our actions?'

'If it comes to, say, murder, or adultery, then I judge the will to commit murder, or adultery, as the uncompleted act. Do you know where my wife is, sir?'

'I will not say.' He was, I sensed, being as scrupulous as he could, and his tone now affected lightness but strove to avoid condescension. I understood the care, and that much of it was care on my behalf – not only as one he shielded physically, but as a listener susceptible to the pain of new wounds, even to Henry's dignity. With an echoing care I held still, though tears broke and ran down my cheeks.

'Then it is true, and you do know where she is. Is she in this house?'

I wondered that Henry's state of heart and mind, after so short a parting, could be more of a mystery to me than the other man's; yet the very restraint with which he put the question pulled on me. My mouth opened, soundlessly; at once Dolly placed her hand over it, without force but with authority. Her collusion in this business, so newly disclosed to her as it was, reflected an instinct unthinking yet

301

strong. Her present reaction, more than any past thing, revealed what close and secret ties bound her to William!

Again part of the exchange was muffled or misheard. It may be that one speaker turned away, and the other followed. I believe there were also passages of actual silence. To me, it was a sequence of new eternities, between each inconclusive noise. I could not know what expressions, gestures, or wrestling for composure might be taking place. I had the greatest sense of William's dilemma, but had more difficulty visualising Henry's. It was my husband who next spoke clearly, and still with calm in his voice.

'I will say this, Evenden. There is no cause and was no warning of her behaviour in this. As you know, we have suffered a loss, and for that and other reasons my observation of her recently may have been clouded.'

My shaking now made Dolly grip me tighter, for he spoke of my Alice!

'But there is no estrangement,' he continued, 'no shadow of one. I can only think that she is affected in her wits. My need to find her is strong, but her need of me must be stronger. I don't know for certain what game you have played, but I will not give her up. I must recover her. That I could be deprived in this way is too wrong and unjust to contemplate –'

'And I will say this, Ryder. Your wife has asserted a claim to be free of you. She is gone from here' (he lied then, for me) '– and it will be for her to decide for how long she stays, when, how or if she contacts you again. To talk of justice or the niceties of good conduct when a feeling creature is at such a pitch is to be blind to humanity to such a degree I pity you, and I begin to understand that perhaps a form of pity for your blindness was the reason she ever cared for you at all.'

'I don't know what language you speak, sir, but it is not that of England, as you will find. You know more, and I will have it out of you. I am not afraid of you, or of the consequences. You have risen very high since she saved you from your deserts, but you stink of the same filth –'

'Leave my house.'

'I believe you will follow her, too, like a beast on the scent. Well, you may get down with her, or more likely tread her under before this is through, since she is not and shall not be free!'

'You will reflect more on this. The only justice can be in the damages payment. You have lost her, and if you refuse to divorce you cripple yourself, for which I care nothing. But as for *her*, I promise you, she will be, and is, free.'

'It is not freedom, to be dealing out pain. I know about pain: as to that, I am not blind; I know what faces me and I care nothing for payments and the law.'

'You will be seen out. Shall it be by force?'

'I am going. But I will *never* leave you in peace.'

There was the noise of his departure. Dolly and I waited until the silence had been unmistakable for some minutes. There were all the dense noises of high summer issuing through the open window, yet the silence was heavy. I have recollected the words exchanged, those recorded above, quite exactly; there may have been more now forgotten, as with all scenes merely enacted in memory. We stood back as we heard William's touch on the handle of the double doors. He came in, pulled the doors to behind his back, and gave a look both serious and whimsical.

None of us spoke for a while. I sat down, on one of those flimsy chairs kept in great houses for ornament. He reached out a hand and I held it. Dolly turned and paced a few steps away from us. He watched her.

'Why did you tell him?' he asked.

'Oh,' she uttered a sigh, 'not because I meant any harm to come to him, or you. It was just a few weeks ago. I had reason to consult him professionally. There were certain alarming symptoms – and I have had such good health for so long! I told myself – you know, one never likes to think of oneself as merely selfish and afraid – that it could not happen now, when my friends seemed to need me so much. So I had become very upset about it and I sent for him. He was able to reassure me almost immediately. It was nothing. There would be no need to alarm my friends. I was impressed, and so grateful and relieved, and all at a time of such sadness and difficulty for him. I had a sense of guilt, and I thought it would do no harm, and possibly some good, for the blind man to have his eyes opened a little. After all, Will, you were not plotting and planning, were you? I did not act against you.'

It must be true then, that William had cared for me more than he should and had told her of it – But while she had been speaking new pains had come upon me, as the sickening remembrance came of what had followed from her caution to Henry. I was as one hearing encoded messages, while trying to decipher another that had been given out by my husband in recent days.

William asked only, 'What *symptoms?*'

'Foolish ones. They are gone. It has all been nothing but foolishness. I regret it, but how were we to know?'

'There should have been no secrets between us,' he urged.

'I agree! But I think *mine* was a very small secret – and after all what difference does it make, except for him coming here earlier than he might have done? I too do not know what game the two of you have played,' Dolly went on tersely, still addressing her remarks to him alone, not me, 'but you had better look to your lady.'

When Dolly drew his attention to me, it was as if he forgot her existence entirely, intense as their exchange had been. He bent beside me. My last words to him had been in anger. Now he touched my cheek, and I his.

'Do you think it is true – that I am mad?' I asked.

He said, 'Insanity may be in the air. For me nothing has been reliably fixed and rational since – the time we first met! So it is all one.'

I dropped my hand and closed my eyes for a time, and we were quiet.

There was a knock and Craig entered the room. It would not be true to say that I did not care any more as to my position and his look, but I cared much less than I might have done.

'Excuse me, sir,' he said. 'There is a man up on the moor now, watching the house. I believe it is Doctor Ryder. The girls are alarmed, because I let slip to them that it looked to me as if he was armed.'

'Armed!' Dolly made a move.

'Wait; stay away from the window!' William called to her. 'Do you think he knows that you are here?'

Dolly merely looked at him, but Craig answered.

'No, sir. Leastwise, the post carrige was sent round into the stable yard when Miss Bowlby arrived. The doctor walked up to the house from this side, off the moor.'

William asked for the sply-glass to be fetched from the library table, and with it he stepped to the open long window, and leaned, for steadiness, against the frame as he put it up to his eye. Keeping back, watching him, I believed his alarm to be not unmixed with satisfied male instinct, at the turn events were taking.

'Hard to tell,' he said, lowering the glass. 'Craig,' he added incongruously, 'have toast, and coffee, brought up for these ladies, will you?'

'Yes, sir.' Craig departed.

'Well,' Dolly asked with aggrieved irony. 'How is Kitty to be got away, now?'

'He does not know that either of you is here,' said William. 'I think he is waiting to see if I should leave; though he is mad to show himself so. He will not harm me if he wants to find his wife through me. I shall go up there, and take him on.'

Dolly looked at me. 'Do not be alarmed; no harm will come,' she made to reassure me.

'You heard what terms he used! It is true enough that the man does not deserve to live,' William protested.

I was, to quote something of his phrase to Henry, at a certain pitch. I was revolted by the casual expression of his sentiment, and showed my feeling.

'You know nothing of him, William! He is a saint.'

He looked up like a spoiled child, then bowed his head. 'You are right. But *you* cannot go to him, certainly, until his passion has cooled. I mean only to try to draw him away. Then when you have

305

breakfasted, you can make haste to Frith. You are to catch the stagecoach, if you can,' he explained to Dolly.

She looked at him intently. 'Will – is it indeed quite safe for you to go after him, after that scene?'

'I shall not be spoiling for a contest. I shall pretend not to see him, as long as I can, and make him follow me while I stroll out to do some sketching.'

He rose and left us, leaving doors open, coming and going as he gathered his things. Dolly and I sat in silence, both uncertain as to his temperament for the plan, and its wisdom; but there was no alternative. The coffee was brought, and toast in a covered dish, and remained untouched. When ready, William went to the window again. He informed us that the figure could no longer be seen, but said we should remain out of sight of that side of the house nevertheless.

I had not seen Henry since the previous evening. I had heard his disembodied voice, his rising anger like something released, long buried. As I looked toward the window I knew his watching presence. The very sky's azure was like his eyes.

William stood before us. 'Until we three meet again!'

I stood at last and embraced him, and felt his arms respond and tighten about me. Only when they loosened did we exchange whispers.

'I will follow you, when it is safe,' he said. 'But shall I await your word, if it will come?'

'What you will. Or – I will write to you. Stay for that.'

With my face against him, I heard him say, 'Dolly – thank you.'

Just as he pulled apart he pressed a small paper package in my hand and he muttered quickly, not looking at me or brooking any question:

'Do not think me morbid but there is very little time for this; I had hoped for more! The note explains.'

Then he left us, but Dolly impulsively ran into the hall after him. Through the doorway I heard them murmuring, saw her give him something, and heard him laugh. As he turned I saw that it was a small gun, which he put in his pocket. Dolly stared after him. She looked anxious, and as if aged.

She returned and we sat in silence. The paper he had given me lay unconcealed in my hand, under her gaze. Without much evident will she urged me to eat, but I shook my head. The silence resumed and continued. Deliberately, I unwrapped the outer sheet of the package. There was writing on its underside, but within was a further sealed envelope addressed more neatly to 'Thos. James Esq., Solicitor' – !

I stared at it, then read the outer note:

I wish this one service of you, that whenever you can you shall address this to your father. May it be enclosed in a note of your own? I know the difficulties, but I think I know your hopes – You have helped me to a new resolve (– to another one, I should say, since the greater one is so plain!). Reasons of pride that seemed adequate before, in my present pass are not so. What more to say? What have we done? But I know what, and pray you will be glad of it as I am, come what may.

Dolly announced that we must be gone. Servants were summoned and the carriage ordered round. She took me in hand like a child and I submitted accordingly. As our conveyance moved off she looked steadily out of the window. I murmured her name; she did not hear.

'Dolly,' I urged more loudly. 'Was William with you, the night his brother was killed?'

She gazed at me then, wide-eyed. 'Why, you always knew my testimony, and you have never asked – !' Then she added, in a flat, offhand way, looking out of the window again, 'Yes. Yes, he was.'

I did not expect her to speak again, but to my surprise I felt my hand taken in hers, though roughly enough.

'I think you may trust whatever he has told you. For now, you must be got out of harm's way. I know a place . . .'

I made no enquiry of her, but was borne away.

*

307

Those events in my life which influenced the fate of Henry Ryder have now been told. The rest is no-one's business but my own. If the account even as it stands is opened to any rational eyes it will be suppressed as a loathsome aberration of nature, rightly repugnant to those of normal sensibility.

It remains only to face the one question in true justice yet before me. Knowing all, what of the evil that befell would I now turn back and see changed, if I could? Unto the last, the worst of this my account abides with me: that *I cannot say*.

PART 5

17th AUGUST 1870

36

Walking to his office early, Tutt had sensed the smoke of Burlas industry settling comfortably beneath the cloud cover. For him, the oppressive heat of the previous few days had been an alien invader from the furnace (as he pictured it) of the continent. He was not built to withstand it; neither was the town. There was a small sense of relief in finding it had retreated in the night.

'. . . The proximate or direct cause of death, therefore, is quite clear, and as you expected to find.'

Doctor Maugham, seated at the far side of the desk, spoke sombrely.

'Yes,' said Tutt, 'as we all assumed. What did you say was the name of the particular agent?'

'Strychnine: a natural poison of formidable power. It is obtained from certain beans growing on the islands of the western Pacific Ocean.'

'Who obtained it, I wonder?'

'Anyone with access to Ryder's dispensary, I would hazard. I keep some myself; it has its medical uses, in low concentration and in cases otherwise hopeless, as a cathartic. But this was no case of accidental misuse. The uningested matter in his mouth, and the surface of the relish in the jar, both contained traces in the pure form; the test for that is very simple. Strychnine has an exceptionally bitter taste, though admixing it with the relish may have helped mitigate that. A morsel would be sufficient; when you yourself handled the knife and jar it is fortunate you did not think to try

311

tasting a speck! The body shows all the signs of the typical consequences.'

Tutt's mouth was dry. 'Which are, or would be – ?'

'Inevitable and direct. Death follows instantly, caused by a single spasmodic paralysis of the brain and of all vital operations of the body.'

The two men shared a few seconds' silence, staring variously at the mess of papers on the desk.

'Thank you,' said Tutt.

'For very little, I think,' said Maugham. 'The conclusion at least as to proximate cause is the plainest possible.'

'Nevertheless, it is a grim business, and I thank you. I am sorry I troubled you to come here; I should have thought to come to your surgery this morning.'

'No trouble, I assure you!'

'I mean, for a particular reason.' Tutt fidgeted but did not delay himself long. 'I believe some three months ago you carried out a post mortem examination on the Ryders' child, a girl. I may require you to consult your notes on that –'

'I doubt it,' said Maugham sharply.

Tutt looked up startled.

The other man offered a thin smile. 'I only mean that I doubt I would need to refer to my notes. What do you wish to know?'

'If the cause of death was as clear, in that case, and what it was; whether there are any grounds for suspicion regarding, say, the treatment the girl received – ?'

'I can answer in every particular. The cause of death was atrophous degeneration of the heart muscle, a congenital disorder, quite rare, but following an entirely conventional path to the expected fatal outcome. Nothing suspicious, as you put it. She had the best of care.' Maugham's voice had a remote quality. He took a breath before continuing. 'She had the best of care; and if I had a child sick, I would have Ryder provide the treatment before myself, if I still could. You may have heard of some recent debating about his methods and his zeal – some remarks attributed to me,

312

perhaps – but I must tell you: his was the greatest talent, and the greatest will to do right, medically speaking, that I ever saw.'

Tutt said, 'I assure you I never meant to imply anything against the doctor himself.'

'Did you not? Well, there are other failings, for which we may condemn – Here is my report.' Maugham passed a card folder across the desk.

Tutt opened it and began to read the single sheet of small, punctilious handwriting.

'You will see,' said Maugham, 'that I have included some references extraneous to the proximate cause. They may have a bearing at the inquest, though at this stage I have refrained from drawing certain conclusions. As *you* will know, it is always a delicate matter.'

Tutt, distracted between Maugham's speech and his writing, took a moment to look up and respond, 'Indeed. Quite so.'

Maugham rose to depart. 'If I might suggest – ' he began, then hesitated.

'Yes, Doctor?'

'If you could locate my colleague's own records: his ledgers and case notes – He was always quite insistent on comprehensive documentation of every decision, every intervention, even,' Maugham gave an awkward twitch, intended to be a disarming laugh, 'in the simplest cases. You may find it useful; and if I may, I should certainly value the opportunity at a later stage to study his papers. In due course, I am sure, the appropriate thing will be to have them deposited with one of the institutions.'

Tutt had risen also. 'I cannot say as to that.'

'The property in them would normally speaking go to the widow, I suppose.' Maugham stood still, reflecting. 'A pleasing woman, with a quick understanding; but has that unfortunate manner, in a lady, of looking *back* at one, you know. She was wrong for him, I suspect. She would want to be inside a fellow's head. Most men are not comfortble with that, except only now and then.' He smiled. 'She is an after-dinner specimen, I would say!'

'Is that what you call it?' The two shook hands. 'I will see you at the inquest.'

After the doctor left, Tutt re-read his report, before rousing himself and preparing to go out. Then Otley entered.

'I am glad I caught you, sir.'

He leaned on the desk, excited and a little breathless. He had raced back with fruits of his warranted search of Evenden Hall. There was nothing of direct assistance, but plenty that was 'circumstantially useful' as he put it: confirmation of depravity and obsession. One alcove contained nothing but the unfinished portrait in oils of Mrs Ryder, and a box holding pencil sketches of her, old and new, and letters whose common factor was only that they all included some reference to her. In the same room there was a quantity of obscene material – none of it, alas, featuring her, but –

Otley, Tutt perceived, stumbled excitedly over the name of Miss Bowlby. Besides his awareness of her involvement in the escape of Katherine Ryder, Otley had studied to impress by acquainting himself intimately with all the old doubts over the case five years ago. He bore with him some of the material. Tutt took it from him and laid it on the desk, in its wrapper.

Otley then produced from his pocket a handbill on orange paper.

'Do you know these are all over town this morning, sir? Asking people to look out for lost property on the moor, particularly a firearm, and to hand it in to the police. Hope it won't cause us too much bother. Miss Bowlby offers a reward, for evidence as to the incident in which –'

'– Mr William Evenden suffered grievous injury, on the fifteenth instant. I know.' Tutt pushed the morning newspaper across the desk. Miss Bowlby's advertisement was displayed there also.

'I see, sir.'

'You'd better advise the men, in case anyone comes in with anything. And send someone up to the moor to see what's afoot.'

'Shall I go myself?'

'No; I have another job for you . . .'

After Otley had gone Tutt examined the drawings he had left. Probably, he thought, the boy had imagined that, beneath their costumes, women over thirty were made up of twisted iron. Tutt sorted the papers, with various others, into his bag and set off.

Katherine Ryder had been allowed to spend the night at her home, with a constable posted guard to warn off the curious, and paradoxically to advertise official interest in her. She had also been permitted – there could be no objection – to send for Mercy Meadows.

As Tutt walked up Water Lane a cab drove past. At a small cry from the interior it drew up ahead of him. Miss Bowlby descended, paid off the driver and joined him. It was plain that she had something to say.

'Good morning.' He tipped his hat to her.

'Good morning, Inspector. You have seen my advertisements? Has there been any response?'

'None as yet. The office has not been open long; but let us be hopeful.'

'Oh, yes. Let us, indeed.'

Her voice betrayed some surprise – she contrived to half-smother it; she would hate to be caught openly patronising him.

She went on. 'We need just that something more, I thought, to clear up that part of the business in William's favour. You will understand why my efforts have been concentrated there, since it was I who put the smoking weapon in his hand!' She shook her head. 'So many innocent errors!'

'As you say.'

'I am sure that we have both now been busy on the poison question.'

'*You* have?'

'Of course. Did I not undertake to give it some thought? Both Kitty and Mercy are in the firing-line, so to speak; so my interest extends everywhere, and I assure you it is very deep.'

'Yes, both of them would be in it. And William Evenden.'

She smiled, as at the opportunity for a diversion from serious

315

labours. 'Really, you must have him, still, for one thing or another, mustn't you?'

He gave an answering smile, but said nothing.

'Well,' she went on, 'as for the poisoning business – we shall continue to assume that it is poison. If so, I believe I have calculated what must have happened. There is only one aspect that is less than satisfactory.'

'You are otherwise satisfied?'

'Now, you know that it must be universally acknowledged a great tragedy. He was young and promised much. I am pursuing an argument, and speaking here of the sufficiency of the argument to its purpose.'

They both moved slowly up the paved incline; she too had spoken evenly. Now she awaited some concession of interest. They marked together six or seven more paces.

'I'll tell you what he did,' he then said. 'He drew a picture of me once. What they call a *caricature*.'

'He did what?'

'I apologise. I was thinking of Mr Evenden still. Pray continue. What matter is it that still troubles you?'

She looked at him. 'Merely, his reasons or motive. I can see some, but not sufficient.'

'It may not be necessary to produce reasons, as well as everything else, depending on the strength of your proof. Reasons are something that may well be said to be yet in the province of the Lord.' Then, heavily, he yielded: 'Well. Sufficient for what?'

'I believe, first, that the examination of Henry's body will reveal the poison to have been one which takes effect rapidly. I am no expert but it was not, for example, arsenic.'

'That much is obvious.'

'Easy for you to say, Inspector! As I said, I am no expert. Mercy and I spent some time yesterday going over the exact state in which the two of you found him. Do not underestimate her, incidentally. I have always found Mercy to be possessed of a sensitive, observant intelligence.'

'I assure you that I think very highly of Miss Meadows.'

'It was itself a merciful death – so swift that Henry, a doctor, and a good, sober, level-headed one, was incapable even in his agony of emptying his mouth of the matter that remained there. Some dribbled out afterwards.'

His stomach soured anew at the memory. 'Yes?' he said.

'Yet slow enough, you think, to allow him to take up his pen and continue writing?'

'I see your point. There is an apparent inconsistency.'

'A very real one, and in your heart you know it. It teaches us several things: first, that Henry took his own life; second, that he was not overly endowed with physical courge; third, that he was an expert on the easiest means to effect his own end, and had those means to hand. Of course, he was a doctor; and we know that where there is both poison and a medical man in a case it is ten guineas to a sixpence that the one was administered by the other –'

'Wait!'

They both stopped. He faced her, and for a moment groped for an opening.

'Did you – sleep well, Miss Bowlby?'

'Why, what do you think? Not a wink!'

'You see, that is it. I do not know what to think where you are concerned. I can believe it possible that you mean to be helpful. I would go so far as to say that you have been. But you should consider me also. It is my task that you set about, the business *I* am charged with; and you go at it to serve your interest. I have never been sure what your interest is.'

She blinked at him. 'My friends are my interest, and naturally I serve it.'

'While I serve only my duty.'

'Ah, duty –!'

'Take me back to what I think was your first proposition. Why are you so sure that Doctor Ryder – laid violent hands upon himself?'

'Why, because he was at such pains to set the scene. He even began an apparently untroubled report followed by a last – ' she rolled her eyes, 'tormented message, before any poison touched his lips! If those last poor scribblings were to any purpose, it can only have been to create an impression as unlike self-killing as possible, and perhaps to raise in you precisely those disgraceful suspicions which I know you outlined to Mercy yesterday: that Kitty poisoned both husband and child.'

He did not reply, but turned aside to continue his progress towards the house. Again she fell in step beside him. At their destination, Tutt exchanged brief words with his man on duty, then he rang and they were admitted by Mercy. From her they learned that young Mrs Ryder was with her father upstairs. Old Mrs Ryder, the doctor's mother, had arrived and taken over the parlour, preparing it to receive the master's corpse; she had enlisted Mercy's help in that.

Tutt stood a moment considering.

'Then I shall stay in the consulting room for now, if I may. The study, do you call it?'

'Yes, sir. This way.'

'Thank you, I recall the way. Miss Meadows,' he called to stop her from walking away at once. 'Er – how was the prayer meeting? Mrs Ryder spared you as promised, I hope.'

'I am afraid the speaker did not appear. It was not a wasted evening, but less comfort than I had hoped. I came back early. If that is all, I shall go back to Mrs Ryder – Mrs Ryder senior; she's brought a deal of funeral cloths, and they are all to be draped –'

He indicated at once that she could go. He had wanted only to feel a little more at ease with her, if possible, in the face of the self-contained, self-effacing manner she wore.

Miss Bowlby shook her head in Mercy's direction. 'I have always wondered what need such a woman had of so many prayers!'

Together, they entered the room where Ryder had died. Tutt stood examining the desk, then looking out of the window. He sat down where the doctor had been sitting, placing a hand before him where the head had slumped. He had brought his case of papers with him and he placed it on the floor beside his chair.

'We must consider all possibilities, you understand. It is possible

318

that a murderer might have come afterwards and forged the final words,' he said.

'I cannot think why. A murderer would thus lose all the advantage of placing the poison in advance and getting away. And Mercy is certain that no-one else was about. But I am glad to see that you have such a scrupulously open mind.' Miss Bowlby remained standing, watching him.

'Oh, there are always the devil of a number of possibilities to consider. Persons acting in concert . . . You said, you were stumped for a motive?'

'Not altogether. I can see why he wanted to cover up the suicide; it would be as great a scandal as Kitty's desertion, and I am sure that Henry cared above all for his reputation. By any standards, given his origins, he had risen to giddy heights. That is in large part thanks to his marriage. I can see his motive for wanting to lay his death to her charge, out of spiteful revenge – to his mind justified, no doubt. I believe William says he uttered some obscure threat against her; is not something like that in William's statement? Of course, he similarly tried to fasten William's own shooting on William! By then, his mind must have been in panic, and losing what little originality it possessed. In both cases, he was half-hearted; by instinct, he seems to have left a trail quite obviously false.'

Tutt raised his eyebrows, and permitted himself an inaudible snort. 'So – your difficulty – ?'

' – Is with the self-destruction itself. The desertion, even following on a bereavement, to me does not seem enough, not for one of his temperament. His relations with others were faultless, but he never himself depended in any degree on external relations. I believe he was essentially a coward. Yet, this was not the act of one. Some would call it so, but not I . . . As the injured party, the obvious course would be to stand fast and redeem himself; it would not have taken long; he would have had all the sympathy. Oh, and to a lesser extent, I am puzzled by the sudden assault on William. I heard their exchange that morning. They were aroused, but neither of them murderous. If anything, Will was more – oh, I can tell you now, I feel sure. Henry said nothing to alter Kitty's view – as stated immediately afterwards, I remember – that her husband was a *saint*.'

'Indeed? You gave Evenden the gun, I assume because you thought he might require it in his own defence.'

'I was anxious, but never truly expected – Had I done so, Will would have had to kill me first, before – !'

'I believe you.'

Miss Bowlby, seeming to have finished at last, had lapsed into silence. Tutt lifted his little case onto the desk, the better to open it and sort the contents.

'Ah, yes. I should return these to you.' He crossed to where she sat, and handed her the sheaf of drawings. She edged them sufficiently open, with a finger, to see what they were, then looked in him from under her brows, a glint in her eye.

He coughed. 'I know that they are not your property, strictly speaking; but I trust that you will do what you think best. I would venture to suggest that you should retain them, given the new – circumstances?'

She smiled. 'Thank you. I will.'

'And – one final matter. This *is* your property.'

From one of his pockets he pulled her gun and held it out to her. She took it, and opened her drawstring bag to put it away. He walked over to the glass-fronted dispensary cabinet and tried the door; it was locked.

'You calculated well, from the evidence,' he said. 'The poison was one of instant effect.'

'I beg your pardon?'

'Doctor Maugham tells me it was strychnine. These labels are all in some form of code – ' He was peering near-sightedly through the glass.

'Don't you think you should tell Kitty?' she said firmly.

'I was just going to send for her anyway.' He rattled the cabinet doors again. 'Oh, I don't like to call Miss Meadows away from her work again, so soon. As you are a friend, I wonder if you would be so good?'

320

With a look of impatience she left the room at once. She returned shortly with the young Mrs Ryder. Mr James followed them in.

'Good-day to you, sir.' Tutt shook his hand. 'Mrs Ryder, I expect Miss Bowlby has told you what has been learned this morning. I need access to this cabinet. I wonder if you can help?'

Without a word she fetched a small key from a corner of a drawer in the desk, and used it to open the cabinet doors. Tutt went to stand beside her, considering the ranks of bottles and jars.

'We may still require some expert help – ' he began.

She reached and took down a small bottle, labelled in scarlet ink, from the top shelf.

'I think you may find this is the one,' she said very softly, handing it to him. 'Take care with it, Mr Tutt.'

'Kitty!' her father exclaimed. 'Inspector Tutt, if you mean to trap my daughter in some way, in her present state I think it most improper –'

'Mrs Ryder told me, yesterday, everything she knew of these preparations,' said Tutt. 'But do you know, Mrs Ryder, if there is an account somewhere of what is actually contained in them?'

She pulled open a drawer at the base of the shelves. It contained nothing but a large bound ledger. She took the book out and held it, studying its cover before handing it to him.

'You will probably find it in here,' she said. 'He told me he kept an exact account of everything dispensed.'

Tutt put the poison bottle down on the desk, and opened the book to read.

'Well,' he said, 'there is no entry for the fifteenth of August at all; I dare say that was not to be expected.' He leafed back through several pages. The others were silent. 'Have you ever looked in this?' he asked.

'No. I never did.' She spoke as softly as at first.

'Do you know, some of these entries are so clear, even such a dull workaday fellow as I can understand! Here, your own name appears –'

'I am sure.'

'Then, going back some months now, Alice Ryder – yes, many times, and the account tells of how her illness progressed, in various particulars.'

He saw that she was shivering.

'Now,' he said, stopping at another page, 'this expressly records that certain medicines were administered at Heysham – it was indeed in early spring, was it not? – by the agency of Miss Mercy Meadows. And here is a mystery explained. Doctor Ryder himself administered an additional higher dose of the same physic, it seems.' Tutt shook his head. 'It must have been awkward for him, to find your servant so conscientious as to notice it in the way she did.'

Katherine Ryder was staring. '*He – ?*'

Tutt now put the heavy book, open, on the desk, and invited her to look. 'He took the same medicine himself; you will see it, and others, identified against his own name as patient, in many other entries. He was ill, Mrs Ryder. Did you not know? If you had ever looked in here, he makes no secret of it.'

Turning the pages slowly, she did not answer. A powerful shuddering came over her in waves.

Into the silence Henry Ryder's mother exploded; rustling through the door in her capacious mourning costume like a giant beetle. She walked straight up to Tutt, ignoring the others.

'Well, sir?'

'Ma'am.' He bowed his head to her.

'Of course, I heard your arrival fifteen minutes ago at least; since then I have been kept waiting. Are you not here with news for me? Have your people done nothing, yet?'

'I am sorry indeed for the delay. I know you are anxious for news. I – do now believe my principal investigations are complete.'

'Then you can take her away; and when she is clear of the place the body may be brought here. I am prepared.'

'I fear that may not be. It will be for the coroner, but he may order the body not to be released in this case.'

She stared at him in utter mystification.

'Poor Henry,' murmured Mr James.

Tutt went on. 'Doctor Ryder died of strychnine poisoning, but he was in any event mortally sick. He told Doctor Maugham that he believed he had only a few months to live. Doctor Maugham already suspected it, and questioned him about it when reporting on the child's post mortem examination. Little Alice's illness was caused by a predisposition inherited from her father; it was from her he learned unmistakably of his own fate.'

'Oh! What a scene it was, then!' said Miss Bowlby animatedly. 'He had been speaking with you at the Infirmary, had he not, Inspector? What a burden he brought back with him here. His reputation was already under attack. I knew that, but thought it would surely recover and reach new heights; in fact, there was no time. He saw his last months further blighted by the desertion of Kitty, to whom he had never dared tell the truth, and now left with neither wife nor progeny. And he had shot Will, and everyone would know it –!'

The old Mrs Ryder lunged at her, and was restrained by Tutt.

'My son did nothing!' she screamed. 'It was that evil creature, who cheated the hangman before, who had the gun!'

'Your son also had a gun,' said Tutt. 'His wife has told me; and it is now missing.'

The woman in his arms gasped. 'No! That was my husband's, his father's; he would never use it so – !'

Tutt loosed his hold on her and took a step back. His eyes wandered about the room for a moment but he fixed them on her boldly as he began what felt like a confession.

'Well, ma'am, we have two accounts of the shooting, and who knows but the truth may be more or less different from either. On balance, I must tell you I now believe what was said by Mr Evenden –'

She stood, panting rather animal-like, he thought, with her pale eyes still blazing at him. Though disconcerted he continued, 'There is what we now know of the doctor's prior state of mind; and what it seems he did later, in this room. The two acts make sense of each other. Each requires us to assume the other. There is a sorry lack of other clear indicators; but one could point to the fact that the bullet he extracted from Mr Evenden, and the portion of clothing he cut away, cannot now be found anywhere among his effects. Furthermore, his gun is missing. He is not here to explain, and it all undermines what he first said to me –'

He felt himself trailing off, unsatisfactorily. Her mouth now opened; considering her appearance, it was astonishing that a voice of such confident, precise power emerged.

'You have no proof?' she asked.

Tutt said, 'None!'

'Then we all know the two persons responsible for my son's death. Arrest them, at once!'

'There is no proof, but on this evidence we require none.'

'On the basis of what has been discovered, and the most probable deductions therefrom,' Mr James expanded, 'the inquest verdict will be "felo-de-se", or suicide, and there will be no further criminal investigation. Crimes will be recorded, both of assault with a firearm and self-destruction, but the perpetrator is beyond earthly jurisdiction. Am I correct, Inspector?'

Tutt nodded.

Addressing Mrs Ryder, the lawyer went on more gently: 'The jury will be instructed to give the most careful consideration to Henry's state of mind, and if they can, *may* bring in a verdict of killing by himself, but while in a state of – insanity. Only if they believe that they can. I fear his body will not be released, however. The coroner, tomorrow, is most likely to make an order for the internment – without funeral rites, after nightfall –'

Mrs Ryder shook her head. 'I knew, I always knew, that he would die young, like his father. A mother sees that in a child. But not this! Oh, it is horrible! There will be *no trial*? And I am not to have his body?' She paused to take in a terrible great breath. 'You!' She swung around. 'All of you are damned to hell!'

Pressing a hand convulsively over her mouth, she quit the room. She tried to slam the door but her skirts caught in it and it opened again after her; they saw her re-enter the parlour. Tutt half-followed, out into the hallway. From there he saw her gulping out painfully some words to Mercy, who had caught her about the

324

shoulders; but she broke away again. The room was curtained and dim, with some kind of extending table in the centre, festooned in black. Those black cloths Mrs Ryder seized hold of and tried to tear, though they were strong. Only little yelping sounds escaped her now. Mercy moved across to her again, concerned and calm. As she did so she caught sight of Tutt, and stopped. Then she moved to the door with authority, and softly closed it, in his face.

He returned to the study. No-one there had moved. At his entry Miss Bowlby spoke, as on cue.

'So he would die alone, beset by scandal, his achievements reduced to nothing, moreover childless. Kitty had left him. He may not instantly have formed his final intentions. He went in search of her; he may have thought to keep watch on Will in order to find her. But Will had crowed over him – I heard it – or it must have seemed so. And then, perhaps in a moment of some especial self-torment, he shot Will.'

'So I too would speculate, now,' said Tutt. '*Speculating*, I say, still: he tried to cover up what he had done. At the same time let it always be remembered that he did return and save Mr Evenden's life. Doctor Maugham confirms it; simply by delaying for a half hour, Doctor Ryder could have ensured that his victim was silenced forever, and his story could never have been contradicted. Instead, he saved him. True, I have been told it is arguable that he should have merely stopped the bleeding, leaving the operation to be carried out in the new antisepsis room at the Infirmary; but a respectable case, medically speaking, can be made for acting as he did. In the process, on the moor, he took the opportunity offered of losing the ball or bullet.'

'But his fate was sealed by then, nevertheless,' mused Miss Bowlby.

'Yes. With Evenden recovering, he was faced, besides all else, with a charge of attempted murder. Prison. The other man, his rival and enemy, having once already been a suspect for murder, would be the less believed at first. If for the present we take Mr Evenden's statement as the truth, he was so to speak inspired in his improvisation of his story by that thought. That Evenden was again

325

accused was not so remarkable a *coincidence* as yesterday's news-papers would imply.'

'Given your prejudice, no!'

'One can see how his difficulties accumulated, almost by the minute,' said Mr James. 'But is there sufficient evidence – in front of Mrs Ryder I did not express any doubt – for the inquest to conclude that he killed himself?'

'Oh yes!' exclaimed Miss Bowlby. 'Henry settled on the nearer exit. Indeed he may have retained the faint hope of leaving everyone deceived and retaining a measure of honour in the public eye. That hope required in turn that his death should appear to be by some means other than the most shaming one of suicide. He could begin his written report on his treatment of Will, just as usual; for him, that would be a matter almost automatic. In his mind, it is clear that the guilt for his fate attached firmly to Kitty and to Will. He staged an attempt to make his death appear as if directly at his wife's hand. He left a clue, as if scrawled in his death-throes; but it could not have been! Furthermore, he mixed the chosen instrument into his jar of relish, replacing the poison bottle itself in his cabinet.'

Katherine stood against the desk, her head still bowed over the ledger. Tutt realised how silent she had been.

'I do not know, quite, about all of that,' he said. 'Certainly his mental state is unimaginable. On the one hand, there was great control. On the moor, he gave me what I now think was a false account, even as he saved the life of the one person who could contradict it! And in this room everything was precisely arranged, including his notes, down to the moment when, having dropped the poison on the surface of the relish, he was ready to take it. That last scrawl may have had some sophisticated intent, as we thought. On the other hand, the tightest-drawn bands break with the most force, do they not? The last words were written before he took poison, I know, but still they may not have been calculated: only the expression of the most bitter sorrows, overwhelming him in his final moments. I do not think it a matter that need be adverted to unduly, tomorrow.'

No-one responded with further comment or contradiction, and Tutt began gathering his things.

'What I did,' murmured Katherine Ryder.

'I beg your pardon?' Tutt approached her, to hear better.

She looked up. 'You know, I told you yesterday,' she said. 'The drug I made him take, unknowingly, in my place. That also can affect the mind –'

'I do not think it a point of any significance,' said Tutt.

'I do. I will say it, tomorrow.'

Mr James was the next to speak, in a low and, affectingly, uncertain voice.

'Kitty, we should talk this through. Shall you come home with me? I wrote to your brother, and expect him shortly.'

Tutt awaited her reply with interest. He could see from the way she looked at hearing his words that she was at least sensible of the magnitude of this paternal indulgence.

'Thank you, Father. But you should know that first I will call at the Infirmary.'

'I doubt that will be necessary,' Tutt interjected. 'The guard has by now been removed from Mr Evenden. He is no longer under investigation in connection with these matters. Excuse me.'

He left the room and stood in the hallway, hesitating and fingering his hat. He heard a door open and close softly and he was joined by Miss Bowlby, pulling on her white gloves. 'Do you think that we are no longer required here, Inspector?'

'Well, I *was* wondering.'

She stopped her preparations, stimulated by another fresh thought.

'Dear Henry,' she said. 'Even on that day, he was helped by the habitual order of his mind, which like iron would never fail. The sketchbook had also to be disposed of, of course, because of the blood splashes.'

'I beg your pardon?'

'They also could have demonstrated that the shot was from a distance.'

'Yes, I dare say. If there had been a trial, it would have been an interesting one. All that rarefied analysis, you know, is regarded with suspicion in the courts. Cases have had to be withdrawn.'

'I know; in the past. Especially against doctors, am I right?' She did not require him to confirm it, going on quickly: 'But the age of superstition is drawing to a close. I am sorry, truly, that the famous issue, which this could have been, is not to be put down to *your* name after all. I am not sorry that again you have failed in your persecution of Will. You accept his innocence.'

They heard steps outside, and a loud ring. The consulting room door at once opened and Katherine appeared, but stopped seeing their eyes upon her. Tutt answered the bell. Evenden, up and dressed, bareheaded, with a coat draped loosely about him, was on the step. He gave the inspector a meagre smile and bow as he entered. He walked stiffly, but on seeing Katherine raised and opened his arms, sufficient to draw her to him.

Otley remained on the step.

'You were right sir,' he said in the tones of one washing his hands of an unfathomable business. 'He was for discharging himself at once, and coming here, so I offered to bring him.'

Tutt put on his hat. Miss Bowlby crossed to join him again. Tutt indicated the pair who yet remained in the deep exclusive ecstasy of their embrace.

'Not guilty they may be,' he said in a grim undertone; 'they are not innocent, neither. She is but forty-eight hours a widow!'

Her only response was to take his arm and usher him from the house.

Otley, still at the door, was given orders to stand down the various men on duties connected with the Ryder case. Tutt would return to the office, to prepare a report for the superintendent and the chief constable.

'It is a good job I was accompanying him,' Otley volunteered.

'Why?'

'Oh, as we were getting a cab outside the Infirmary a wild woman was waiting about the gate. She heard me use his name and started berating him as the Devil!'

'Did you put her in charge?'

'Well, no – I couldn't really. But I saw her off.'

Miss Bowlby had dropped the detective's arm but still she walked with him down the lane. For a few minutes she respected his mood of silent reflection; but plainly she was so full of a sense of new-discovered revelation herself it must spill out.

'Henry's feelings were always very fine,' she said, 'but I used to think that there was a thinness, an insubstantiality, to them. His final acts showed true passion. Somehow their very wrongness, their thorough wickedness, make me think more kindly of him. I suppose it would be no comfort to him to know that *I* shall respect his memory!'

'He was provoked beyond all endurance,' said Tutt. 'Are you still puzzled as to his motives? After all, might it not have been possible that he died for – ah – love,' he coughed over the word, 'alone?'

'*Can* one die for love alone?'

'In my experience, no.'

'In mine, one cannot even so much as experience love, alone. It comes always accompanied with envy, or gratitude, dependency, cowardliness or covetousness, or vanity, or some such. Which is the rooted emotion and which the parasite – who can tell even as to that, Inspector?'

Step by step and step for step, they put distance between themselves and the late doctor's house, and drew near to the rude and curious world. Her question went unanswered and after a while she went on.

'When he shot Will – that was his principal mistake, and that may have been on account of love. There's a place – I must confirm sometime, if that was where Will stopped. He described it to me once, as a resting-place above the path, which affords a picturesque outlook . . . It has a special meaning for him, and a particular association with Kitty, I believe, for some reason. There may have been *that*, in Will's countenance, as he turned there that morning, that if for once Henry could read it, would have been gall and wormwood.'

She dipped her face, briefly, and Tutt could almost imagine a tear being stopped there. Burlas spread before them now, in that sootiness against which her womenfolk went into battle, repetitious and without end; the soot never failed, and crushed them all. Alongside Miss Bowlby, Tutt felt his age; felt the years ahead shorten, his opportunities contract and harden. Her presence acted on him like a heady yet suffocating miasma. An age without benefit of superstition dawned, for him, cold and unforgiving, and he trod forth into a narrowing passage, while by his side she seemed a creature flying free.

Out of nervous habit, he began to dig in his overcoat pockets as he walked, taking out and sorting the detritus of days past. A small hardness in the corner of one proved on examination to be the yellow metal cartridge case she had presented to him. His other hand found a piece of paper which had spent almost exactly as long about his person. It was the tract thrust upon him by the strange woman in the street . . . He uncrumpled it quickly. It was not a tract at all, but a handbill advertising a prayer meeting:

. . . Miss Deacon speaks with the power of Plain Truth . . . Her irreproachable Dignity and Humility . . . The Elixir of Redemption!

Tutt read it twice then returned it to his pocket. He wondered what young Mrs Ryder's future would be, supposing her lot to be thrown in with Evenden. He heard his own voice, brute and sudden.

'We are forgetting John. Did he batter himself to death merely to spite his younger brother?'

Moments later, alone, he approached the police office. He saw a man dressed in the comfortable rustic colours of the hill farmer, wearing also a complacent and hopeful expression, turn in from the opposite direction. The citizen carried in one hand, muddied but unmistakable, a heavy old-fashioned pistol. The fingers of the other were fastened gingerly upon a tattered and rain-soaked sketchbook.

PART 6

FOUR YEARS LATER

37

As the world turned, the little world of each went also in tow. Scandal does not so much 'die down'; it is put by, when other business presses its claim.

Mrs Molsworthy had come at last to know what it was to be addressed as 'My lady mayoress'. She had not yet succeeded in re-housing herself; to everyone's surprise Evenden Hall still was not vacant. She tried to be patient.

Mrs Treves survived but had been somewhat left behind by her former friend. Wasted, faded, forgotten and discounted, the only variation in her days was that she was sometimes more stimulated by the tedium and neglect she suffered. Then she would shed a tear of temper, called it the vapours, take to her bed, and in the dark picture again the fair features and gentle manner of the one man who ever had cared for her welfare; and she would hug to herself the richly mournful name: 'Oh, dear Doctor – !' In that, she was not alone among his former patients.

Burlas council *had* now at last taken up the old recommendation and appointed a Borough Surveyor and a Medical Officer of Health (the latter a new man, from outside, and a great enthusiast – as well he might be, since considerable fame of a regionalised sort awaited him). An editorial acclaimed the decision, while explaining it in part: 'If existing conditions themselves do not horrify, the lack of chasteness they encourage must.' By the turn of the century, Burlas would take pride in its fresh status as a 'sanitary city', flaunting statistics as much as manufactures.

Inspector Oswald Tutt did his duty as required, and saw the ranks of Burlas detectives double with the promotion of Otley. That made his days less dull, and took the edge of disappointment from some of them. A further, less expected source of interest had appeared shortly after the inquest of Henry Ryder and while the town was still offensively buzzing. Anonymous friends of the late John Evenden had put in his hands new information as to the history and movements of the poor woman, the last witness to his murder. Tutt believed his benefactors were probably relations on the late Sarah Evenden's side, since the contact with him was effected by a firm of London lawyers. Their assistance had continued intermittently. The trail often seemed warm, but was more frustrating and difficult than anything. It seemed that one who had nothing, truly nothing at all, could pass through the eye of a needle. Those with name, property, family, on the other hand, could never hide.

William Evenden's continuing presence at his family seat was an outrage at first, accepted more calmly in time. He had maintained himself in reasonable prosperity by being an interested landowner and by letting fall his artistic ambitions. He remained a detached member of the landed interest, tolerating the followers of Arch among his labourers, and declining urgent invitations to join the country set in putting them down. His fellow landowners, for whom the Sheffield outrages resounded as the most tragic portent of evil in modern times, thought Evenden betrayed the greatest blackness of heart, though it was no matter that ever impinged on the consciousness of any police inspector in smoke-blinded Burlas.

His disloyalty merely completed his social ostracism. The country set were never going to accommodate themselves to the second scandal, the way they had to the trial. The precipitate way he had married the widow – one wholly unsuited, in every aspect, to claim a place in the drawing rooms of the solid and respectable – ! Why, it had been better by far to marry the Bowlby woman after all. When the birth of a son and heir was announced, a scant half-year after – then was no more pretence possible, as to what she *had been*, under the oh-so-noble profile of the upstart doctor. Most condemned Evenden and his wife equally. Many still maintained the view that a widow ought not to remarry, ever. A very few, like her father, believed that he had taken unforgivable advantage of her acute distress. But most would happily see the couple in hell together. Sometimes, on a Sunday, it was the more thrilling then to pray for them and renew oneself in righteousness and a sense of one's own forbearance.

For four years he and his wife endured in their sanctuary, each admitting to the other that they had little real love for the place. They tried each other's strength in subtle ways, as when discussing their mutual friend Dorothea Bowlby.

'Her concern for the poor and oppressed is certainly genuine,' he said, 'but, never having had any real prospect of being numbered among them, it is tainted with a kind of half-envious aesthetic regard.'

'Now *that*,' she said, 'Henry could not have begun to comprehend, even if patiently explained. It simply offended his concept of plain reason that improvements were always so difficult to put in place.'

'Your first husband was a better man than your second,' he said.

'Ay, and the rightest thing he ever did was shoot you.' Her gaze penetrated his and held steady as she said it, and after, until he closed the appraising look with a kiss.

She sometimes withdrew to her scribbling, making no secret of it; but when he protested an interest he was dismissed: 'Oh, it does not concern *you!*'

Though he never wished to pay heed, he could not be quite immune to the relentless propaganda of the age, and must speculate that she, too, might be prey to the self-deceptions and sad awakenings said to be the certain lot of any woman who, whilst married, submits to be wooed by another. She would know it now for that – a wooing – that series of charged encounters, in which he had sensed (a sense amplified with hope) her reactive response to his presence. She must also know that, even so, nothing might have

335

come of all his covetous interest and mild intrigue, had it not been for a bolt of lightning.

Their life offered solace and compensation. Tommy was the first and abiding joy. Once a child takes a portion of your heart it is never returned. That was indeed lucky for this child. When the baby was born the unspoken pretence before the world had to be that it was the first husband's. Everyone had *known* that was false. Now, he and his wife saw day by day the fairness more established and the features ripen. The truth hurt, though if it could ever have been made believable to the world it must have redeemed them in the smallest degree. In his eagerness to marry, he had legitimated as his own heir the son of his enemy – and this child *was* as lusty as anyone could wish!

Evenden strolled along the avenue where the boy played, rubbing the yellow head in passing, for he had seen the Mercury turn in at the gate and decided to meet him. Never was the name less apt than when applied to the stout man who toiled daily with his bony mule on the road from Burlas to Frith. Seeing the master, he pulled up with relief, handed over the bundle of mail and turned to go on his way without a word. Evenden, quickly sorting through the expected catalogues and bills and picking out the two items of 'real' post, called after him. One was a letter from Dolly in Paris; there should have been eightpence to pay. However, when he confessed to not carrying the required small change about his person, the postal official merely shrugged and turned again; he could not be bothered to wait.

Evenden was reading Dolly's letter as he entered the drawing room and dropped the rest of his mail onto a table. Having, against many difficulties, removed herself to the French capital the moment the peace was signed, her sharing in the upheavals which followed had made her almost in fact what she had long been in spirit: a Frenchwoman. As ever, her report this time was zealous and didactic. She was furiously suspicious that the after-effects of the war in France were not being marked as closely as those in Prussia, and prophesied that future conflicts would be waged as much with the passions and beliefs of the people as with guns.

The ink changed colour where the long letter had been taken up again by the sender:

You write that the young lady *remains an enigma. I can only remind you that even if she cares nothing for you it is better than you deserve. Wm. Evenden always had the devil's mark on him for good fortune. And mind you show her this.*

This set him thinking of his wife. He did not expect all about her to be always clear to him. Did any cause for agitation remain, when such a woman pledged her faith? It was incredible that she should still doubt him, yet give the sincere affection of her heart – as she assuredly did, Dolly's jest notwithstanding. In any other person, it would be incredible.

He recalled an instance when the old subject of the trial had arisen. She had quite calmly told him that she had come round to the Crown's view: that on a rational assessment her own evidence was valueless. It might have been different, had he proved his lack of concern by leaving the newspaper on the train.

'. . . But you did not leave it behind. I did. The only witness who knew that you were innocent, as a fact, was Dolly.'

He had thought for a moment. 'Howsoever that may be, the defence, your father, rightly calculated that you would be more likely to impress the jury than she. Certain things cannot be hidden. *If necessary*, she would have lied to save me. You would not. Not even now! There is, of course, one other person who knows the truth.'

She had looked up. 'Who?'

'My brother's murderer.'

That was the closest he had ventured to proclaiming his innocence. She had never questioned it again, after the night of the storm. He had the feeling that she did not care; but if he found himself bitter over that, he would remember the question *he* had once asked *her*. When he saw her at her house, after first rising from his bed in the Infirmary where he had spent long hours turning over in his mind the implications of what he had been told:

'What have you done?' he had whispered, holding her.

She had replied, 'Nothing!'

Evenden broke from his reverie and picked up the other envelope. On opening it, he was initially disappointed. Most of its thickness proved to be an official-looking copy document – probably a draft lease or some such. He separated the covering letter. A glance at the signature intrigued him anew. So far as the matter was concerned, the letter was perplexing, carefully but haltingly phrased. After a hasty perusal, he put it down, and took up the main document.

Certified Copy of Statement before Witnesses, made by Zillah Dixon otherwise Deakin –

I make this statement in full confession of my crimes before GOD, of my free will and right readily. I know not whence I came, but that I was born in the workhouse of the Linden Union in the year 1836 or thereabouts – it was the new Union. I knew no family there but the band of children in like situation, but of them I recollect I was the only one to live out many years. By the time I reached my grown senses I was ruined, for though the men were kept from us the women and boys were creatures low as myself, and overlords at best uncaring. The only gentler pleasure to be had was when a bottle or powders could be got. Nothing do I pray to excuse my foul wickedness, though true it is I knew not good or bad then, but I would not seek in my heart for it.

I grew strong and had my appetites, being a great manly girl and looked on as something droll and witless merely on that account, which treatment will force on that which it prematurely sets down to one, in my view. Being about thirteen years I left the workhouse and laboured for a time on a farm, but was cast off from that when my condition was divined by the foreman's wife – by witchcraft, so others told me. I never would return to any workhouse but made my way, staying in each parish until I was run off. Sometimes men would come after me in a band and do as they would without penalty, but generally when they were flush and in drink I got something from them. I drank much gin so bad it does not merit the name, got from low tradesmen or the back windows of ordinary shops, and therefore the sickness in my head did ever increase so that I scarce knew who I was or cold, heat, night or day much of the time. I knew children baited me and ran from me as a madwoman. Yet if I did any damage or hurt, it was in the blackness sent over me, and that may be,

338

for which I do therefore beg pardon. I did keep hid whenever my time came, in the woods, but can swear all the babies died natural which is more than many another can. As for those that did suck, I think my milk was something off.

I had been two winters at Critchley, long enough to have a name and be known as a fool of last resort. I had a home in the wood with four walls and a roof, but I knew it was mean and stinking for I never saw such pretty dainty homes as were a few thereabouts, hobby-houses about the estate. There was a cleric there took special delight in hurling words with me in the public way when we met, and finding me pure ignorant, a gentle liberal man. I offered him a slug once, being out of wit, and he took it. But he choked and lost his voice, and croaked God meant even me for better than that. Which I mention in confirmation that the gin was much at fault; indeed I believe mine was on purpose poisonly intermixed worse than anyone's for many felt called to deal to me the punishment the world thought me fit for, though I paid money the same as another. I have learned now the stuff that oftentimes goes into such brews, and curse the inhumanity of such practice, which then was lawful.

In the summer of 1865 I would be cried often 'old Zil', 'old daftie' or similar, being old in my life if not so much in years – my hair was gone white and my back curled. One night I was a dangerous thing abroad, like the spirit of the world's crookedness, so I think, having buried twin girls as sweet and small, for once, as dolls you might see in a city shop. I passed by John Evenden's house. I knew who he was; many thought I could not follow plain English but I knew all the village talk. There was a light at one window by which I could see within, and the glass was like the plane between Heaven and earth, though I did not think of Heaven then. I knocked at his door and when he answered I said that I was taken with a powerful thirst, which was true. He went to fetch water and I followed him in – he knew me and was unafraid, being friendly with the cleric of whom I have spoken. I just stepped quick into his parlour and drained the brandy glass from which he had been drinking. I had never drunk brandy. I cannot tell you what came over me, with the taste of that nectar! I have often thought since, but never dared say, that 'the love which passeth understanding' though it cannot be sensed direct in this life, our frames not being made for it, will course through our souls as the brandy did my body. The open bottle stood beside the glass, and I had taken it up when Evenden came back and shouted at me: 'Hoy, leave that now, you thieving natural!' He tried to take the bottle from my hand but misjudged my size and my determination, so I guess. What made me mad though, was to see the bottle smashed against his head and its contents run away down him, all lost, when had he valued it at all he had simply let me have another drink, and reasoned with me as one human creature to another. The poker was before my eye, as something meant, and I took it and dealt him blows as hard as in my power, in that moment wishing it more. My first frenzy being gone, I stood dazed. My fingers touched brandy and blood mixed, and I tasted, but it was nothing the same.

I was out of the room, when I heard him stir, and call, in a voice which cannot have been much but was loud to me. He caught his breath as if he heard something, and cried 'Will!' Then, again, 'Will, is it you? Murder!' I went back then, and though not aided by the same passion as before I beat him again with whatever was heavy that I could find, until he was still, and then some. Of that, I say, that I know I had killed him in my first attack, by the dints in his head and the look of him, but I had to stop the noise.

But there could be no stopping of all noise. I listened for footfalls, thinking he had known someone was approaching, and thinking that someone must have seen what I had done, and was yet watching me. The sense of a 'Will' watching me was something I was to carry like a burn that would not heal!

The only thing I thought I knew was that gaol was worse than the workhouse, which I can say now is not true; I know not why but I did not think of hanging, and being ended thus. I took the light with me. In the hallway, I found a paper, a telegraphic dispatch. I could not read much, but made out that the last word began with W, and in my superstition thinking of the name Will again I took it. Such was my confusion. I closed all doors, put out all lights, and took myself off.

Next I cast myself in the river. My babies and Evenden had bloodied me, and this was how I would always clean myself, though I must often go about smeared being afflicted with a kind of flux – on which account also I was spurned and mocked. I stayed in the river a long time, then I went home. I set the place afire. I must have got out at the last, for I came to myself elsewhere, with my clothes dry again. It was in the next parish I heard that Evenden's brother had been charged with the murder.

In my old shifting way I got to great Burlas for the trial time, a place where I had never been. I had no wish then to tell the truth, but yet must know what was to happen, and be determined by the honoured people about the doings of *that night. I wanted the man to hang; it even seemed just to me to want it, for the scalding heat I felt on me still, from his watching eyes. I was thus all but maddened into my true wits for once, and indeed it seemed that after that brandy I could stomach no more gin, or so I thought. I could not get in, and like the rest of the ordinary people was pushed along outside of the castle wall. In the close there, as the time for decision drew near, was a press of folk, the greatest crowd I ever saw, and the greatest trading of goods and passions and ideas, as if I was the only one intent on what mattered. I was followed by a stranger who claimed he saw something in my eyes. I tried to escape him, until seized by the message in his words, which fastened on me like a collar of iron. He asked if I knew a man who lived among us, doing only good works, but was repaid with death. That I did: I never knew other than that he was a good man. He said He was slain most cruelly, but did not die. That also was true: at first he would not die. Then he told me more of the One who died for our sins, and now sits at GOD's right hand and will save us all . . .*

A moan ran through the crowd when it came out that the brother was found not guilty. I had been separated from the preacher again, and if I did not make a sound yet I felt it worse than any. The hand of vengeance would be out again, for me, was all I thought – being still a creature in darkness. I wandered about, and even found a gin-shop, but could not approach: I stood in the street before it trembling like with an ague, at the smell.

I know I may tell only briefly of the years that followed, though they mark for me the only span of my life when I was favoured, in His mercy, with fitful glimmerings of grace. I did not find the preacher again, but found others to teach me, even to read the story for myself. I was granted a voice to tell the gospel, a sober head, and at last a heart at peace. So my new travels came about. I was riven at times, in prayer begging to know if it was not meant, all of it, that those who found the path to joy and resurrection in my words should be ready to receive also the dark tidings of my soul. I carried the same fear as ever, but had a truer understanding of what I should fear. I feared most the judgment of the Lord, next that of men. I feared William Evenden still, but in reason: that on me he should avenge his good brother's death, and the calumny and peril endured by himself, through my silence! Having learned my letters, I wrote once to the family. I meant always to do so again, in true confession.

I never did confess; for most of each day time I was in such peace the truth seemed a tale of an unfortunate other, not me. Once, at a meeting, I saw the

341

former cleric of Critchley. It was as if a terrible angel of GOD was revealed to me, though his face was in shape all puzzled kindness. He waited until I was finished speaking, and next appeared close at my elbow. 'Is it you, Zillah? Did you see anything before you went away from us? Were you afraid?' I could not speak, but only shook my head and ran from that country.

That time is like a happy dream, which was shaken out of me after a few short years. I happened to be back in Burlas; I do not question what powers ordained it. It is not a pretty place, but there came a morning when it was touched with glory in my eyes; you never saw a dawn like it, and I was up with the dawn in the hills, seeing the place spread below me, and thought myself full ready to lie down and die, grateful to GOD.

As soon as I was back down in the town, I heard the name Evenden. It followed me so, I thought it addressed to me, spoken after me like a curse. Many were reading the newspapers and, with some very forced speech, I obtained one. I could read well enough by then, though most accustomed to scriptural language. The words began to tangle in my head, but it seemed now that the brother had killed another man, a doctor who had saved HIM from death! I had failed in my ministry. I had deceived myself, and closed my heart against the true message of my Saviour. This was the judgment being prepared for me, all chance for escape gone. My mind was all weak and broken, back into its old sickness. I recall little of those days, save that it was somehow borne in on me that the brother went free again, but that was all one. I was pursued by visions, in which Mr John Evenden and the poor doctor lay before me in fear and torment, sometimes two, sometimes one; and I with the brother circled round, and sometimes we were two, sometimes one, but for the most part he mocked me, and I fought with him for dominion over the dead. In my better senses, I tried to recall if 'Will' had indeed been there, when his brother called to him, since I dreamed so clearly of him. But thereafter my wits were gone, and what I comprehended of my existence was worse than before.

I know that this is Lincoln gaol, and that last week in the streets of this city I did set on a woman and steal a necklace. I have no memory of it, but confess it and ask pardon. A deeper shadow is coming over me which is to the darkness of my life as night to day. Soon I will stand before the judgment seat. His mercy is infinite, and so is His might. I have known but the echo of His undying passion, and I am afraid. I urge all who read this to sincere

342

repentance and striving always after the good, and I say it who am the worst upon the earth.

(Signed under assistance, given under her oath, notarised and witnessed)

38

Murder generally has a cause, he thought; but his brother had been snuffed out almost at random. The death, without cause, had instead become the cause of so much else. As a result his own grief had always been of a warped kind at best. For a time, he had embraced the outstanding suspicions against himself as a badge of honour.

He had known the general belief from the first: that this near-mythical person about whom he knew nothing could in some way prove his guilt. Such is the suggestive power of common belief, he himself had even come to regard the possibility of her discovery with trepidation. However, with the change in his circumstances four years before, he had overcome that superstitious reluctance. He had put into his father-in-law's hands what had been left to him on his mother's death: a single letter, strange, startling but inconclusive. He had instructed Mr James to see that it, together with whatever other information could be found, should be delivered to Inspector Tutt. His father-in-law had kept the secret well, even from Katherine.

He walked through his house, looking for his wife that she might hear from him the news that had so dazed him, and yet wondering how he would mete out the words, in facing her. He would have found her sooner, could he have applied his mind fully to the task; but he was abstracted in his wandering, seeing his surroundings not simply as they were but as they had always been.

He found her at last in the nursery, where the two younger children slept in late morning. The girl was asleep already, he saw:

she who meant most to the mother who feared to love her. The baby, who could keep a tenacious hold on consciousness, was just drowsing, so Evenden stood noiselessly in the doorway. Katherine bent to lay Fred down. Even as sleep overcame him his little palms stuck to her bosom like burrs, which she tugged away at last, then she saw her husband, and they crept out of the room together. He embraced her, sensing her quizzical half-formed thought and pressing her to patience, his hand behind her head. With unconfessable pleasure he noted white hairs among the brown; like the children, they were outposts of the future.

He pulled apart and stroked her nose with the document in his hand. He had been calculating what words to use.

'It seems my brother died bravely,' he said, 'and of all things, thinking of me.'

Intrigued as he had intended, she took the folded papers from him, and moved across to a kind of gallery window; they were almost at the top of the house. She read soundlessly, but in watching he anticipated her voice, with its well-known soft yet definite trace of Burlas accent. In unguarded repose her face bore the imprint of remorse which, though to eternity he would resent the cause of it, sealed her beauty for him.

The reading would take some time, and at length to school himself in waiting he turned again to Tutt's covering letter, now explained.

. . . The document enclosed will be made public shortly, by agreement between the coroner and two Chief Constables. Should you, as present head of the family, have any observations as to the form to be adopted or information restricted, in courtesy I shall convey the same to those authorities.

I have broken the silence between us, thinking it lay to me to own that the truth has thus been furnished, not through any of the efforts of the friends of your brother above mentioned, but merely in its due time. Upon being notified I went to Lincoln and saw the woman, but she had determined to speak no more and died soon after. She was a strikingly big woman, who you would think to look at of sixty years at least: altogether a vile aberration.

My respectful regards to you, and apologise for past injury, but must maintain in fairness that I had grounds, as it was presented: as also with regard to Mrs Evenden. At the close of three months I retire from my present position, not being blessed as you are but with notwithstanding my pipe and cottage ready waiting, and a place above the mantel where shall hang the picture of a man in error, which I have kept, I find, and shall now have framed for the purpose.

If, in conclusion of this drawn-out piece of business, we are judged not merely by our acts and their consequences, but by our reasons and regrets – I hope for a merciful reckoning – I dare say it – for all parties. Sir, I remain

Yr. Servant
OSWALD TUTT